THE PRESSURE INSIDE MARDI'S SKULL WAS IMMENSE. THE VEINS ON THE BACK OF HER HANDS SWELLED HIDEOUSLY. . . .

Mardi grabbed a cutting knife, whipped around, and drove the blade into Chris's chest. He grunted and lurched back, his hands grasping the knife. Blood began to ooze around the wound. Mardi was pleased. . . . Suddenly Chris gave a convulsive shudder, his body went limp, and he crumbled to the floor.

Only now did she hear her name being called. Her mother was shouting up the stairs to her. "Mardi? Mardi, is everything all right?" Mardi stepped over to Chris's body. She took hold of the knife and pulled until it slid out of Chris's chest.

Suddenly a scream rent the air. Her mother's scream. Mardi turned slowly. It was so strange, how effortlessly she moved; it was like floating in air, as if she didn't exist. Her mother stood rooted to the spot. "No, no, Mardi!" she kept saying, her voice dying little by little. All Mardi wished for was silence. She'd lived with her mother's voice for too long. . . .

LESLIE HORVITZ

Blood Moon

PUBLISHED BY POCKET BOOKS NEW YORK

This novel is a work of fiction. Names, characters, places and incidents are either the product of the author's imagination or are used fictitiously. Any resemblance to actual events or locales or persons, living or dead, is entirely coincidental.

Another *Original* publication of POCKET BOOKS

POCKET BOOKS, a division of Simon & Schuster, Inc.
1230 Avenue of the Americas, New York, N.Y. 10020

ISBN: 0-671-61169-0

First Pocket Books printing February 1987

10 9 8 7 6 5 4 3 2 1

Printed in the U.S.A.

AUTHOR'S NOTE

In 1831 a plague of cholera swept through London, its cause unknown until one doctor—John Snow—traced it to one of the city's water pumps. By shutting the pump down he effectively eliminated the source of the epidemic and at the same time became the father of epidemiology. His spiritual descendants can now be found at the Centers for Disease Control in Atlanta, Georgia. Founded in 1942 (as the Malaria Control in War Areas Agency), the CDC employs more than four thousand people who are engaged in monitoring and investigating any threat to public health in the United States—and in some instances abroad. Its labs are among the most sophisticated in the world; its equipment can measure the presence of certain chemicals down to parts per trillion or determine the strength of a rare Class IV virus like Maburg fever in a tissue specimen. The CDC is home for what is widely regarded as the best medical detective agency in the world—the Epidemic Intelligence Service. Only sixty people a year are chosen to serve a tour of duty with the EIS. On call twenty-four hours a day, they must be ready to go anywhere an outbreak of a disease occurs—as long as they are invited in by the state affected. About one thousand epidemics come to the attention of the CDC each year. Most of them are known quantities: salmonella, hepatitis, botulism, diphtheria, and so on. But every once in a while Nature comes up with something altogether new that defies the best efforts of researchers and investigators to figure out what it is and then—more importantly—put a stop to it.

Blood Moon

one

Mardi Lloyd was sitting, talking with her mother, when the episode began. It came on the way it had the last time, so gradually that she was not even aware of it for several minutes. The sensation was not unpleasant—not at first.

What was most striking was how her senses became heightened. Colors were suddenly endowed with freshness and vigor until she found it too painful to look at one thing for very long. Smells she would otherwise have ignored, registered with particular urgency. When Mardi looked at her mother, her eyes were drawn to the smile that had formed on her mother's lips. It was a meaningless smile, a smile practiced for the camera.

"Are you all right, honey?"

"Oh yes, fine, Mother."

Her skin was beginning to tingle just as it would after a prolonged bath. She was becoming disconnected—floating. She suspected that all she would have to do was cast a sidelong glance and she would see herself—another self—right beside her. But she didn't have the nerve to do this, afraid that her suspicion might not be unfounded.

This was like being on mescaline, she decided, only she hadn't taken any drugs, not unless you counted the joint she had shared with Sean the night before. But no amount of weed she'd ever consumed produced an effect quite like this.

"Are you sure you're all right?"

Her mother was leaning forward, her scalloped blouse loosening with the motion.

"Absolutely."

"You look distracted."

Distracted is right, Mardi thought. She knew what came next and it terrified her.

These episodes usually lasted for twenty minutes, half an hour at the most, and they always came in two stages. In the first she floated; in the second she came crashing down to earth. It was as if someone were playing tricks with her mind, pushing buttons at random.

Her throat was going dry. She desperately wanted a glass of water, but didn't dare stand up for fear that she would collapse.

"No, really, Mother, I'm okay."

The dubious expression on her mother's face told Mardi that she was not convinced. But nonetheless, her mother resumed where she'd left off, discussing what one lawyer was advising her to do regarding her divorce settlement, and what another lawyer was advising her to do regarding her suit against her last recording company over breach of contract. In the best of circumstances, Mardi wouldn't have paid any attention to her, but now it was impossible to listen. Her mother's words sounded like the droning hum of distant machinery.

The tingling in her skin was becoming more pronounced and an insistent throbbing in her temples was followed immediately by exploding lights, like hundreds of flashbulbs going off. She couldn't decide where these lights were coming from. A disturbance of the optic nerve maybe. She knew she would have to hold on—literally. Her hands gripped the arms of her chair so tightly that the knuckles were white.

Her body seemed to be filling up with a violent electrical current. She looked dumbly ahead but could see nothing, not even her mother less than ten feet across from her, not the window with its view of Australian pines just to the right of her, not even the tiled floor on which she'd planted her bare feet. She could only see lights exploding, and smell a noxious odor, like rubber burning.

Somehow she still had the capacity to know when to nod or to mumble a response so that her mother would think she was continuing to follow what she was saying.

It was all she could do in the meantime to keep herself from springing up from her chair. But if she did that, then she knew she would do something terrible, something she couldn't bear to think about.

Then, as suddenly as it had come upon her, the episode passed, the lights stopped, and the smell vanished along with the tingling. In its aftermath she felt drained, washed out, barely able to keep her eyes open.

"Mardi, come over here for a moment."

It took all the energy she had to comply with her mother's request. Her mother placed her hand on Mardi's brow. No fever. But this finding didn't reassure her.

"Mardi, I'm worried about you."

"There's no reason to worry, Mother."

"You're not taking very good care of yourself."

Mardi could sense what was coming: another threat to send her back to Dr. Ableman to explore the possibility of a nervous breakdown. Nervous breakdowns were something Carol Lloyd could understand. Nervous breakdowns were what she kept having, so she no doubt assumed that her daughter would inevitably have one as well. It was like an inheritance.

At that moment Mardi realized what she would have done if she'd gotten up from her chair during her episode. Without any hesitation she would have laid her hands on her mother's neck and strangled her to death.

Mardi left her mother and began walking. She was bored with the resort, having explored everything that it had to offer. Actually there were two sections of the resort—two Shadow Pines—and she couldn't stand either one of them.

One was the Shadow Pines that catered to the middle class, the ones who wore loud Hawaiian shirts and were constantly bawling out their kids. The other was the restricted area, guarded by security men who looked like they'd been imported from Scandinavia; they made sure to keep out the trespassers and prying members of the press, particularly the photographers who were desperate for shots that would titillate the public.

But as far as Mardi was concerned, the people who lived in the restricted part of the resort were no more interesting than the ones with the Hawaiian shirts. She'd known celebrities and millionaires since she was a little girl growing up in L.A. and they didn't do anything for her anymore.

About the only person who did interest her here was Sean

Laramie, a tennis instructor. All he'd had to do was take one look at her and he was so completely smitten that he could hardly get a word out.

Mardi found him on the courts giving the last lesson of the day. He didn't like her intruding on his lessons. He told her she was too distracting. Well, that was true enough; with just a T-shirt and cutoffs on there was no way she could *not* be distracting. It was what she did best in life—take people's minds off what they should have been paying attention to.

But she knew that Sean's show of irritation was just a cover. She could read his eyes; they were drinking her in. He'd have her on the tennis court if he could.

"What do you want, Mardi?"

"I want to show you something. After you're through I want you to come with me."

Want was all she felt. Nothing but want.

He said that he hoped it wouldn't take forever, whatever she had in mind, because he had other things to do. He was only twenty-four and yet he was acting like he was a big shot, a man with authority. Sean was bullshit and Mardi wouldn't have bothered with him except that she was so bored. Coming to Shadow Pines all these years, what did anyone expect?

She'd discovered a secret place halfway up Mount Sycamore. No one ever went there, and no one ever would. People who came to Shadow Pines wanted everything done for them; they were too lazy to go hiking up some damn mountain.

The mountain was half in the resort, and half out. Mardi had once climbed to the top, and while the view was okay, it really wasn't what made it worth trudging all the way up there.

The walk up was fine, exhilarating really. She could even put out of her mind the memory of the episode. It might never have happened.

The path that wound its way up the 2,200-foot mountain was pebbly, covered with lichen and moss. About a quarter of the way up they came upon an abandoned quarry, cut deep into the mountainside. Mardi felt that no one had been this way for years, until she had come. It was her private preserve. She was beginning to wonder whether she might have been better off leaving Sean on the courts. He probably wouldn't know how to appreciate what she was about to show him.

Suddenly the path wasn't there anymore. It didn't peter out, it just disappeared. They were at the place Mardi had found on her own; it was a lake, the strangest, most bizarre lake that Mardi had ever laid eyes on.

Even Sean was impressed. "What the hell is it?"

"A lake, brilliant, what do you think it is?"

"I know it's a lake but I've never seen one that looks like *that*."

"What you want to know is what makes it look that way?"

He nodded.

She'd given this matter considerable thought but had arrived at no conclusion. "I haven't the slightest."

What made this lake so extraordinary was that it was as black as pitch; a black so profound that it was impossible to determine how far down the water went. At the same time, the blackness of the water acted like a mirror, casting back their reflection with practically no distortion.

On her last visit to this lake Mardi had circled around it all the way to the opposite side; there she'd discovered a dam, a jerry-rigged structure constructed of branches, lightning-scorched boughs, and rotted-out tree trunks, fortified by thousands of twigs and chunks of earth. Clearly it hadn't been made by humans. Only beavers could have been responsible, even though Mardi hadn't spotted any on her excursion.

She stooped down and, cupping her hands, gathered up some water to drank.

"Mardi, don't do that."

"Why not?"

"Well, it looks . . . it looks dead."

It did look dead, she supposed, but that was why she'd drunk it, to find out what death tasted like.

But it wasn't enough for her.

"What are you doing?"

"Really, Sean, you can be such a drag sometimes." She was getting out of her clothes. Since she was wearing so little in the first place, this did not take very long. She kicked off her seventy-five-dollar pair of running shoes first, slipped off her shorts next, and hesitated only a moment before pulling off the T-shirt. Her T-shirt today read WHOEVER HAS THE MOST THINGS WHEN HE DIES WINS.

Sean looked absolutely aghast that she was about to go swimming in water that was this incredibly black; at the same time he was held nearly spellbound by the sight of her nudity.

"Well, are you going to join me or not?"

"I don't think so. Mardi, don't go in there."

What he didn't know was that this was something she'd done before. Let him think this was her first time; it made everything more exciting somehow.

The lake deepened suddenly; one instant the water was up to her ankles, the next it was up to her neck. Gazing down, she could barely see her breasts, which were just a blur of white amid so much black. Tatters of leaves and pine needles floated leisurely around her.

Sean hadn't moved from the edge of the lake. His look of astonishment changed to one of irritation when she splashed him. He jumped back as if he'd been singed. Then he inspected the water on his hands as if he expected that it too would be black.

"See, it's just like any other water, only it looks different."

"Goddamnit, Mardi," he said, unhappy that his precious tennis instructor's uniform was now sopping wet.

"Now you're going to have to take them off to dry."

Nothing doing. He was adamant in his refusal to come in. So she went out and got him. By throwing herself on him, pressing her soaked body against his, she accomplished her objective. When she undid the buckle of his belt, loosening his shorts, she failed to hear any protest.

As she was doing this she began to sense that something else was happening. The strange tingling of her skin, she knew, was not accountable to the water she'd just come out of. It was beginning again.

Mardi drew him down with her on a bed of pine needles and moss. He was kissing her everywhere, sucking one nipple, then the other, with great concentration and fervor. She was burying her fingernails, those she hadn't eaten down, into the back of his neck, but he seemed not to notice.

What he would have no way of knowing was that she was holding on to him not in desire, but simply to hold on. This time it was happening much more quickly than the last; already she felt as though she were becoming disconnected.

Sean maneuvered one hand down between her thighs. When she arched herself to allow him to penetrate more easily, she felt something let go inside of her. She began to heave and buck so wildly that Sean struggled to keep her in one place. She had no idea what was happening to her; she felt as if she'd lost control completely. She clung to him more fiercely if that was possible. She threw her head back and forth, whipping her hair against his face.

It began to occur to her that there was hardly any sensation in her legs, just a cold and clammy numbness. She felt as if she were going dead inside. She cried out. Sean, undoubtedly believing that he'd succeeded in arousing her to new heights of passion, drove into her with more frenzy than before.

She couldn't take it any longer. The numbness had reached her thighs, and although she still was capable of movement below her waist, she could register neither the sexual pleasure Sean was attempting to give her, nor the discomfort of the hundreds of pine needles and pebbles digging into her buttocks.

"Stop it, stop it, Sean!" she screamed, pounding his back with her fists.

"What . . . ?" He looked down on her with incredulity, certain that she could not possibly mean what she'd just said.

But she meant it all right. She fought against him, pummeling him until he loosened his hold on her. "Mardi, what's wrong?" he kept saying. "What the hell's the matter with you?"

As soon as she could squirm out from underneath him she stood up, hoping that by doing this she could restore some sensation to her legs. But this did not occur. It was as if half of her body were encased in ice.

She didn't know why, but she was seized by the impulse to jump back into the lake. She ran. Sean was pursuing her, but he skidded to a stop at the edge, still too apprehensive to take the plunge.

But Mardi was already immersed. She swam down, down farther than she'd ever gone before. Her eyes open, she still saw nothing—just darkness.

And then, a second before she lost consciousness, she saw—or thought she saw—a hand reaching out to her, hovering in the obscurity. Not Sean's hand, but the hand of someone at the very bottom of the lake.

two

"I'm sorry Gordon couldn't be here," Neville Green was saying. "I'd looked forward to meeting him for some time now."

Jessie Palmer had very much wanted to introduce her husband to Neville, one of her oldest friends from Radcliffe. Although Jessie and Gordon had been married for nearly two years, most of Jessie's friends, who lived outside the Atlanta area, had yet to meet Gordon. Either he was abroad, as he was this July Fourth weekend, or he was so preoccupied by his work at the Centers for Disease Control that he could never spare the time to get away.

A former researcher at the Sidney Farber Cancer Institute across the Charles River and an ex-professor of genetics at Harvard, Neville Green was a donnish figure with an expanding bald spot on the very top of his head which each summer turned a startling shade of crimson.

They were sitting in his backyard under the shade of the gnarled old maple whose sturdiness and creaking boughs seemed to embody the spirit of its owner. It was close to seven o'clock and evening was settling in, though not with its customary Cambridge stillness. In anticipation of the festivities ahead, firecrackers and cherry bombs were being detonated with enough frequency to make it sound as if a civil insurrection were in progress.

"So I take it you two are getting along? I mean, you're finding marriage not to be as bumpy a road as all that?"

Ever since the spring semester of her junior year, when Jessie attended Neville's seminars in the history of eugenics, he had taken a paternal interest in her. There were occasions when he would hint that the man she was currently dating might not be exactly suitable for her. He was often right, although it required more than his advice for her to see it. She wondered whether he would approve of Gordon.

"There are problems as there are in any marriage. But I'm happy."

"Splendid. You seem happy. It wasn't so long ago, if my memory serves me right, that you were quite a moody young lady."

"I still have my moods," she laughed, "but they're not so pronounced. Gordon is a pretty stabilizing force. I've never met anyone who was so grounded, so certain of his path in life. And you know how I could get sometimes? I'd be all over the place."

"Where did you say Gordon was right now?"

"El Salvador."

"That sounds rather dangerous."

"He's been there before. He founded a clinic about a hundred miles from the capital twelve years ago. When he first went down there for the CDC, it was to direct a mass immunization program for the peasants. Then he realized that that wasn't enough. So he set up a clinic and trained people to assist him and eventually to take over themselves. At the time no one did things like that. I understand the CDC wasn't too pleased, and certainly the government wasn't exactly enthusiastic. They probably believed Gordon was a subversive and that the clinic was a part of some left-wing plot. But he stuck with it, training the peasants and making them into paramedics, barefoot doctors."

"Your husband sounds like an amazing man."

"I have a picture of him, if you'd like to see it."

"Absolutely."

Jessie opened her wallet and first removed a photograph of Gordon alone, a bit faded now and frayed along the edges. It showed a face remarkable in its ability to capture and hold experience; it was a patrician face, but not handsome; the eyes less piercing and blue in the photograph than they were in real life, the beard peppered with more gray since the picture had been taken. The lines in his face made him appear older than his forty-eight years. But if the camera had managed to project him ahead in time, it had not done so to his detriment. Age, Jessie thought, would sit well with him.

Studying it, Neville said, "He looks like a man one could count on as a loyal friend, but one who would not hesitate to tell you where he thought you'd gone astray."

She laughed. "Here," she said, holding out a second photograph for his inspection.

This photograph showed the two of them together, she and Gordon caught by a 35 mm less than a week before their wedding. Gordon was squinting into the sunlight, an uncustomary smile perched awkwardly on his lips, his arm about Jessie's waist. Her hair was tied back in a fashion that she'd long since given up. The way the sun dappled her hair had caused the red in it to turn a russet gold. This effect only occurred in summertime; winters, the color would revert to brunette.

The Jessie Palmer revealed by the photograph could have been a jazz dancer, leggy and lithe, with fine features set into a pale, oval face. Her eyes dominated her face, dark Mediterranean eyes.

Looking at the two of them together, frozen in time on the front lawn of Gordon's house in Atlanta, Neville was moved to tell her, "I'd have to say that the young lady in this picture looks like she was trying to learn how to become happy, but hadn't quite gotten the hang of it yet."

Jessie's laughter this time had an edge to it. Recalling the day the photograph was taken, though, she realized that he had hit upon something. She was nervous about the prospect of her impending marriage, as any woman might be, especially one who was about to go to the altar for the first time; unlike Gordon, who'd gone through the whole business before. But a part of her uncertainty stemmed from not knowing whether a man like Gordon, so set in his ways, so goddamn stubborn, and so many years her senior, would make the match she'd always believed was her due, like an inheritance you knew you would in time come in to.

Two years had passed since that photograph; so many things had changed which had surprised her. And so many things hadn't, which surprised her more.

Neville returned the photographs to her, then asked about her career which, after all, he had something of an investment in. Not for nothing did he attempt to drum into her head the basics of genetic theory and the principles of research.

Jessie had just finished the second year of the CDC's two-year Epidemic Intelligence Service program. Because she was such a recent graduate she'd had little occasion to work in the field. "One hepatitis outbreak in Oklahoma," she told Neville a little apologetically. "It was traced to a restaurant that was ultimately shut down. Unfortunately, most of the investigation had already been completed by state health authorities before we were called in. So I can't say that I've really had my baptism under fire."

She envied one former EIS graduate who had no sooner finished his training than he was dispatched to Philadelphia to contribute to the investigation into Legionnaire's Disease. There was an extraordinary opportunity, she thought, a chance to be in on the making of medical history.

"Tell me, Jessie, how did you feel when you were given your first assignment, small as it turned out to be?"

"Excited," she answered. "Scared. I'm still scared."

"That's not such a bad thing if you know how to put your apprehension to good use."

Unlike a physician who operates in controlled circumstances, his diagnosis likely to be backed up by second opinions, CAT scans, X-rays, and a vast arsenal of modern medical technology, a member of the Epidemic Intelligence Service was thrown into the field, often on his own, and asked to track down the source of an outbreak. Three children come down with hepatitis in the same household? How were they infected? Half a dozen men stumble into a hospital suffering from botulism poisoning? How did they come by it? Did they all eat the same contaminated food, perhaps in the same place? Is there the danger that others might be similarly poisoned? It was basically medical detective work, what authors on the subject tended to refer to as "shoeleather epidemiology."

Without asking, Neville went to get a refill for Jessie although she did not think that a third gin and tonic was absolutely essential at the moment. Apart from the distant explosions of firecrackers, she felt more at peace than she had since Gordon had left. In spite of all his assurances that he did not expect any trouble, the unstable political situation in El Salvador was nothing to take much comfort in. When she'd married Gordon she had to accept that he would often be on the move, working in countries where there was as much danger from gunfire as there was from malaria or dysentery. If for no other reason than this, she found the din of bursting firecrackers disturbing.

Neville returned to his chair and set her drink down on the table. "You know," he said, "I was anxious to meet Gordon not only because he happens to be your husband, but also because I've heard of a case, actually three cases, that might intrigue him."

"Here in Cambridge?"

"Well, in Boston really." Neville folded his hands and drew himself up in his chair. An expression formed on his face that Jessie remembered most particularly from his lectures; it was an expression that suggested the delight of a magician about to pull pigeons, rabbits, and silver dollars out of thin air.

Neville was a collector of rare cases, practically a connoisseur of them. Incidences of Lassa fever, African sleeping sickness, mysterious poisonings (an overdose of saltpeter, say), Wilson's disease, even a phenomenon known as carotenemia-lycopenemia which could turn someone's skin a disquieting shade of orange—all intrigued him. Armed with facts and anecdotes and all sorts of explanatory hypotheses, he was ready at a moment's notice to discuss these cases with anyone who would listen. He kept an account of these cases in several volumes of notebooks which included not only his own commentaries, but also clippings and lab reports sent to him by his many friends who were still active in the medical profession, friends who could be found in all corners of the world.

"What is most striking about these three cases is that as far as I know I am the only person to see a relationship between them. The first case is a young white male, about thirty-two years of age; the second two are both females. One a woman of Oriental extraction, in her mid-thirties, the other a Caucasian about forty-one years of age."

"How did you hear about these cases?"

Neville explained that he'd learned about them from different sources, no one of which was aware of the other. That was why he believed he was the first person to link them together. "But it's all speculative at this point," he cautioned, "and it would be premature to alert the health authorities that something might be occurring to warrant their attention."

He went on to say that the Oriental woman had been admitted to a psychiatric hospital a few days ago; the Caucasian woman had lapsed only that morning into a coma at a local hospital; and the young man . . . well, the young man had died in the last forty-eight hours. An autopsy was to be conducted on him tomorrow morning.

"I don't know whether you'd be interested or not, but if you like, you can accompany me tomorrow and we can witness the autopsy together."

Although Jessie had seen autopsies before, the prospect of spending part of her vacation observing the dissection of a cadaver did not exactly enthrall her. "But you haven't told me why you think these cases are related. You haven't even said what's wrong with any of them."

Neville gave her an odd, mischievous little smile and said, "Come with me tomorrow and I'll enlighten you. And in doing so I may become enlightened as well. You know how I like to work; start at the end and find my way to the beginning."

He gave her the upstairs bedroom. He preferred the one downstairs because of his legs. His knees were really shot in spite of the surgery repeatedly done on them, and climbing the stairs was too painful an ordeal for him. Besides, the upstairs bedroom was the one where he and his wife had slept until her death. Jessie imagined that the memories contained in the room were far more painful than his debilitated knees.

It was hard for her to get to sleep. The double bed was much too big, and perhaps because it was so unfamiliar to her, she was particularly sensitive to Gordon's absence. She lay awake for what seemed like hours. There was no clock in the room and she hadn't the energy to go to the bathroom where she'd left her watch. The room looked like it probably did on the day after Neville's wife had left it for good.

Listening to the firecrackers shattering the silence, Jessie reflected on her decision to go with Neville to see the autopsy. There was more to it, she decided, than he'd let on, not just in terms of the particulars of the cases, but in terms of his motive in introducing them to her. The Greeks, Druids, and Indians all had their secret mysteries into which select individuals were initiated. Neville had his mysteries, too, and Jessie had the feeling that tomorrow morning she would become an initiate herself.

three

The pathology department of St. Giles Hospital was reached through a subterranean corridor lined by cinderblock walls and kept brilliantly lit by incandescent lights. The faint odor of formaldehyde signaled the proximity of the department more forcefully than the names embossed on the doors.

The approach Jessie and Neville were making to the pathology department was necessarily slow, almost agonizing for Jessie. Neville relied on two canes to propel himself forward, and each step was accompanied by a slight grimace or an occasional sigh.

A secretary Neville addressed as Anne greeted them, saying, "Dr. Whitmore has just started. If you'll follow me, I'll show you the way."

She led them through a room given over to several cubicles occupied by clerks and secretaries, most of them female, and most of them, curiously, resembling Anne. Digital computer terminals, emitting an eerie greenish glow, rested on virtually every desk they passed.

"The fact of the matter is," Anne said, "I only have a vague notion as to what Dr. Whitmore is going to find. But from what I understand, the X-rays taken of the patient in the final hours of his life led him to believe that the results might turn out to be quite interesting indeed."

Anne opened a door which, unlike the others they'd passed through, was made of steel, and when it shut behind them, it did so loudly, with a finality that was appropriate to the purpose the autopsy room served.

Everything about the room—actually composed of three adjoining sections separated by partitions of translucent glass—reflected the utilitarian nature of the work that went on in it. It was spartan and unadorned save in Dr. Whitmore's office where, Jessie noted, postcards and pictures of his family had been tacked to a corkboard above his desk.

Visible along the farthest wall were banks of trays where bodies were stored, filed away for future reference, Jessie thought. There was, in addition, a walk-in refrigerator. If St. Giles followed the policy set by other hospitals and coroners' offices, this would be where the bodies of children and infants were kept.

Right behind the first partition they found Dr. Whitmore and his assistant. Whitmore was an affable, bearish man, with a carefully nurtured beard, who went about his business as if he were doing nothing more remarkable than ringing up sales in a department store.

The body of the young male, identified on his record and on the tag tied by a string to his right big toe as Perry Atwater, was stretched out on a table. On a second table specimen jars were laid out; some already contained bits and pieces of vital organs that would later be subjected to lab examination.

Jessie had seen cadavers—not many, but a few—that didn't appear to be dead. In dying their faces had assumed an expression of tranquility, as if they'd succeeded in making peace with themselves. But there was nothing about the look on this young man's face that suggested tranquility. Rigor mortis had frozen on it an expression of anguish; his features were so contorted with pain that his face was askew. His lips formed a crooked smile, a horrific grin.

"What did he die of, Dr. Whitmore?" Jessie asked.

She hoped that the pathologist would prove more forthcoming than Neville had been so far.

"That's what we're trying to find out." Dr. Whitmore was skewering the belly with a deft motion, extending the opening up into the wall of the chest, past the sternum. "The fact is that we really have no idea. Some sort of virus seems to be at work. You can look at the records if you'd like."

After perusing the documents Jessie could see why the physicians treating Perry Atwater might be confounded. Here was a white male, thirty-two years old, with nothing out of the ordinary in his medical history, apparently stricken quite suddenly by something, possibly a virus, that had lain dormant for some while before manifesting itself. He'd been admitted to St. Giles six days before. Conscious and relatively alert during the first forty-eight hours after his admission, he then lapsed into a coma from which he never recovered. His condition steadily deteriorated despite all the antibiotics administered to him. His protocol showed the use of three antiviral chemical agents which required permission of the patient's family to employ. At the end his doctors were ready to try anything.

"What is so really unusual about this case," Dr. Whitmore said, speaking more to Neville than to Jessie, "is that all the symptoms he exhibited, including those he experienced before his admission, point to a slow-moving virus."

Slow-moving viruses, which included rare ailments like Jakob-Creutzfeldt and possibly Alzheimer's diseases, act on the brain and, over the course of years, gradually destroy the tissue and central nervous system. No drugs or vaccines of any kind have been produced to arrest the inexorable progress of these diseases, let alone cure them.

"You feel this is unusual because it's so rare?" asked Jessie.

"It's rare all right. But that's not what makes it unusual. Most slow-moving viruses, once the initial symptoms appear, take anywhere from one year to four or five, in some instances—if we're talking about Alzheimer's—even longer, before the brain is gone or the victim dies." As he spoke, he stared down into the chest cavity which he was speedily and methodically in the process of emptying. He resected the organs on the left, then on the right, depositing a representative sampling from each in the appropriately labeled specimen jars; there they were left to swim in formaldehyde.

"But not in this instance?"

"Not in this instance. The disease, if it is a virus, is so acute that it accomplishes the same result in just a few weeks."

Neville, from his chair, regarded Jessie. "Didn't I tell you this might be interesting?"

"What you're saying then is that this is a fast-moving slow-moving virus?" Jessie said.

Neville and the pathologist found this amusing, but not Whitmore's dour assistant.

"You might put it that way," Whitmore said.

It was customary in performing autopsies to save the

brain for last. In this case, the examination of the brain would allow them to see just what impact the virus had had. This, after all, was the organ that had suffered the brunt of the attack.

First Whitmore peeled away the skin guarding the back wall of the skull, a task he accomplished with surprising quickness, bringing into light several square inches of bone.

After donning a face mask, Whitmore took hold of an electric drill and positioned its tip against the skull. The drilling made a racket, dislodging chips of bone, some as fine as dust, into the air. In less than a minute he'd succeeded in exposing Perry Atwater's brain.

Peering into the gap he'd just produced, Whitmore whistled in astonishment as he gathered up the organ in his gloved hands. "Well, isn't this something?" he said.

Looking over his shoulder, Jessie observed several patches of white scattered over the surface of the brain. There were specks of orange, too, like confetti. But that wasn't all.

"Jesus, I've never seen anything like this," Whitmore said. "Part of this fellow's brain seems to have just rotted away. See those holes there?" He was pointing to what, to the untrained eye, had the appearance of small cracks or fissures. "What we have here is a man with Swiss cheese for a brain," he declared, turning toward Jessie. "By the end of his life your average pet poodle probably had more smarts than he did."

Perry Atwater's autopsy was not the only thing that Neville Green wanted Jessie to see on that morning of July fifth. Once they were back in his car he said that he had one other destination in mind. By this time Jessie knew enough not to ask any questions, understanding that Neville wished her to draw her own conclusions.

Their second stop was situated close to Northeastern University, in a building whose indifferent postwar architecture gave no hint of what went on inside. It was fourteen stories tall and all of industrial gray brick. Only when Jessie raised her eyes to the top two floors did she notice anything unusual; on those two floors the windows were shielded by bars.

Above the entrance, the words HALBRITTEN INSTITUTE

were engraved in stone. Jessie hadn't heard of the Halbritten Institute, and there was nothing about the lobby which was helpful in establishing an identity for it. Ahead of them, a man wearing the uniform of a private security agency was seated at a desk, talking with a Boston city cop. There was a bank of elevators just behind them.

Jessie felt certain that this must be a psychiatric institution. It was the feel of the place, something in the air.

"We're here to see Dr. Scotto," Neville said. "We have an appointment."

The guard confirmed this, and after they signed in, he directed them up to the seventh floor.

On the seventh floor, no effort had been made by interior decorators to lift the spirits of the patients or the staff; it was, if anything, drabber than the lobby. From what Jessie could see by the names on the doors they passed, this floor held mostly administrative offices.

Dr. Ernest Scotto was a trim, dapper man with pinched features. A bowl of peanuts rested on his desk and every few minutes he'd take one, break apart the shell, and pop the nut into his mouth. He didn't offer any to his guests.

The records pertaining to the case that he'd alerted Neville to were spread out in front of him. "An unusual case, to be sure," he said. "In my opinion Miss Chong should not be here. But the court ordered her remanded here for observation. It's what her lawyer requested. So what can I do?" He threw up his hands in a gesture of resignation.

Jessie was wondering what this woman had done to have been remanded into the custody of a psychiatric institution, but the inference was clear: she was pleading not guilty by reason of insanity. The question was: Not guilty of what?

"Describe for my friend here what kind of behavior Miss Chong has been exhibiting since she was admitted—what was it, five days ago?" Neville said.

According to Scotto, Miss Chong had engaged in acts of self-mutilation, had repeatedly soiled herself, had attacked nurses and orderlies and guards alike with the result that she needed to be heavily sedated. On three occasions she'd attempted suicide, twice by trying to hang herself with a bedsheet and once by pounding her head against the wall until she'd produced a scalpal laceration nearly three inches long.

"You told me over the phone, Ernest, that this woman had no previous history of violent behavior—either toward herself or others," Neville said.

"That's correct, as far as we know. She committed no act of violence until she slit the throats of a couple in a nightclub—people that she had never met before in her life."

Each time Jessie thought she had caught a glimmer as to how this case related to Perry Atwater's, some new shred of information would emerge to throw her into even more confusion than before.

"Now, could you tell Miss Palmer what other symptoms you've observed since Miss Chong was admitted?"

"Let me caution you that at this juncture, until further tests are conducted, we have no way of knowing whether these symptoms are the result of a psychological disturbance or represent some physiological disorder such as a brain tumor."

Like a priest rattling off a litany he knows by heart, Scotto proceeded to catalog the symptoms: ataxia (lack of muscle coordination); spasticity; myoclonic jerks (involuntary contractions of the muscles); tremors; rigidity of the neck; petit mal seizures followed by blackouts and the loss of short-term memory.

"At intervals the patient is lucid enough to describe some of her symptoms as she experiences them," Scotto continued. "One of the more curious she reports seems to involve some sort of optical illusion."

Scotto consulted the records again and said, "Just before her blackouts she sees lights, brilliant lights. She says they're like flashbulbs exploding in her eyes. They last for as long as half a minute." He poured out a handful of peanuts and began cracking them open. "Let me caution you again that there may be nothing physically the matter with the woman. So far none of the lab tests we've performed, blood and urine analyses and such, have shown up positive for anything. Even such a bizarre range of symptoms as I've just enumerated can be attributable to some grave psychological disorder—a paranoid-schizophrenic reaction, let's say."

Jessie had the sense that, as a psychotherapist, Scotto might have had a certain vested interest in viewing the patient in this light. Nonetheless, the symptoms that he'd just described were all compatible with the diagnosis of a slow-moving virus—or a fast-moving slow-moving virus, as she'd dubbed it.

"Would you like to see the patient for yourself?" Scotto asked. "Not in person," he added. "We monitor patients in the special wards through video cameras. Without constant surveillance I'm afraid that Miss Chong would have succeeded in her attempt to put an end to her life."

"I don't know about Miss Palmer, but I would be very interested in seeing the patient," Neville said.

"Sure, why not?" said Jessie.

What she imagined she'd see was based on her previous visits to hospital psychiatric units, where almost the entire spectrum of human derangement was on display: a museum of dementia. But precedent proved to be of no help in this instance.

At first all that they could see was the room itself, painted a shade of green more soothing than what she'd seen on the corridor walls; dominating this room was a bed, distinguished by the leather constraints attached to the mattress. The mattress was bare. A pillow, stained with what looked like dried blood, lay at its foot; a blanket had also fallen—or been flung—off the bed.

As the video camera slowly began to pan around the room, Jessie caught sight of a part of the wall previously unexposed to view. Although a valiant effort had been made to wash it away, she could still make out the place the patient had banged her head repeatedly; not only was there evidence of dried blood, however faint, but there was a conspicuous depression in the wall itself where it had begun to yield to her blows.

The camera continued to pan until it came to focus on her.

Her head was buried in her hands; her hair, tangled and matted, but still lustrously black, hung down so that it touched the floor. The johnny she wore had come loose and looked about to fall off her shoulders. She was huddled in a corner, her bare legs drawn up so that she was practically sitting on them. She was oblivious to the exposure of the pudendum; the triangle of hair there was wiry and sparse. Small cuts and several bruises were visible up and down her legs, and although most of these wounds were dressed, gleaming with new applications of antiseptic ointment, there were more recent wounds, still oozing blood, that evidently no one had had a chance to attend to. Her body was shuddering in response to tremors coursing through it. From time to time she'd stiffen suddenly, or an arm would begin twitching uncontrollably.

Jessie cast a sidelong glance at Neville, but there was no telling from his detached expression what he was thinking.

"Wait," said Scotto. "In another couple of moments she should show us her face." He made some adjustments on the panel from which the camera was operated, bringing the woman into closer focus.

There was something repulsive about all this, Jessie thought, observing this poor woman through the intervention of technology as though she were a dangerous, but very rare, caged animal. In a way, of course, that was exactly what she was.

"It's a bit uncanny," began Scotto, "but she seems to sense when the camera's aimed on her even though it's completely concealed from view. Look."

Very slowly Lucy Chong raised her head and glanced up toward the camera just as Scotto had said she would. The effect was unnerving; Jessie had the feeling that she could see them, that not only did she know the camera was there, she knew that *they* were there, and that no matter how shattered her mind and body might be, she still retained a dignity that they, by the very act of spying on her, had lost.

At first, because of the way her hair draped her face, like a badly frayed curtain, they were unable to get much of a look at her. But then she pulled at her hair until it parted enough so that they could see what they liked. It was as if she were saying: All right, you want a show, I'll give you a show.

Jessie sucked in her breath; it was all she could do to keep her eyes on the screen. For there was hardly any flesh left to the woman's face; it was a maze of welts and lacerations, oozing with pus and blood where she'd ripped off the dress-ings. Her lips were bitten through and bleeding as well. One eye was half shut and veiled with creamy yellow pus. But the other eye was still open and functioning; and in that eye Jessie beheld such despondency and defeat that she stood up from her chair and said to the two men, "I think I've seen enough."

As she fled the monitoring room Jessie felt that she had looked into the eye of someone whose brain was rotting away, becoming as riddled with holes as Swiss cheese, in Dr. Whitmore's phrase. The horror wasn't that the woman was dying or that she might be despondent; the horror was that she might not be human anymore.

Only when they were on their way out of the Halbritten Institute did Neville hazard an opinion as to what they'd just witnessed.

"There's no question in my mind that in spite of what Dr. Scotto said, Miss Chong is suffering from the same disease that struck down poor Mr. Atwater. Did you happen to notice the extensor plantar reflex?"

"The what?"

"Two of her toes on her left foot were curled upward—it's a symptom often associated with brain damage."

"How much longer do you think she has?"

"Let's hope not long. What she's doing now could hardly be termed living."

"What about the third case you mentioned?"

"Oh yes. Her name is Leiter—Ellen Leiter. I haven't been able to learn much about her, but I'm working on it. At the moment this is really all I have to show you."

Supporting himself on Jessie's arm, Neville drew three neatly folded clippings from his inside jacket pocket. One was from the Boston *Globe*, the other two from the *Herald-Traveler*. She scanned the headlines of each:

BROOKLINE MAN ON WILD SPREE
Kills One, Injures Four in Braintree Mall

MOTHER OF THREE HELD ON CHARGES OF
ATTACKING 12-YEAR-OLD SON

WOMAN SLAYS TWO IN NIGHTCLUB INCIDENT

These tales of urban mayhem and death would have been unexceptional except that they all involved people who fell fatally ill in the aftermath of their violent crimes.

"Notice not one of them had any previous record of criminal behavior. On the contrary, all of them seemed to have led untainted lives." Neville went on to say that while it was not unknown for people to become suddenly deranged without showing any sign of mental imbalance, it struck him as more than coincidental that this should happen to three individuals in a one-week period. And beyond the bounds of probability that each should then exhibit the same symptoms.

"If this thing does turn out to be a virus, that would mean others might be infected as well," Jessie said, drawing the obvious inference.

"That is quite correct."

"So I take it you expect more stories like these."

"It wouldn't surprise me," Neville said, "if the situation did not deteriorate, perhaps to the point of an epidemic. What you might call a plague of madness."

four

The roar of the 747 as its engines went into reverse jolted Gordon Markoff awake. Blearily he turned his eyes toward the oval window and saw that this was Hartsfield Airport, Atlanta. He was home, only he didn't feel home. His mind was still back in El Salvador. Whenever he slept his dreams were full of automatic fire and the thud of artillery. The mutilated bodies of peasants, executed for some forgotten offense, would regain their lives in his dreams and begin to crawl along the ground, making threatening gestures, as if he alone were responsible for their plight.

His body, fatigued and aching, wasn't made for the confines of a 747 seat. He was too tall, too thickly built. It was painful getting up; his feet were numb, they didn't want to move. Hell, *he* didn't want to move. The smile the stewardess gave him, he thought, was inappropriate, intended for people who actually liked being swept through the air from one place to another.

Jessie was waiting for him by the gate. She still hadn't spotted him yet. He saw her as a stranger might, attractive, certainly enticing, but vulnerable. A con man would be able to pick her out of a crowd, move right in on her. Always when he went away he was seized by dread, by a nameless fear, not about what would happen to him but what would happen to her. It was his belief that she needed him more than she thought or wanted to.

He would have liked to buy a present, something exorbitant, something one of a kind, but in El Salvador what they had to sell didn't come close to fitting those criteria. Nor was there any time on the stopover in Miami to shop around.

She never expected gifts from him, really. When they'd met he had just finished delivering a talk to her epidemiology class on schistosomiasis, detailing how the little buggers could eat their way into you if you were so unlucky to step barefooted into the African waters where they thrive and cause no end of trouble, not the least of which was blindness. She told him she'd never heard such a thoughtful analysis and such a colorful one. She seemed to revel in his words; his words were his gifts to her and she made it clear that they need not take material form so long as he never committed the crime of boring her.

But now he wondered. Now he might be guilty. Things had changed between them; he'd felt it before he'd left this last time.

Yet the sight of her, wearing a white shirt, open (a little too much) to reveal a simple gold necklace, and white slacks, caused his breath to catch in his throat and a sharp pain to stab at his chest. How much longer would it be, he wondered, before she protested his frequent absences and stopped coming to Hartsfield Airport to wait patiently at the gate for him to return?

She saw him now, the exhausted veteran of foreign places, the medical missionary back from the war zone, and her face lit up.

He took her in his arms, registering the scent of her perfume. She was warm; her skin felt like it was on fire from the heat of the summer day.

"You look terrific," he said. He kissed her.

"We have to get out of the way," she told him, drawing him off to the side so that other deplaning passengers could go by.

She was hardly about to tell him how terrific he looked; he wouldn't let her get away with an obvious lie like that.

"It didn't work out, did it?" she asked in a soft voice.

"Let's get my luggage and get out of here and I'll tell you what happened."

But once they were in the car, stalled in a gigantic traffic jam that seemed to have brought everything to a halt all the way from the airport to the Druid Hills district where they lived, he was no more disposed to talk.

"Say something," Jessie urged him. The silence was getting to her. The heat, the traffic (she was the one doing the driving), were no doubt contributing to her irritability. "Please, Gordon."

Gordon struggled to get his voice back. "It's gone," he said finally.

"What? What's gone?"

"The clinic."

She looked at him, not quite comprehending what he meant by this. "Your clinic? You're talking about the one you built?"

It was difficult to talk just now. He needed to sleep for hours, for days, before he could make a coherent thought come out right in words.

"About the third or fourth day I was there, the guerrillas came. They didn't do anything to us. But they were insistent we treat some of their wounded. When someone's wounded I'm not in the habit of asking questions. We did what we could for them."

He fell silent. For a moment he might have dozed off. He went on, "Then the army came to dislodge the guerrillas. The battle began outside of El Divisio, then it somehow spread into it. The government sent planes. They must have thought they were losing. OV-10's they're called—counter-insurgency. They came low over the town, obliterated half of it. They must have figured the guerrillas were still there."

"But they weren't?"

"No, not anymore."

"And the clinic? It was bombed?"

"Right out of existence."

"Oh, Gordon."

"We'd evacuated most of the patients and the paramedics. It could have been worse. I was thinking of calling you and saying I was staying down there to build another clinic. In El Divisio or somewhere else. But then I decided that that was for another time."

"I'm glad you didn't. I was worried when you were there. I knew something terrible had happened. I wish you'd have let me know."

"It's not so easy making telephone calls out of a town like that."

"You don't have to go back there, do you?"

His renewed silence was in itself an answer. It was something that he felt he had to do, go back, and he wished that he could make her understand why.

The house at 54 Corcoran Road was built to keep books. The furnishings were incidental, the decor more so. Books were what counted; and enough shelf space to accommodate them all so that they were well displayed and easily found. Little by little, Jessie was trying to change all that. Gordon noticed that there were new curtains and that the wallpaper in the dining room had been changed, and there were undoubtedly other alterations he'd find if he looked for them. He wasn't certain whether he liked these changes, but he was in no position to judge now. He just kissed Jessie good night and went upstairs to sleep.

Darkness was in the sky when he awoke. The cicadas were making a racket under his bedroom window. Ten after midnight. That meant six hours of sleep. Not nearly enough. But he was relieved that he couldn't remember dreaming about screaming warplanes and dying children.

Now he became aware of sounds downstairs, possibly from the living room. Footsteps. Something clattered to the floor.

He assumed that Jessie was cleaning. Occasionally, when she couldn't sleep, she would get up in the middle of the night and attack every last grain of dust that had collected in the preceding week, no matter that a woman named Mrs. Sanchez came at regular intervals to do exactly that.

With a groan Gordon got himself out of bed. He opened the door and gazed out into the hallway. No lights appeared to be on anywhere in the house. Obviously, if Jessie was engaged in some insomniac housekeeping she would want a bit of light to assist her efforts.

But there was definitely someone down there. From his experience objects did not generally tumble to the floor on their own. Discounting the intervention of mischievous poltergeists, Gordon concluded that there was an unwelcome human presence in his house. That was bad enough, but what was far more disturbing was not knowing his wife's whereabouts.

For fear of alerting the intruder he dared not call out to

her. He stood at the top of the stairs, peering down into the gloom, unable to make anything out. Cocking his ear, he listened intently, hoping to track the intruder by sound alone.

But to his frustration he registered no sound other than what the damn cicadas were making. He started down the stairs, his bare feet so soft against the carpeting that he doubted his approach could be heard.

It was only when he reached the bottom of the staircase that he realized he had no plan of action. What exactly would he do if the intruder was armed? He had in his time done some wrestling, but years had passed since then, and the ability to maneuver an opponent into the best armhold was certainly going to be of no avail in the face of a .38-caliber pistol.

From where he was standing he had only to extend his hand a few inches to turn on the switch that would throw the entire living room into light. Yet, until he had some idea as to where the intruder might be, he didn't want to do this.

Certainly, whoever it was couldn't stand stark still forever, he thought. He would have to move, and in moving, make some sound. But this belief, however rooted in logic, was not confirmed by reality. At last his impatience got the better of him. He depressed the switch.

The lights—and there were three of them triggered by the switch, two lamps and one brass fixture directly overhead—momentarily blinded him. When he could finally be sure of what he was seeing, he found that the only thing that greeted his eyes was an empty room.

This infuriated him. This enraged him. He was tired, yes, possibly exhausted, and quite definitely depressed. But he could not for one minute accept the possibility that his depleted emotional and physical state could account for a distortion of his senses. It was almost as if he would've preferred to discover a burglar in the act of carrying out his crime.

Had the man (he couldn't quite bring himself to imagine it was a woman) simply, Houdini-like, vanished into thin air?

As he walked into the parlor which adjoined the living room, the first thing he noticed was that the sheet music on the more-or-less out-of-tune Baldwin was one of the Goldberg Variations. When he'd left for El Salvador, Jessie had been playing Strauss waltzes. He supposed that this was progress of a sort.

Only then did he see that one of the screens wasn't quite closed. About an inch separated it from the windowsill. Inspecting it, Gordon observed also that it was not quite fitted into its frame. Of course, it was conceivable that Jessie had been careless, but it was hardly likely.

Dousing the parlor light so that he could better see outside, he observed that the shrubbery immediately below the window had been disturbed. Some branches had snapped off, some leaves stripped away.

Venturing outside, still in his bare feet, he found all the evidence he needed that someone had broken in. Footprints were easily distinguished in the dirt out of which the shrubbery grew, and tracked across the lawn.

The satisfaction he gained knowing that he hadn't been hearing things was outweighed by the great bewilderment he experienced after making a hasty survey of the house. Nothing had been taken. All of Jessie's jewelry, all of the silverware, the RCA portable color TV, the Pioneer tape deck—everything was there. It was almost insulting; had the burglar found nothing of interest? Were he a bibliophile he might have stripped the shelves bare, and then Gordon would have been in a lot of trouble.

But while Jessie's jewelry might be safe, that did not answer the question as to where the hell she was. Only when he went into the kitchen did he discover a note from her which read: "Had to go to the office. Dinner in the fridge. See you later. Love, J."

The thought occurred to him that the note was so prominently displayed that the burglar could have read it, too, but why should it matter? No burglar would ordinarily be interested in the whereabouts of the house's occupants in their absence. Besides, even if, on the off-chance, he was, how could he possibly know which office the note was referring to?

five

Jessie knew that she should be at home even if Gordon was still asleep; he would want her there when he woke up. She felt terrible about what had happened to his clinic but realized at the same time that she resented the hold it had on him. One day he was going to go back and get himself killed—and who knows, he might welcome a martyr's death—and the thought terrified her.

Her office was a refuge. Here, *she* was in control. For the first time she had the feeling she was onto something, that Neville wasn't joking when he'd called the specimens of tissue and blood taken from the three victims in Boston, her belated wedding present. Chong, Leiter, and Atwater: the names were like a litany, a promise, or, more appropriately, like the writing on the wall described in the Book of Daniel: Mene, Mene, Tekel, Upharsin.

Along with the specimens had come the news that Chong and Leiter had followed Atwater to the grave, their deaths coming within just hours of each other. Jessie wasn't surprised. Recalling the hideous, half-human look on the Chong woman's face she was actually relieved to hear that she'd died. How would it be possible for anyone to live on with their brain rotting away, helpless to arrest the loss of memories, thoughts, emotions, even one's own identity—it was too much to imagine.

The specimens, sent to the CDC by the victims' physicians, were now being analyzed in the maximum containment lab, better known as the hot lab, where the strictest precautions were enforced to prevent any contamination. No one wanted all Atlanta to catch whatever Perry Atwater, Lucy Chong, and Ellen Leiter had had.

If the tests confirmed that the same organism—the same

disease process—was harbored by all three victims, then Neville would be proven right.

The next question was: Did anyone else have it? Did it have the potential to spread widely enough to turn into an epidemic?

Not that Jessie had such a perverse sensibility that she welcomed epidemics into the world, but if there were to be an epidemic, she wanted to be in on the investigation that would look for its cause. Of the thousand epidemics brought to the attention of the CDC each year, only relatively few of them were cause for alarm and even fewer were, like Legionnaire's Disease or AIDS, without precedent, epidemics as historically important in their own way as Waterloo or Hiroshima.

In the basement of Building 1, where Jessie had her office, was a refrigerated room. Stored in the room were specimen bottles containing approximately a quarter of a million organisms—bacteria, viruses, retroviruses, prions, and parasites—which had afflicted mankind for generations. They were preserved so that they could be compared with other deadly agents still at large.

So it was possible that whatever had eaten away the brains of the three Boston cases was already known and identified, even if no cure existed for it.

Jessie had a feeling, though, that she—or rather Neville—had stumbled onto something that was altogether unknown. She imagined that explorers must feel the way that she did, exhilarated by the prospect of charting for the first time territory that was unmapped, never before visited by Westerners; and frightened, too, for the territory was inhospitable and the natives there were decidedly unfriendly.

There was a rap on her door, which she'd left partially ajar. She looked up to see Pat Flanigan standing in front of her, a sheaf of lab reports in her hand. Pat, who worked at the hot lab, was a wiry woman with a penchant for big looped earrings, short, boyishly cut hair, and dresses intended to keep the eye on her legs, where there was much to admire, and not on her face or breasts, where there wasn't.

"Here you go," she said, laying the reports on Jessie's desk.

The reports were, as always, couched in the formal language that was peculiar to lab technicians everywhere: "Cells were harvested, centrifuged into a pellet, fixed in glutaraldehyde, postfixed in tetroxide, dehydrated, and embedded in Epon-Araldite . . ." The words advanced in dizzying array across the pages: Porter-Blum MT-2 ultramicrotome . . . uranyl acetate . . . lead citrate . . . Philips EM 200 electron microscope . . . titering . . . lethal dose 50 . . .

She stopped when she came to the words "potentially virus positive." Glancing up at the top of the document, she observed that this test on brain tissue pertained to Perry Atwater.

Although Pat hadn't spoken a word since sitting down, her expression betrayed her curiosity at Jessie's reaction. Jessie turned to the report on Chong—in this instance, a serum analysis. Her eyes ran down the page until she again came to the words "potentially virus positive."

The phrase was echoed once more in a report on a section of brain extracted from Leiter.

Jessie raised her eyes and looked at Pat.

"It's the same in all three cases," the assistant lab director said.

"But what do you mean by 'potentially positive'?" Jessie asked.

"Well, it appears to be a virus, but we can't be certain. For one thing, it's so small that even with the Philips microscope we aren't able to clearly distinguish it. And that means that an enlargement of one hundred thousand times isn't adequate to the task. And measured by its radiation and heat, we're pretty certain that it's an entity distinct from all but a few known viruses."

Just as Dr. Whitmore had surmised from his autopsy on Atwater, Pat noted that there was a remarkable similarity to such slow-moving viruses as Jakob-Creutzfeldt disease and even more obscure diseases like Gerstmann-Straussler syndrome. "Certainly, what we've seen of the brain tissue samples bears this out. There were gaping white holes—vacuoles—where the nerve cells should have been. And way too many plaques—and fibriles that are unlike any virus I've ever seen—they resemble viruses you find in plants or animals. We also observed an astonishing number of astrocytes."

Astrocytes, which showed up only under microscopic examination, were like spiderwebs of multiplying brain cells, further evidence of the spread of the disease.

"But in any event," Pat went on, "this virus—if it is one—follows at least two of the Henle-Koch Postulates. We'll have to wait to find out about the third."

These postulates were like scripture for lab researchers wherever in the world they might be working. Simply put, they stated the following:

1. The same organism must be present in all cases.
2. The organism must be capable of being isolated from the patient and grown in cultures.
3. When the pure cultures are inoculated into susceptible animals, these animals will reproduce the symptoms of the disease.

It was this third postulate that remained to be tested. Since the mice (the susceptible animals in question) had just been injected with the virus, there was nothing to do but wait to see whether they would fall ill and behave erratically, maybe to the point of exhibiting what, for a mouse, would be considered psychopathic behavior.

As Pat was about to leave she turned and said, "There's one other thing you might find interesting when you have a chance to read those reports."

From what Jessie could see there was more than enough "interesting things" about these cases to keep her occupied. "What's that?"

"We found positive chemical findings for choline and succinic acid in the brain tissue we analyzed—findings that the autopsy reports we received from Boston failed to indicate."

"You're going to have to explain to me what relevance that has, Pat. I'm no toxicologist."

"Generally speaking, neither choline nor succinic acid will show up in a test. They're byproducts of succinylcholine after it breaks down in the body. Since you're not an anesthesiologist, either, let me explain that succinylcholine is a muscle relaxant. Enough of it, you paralyze the muscles, including the lungs, and essentially produce death by suffocation. An interesting thing about succinylcholine is that it has the capacity to leave the body without a trace. Only in this instance, such a large quantity must have been used that we found evidence of it in the brains of two of the cases—Chong and Leiter."

"So what you're saying is that it was the succinylcholine that killed Chong and Leiter, not the disease."

"In such a large quantity as it was administered, I would have to say yes. All it did was to hasten their deaths maybe by a few days. While I don't like to speculate about these things, it's just possible that someone with access to an anesthetic like that—a physician or a nurse perhaps—might have performed . . . well, a mercy killing."

"But that would mean there had to be two different mercy killings, committed in two different hospitals on two individuals who were not in any way related or being treated by the same physician."

"Yes, I've thought of that. It is rather odd. But I don't think we can rule out euthanasia."

"Did you find any trace of succinylcholine in Atwater?"

"We went back and looked for it, but there was no trace of it at all. That doesn't mean it wasn't used. It might only mean it was administered in smaller doses so that it didn't show up on our toxicology screens. What you would have to do is to analyze other tissues—the liver, say—to see if they were positive for the drug. And you still wouldn't know for certain even if they weren't."

Pat glanced at her watch and announced that she had to get home. "Once you're through reading the reports, if you have any questions, give me a buzz."

All Jessie had were questions, but she doubted that Pat Flanigan was the one to answer them.

She realized that there was nothing to be gained by reading the reports now; she was too tired, her mind would not absorb any more data. Tomorrow morning she would get to them, when she'd had the benefit of sleep.

Before she left her office she made a note to herself to call Neville.

She not only wanted to inform him of the findings, but she was anxious to solicit his advice in regard to whether she should get in contact with the DA's office in Boston. *Euthanasia* made it sound nice, really quite palatable; it was just that in certain instances what started out as mercy killing turned out to be killing pure and simple.

six

It was only when Pat Flanigan was halfway to her car that she detected the presence of a man walking behind her. Since it was nearly one in the morning, she could only assume that it was another researcher working late on a project. What caused her to think otherwise was how synchronized his pace was with hers. The rhythm of her step was echoed almost exactly by his.

When, as an experiment, she tried to accelerate her pace, perceptibly but not so much that it would hint at any alarm, she noted that his picked up speed as well.

Pat didn't like the idea that they were now farther up Clifton Road, beyond the range of the lights from the CDC complex. It seemed to her that she had three choices: she could continue on to her car in hope of outdistancing the man—assuming that he was following her; she could go back the way she'd come; or she could walk across the street and take temporary refuge in the lobby of the Sheraton Hotel.

She decided on the Sheraton, abruptly veering out into the road and doubling back. No longer concerned about what impression she gave, she broke into a run.

While not large, the Sheraton had the advantage of convenient access both to the CDC and to Emory University about half a mile to the north on Clifton Road. With the night this far advanced, there weren't many people about; the bar had closed and the lobby was empty save for one pair of drunken businessmen and a disconsolate-looking clerk.

Pat's breathless arrival in the lobby stirred absolutely no interest from the three. But it didn't matter; she took comfort in their presence. Only now did she risk looking through the window. But there was no one there. She knew that she hadn't imagined the man, but it was possible that he hadn't been following her, that he was simply on the way to his own car.

Now that she was safe, at least for the time being, she had to make yet another decision. It was silly to call for a taxi. What was she going to tell the driver? That she wanted him to drive her a sixteenth of a mile down the road to her car? Certainly she couldn't remain in the lobby all night.

For the first time the night clerk seemed to notice her. In light of the somewhat flamboyant style of dress she favored, he might have suspected that she was a prostitute. Why else would a solitary woman, who was obviously not a guest, be hanging around a hotel lobby at this hour?

Giving the clerk an apologetic smile, she rose from her seat and went outside.

The night was still and warm. Scanning both sides of the road, Pat could see no one. That didn't provide her with much assurance, however, for it was always possible that someone could be lurking among the trees that grew thick in places on the perimeter of the CDC complex.

Nonetheless, she set off, thinking as a precaution that she would walk along the shoulder of the road where she could be easily spotted by passing motorists.

Her car was parked on a narrow side street just off Clifton. Her keys clutched in her hand, she reached it without incident.

Once inside she made sure to lock the door. As soon as she turned the ignition a Hank Williams ballad came blasting out of the radio.

Reflexively, her eyes traveled to the rearview mirror just before she shifted into gear. It was then that she saw him. The eyes first, dull and unreadable, then the hair, half blond, half white, slapped down both sides of his skull by a part in the middle.

What she didn't see was the gun, but she felt it pressing lightly but emphatically against the back of her head.

A scream died in her throat. Her mouth hung open, but not a sound escaped. Her knuckles turned white as she tightened her grip on the steering wheel. She realized that the wetness trickling down her leg was urine.

It seemed to take the man forever to speak. "Where are the specimens from Boston?" he asked.

She was so astounded at the question, for a moment she almost forgot about her panic. Expecting to be robbed or raped, she had not considered the possibility that this man might be interested in anything connected to her work.

"What specimens are you talking about?"

The tip of the gun pressed closer, through her hair, against the wall of her skull. "Don't give me that shit," he said. He did not sound angry or even irritated. His voice was flat, possibly Midwestern.

But she hadn't been trying to evade the question. It was just that her mind was blank. She could scarcely articulate a single word, much less think.

"Talk to me," the man commanded.

"In the hot lab . . . the maximum containment lab."

"Then why don't you kill the motor and let's you and I take a walk over there."

The maximum containment lab was isolated from the rest of the CDC facilities and only those authorized to work in it were allowed to enter. It was designed especially so that the risk of contamination would be minimized. In effect, it was a building within a building, equipped with elaborate filtration devices. Inside, researchers handled disease organisms for which there was no known antidote.

As they were heading toward the hot lab the man told Pat that if they passed a colleague or a security guard, she was to make no sign that she was in trouble. He did not have to tell her what would happen if she did; the threat posed by the gun he carried, bulging against the olive army surplus jacket he wore, was a sufficient reminder of the consequences.

"I should warn you that there might be a guard at the entrance of the lab," she said. "He won't let you in."

"You let me worry about that."

"But what am I going to tell him when he asks me what you're doing in a restricted area?"

Pat was anxious that this man understand the risk he was running. The last thing she wanted was for him to react in surprise by shooting her.

"If he asks you who I am, tell him I'm an official visitor, make up some kind of story." Obviously he found such considerations irrelevant.

"I don't think that you realize—" she started to say, but he abruptly cut her off.

"Shut the fuck up, just shut the fuck up, will you?"

No security man was in sight outside the lab. Pat didn't know whether to be grateful for his absence or not.

In order to gain admission to the outer shell of the lab, it was necessary to punch out a personal code. Pat toyed with the idea of telling the gunman that the code had been changed and she couldn't remember it, but she decided that this was too transparent a lie.

Immediately beyond the door to the outer shell were chemical showers which each worker had to pass through before entering the laboratories themselves. The man had no interest in the showers, nor would he permit Pat to take one in spite of her protest that certain precautions were necessary. "You don't have any idea just how lethal the materials are in there."

He might have thought that all she was trying to do was stall him. From the implacable expression on his face it was obvious that he was not to be deterred from carrying out his objective.

The containment area was divided into two sections. One was known as the cabinet room, where specimens were examined in specially pressurized glass cabinets, passed from one researcher to the next with tongs. In this section researchers were obliged to wear only gloves. It was in the other section that they needed to don seamless blue space suits, each equipped with its own filtration system attached by a hose to the ceiling. These suits were mandatory because the air inside this section of the lab was considered contaminated.

Pat explained all this to the man, but when she was through, he looked as blank as before. She wondered if he was retarded, or of such low intelligence that certain ideas failed to penetrate. But then he nodded and agreed to put on a suit, making sure in the process that he never once surrendered hold of his weapon.

When Pat went to do likewise he shook his head, saying, "Not for you."

"What do you mean? I can't go in there without a suit."

"Of course you can. I say that you can and will."

"If you don't let me put on a suit I'm not going to punch out the code to get us in there."

The personal code needed at this point differed from the one giving access to the outer shell.

"Then I will have to kill you here." Astonishingly, his voice remained as toneless, as flat, as before. It seemed to Pat that he was incapable of registering any emotion whatsoever; he was altogether dead inside.

He brought his gun up to her head and cocked it. She had not the slightest doubt that he would discharge it should she continue in her refusal to punch out the code.

Quickly calculating the odds, she concluded that, whatever risk she might incur by breathing in potentially contaminated air, she still had a chance of survival. The other alternative left her with none. She punched out the code.

The door yielded into the airlock leading to the suit room. They were now in a world of Class IV viruses—the most dangerous in existence.

Pat presumed that this environment would be completely unfamiliar to this man. Here, among the microscopes, ultracentrifuges, incubators, refrigerators, freezers, and cryostats where frozen tissues were prepared, he was as lost as he would be on another planet. That gave Pat some solace. What she planned to do was to present him with specimens of relatively little importance and tell him that they were the ones that had arrived from Boston.

The suit was designed so that voice communications could be maintained without any trouble; all that it did was make him sound even drier than he was already.

"They're over here," she told him, leading him to the refrigerator where specimens used in a score of tests were being kept. Although she recognized that the effort was going to be of little avail, she tried to breathe as little as possible.

The shelves of the refrigerator were lined with a variety of containers—Roux bottles, French Square bottles, test tubes, and plaque bottles.

Pat examined these tubes and bottles, looking for four whose loss would cause little harm. The labels were coded according to a system used by the Data and Specimen Handling Section (DASH). It was this department that received the specimens and then decided where to route them for diagnostic testing.

"I don't have all day," the man said.

Without displaying further hesitation, Pat extracted four French Square bottles.

"Let me see them."

She handed the bottles to him, certain that he would be incapable of distinguishing between one kind of tissue and another once it had been sectioned and submerged in formaldehyde.

She noticed that he wasn't looking at what the French Square bottles contained, but rather at the labels.

"These aren't the ones," he said as he dropped them—one by one—on the floor. Each shattered in turn, releasing an odor of formaldehyde and no telling how many millions of lethal microbes into the air.

She realized that this man knew very well what he was after, that any further attempt to deceive him would be foolish.

It was of little consequence now how he'd acquired the information he had. All that mattered to her was getting out alive.

Having placed the relevant specimens in storage only an hour before, she had no difficulty in locating them. He examined the French Square bottles she gave him now and grunted, apparently satisfied that he had what he wanted. Then he told her he wanted them destroyed.

Pat led him to the solid-waste disposal unit. Before the specimens were destroyed they would first be rendered harmless—inactivated—by passage through an extended cycle of the interlocked autoclave. She doubted whether such protective measures interested the man.

Having done what he wanted, she assumed that he would allow her to leave the containment area. But evidently he had other ideas.

"You have syringes here?"

"Yes, why do you want to know?"

"Get me a few bottles, three of them—I don't give a shit what they are so long as they're from that refrigerator."

He was obviously aware that no matter what she chose it would be highly contagious.

Seeing her hesitate, he brought his gun up to her head.

Her hands were shaking so badly that one of the syringes dropped and shattered, forcing her to go back to the cabinet where they were kept and retrieve another. The syringes were disposable, with blunter needles than usual to minimize the risk of accidental puncture.

The man then seized hold of her left arm and led her back to the refrigerator. "Close your eyes," he told her.

"What are you going to do?" Her throat was so dry, she could barely speak.

"Close your eyes," he repeated.

She closed her eyes. He threw open the refrigerator door.

"Reach in. Reach in and give me those damn bottles."

One by one she plucked three at random off the refrigerator shelves. He took them from her.

"You can open your eyes," he said.

She felt her legs giving way; it was all she could do to keep herself upright by leaning against the counter. Tears flooded her eyes. "Please," she said, "please . . ." She couldn't seem to get another word out.

He wasn't paying any attention. With the practiced hand of either a doctor or a junkie the man began to fill the syringes with serum, blood, and urine. "Bolivian Hemorrhagic fever," he said, naming one specimen. "Lassa fever," he said, naming another. "Lassa fever again."

Before he could lift the third bottle to his eyes to study the label, Pat understood what he was about to do. Taking advantage of his momentary distraction, she ran.

Her breath coming in gasps, she stumbled, catching herself before she could fall. Unable to help herself, she turned her head to look back. She couldn't see him. But he was obviously there. The interlocked door loomed just ahead of her. She guessed the distance to be about twenty feet, maybe twenty-five.

It occurred to her that she was making a mistake by heading for the door; he would be expecting her to do that. There was an emergency exit located between the suit room and the cabinet room. While her assailant had demonstrated a frightening awareness of how the hot lab operated, it was possible that he didn't know about this emergency exit.

Yet to get to the exit she would have to double back, and

that might prove more foolhardy than continuing on in the direction she already was. Less than half a dozen feet from the door, she decided it would be absurd to change her mind.

Just as she put her hand to the mechanism that would release the door, a hand was slapped over her mouth. How stupid, she thought, to have believed she could escape.

But it wasn't being caught by her assailant that came as such a surprise; rather it was the sudden searing pain of the needle that was jabbed into the back of her neck. She cried out and reached around in a futile attempt to extract it. His hand smothered her mouth. Then a second needle was driven into her shoulder and left dangling there, producing a bead of blood where it had gone in. Before she could react to this, a third was plunged through the light fabric of her dress, straight into her right buttock. She nearly sprang away from his grasp with the shock and pain of it.

She didn't know what was happening to her. She felt woozy, like she'd been drinking too much. Her legs were refusing to support her. Her eyes were losing focus.

When the man decided to release her, she stumbled, then collapsed to the floor. Her heart was thumping wildly as she gasped for breath. A hand seemed to be tightening around her throat, but it wasn't his hand.

He wasn't even looking at her; rather, his eyes were fixed on one of the French Square bottles she'd given him—the one containing tissue from Perry Atwater's brain. He gave her a faint, enigmatic smile and dropped the vial into his pocket.

Then he stepped up to her and put the gun to her head and said, "Would you like me to spare you the agony?"

She nodded yes. Knowing she was dying, scarcely able to breathe, she was ready.

"Too bad about you," he said, lowering the gun. Then he turned and left her where she was.

seven

Just before Larry Fallon was ready to leave Los Angeles, deciding that the city (or county or whatever it was) was just as bad in reality as it was in his memory, what with all the damn pollution and all those highways that never seemed to lead to where you wanted to go, he received a call from his old friend, really his former friend, Stuart Erickson.

"I heard you were in town for the pathogens conference," Stuart said.

"I meant to look you up, Stuart, but there was just no time. You know how these things are. When you're not freezing your balls in some air-conditioned lecture hall, you're trying to dry out from forty cocktail parties."

All this was bullshit, he thought. But Erickson had decided to play along. "Listen, if you have some time to spare—"

"Well, the truth is, Stu, I was just on my way out of town. I have a flight back to Atlanta in a few hours."

If that wasn't a lie it was certainly an exaggeration. His flight wasn't departing LAX until ten o'clock, which left him eight hours, more or less, to do as he wished.

"It's up to you, Larry, but after what I tell you, you might be interested in getting the next flight out."

Larry hesitated, then said, "Go ahead, I'm listening."

Larry Fallon and Stuart Erickson had been in the Epidemic Intelligence Service together. Fallon had gone into Special Pathogens, a division charged with investigating organisms that were seldom inclined to do what you expected. Erickson had left Atlanta and gone into private practice, and a very lucrative one at that. It showed, too, in his smugly satisfied face and his expanding girth. The ill and the dying and the hypochondriacal from Beverly Hills and

Malibu and Laurel Canyon sought him out as if he were some kind of miracle worker. He was good all right, but Fallon looked on him like a heretic whose acquisitiveness was a betrayal of the ideals that they'd once shared, many years before, in Atlanta.

Disinclined to see Erickson as he was, Fallon couldn't resist. His curiosity got the better of him. And even if he were the most idealistic person in the world, which Fallon was not, he couldn't say that he was totally indifferent to celebrities. Nor could he ignore an invitation to give a second opinion on a patient who was either suffering a grievous psychological problem or was coming down with a very mysterious disease. If it turned out to be intriguing enough, he might consent to staying another night in L.A. even if it was at the expense of his lungs.

Erickson picked Fallon up in front of the Beverly Wilshire, where he'd been staying. Fallon reckoned that at least five years had passed since they'd last laid eyes on each other. Fallon told Erickson he looked well. But the truth was that he only looked larger, more settled, like a building gradually sinking into the ground because of an unstable foundation. Gravity was working harder and faster on him than it was with most people his age, Fallon thought.

Fallon, on the other hand, looked younger than his years. He was tan and fit and radiated enough good health to make certain women wonder what really went on inside of Special Pathogens. One of those weird organisms he was investigating, they might have reasoned, must have done something miraculous to him. He was always in motion. He was more clever than smart: the kind of person whom you used to hate in high school because he never studied and still came out ahead on his exams. If he wasn't an epidemiologist he might have been a pro athlete; that was the type of build he had and the aura he gave off.

On their way to the home in Laurel Canyon, where Larry was to make his discreet consultation, Erickson exhausted him with questions about the CDC and about his personal life.

He wondered how Gordon was doing after he'd lost his job as the director of the CDC. "I heard he got booted out," Erickson said. "Some dispute with Washington."

"Let's just say that he left by mutual agreement. Gordon wasn't an administrator, that was the real problem. He hated paperwork, he wanted to be out in the field. At heart he's a missionary who wants to convert the heathen. Give up smoking, reform your life, learn how to heal yourself—that's the message he delivers from on high."

"I remember how he was," Erickson said. "He was always too abrasive; too—I don't know—I guess the word's *arrogant*, for my liking."

"He got married, you know."

"Really?" Erickson was taken aback by this. "I hadn't heard. Which shows you how much I've lost contact. I always figured that after that first marriage to that Costa Rican girl went sour, he'd forget the whole thing."

"She was Guatemalan. A real piece of work too. I saw her a few times at parties."

"Who did he get hitched up to this time?"

"Girl he met in the EIS. She fell under his spell, I suppose, drinking in those golden words of his."

"Shit. I mean, he can speak eloquently when he wants, but that's a little bit much to take. Pretty?"

"Oh yeah, she's pretty, no question. He has taste, Gordon does. But she's, I guess, fifteen years younger than he is. I can't see what keeps them together. He's always running off somewhere anyhow, leaving her to mind the store in Atlanta."

"What about you? How's Cynthia?"

Fallon considered this question for a few moments. "Now that's a very good question."

"You aren't together anymore?"

"And that is a very good deduction. No, we split up about two years ago now."

"She got the kids?"

"I see them summers, Christmas vacation. Easter, too, sometimes."

He didn't want to think about how much he missed them. When they'd gone it was if somebody had gouged out a vital organ of his and nothing had yet grown in to replace it.

"Must be tough." Erickson had been married to the same girl he'd been dating since his junior year in high school; it was a phenomenon, being married that long, practically unimaginable to Larry.

"So are you seeing someone special now?"

"No, no, I'm not. There are women, you know. They're around for a while, then one day you think: this isn't what I want. Whether they reach the same conclusion you do, or whether they just want to stay one step ahead of the game I can't tell you, but usually, when it's good-bye, they don't seem to mind."

"Oh no?" Erickson appeared skeptical.

"Well, I suppose they do," Fallon acknowledged. "I suppose that it's always harder on them."

"But you aren't planning to, let's say, commit yourself for a while?"

"Not unless some girl comes and knocks me off my feet."

"But how often does that happen?" Erickson was being practical now.

"More often than you think." And Fallon was stretching the truth.

eight

It was happening again. The episodes were becoming more frequent now. Up until a certain point she could resist them, keep the worst of it at bay. No longer. She kept pillaging her mother's medicine cabinet, popping whatever pills were handy; uppers, downers, amphetamine and morphine derivatives, tranquilizers guaranteed to soothe even the most rattled nerves, but nothing she took did any good.

Like her mother, she hated hospitals. Hospitals were where you went to die horrible lingering deaths. Like her mother, Mardi believed that there was nothing physically wrong with her, that what she was going through was the result of some bizarre mental dysfunction—a favorite phrase of her shrink's—or some hysterical reaction.

When all else failed she called Chris. Chris was never without an interesting collection of controlled substances: everything from sinsimilla to pure Colombian coke to Ecstasy. Whatever you ordered could be in your hands within the hour. Her mother disapproved of Chris, not so much because he was a dealer, but because he reminded her of the type of men she herself had hung out with in the days before she'd earned a certain respectability, at least by Hollywood music industry standards.

In the past Mardi used to call on Chris maybe once every couple of weeks, but now she called him every day. The Hawaiian grass he brought her ($200 an ounce), combined with what he claimed to be nearly pure Peruvian coke ($120 a gram), was doing nothing to alleviate her condition, but at the very least the drugs made her high enough not to care so much about it.

He would come in through the back way, where the help entered. The guard at the gate knew him.

Mardi remained in her room, most of the time watching

her favorite movies on the VCR at first, but later on abandoning them for reruns of old cartoons: Bugs Bunny, Roadrunner, the Pink Panther, and Davey and Goliath. The problem was that she couldn't concentrate on anything longer than a ten-minute cartoon. The episodes, coming on every three or four hours now, left her so disoriented that she could scarcely recall her name, much less follow the narrative line of a two-hour feature. Besides, her eyes hurt if she focused them on anything too long.

She had practically no appetite, but she had no idea whether this was due to these episodes of hers or to all the coke she was ingesting. If her mother, or one of the women who worked for her mother, insisted that she eat, she got what she could down, then went into the bathroom to throw it up. She hated how thin and drawn she'd become; worse, she was pale. She couldn't stand being pale. Pale was what happened to people who lived on the East Coast.

To complicate things, her period was late. It was possible she was pregnant. She'd been pregnant once before, when she was fourteen and a half; she'd waited until the second trimester for an abortion and had to be suctioned out.

What baffled her was how oblivious her mother was to her condition. Even after Sean rescued her from that lake and explained to Carol what happened, she still didn't show much concern. Her mother didn't know when she was pregnant and now she didn't know—or didn't want to know—when she was sick. If a shrink couldn't help her then it wasn't real; that was how Carol Lloyd looked at life.

It was now early on a Friday afternoon, a little over a week since their return from Shadow Pines. The air was yellowish, like weak consommé. Continuous air conditioning sustained the interior of the Lloyd house in comfort, but Mardi could well imagine how it must be outside, how relentless and polluted the heat must be. The radio announcers spoke of a thermal inversion over the whole basin.

On this particular Friday afternoon, with nothing to occupy her until Chris showed up with his latest offering, Mardi lay in her room, distantly aware of her mother's voice filtering up through three floors from her sound studio.

In theory, the studio was soundproof; she shouldn't have been able to hear her mother. And ordinarily she wouldn't have. It must mean that another episode was about to occur; otherwise she wouldn't be so sensitive to sound to pick up a voice that acoustical engineering had intended to mute.

She didn't think she could endure it another time. Not alone, not like this. She needed her mother to understand how bad it was becoming.

Wearing only a flannel robe, one she'd had for so many years that it was faded and frayed, she started down the stairs, silent on bare feet.

The walls alongside the stairs were decorated with photographs of her mother, mounted glossies. They were mostly publicity shots; portraits of her when her hair stretched down below her waist and she was playing acoustic guitar in Greenwich Village clubs; portraits of her when her hair was cropped like a boy's and streaked across the middle with silver when she was playing electric guitar in the Fillmore West; portraits of her in Hamburg, Amsterdam, Tokyo, and Golden Gate Park, entertaining thousands of enthusiastic fans. One by one Mardi tore the photographs from the wall and ripped them to shreds. It was almost reflexive, committed without giving the action the slightest thought. She didn't even quite realize what she'd done until she looked back up and saw hundreds of bits and pieces of her mother strewn on the stairs behind her.

I've done it now, she thought. But in thinking this she didn't quite believe it. It was as if someone else were in control; so why should she have to answer for it? It was another self that was responsible. Downstairs it was quiet, except for the strains of her mother's guitar, whining plaintively from the studio two floors beneath her. The floor registered its vibrations.

It seemed to Mardi that she was only responding to a plan that had been devised exclusively for her; she might just as well have been programmed. Certainly it seemed entirely appropriate that she should now be stooped down in front of the shelves containing her mother's records, many of them foreign editions still neatly wrapped in cellophane.

She hesitated, thinking that maybe if she fought hard enough she could still exert some control over her mind, her body. But no, it was impossible. The pressure inside her head was too immense; it demanded that she go ahead and pull out the records. Gazing down at her hands, she was astonished because they did not appear to be her hands. They were white and cold and much too big to belong to her. The veins on the backs of them swelled hideously when she flexed them.

There was something oddly satisfying, almost reassuring, about the sound of vinyl breaking apart and sending black splinters flying across the room. Wherever she looked there was her mother's face staring back at her. Carol Lloyd . . . Carol Lloyd . . . Carol Lloyd. The face repeated endlessly, the name repeated endlessly.

She was crying, she was screaming, but no one heard her or, hearing her, was troubling to respond. Blood began to stain the record covers, the shattered bits of vinyl, the deep white fur rug. It took Mardi a few moments to realize that the blood was coming from her, that her hands had been cut up by the fragments of her mother's records. But as she could not quite accept the fact that these hands were hers, by the same token she could not identify with the pain that they were causing her. The blood belonged to someone else too. Her robe was covered with it. But it didn't matter to her. Nothing mattered.

After a while none of her mother's records remained to be demolished. By trying to grind the debris into the rug, all she succeeded in doing was to slice up the soles of her feet. But this pain was no more able to make itself felt than the pain in her hands.

Descending the stairs to the ground floor, she became more conscious of her mother's voice, no longer as forceful or insinuating as it had been in her prime, half an octave lower because of all the packs of cigarettes she'd consumed over the years, Camel Filters and Dunhill Lights. The song she was singing was new, written especially for her. Mardi had heard her practicing it for weeks; it was a loathsome song, she thought, vulgar and cheap, and she detested it.

When she reached the ground floor she heard the sound of the doorbell. The back doorbell. Chris.

Behind her, when she glanced back, she saw a trail of blood, like animal spoor. She wondered, distantly, whether she might bleed to death, but the prospect of that happening did not alarm her. Nothing could alarm her. She felt as though she were hovering several feet above the ground. Everything would be fine, she thought, if only the terrific pounding in her head would go away.

At intervals the lights would seem to dim and go out and then she would have to stop, unable to penetrate the pitch blackness into which she'd just been plunged. Then a moment later the lights would come on again and she could make out where she was. The back door. It was essential that she have a destination, a point by which to navigate herself.

She threw open the back door and looked up into the face of Chris. His eyes were gaping, his jaw hung open. She imagined that the spectacle she presented must have shocked him. Well, the hell with him, she thought.

"Mardi, what happened to you?" he said. "You're bleeding."

She wanted to tell him but couldn't, couldn't get a word out. She turned and began to run. But where? She hadn't the faintest. All she knew was that she couldn't look at him. His face was grotesque; the beard he wore was thick and dirty, his eyes black pinpricks of light, the eyes of a devil.

"Go away!" she was shouting.

But maybe not. Maybe she was only imagining that she was shouting, maybe no sound was emerging at all.

He was following her in, the crinkle of his leather motorcycle jacket audible to her as he moved.

Go away, go away, go away, she thought. Why didn't he understand that he could not be here now?

There was no way that she could make him understand. *I am going to do something terrible, please go away, I am going to do something that cannot be called back—ever.*

He was still coming into the kitchen, the fall of his steps against the linoleum a relentless tattoo.

"Mardi, what's wrong? Let me call a doctor. Mardi, where's your mother?"

Unanswerable, all unanswerable questions.

Then she knew, knew absolutely, what she would do. Seizing hold of a cutting knife, its surface moist from recent washing, she whipped around, surprised to see that Chris was not more than half a foot from her, and then drove the blade into his chest.

He grunted; it was a very small sound really, more of surprise than of pain. Lurching back, he carried the cutting knife in him, grasping at it, but not successfully. His hands kept slipping. Blood began to ooze around the wound. Mardi was pleased to see that it was someone else's blood for a change.

"Mardi," he said, no doubt dumbfounded that this should have happened to him and that it was she, surely one of his best customers, who was responsible.

He choked as if he'd swallowed something the wrong way. He gasped and spit, and when he spit it was blood, not saliva, that came up.

It was so strange, knowing that she should feel something, but feeling nothing all the same.

Had Chris suddenly collected his strength and attacked and killed her, she would have been neither surprised nor upset. On the contrary, she would have welcomed it. But this was not what happened.

Chris gave a convulsive shudder, his body went limp, and he crumbled to the floor. He was looking straight at her, his lips moving in a fruitless effort to speak. His eyes fluttered and he slumped forward. To Mardi it looked as if he were praying. But he wasn't praying. He was dead.

Only now did she hear her mother shouting up the stairs to her. "Mardi," she was saying. "Mardi, is everything all right? What's all that commotion I hear?"

Mardi stood amazingly still for several moments, but she wasn't scared, she wasn't distraught, she wasn't anything at all. *I am not doing this,* was what she kept telling herself. *I am not in charge, I can't be blamed, I do not exist.*

The sound of her mother's footsteps on the stairs reached her as if from very far away. Mardi stepped over to where Chris sat as immobilized as he would be in a photograph, already going stiff. Blood was coursing down his pants legs, pooling on the linoleum floor. Mardi almost slipped in it. She took hold of the knife and pulled until she'd succeeded in freeing it from Chris's chest. It was easier than she'd thought it would be. More blood eddied through the wound now that the knife had been withdrawn.

Suddenly a scream rent the air. Her mother's scream. Mardi turned slowly, in no hurry at all, to gaze upon her mother's face. But all she saw was the face from the scores of record albums and publicity photos she'd ripped apart, not the face of the woman standing before her, her features distorted by horror and fear.

It was so strange, how effortlessly she moved; really, it was like floating through air, meeting no resistance whatsoever. Her mother, on the other hand, didn't appear able to move. She stood rooted to the spot, her hands grappling at her face, perhaps because she didn't have any idea what else to do with them. "No, no, Mardi!" she kept saying, her voice dying little by little until it was practically inaudible.

All Mardi wished for was silence. She'd lived with her mother's voice for too long.

It took well over an hour to reach the canyon, with the Friday evening traffic bumper-to-bumper on most of the city's major arteries. Carol Lloyd's house wasn't immediately visible from the street, being shrouded by palms and eucalyptus trees sprouting up from a bed of shrubbery and spectacularly colored bougainvillea.

"Now, remember to tell her that you're from Special Pathogens, that you've had experience dealing with rare diseases," Erickson said. "Or better yet, leave out the part about Special Pathogens. It sounds too ominous. Just say you're with the Centers for Disease Control and you're seeing the girl as a favor to me."

When they approached the front gate, a security guard appeared. He was black, in his forties, and clearly uncomfortable in his starched uniform. His brow glistened with sweat. Recognizing Erickson, he greeted him warmly and said, "Miss Lloyd's expecting you."

The gate, operated from a small guardhouse, swung open for them and they continued up the length of the driveway toward the house.

Except for some obstreperous cockatoos in the branches overhead, the only sound to be heard was the hiss of sprinklers maintaining the lush green of the lawns. Roses, tulips, and forsythia, wound around the side of the house. The house itself was big, but humanly proportioned, designed in a hacienda-like style typical of many homes in the L.A. area.

They walked up a path of crushed stone, then climbed the four steps to the porch. A narrow arched door, with a small round window in the middle of it, loomed in front of them.

Erickson rang the bell. Two chimes sounded in response. They waited. Several moments passed.

"That's funny," said Erickson. "I would've thought that John phoned Carol from the guardhouse to let her know we were here."

Again he rang. All at once they heard footsteps, a female voice calling to them, but they were unable to make out the words. Then the door was thrown open. The two men stared in disbelief, for the sight that greeted them was unlike anything that either man had ever seen before.

nine

The man in the chauffeured Mercedes needed to take only a single glance to realize that he was too late. An hour earlier, possibly, and he might have been able to contain the situation.

Seeing the presence of so many squad cars—five in all—not to mention two ambulances, the chauffeur asked his passenger whether he still wished to pay a call on the Lloyd residence.

"No, I think that that'll have to wait. But I tell you what you can do for me. Let me off here and take a spin around the block. I'd like to see what develops."

The man who'd come to this place in a chauffeured Mercedes was named Stanley Koppleman. That he was dressed fashionably enough to satisfy the rarefied sartorial standards of Savile Row no doubt contributed to the air of authority he exuded. Certainly, the red handkerchief protruding from his jacket pocket, matched to a tee by the red rose leaping out of his buttonhole, hinted at an attention to style that many men in his position generally tended to ignore. His hair, what there was of it, was expensively coiffed; rusty brown, it rolled along his scalp until it yielded to ruddy skin that, in certain light, would glimmer brightly. He had a generous face, piercing eyes accustomed to reading the faults in the people he met, flaring nostrils, and lips that were of a natural red shading so startling that it was unlikely any lipstick could duplicate it. He was heavyset and moved with slow, purposeful motions. He was one of those rare people who, even without the clothing and the expensive accessories, could expect to be listened to and obeyed.

When he went over to one of the policemen standing by the gate, uneasily eyeing the small crowd gathered in front of him, it was with the expectation that any question he asked would be answered.

"What happened here, Officer?"

The policeman had no chance to respond. Two ambulance attendants were propelling a stretcher down the length of the stone path and he was obliged to open the gate for them.

A tangled mass of blondish hair was the first thing that Koppleman saw. Mother or daughter? he wondered.

It was the daughter, Mardi.

Unconscious, not dead. Surely, he reasoned, if she were dead, they would have had the decency to cover her. But he had only to catch a glimpse of her to see that, barring some medical miracle, it should not take death too long to get to her. Her eyes were open but glazed, unseeing. Her face might have been coated with a fine white powder; no natural skin tone remained to it that he could see. A slight amount of blood was visible at the edge of her lips.

Looking up the path, he saw two more officers. They were in turn followed by a man who, while unknown to him, he assumed to be a doctor. He looked shaken and bewildered.

This procession was brought up finally by yet another stretcher.

This must be the mother, Koppleman decided.

But it was not. It was someone too tall, with too much bulk, to be a female. Whoever he was, though, he was dead. The sheet draped over him had sopped up enough of his blood to indicate the extent of his injuries. A chest or belly wound was what Koppleman surmised.

Carol Lloyd was in a wheelchair, being pushed down the path by an attendant. To one side of her was a police officer, to the other a doctor, most likely the family physician from the way in which he kept hold of her hand, from time to time leaning down to say something into her ear.

But Koppleman doubted whether anything was registering. She appeared to be in shock, her eyes empty, her face devoid of all expression. Her off-the-shoulder top had slipped down her arm much farther than the designer could ever have intended it to go, bringing into view a good deal of her right breast. Every time the doctor would adjust it she would shrug and it would slip off again.

She looked small and vulnerable sitting in the wheelchair; if she was conscious of the attention she was drawing it wasn't noticeable.

As the attendants were assisting her into the back of the ambulance where her daughter was already installed, Koppleman's Mercedes reappeared.

Having witnessed all he wished to, Koppleman returned to his car. "Where to now, sir?" the chauffeur inquired.

Koppleman gave him the address of a place on Western Avenue to which chauffeurs at the wheel of Mercedes XL-100's were unaccustomed to going. But whatever surprise the chauffeur might have felt at hearing his next destination, he kept to himself.

Such discretion, however, was not duplicated on the part of the locals who habituated the block on Western where they were headed. The hustlers in their fedoras and seersucker suits gave him long inquisitional stares. Seldom did anyone looking so well-heeled come to this neighborhood of fast-food joints, Chinese laundries, rundown motels where no names entered on the register were ever true, and bars where White Label scotch sold for eighty-five cents a shot. When such a rare specimen did turn up, it was widely assumed that he was in search of something illicit or sufficiently depraved that he couldn't find it in more affluent parts of the city.

Koppleman's chauffeur, sitting in air-conditioned comfort behind bulletproof windows, watched unhappily as he entered a building that looked only slightly less derelict than its neighbors.

Should the need arise, and with Koppleman it almost never did, he could protect himself. Within easy reach was a Beretta, lodged in a holster strapped into place under his jacket. Unlike many of those individuals with whom Koppleman had dealings, he had a license to carry a weapon. It would not do to risk arrest for violating gun control laws; it would accomplish nothing and get him disbarred.

There was an elevator in this building, but a handwritten sign had been taped to its door indicating that it was out of order. Koppleman took the stairs.

At the door of 4E, he knocked. The man who welcomed him was a stubby fellow, with the ascetic features of a defrocked Jesuit and hair swept evenly down both sides of his head from a part in the middle. The hair was half yellow and half white. The whiteness was premature; the man was only in his mid-forties. His name was Hal Jarvis.

The apartment Hal Jarvis occupied—at least for today, for he was constantly on the move—was nearly empty; there was a tattered couch, a couple of folding chairs, a table encrusted with wax from a candle that was no longer in evidence, and a cheap, faded picture, framed, of the Virgin Mary. Jarvis must have been doing some cooking when Koppleman walked in, for there was a strong, rancid burning smell coming from the kitchenette.

Koppleman, without invitation, took a seat on the couch. "How was Boston?" he asked.

"Boston," Jarvis said as if it wasn't a town he was familiar with. "I don't know. Boston was all right. I got something done."

"But not enough."

Jarvis said nothing.

Koppleman had had what might be termed, loosely, certain business transactions with Hal Jarvis for five years. Ordinarily Jarvis didn't disappoint him.

"You should be grateful to me," Jarvis said after a long pause. "I got two of them, Chong and Leiter. Atwater died, never said a word to anyone."

"You're sure of that?"

"He was in a coma, never came out of it. How was he going to say anything?"

Koppleman acknowledged that Jarvis might have a point.

"And Atlanta?" he asked.

"Atlanta went well. The specimens were destroyed. All down the drain. Finish, kaput!" He clapped his hands together as if he were applauding his own action. "There was some bitch there I had to deal with. She went kaput too."

"I see." Koppleman would rather not know the gory details.

There was a certain way that people got when they were anticipating money, and that was the way Jarvis was acting now.

From his inner jacket pocket, Koppleman took out a sealed packet. "I think this should prove satisfactory."

Jarvis tore the packet open with unseemly haste and inspected its contents, counting out the hundreds with his long spindly fingers.

"It's all here." He sounded surprised.

"Is there something else you'd like to tell me?" Koppleman had a feeling that the reassurance of having a large amount of cash in his possession might loosen Jarvis's tongue.

"Well, come to think of it, there is. There was some son of a bitch in Boston asking around about two of those wasted fuckers, that Chong bitch and that Atwater dude."

"Who was this man?"

"Guy named Green. Queer name for a first name. Neville or something like that. He was palling around with some bitch from the CDC. You want to find out more, it'll cost you."

The society Koppleman customarily kept rarely included people like this. He found Jarvis something of a novelty actually. It was interesting how people like this were motivated solely by money, allowing neither morality nor love nor righteous indignation to keep them from their appointed rounds. They were pure in a way, like death itself, whose agent they were.

"What would you say if I gave you five K to start with?"

"For what?" Jarvis was suspicious of people who were ready to give him so much all at once.

"For neutralizing this man you mentioned in Boston. And for keeping track of that girl from Atlanta."

"I've got her name written down here someplace." Jarvis began looking through a paperback titled *Smart Men, Foolish Choices,* which looked like it was the only book in the place, and plucked out of it a slip of notepaper. "Jessie Palmer. An epide—something."

"Epidemiologist?"

"That's it. An epidemi—" He gave up, throwing the book down.

Koppleman wondered what he was doing with a book like that.

"Tomorrow morning you'll have the cash. I'll make the necessary travel arrangements for you."

"Pleasure doing business with you, Mr. Wilder," which was the only name Jarvis knew him by.

"You'll hear from me tomorrow," Koppleman said. Stepping out into the corridor, he closed the door behind him with relief. He took a deep breath. Even the stench of urine and marijuana was better than whatever it was Jarvis was burning in his kitchen.

ten

The first thing that Larry Fallon did when he got back to Atlanta was take a taxi straight to CDC headquarters on Clifton Road. A hermetically sealed box, labeled BIOHAZARD: DO NOT OPEN, rested in his lap. Inside were specimens of brain tissue and blood and urine from Mardi Lloyd, dear, demented, and now dying daughter of the famous singer. Unable to cope under the best of circumstances, from what Larry understood (basing his information on Erickson's confidential disclosures and all the stories he'd read over the years in the *Star* and the *National Enquirer* while waiting at supermarket checkout lines), Carol was reduced to a semicatatonic state. Columnists who were paid to know such things said she'd gone into seclusion.

It could have been worse, Larry figured. Her daughter could have gone through with it and sliced her up the way she had the "reputed drug dealer," Chris Bonaventure. But from what he and Erickson had deduced, at the last minute she'd faltered; most likely, she short-circuited, her fuses burning out, leaving her without the energy to actually drive the blade into her mother's chest. Larry doubted that it was the stirrings of a dormant conscience that stopped her in mid-motion.

Pulling up to Clifton Road, he experienced a sensation of déjà vu. Four patrol cars were lined up in front of Building 1.

Was this going to be how it was everywhere he went? he wondered.

He hurried from the taxi and entered Building 1 where he spotted someone he knew and asked what had happened.

"Somebody was killed last night in the hot lab," said his acquaintance, a microbiologist whose eyes looked too big for his face, which might have been an occupational hazard from peering into microscopes too long for years on end.

"What are you talking about?"

This was unfathomable to Larry. People maybe got infected accidentally in the hot lab, but they were not killed.

The microbiologist, whose name was Gregory Mars, explained that the death had been a gruesome one, speculating that it must have taken "the Flanigan woman," as he called her, hours to expire.

"Specimens were stolen out of the lab too," he added.

"What were they?"

"You'll have to talk to somebody who works there. I don't know myself."

What madness, Larry thought, what excitement.

Having pumped Mars for as much information as he expected to get, Larry thanked him and headed in the direction of the Data and Specimen Handling Section.

DASH was located in the basement of a building close by, where he intended to present his little package from L.A. As accustomed as he was to dealing with unknown and insidious organisms in Special Pathogens, he didn't mind carrying around specimens like this. On the other hand, he had to admit he was happy to have it taken off his hands.

Harry Vaughan greeted him as soon as he walked in. Vaughan had been with DASH ever since anyone could remember. He had the look of eternity about him; give him a long snowy beard and he could have modeled for God. His voice came from down deep, and perpetually sounded like he'd just been roused from slumber.

Spying the package borne under Fallon's arm, Vaughan said, "What have you got there for me?"

They sat down. Vaughan took a blank 3.203 form and went through the ritual.

Fallon gave him the patient's name, birthdate, sex, all the information he knew about the case and the particular specimens he was consigning into DASH's custody.

As he spoke he began to observe a change in Vaughan's expression; recognition lit up his eyes. "You know, what you're telling me reminds me of something."

He motioned Larry over to a computer terminal stationed on another table. He typed in the relevant CDC number and in moments the computer responded with the exact location of a record which was titled "Atwater, Perry."

"What's this?"

"Wait, let me see something," said Vaughan. He now called up the Atwater file. The screen filled with its first microfilm frame.

Looking over his shoulder, Fallon perused the file as Vaughan went through it, frame by frame. He didn't have to be told why the specimens he'd just turned over had drawn the reaction they had from Vaughan. "It sounds like Atwater had the same thing Lloyd did," he said.

"Same type of symptoms certainly."

Vaughan keyed in the CDC number for Chong, and after calling up her file, he read through that. He repeated the process for Ellen Leiter.

"When did these Boston cases come in, did you say?"

"A few days ago. They were being tested in the hot lab when they were stolen. We suspect that the same son of a bitch who murdered Pat took them. I guess it's up to the police to find out why."

"Oh, so those were the specimens that were taken. How curious."

"Whoever the hell it was who did this thing must have thought he could destroy all record of the specimens. He broke into an office in Building One and lifted all the preliminary test results Pat had brought to Miss Palmer."

"Jessie, you mean?"

Vaughan looked up, surprised. "You know her?"

"Just enough to say hello."

"She's the gal who told us about these cases in the first place. We're trying to get more specimens sent down to us from Boston. But maybe we don't have to wait to find out what we're dealing with if your specimens turn up the same virus. And that we do know—that it was definitely a virus that did these people in. Your girl Mardi's still alive though, isn't she?"

"Barely." Fallon stood up. He knew exactly where he had to go. "I hope you people have better luck hanging on to the specimens this time."

Vaughan shrugged. "Once they leave here, they're someone else's responsibility."

The door to Jessie's office wasn't altogether closed. Was this an invitation or an oversight? Fallon decided to enter at the same time he knocked, giving her no opportunity to ask him to come back later.

She looked lost as she sat at her desk in the middle of what might have been thousands of pieces of paper strewn at her feet. Looking lost suited her, he thought, made her somehow more alluring.

Her hair was almost in as much disarray as her office was; it had come loose, and she hadn't quite gotten around to doing anything about putting it all back in place again. When Larry appeared she gave him a quizzical look, no doubt trying to figure out what he, of all people, was doing here.

"Oh, I thought you were security."

"Believe me, I'm no security at all."

At first she didn't seem to get it. Then a smile flickered on her lips. "I'll remember that."

"I heard about the break-in here."

Her eyes traveled around the office, as they must have a hundred times already. "Better this than what happened to Pat. I can't believe it. It could have been me instead."

"Are the reports missing?"

She nodded. "Security told me to leave everything the way it was. I suppose they're thinking they might find some piece of evidence that will lead them to whoever did this. I doubt it."

"So do I."

"Oh, I'm sorry, why don't you sit down?"

Larry upended a chair and planted it where there were no loose papers on the floor.

"Tell me what brings Special Pathogens to my door this morning? You want to get a look at how the other half lives?"

She had such a graceful neck, he thought, admiring how long it was, what elegance it offered the viewer. But it was her eyes that he liked most of all, and the intelligence and wit he detected there. Too young for someone like Gordon, but who knew what drew two people together?

"Not exactly. I was just talking to Harry Vaughan at DASH. He told me about what you found in Boston."

"It started out as a vacation. Next July Fourth weekend I think I'll go somewhere else."

She was nervous and edgy, and no wonder, after something like this. Larry thought he had a knack for meeting women—at least getting to know them better—when things began unraveling on them.

"Weren't you with Gordon?"

"He was in El Salvador."

"Now, there's a place to spend July Fourth! All the fireworks—it must be something else."

This attempt at humor failed to elicit a smile from her.

"What does he think about all this?"

"It's hard to say. He just got back yesterday and I really haven't had a chance to fill him in. I talked to him a few minutes ago and told him what happened. He sounded concerned. I'm sure he is concerned. But then he's always concerned about so much that I wonder whether he's got room for one more concern." Her voice had a rueful quality. Raising her eyes toward Larry, she said, "Now, why am I telling you all this?"

"Because I'm here and I'm a good listener. And—"

"And you're not security."

"And I'm not security. Now listen, I have a story to tell you about what happened to me on the way to L.A. airport."

"Is this relevant to anything?"

"Believe me, it's relevant."

He began to recount the story of Mardi Lloyd, with such drama and suspense that he could see he had her hooked. It wouldn't have mattered if it didn't turn out to have any relevance. "And when they did a CAT scan of the Lloyd girl's brain," he said, "you can't imagine what they found."

"Tell me." She was leaning toward him, the scent of her perfume drawing him closer to her too.

"They found that a chunk of it wasn't there anymore."

"It sounds like the same thing those three in Boston had," she agreed. "Was Mardi in Boston anytime recently?"

"From what we could get out of the mother—and given her condition it wasn't much—she hadn't been to Boston for maybe ten years."

"That doesn't make our job any easier, does it?" The question was rhetorical. "Did Harry tell you that two of the

Boston victims were murdered? And possibly the third as well?"

"Murdered? Jesus."

The only murders he knew about were in the papers and on the nightly news, but now it seemed murder was becoming much too personal, yet vastly more interesting.

"Then I guess it's your turn to tell me a story," he said.

eleven

Stanley Koppleman did not like New York City. He liked L.A. He liked Chicago. He had a thing for Miami, but he did not like New York City. Too much needless commotion for his taste. It was worse in summer, unbearable; although there was no garbage strike on, it certainly smelled as if there were. The dead air held the stench of waste long after the sanitation trucks had come and gone.

For the purpose of traveling through Manhattan, Koppleman relied on a white Bentley driven by a man named Gibson. Whether this was his first or last name, he never said. He was, like the Bentley, like the Moët de Chandon kept on ice in the rear, one of the many perks awarded to contract employees of Wisdom-Templar Corporation.

Headquarters for Wisdom-Templar could be found in a building shielded completely by ice-green glass overlooking Battery Park on one side and New York harbor on the other. At the time Koppleman entered the thirty-third-floor office suite of Jeremiah Mack, vice-president in charge of Wisdom-Templar's resort and entertainment division, a Circle Line cruiser and a tug bearing the city's refuse out to sea were making their way across the harbor. A lovely view. A spectacular view. An air-conditioned view.

Jeremiah Mack was a tall man who didn't seem to know what to do with his outsized frame. Because of the way his hair had receded, a vast expanse of florid brow dominated his face. He projected an air of affable neutrality that made it difficult for people to take offense at anything he did, and it was probably because of this quality that he had advanced to his high corporate station.

Wisdom-Templar, begun as a manufacturer of radio components in the early 1950s, had in the last three decades gobbled up so many other companies that it could no longer be said that Wisdom-Templar *did* anything; rather it owned everything. Its CEO, a man with the cultivated sensibility of a renaissance man and the moral scruples of a marauding buccaneer, was an artist when it came to mergers. He couldn't pick up *The Wall Street Journal* in the mornings without spotting a company that didn't strike him as a possible takeover target. A multimillionaire at the age of forty-five, he was once asked why he worked so arduously to make yet additional piles of money. To this question he replied, "It's a way of keeping score."

His philosophy permeated every aspect of the conglomerate, seeping into all its thousands of nooks and crannies so that even those who manned the mailrooms or rolled the coffee wagons through the corridors of corporate headquarters were subject to its influence. It was a wonder that the corporate logo wasn't a dollar sign. Instead it consisted of a heraldic shield, with a background of deep blue, on which a silver leopard crouched in the upper left-hand corner.

This shield was duplicated on the flag in the Wisdom-Templar plaza, flying from a pole exactly two feet lower than the pole flying the American flag. It came as little surprise to see it hanging on the wall immediately behind Jeremiah Mack's teakwood desk.

Mack and Koppleman had met perhaps half a dozen times over the last two years, ever since the attorney had been put on retainer for the conglomerate. Koppleman's reputation had preceded him; deference was accorded him more on the basis of the controversy that his unconventional behavior invited than on any successes he might have achieved in a court of law. It didn't matter to Koppleman what people thought of him, though. He was quite pleased with his notoriety.

"I don't know whether you've talked to our people at Shadow Pines in the last few days," Jeremiah Mack began once the formalities were dispensed with, "but we seem to have a little problem on our hands."

Koppleman had a good idea as to what he was referring to, but he didn't let on.

"It seems that four days ago two of our staff members were embroiled in a dispute."

"A dispute." Koppleman repeated the word as if he wanted to feel it out on his tongue.

"The man who initiated this dispute—his name, for the record, was Sean Laramie—was a tennis instructor. From what I'm told, there was no indication that he had a violent personality. On the contrary."

"And what was the outcome of this dispute?"

"Well, apparently it took place in the kitchen. Late at night, long after dinner was over and done with. Someone saw Laramie wander into the dining room looking glassy-eyed, as though he was on drugs. Then he went into the kitchen."

"For any particular reason?"

"Who knows? There was only one man in the kitchen at the time—a janitor who was in the process of mopping the floors. I can only conjecture what happened, but I suppose the janitor asked Laramie what business he had in the kitchen. A fight broke out. Laramie grabbed hold of a knife—the kind they use to slice meat."

"A butcher knife."

"Right, a butcher knife."

"Then what did he do?"

"Oh, well, he cut the janitor's head off," Jeremiah Mack said as if it were the most natural thing in the world to do with a butcher knife.

A tennis instructor decapitating a janitor; it seemed extraordinary to Koppleman.

"What happened to Laramie?"

"He collapsed and lost consciousness. We found him next to the body."

"The headless body?"

"Well, the head hadn't gone very far. I understand it was still attached. Barely."

"You mind if I smoke?" Koppleman removed a pack of Lambert and Butler's. He was not waiting for Mack to say whether he minded or not. "Tell me, Jerry, what do you suppose prompted Laramie to go on this rampage?"

"You were out in L.A. recently, weren't you?" It was on company business; of course he was aware of where Koppleman had been. "You know what happened to Mardi Lloyd."

"You suspect that the same thing was at work?"

"Gossip has it that the two were sleeping together."

This was something else that Koppleman hadn't known.

"I am not an authority on such things, but it is my suspicion that some toxic agent may be responsible. Contaminated water, spoiled food, I don't know. So far we've managed to keep this thing quiet."

"Just how quiet?" From his practice, Koppleman knew that there was quiet and there was quiet.

"Naturally, we had to advise the police."

"Yes, I understand that they take a particular interest in decapitations."

Jeremiah Mack did not appreciate the humor in the situation. He went on to say, "We were able to prevail on them to pursue their investigation discreetly. The local authorities are appreciative of the delicate position we're in."

What Mack was saying, in so many words, was that the police knew better than to cause trouble for a resort which catered to VIPs on both sides of the law, former presidents of the United States, and Mafia dons alike.

"And the janitor's family?"

"The body—that is to say, the body and the head—was unclaimed. He was, you know, just a janitor."

"They're hardly worth the trouble until they advance to the level of a dishwasher."

Mack looked sharply at Koppleman as if he suspected the attorney might be mocking him. Still unsure, he leaned back, glancing abstractedly out the window, toward the harbor. "Given the fact that this violent incident has come on the heels of another, similar one, I think we have reason to be concerned."

"You're afraid that someone will connect what happened to Laramie and Mardi Lloyd to Shadow Pines?"

"That's not the worst of it. There's no reason to think that we won't be seeing more incidents of this type."

"What do you propose we do then?"

"I'm going to leave that up to you. I'm told you have an ability to work miracles. Prove it. One thing, though, we would like you to do whatever possible to make sure that the Northeast Classic is held on schedule. Here, by the way, is the list of those who've indicated they'll attend."

Koppleman perused the list, noting that it included an array of dignitaries, congressmen, governors, and high-powered corporate executives more impressive than last year's participants. He was gratified to see that among them were three Pentagon officials who handled billions of dollars in defense industry contracts.

For it was not only the publicity that was important to the resort as a result of the televised golf tournament, it was also the opportunity the tournament provided for an intensive lobbying effort.

The operation of Shadow Pines was only a small part of Wisdom-Templar's business. Arms and aeronautical technology firms under its rubric brought in far more money. In the relaxed atmosphere of the resort, the CEO of Wisdom-Templar believed that its business interests might be advanced with greater speed than in the corridors of the Pentagon or on Capitol Hill.

It was one of Koppleman's responsibilities to promote the conglomerate's business interests among the VIPs who turned out for the tournament. That he chose to use such ancient but effective techniques as women and drugs in executing this mandate was something that Jeremiah Mack and the executive board didn't wish to know about. Whatever worked, worked.

"So I take it that you're alarmed because something might occur to disrupt the tournament," Koppleman said.

"Worse than that. Suppose, for argument's sake, that another one of our employees or maybe one of the guests starts to run amok like Laramie."

"And in the course of his murderous binge kills the chairman of General Motors on the fifteenth hole or delivers a fatal wound to a deputy secretary of defense who served during the Ford administration?"

"I'm glad that you see my point."

"So, as I understand it, you want me to see that nothing like this Laramie incident recurs?"

"Exactly."

"And why, Mr. Mack, do you believe that a toxic agent might be the cause of such . . . well, extreme behavior?"

"I heard that there were some cases in Boston like this. I read in the papers that drugs of some kind were suspected."

"Let me fill you in, Mr.Mack. I've done some investigating myself and from what I've discovered, it wasn't a drug."

"No? What was it then?"

"A virus. Or something that resembles a virus."

Mack was incredulous. "What kind of virus could drive a man mad like that?"

"It's like Legionnaire's Disease or AIDS. It's new to the world. At least this part of the world. I've done my homework on this."

Mack was shaking his head, a look of irritation on his face. "Jesus Christ," he said, "a goddamn virus." Then he met Koppleman's gaze. "It's possible that the girl or Laramie had it before they came to Shadow Pines, isn't it?"

Koppleman agreed that that was possible.

"It's also possible that no one else will be infected."

Yes, Koppleman agreed, this was also possible.

"Then maybe my fears are groundless."

"Precautionary measures can never hurt." Koppleman dwelled in a world of precautionary measures.

"That's why I wanted to talk to you today. It seems to me that after what happened with Laramie, we can't be too cautious. We've got to make sure that this thing is contained."

Koppleman understood what he meant; it wasn't the prospect of a disease spreading through the resort, nor the potential for violence that the disease might unleash, that had him worried. It was the prospect of bad publicity. Nothing in his business was quite so bad as bad publicity.

twelve

The music was by Bach; majesterial and stirring, it filled the church with an almost physical presence. The whole floor vibrated with the organ's drama. But what composition it was, whether a fugue or an excerpt from one of his oratorios or cantatas, Paul Leiter didn't know. All he could say for sure was that it sounded familiar; in fact, it sounded very much like something that his mother used to play on the stereo.

His mother had had a great many friends. He remembered parties that were so crowded they reminded him of Times Square on New Year's Eve. His mother had taken him there once when she was still married to his father. She'd told him, "This is something you ought to see once."

Where were all those friends of his now? Paul wondered, looking around and noticing how many empty pews there were. They were afraid, he thought. *They are afraid because of what they read about Mother in the papers. I am afraid, too, but they are more afraid.*

Reverend Reingold, a young, softspoken man who didn't wish to offend anyone, had made no mention of what had happened Thursday night two weeks ago. But why should he? Everyone knew. It was embarrassing. For Mother there was only praise, a flowery good-bye. Reverend Reingold had quoted a good deal from Psalms. Paul had scarcely been paying attention. He couldn't concentrate, but he didn't know whether this was because there was too much on his mind or because of the knock on the head his mother had given him with the half-full bottle of Gordon's Vodka.

Everyone was staring at him. Although he tried not to, he kept getting red in the face. He knew that they were looking at the bandage on his head where the nurses at the hospital had had to shave his hair off. He knew that they were looking at the black eye and the bruise on his forehead. He knew what they were saying: How could such a wonderful woman like Ellen Leiter do such a terrible thing?

They told him at the hospital that it was because his mother had something wrong with her, something that made her funny in the head, and that he must forgive her because she couldn't help herself. He wanted to believe them, but he couldn't shake the feeling that maybe they were just trying to make him feel better.

Aunt Betty, who stood beside him now, and his older sister Annie told him that he had no obligation to come to the funeral and that everyone would understand if he didn't. But he remembered one thing his father had said, when he was very little, and that was that you should always show people you're not afraid even when you are. And he was certain, although he wouldn't have been able to explain why, that he would regret it if he refused to go.

He felt Aunt Betty's hand on his shoulder.

"You don't have to go up there if you don't want to," she was saying.

At first he had no idea what she was referring to. Then, directing his eyes down to the head of the aisle, he understood that his mother was waiting there for him. The casket shone in the light from the altar. It was made of wood so highly polished that it reflected the giant cross that rose above the pulpit. And it reflected Reverend Reingold's face.

"No, I'll go," Paul said. "I don't mind."

People were beginning to file down the aisle. Suddenly it became very important to him that he be first, that he show everyone that he was not afraid, that he loved his mother. No matter what she had done, he still loved her. Whether she was funny in the head because of some disease or whether everyone was lying to him and she really and truly hated him, he still loved her. That was what counted.

All at once he tore down the aisle. He heard somebody's muffled protest. He didn't care.

Cutting in front of everyone else, he went to the head of the line. Some sort of perfume or incense floated up from the casket. He didn't like it at all. His mother never would have used such a perfume. His eyes were closed; he wasn't sure he could look.

Opening his eyes and gathering all the courage he had in him, he leaned down so that, instead of smelling the strange perfume, he could smell another smell, a smell of dead bodies after the undertaker has done something to them. He puckered his lips to kiss his mother, but then he drew back as if somebody had smacked him right across the face.

It seemed to take the longest time in the world for him to be able to scream. And by then he was already racing back down the aisle, no longer worried about what people saw.

How could anyone doubt that the boy had been overcome by grief at the unfamiliar sight of his mother preserved by the embalmer? But that was not it at all. For when Paul Leiter's aunt stepped up to the casket, she understood immediately what had prompted his flight. One glance was sufficient to tell her that whoever the woman was lying in the casket, it wasn't Ellen Leiter.

Eight and a half hours after the funeral of Ellen Leiter came to its abrupt and puzzling conclusion, a tan Datsun pulled to a stop at a vacant lot a few miles south of the town of Milton. The lights of nearby Boston had infused the overcast sky with a hazy glow. The smell of newly fallen rain hung in the air. There was a smell, too, of waste, of sewage, of rubble.

No one used this lot. The FOR SALE sign posted at the entrance was rusted like every other piece of metal on the lot. Clearly, this was not what anyone would consider prime real estate. The wire fence meant to discourage intruders had long since been broken through and there was no evidence that anyone had seen fit to repair it.

Satisfied that he was alone, Hal Jarvis opened the Datsun's trunk and removed from it first a shovel and then a duffel bag which contained all of the earthly remains of Ellen Leiter. In death, and probably in life, too, Hal Jarvis suspected, she weighed very little. Ninety pounds, a hundred at most. He slung her over his shoulder, at the same time using his foot to close the trunk.

It was his belief that his break-in into the Fabrizzi Funeral Home on Massachusetts Avenue would never be discovered. The lock had been jimmied so well, he thought, that he'd left behind no visible sign that it had been forced. Some mix-up would be assumed, a confusion of cadavers laid out for the embalmer's ministrations. It pleased Jarvis to know that no one would ever figure out that the woman they were eulogizing at the Church of the Sacred Heart had been eulogized and buried once already. As for Ellen Leiter, her final resting place would be here, in this foul-smelling, pestilential lot. For her there would be no well-tended grave, no visits from bereaved family members, no flowers.

Jarvis began digging. The ground was thick with mud from all the rain that had fallen and it proved heavier to scoop out than he'd expected. But he didn't want to wait for it to dry. There wasn't any time for that.

Actually, it wasn't the backbreaking labor that bothered him so much, it was the bugs, particularly the mosquitoes. Constantly he had to stop digging in order to swat at some marauding insect supping on his blood.

He planned it so that Ellen Leiter would occupy a spot not far from where Chong had been interred the previous night. Chong's disposal had been simpler, involving no break-ins, no switches. In his case, all that had been required was an exhumation from the grave he'd been put in originally and a relocation to the lot.

It was possible, of course, that all these efforts on Jarvis's part weren't entirely necessary. The specimens destroyed in Atlanta might have contained all the succinylcholine left in their bodies. But he knew enough about the action of the anesthetic to realize that, in the quantities he'd used, traces of it might very well turn up in other organs. Neither he nor Mr. Wilder, who'd contracted him for this job, could afford the risk of a court-ordered exhumation of the two corpses.

After three-quarters of an hour Jarvis decided that he had no need to expend himself further. He untied the duffel bag and reached inside, his hands meeting the cadaver's hands. He pulled.

Naked, the body was so incredibly white that it seemed as though there must be an incandescent light lying just below the surface of its skin. Ellen Leiter's face, he noted, was composed and tranquil; it was no longer a face, it was a mask, a tribute to a mortician's magic.

The grave he had dug for her was shallower than he would have liked, but at least it had the added camouflage of the rotted-out hulk of a Ford Toreador.

Another hour was consumed in burying her. By the time he was finished he was covered with mud, his hands were raw and scraped, and he smelled of the death that had claimed Ellen Leiter for its own.

He hadn't any opportunity to wash or change. As soon as his work was completed he returned to the Datsun and began the drive back into Boston. He arrived in front of the Copley Plaza at five minutes to eleven.

Waiting across the street in his car, Jarvis kept his eye on the main entrance. According to the schedule he'd picked up earlier in the day, the Chamberlain Awards Dinner for Medical Achievement should just be letting out.

The man he was waiting for was easily picked out of a crowd, for in order to get around he depended on the use of a walker.

He appeared, in the company of three men, at quarter past eleven. But he soon separated himself from them and proceeded to his car alone.

A slow walker, he wasn't a much faster driver. Moreover, the streets of downtown Boston this overcast night were unusually devoid of traffic. Hal Jarvis had no difficulty following him home.

thirteen

In the dying summer light Jessie's skin turned darker, almost amber, the color of Gordon's first wife's skin when the sun was shining. The darkness favored Jessie; it gave her a beauty that was more serene, more ethereal.

She lay stretched out alongside him, leg to leg, a damp sheet draped indifferently over them. Propping her head up with her hand, she was looking not at him so much but at something out in space. She held her gaze steady and he asked what she was thinking.

"I was thinking about how nice it was to have you back."

"It's nice to be back."

"But then you'll be gone again. Back there."

Back to El Salvador, she meant. Back to where his clinic was no more.

"Yes, I will. But that's my life. And yours too."

She would be on the road more often now, investigating outbreaks from out of badly furnished hotel rooms.

It was in one of those badly furnished hotel rooms that they'd first made love. She'd come to see him while he was on assignment in Charleston, South Carolina, trying to discover why teenagers were coming down with salmonella poisoning. Turned out that the salmonella was being transmitted by contaminated marijuana. Jessie liked to smoke grass in those days. Gordon couldn't abide it. They used to argue over that and everything else. Then they'd fall into bed together, wondering why they were always fighting with each other and were still in love. Couldn't figure it out. Couldn't figure it out now, either.

The difference was that Gordon accepted the love as a given, as an expression of whatever fate was operating on their behalf. Not Jessie. She was always questioning it, always trying to dissect the attraction, see what made it tick.

"Are you ever interested in being with another woman?" she asked, shifting position enough so that he could now see both of her breasts, the tips rising toward him.

"No, no, I'm not," he said, and he was being truthful. He didn't want anyone else. Even if he had, he couldn't have spared the time that a courtship, particularly an illicit one, would demand. He barely had time for his own wife.

"Oh," she said. She looked puzzled. Then she smiled and said, "I'm glad."

He was about to ask her if she'd ever thought about other men but then stopped himself, not only because he didn't wish to know, but also because this was her type of question and not something he would ever feel comfortable in asking.

"Neville says that in the picture of the two of us it looked like I was trying to get the hang of being happy. You know, the photo I carry around in my wallet?"

He remembered; he didn't care for it; he thought it made him look too haggard, too old, too old for her anyway.

"Have you?"

"Have I what?"

"Gotten the hang of it."

It seemed to him like a simple thing, happiness; complicated, too, of course, but not nearly as difficult to achieve as people thought. The problem, Gordon believed, was that everyone worked too damn hard at it. His work made him happy. That is, when it didn't go down the tubes. Work should make everyone happy; if it didn't they should find something else to do: that was his conviction. On the other hand, love was something people made too much of, put too much weight on: that was his conviction too.

"Maybe, maybe I have," she answered. "Neville would like to meet you someday."

"He sounds like an interesting fellow."

"No, really he would."

"I believe you."

"Will you go up to Boston with me sometime later this summer and meet him?"

"If I have the time."

"You never have the time. Make the time."

"All right." He had the sense, which had begun as a dim

awareness and was now growing a lot clearer, that her mood was altering. A certain irritability was taking hold. As it did so her posture changed; her leg was no longer flush against his and she was now beginning to move away from him. Not much but enough.

"All right, I'll make the time."

He couldn't see why it was so important for him to meet this former professor of hers. But to accommodate her he'd go along with it.

His words, however, didn't appear to have appeased her. "I wonder sometimes whether you really care what I'm doing."

Do we have to get into this again? he thought. He wished that their lovemaking could be somehow more definitive, its effects more lasting. How easy it was for things to come undone. And mostly, he felt, it was her doing, her provocation, her infuriating habit of analyzing everything, questioning everything. Those were good traits in tracking down diseases, not emotions.

He breathed in deeply, intent on keeping his temper. "I don't know why you say that, Jessie. Of course I care."

"Then why don't you want me to pursue this thing?"

"What thing? Are we talking about that damn virus again?"

She'd told him about all that had happened since her meeting with Neville in Cambridge, how she'd witnessed an autopsy and visited a psychiatric institution, how she'd then acquired the specimens which had been taken from the hot lab. He didn't know exactly how she expected him to react. But it was obviously not the way he had.

"I thought we'd settled all that," he said now.

"No, we haven't."

"Listen to me, Jess, it would be one thing if this were an outbreak. Right now we have three isolated cases."

"Four with Larry's."

"All right, four. At this point, though, we don't really have any idea what we're dealing with. And after what happened last night to Pat and the break-in here and at your office, my advice is stay away from it. There's enough work for you to do already and I don't give a damn how much it means to Neville or whoever else. As far as I can see, it's more of a case for the police department than for an epidemiologist."

That was almost the same thing that he'd said hours earlier during the heat of their argument. He'd hoped that it would have penetrated. Evidently it hadn't.

"Where are you going?"

She was getting out of bed and beginning to dress, pants first, blouse next, in too much of a hurry to put on a bra. Frustrated and angry as he was, he still couldn't help admiring her. He wanted her all over again.

"I'm going to do some work."

"Jess, would you come back here?"

By the time he got on his slacks he heard the front door slam—a bit too melodramatically, he thought. Moments later the car came to life and she was pulling out of the driveway.

"Goddamn you, girl!" he shouted, but he doubted she heard over the motor of the car.

Hell, it made no sense chasing after her. It would only compound the enormity of his sin. If only he could understand which sin he'd committed.

He decided it must be the sin of telling people what they don't want to hear regardless of the wisdom of your advice.

But what did she want him to say? You're right, keep on the case, work with Larry, get yourself killed?

The more he thought about it the more furious he got. It was terrible being angry alone. He began to think that maybe it would have been better staying in El Salvador. Dodging automatic weapon fire and detonating explosives might be preferable to this.

It's all right if he goes all over the goddamn world and puts himself at risk, never giving a rat's ass if he leaves me a widow, Jessie was thinking during the drive to the CDC, *but somebody breaks into my office and all of a sudden I have to be locked up in an ivory tower. Well, goddamnit if I'm going to stay put.*

She was so enraged that she nearly smashed into an oncoming car when she turned onto Clifton Road. The fearsome screech of tires, followed by an even more fearsome blast of the other driver's horn, didn't do anything to calm her down.

The guard on night duty greeted her warmly but was reciprocated only with a curt hello. The guard knew enough not to ask her how she was doing, having a good idea as to what the answer would be.

There was a new lock on her door. Inside, her office had been restored to order; there was no sign that it had been torn apart the night before.

She sat down at her desk and dialed Neville's number.

This time he answered. "How are you, dear?"

She lied and said she was doing just fine. "I was hoping to find you in. I get worried about you, living like that, all alone."

"I'm used to it. I'm quite all right. Now tell me what news you have for me." She could sense from the sound of his voice how much he must be anticipating something startling, something that would absolutely bowl him over.

Three murders, she thought, ought to bowl anyone over. She started to tell him and, as she went on, he would interrupt her only to say, "How extraordinary, how astonishing, are you quite certain of that?"

He really was like a kid, she thought, with a jigsaw puzzle, all in pieces, spread out on the floor in front of him.

"Excuse me," he said after she'd gone on for maybe ten minutes, "there seems to be somebody at the door. Let me go see who it is."

He put down the phone. There followed a long silence. The silence grew longer. And then the phone went dead.

fourteen

It was unforgivable that no one had gotten around to fixing the air conditioning in his car, Ned Hollister thought. There was some department that took care of such things; he wasn't sure which department it was, but that idiot Luther Riley knew. Repeatedly, he'd told Luther Riley to contact the relevant people and look after it. Either Riley had forgotten or he'd not impressed upon the relevant people, whoever they might be, that it would not do for the acting commissioner of the New York State Health Department to be driving around in an official state car dying of heat prostration.

In the five months he'd occupied his job, Hollister had seen parts of the state that he hadn't known could possibly exist in the twentieth century. Especially the part he was visiting on this particular July day. He wasn't sure, but he believed that he wasn't far from where Washington Irving had set many of his famous stories. He could see why Rip Van Winkle might have felt right at home here. From what he'd glimpsed of the people he'd passed along the road, the whole area was populated by his descendants, people for whom the passage of time had an entirely different meaning than it did for city dwellers. They looked archaic, their faces weathered and alien the way they were depicted in folk art from the middle nineteenth century.

The pastoral beauty that presented itself to the eye of the visitor—acres of woodland crisscrossed by unpolluted streams, verdant valleys that seemed to hold the promise of bountiful harvests come autumn—was deceptive. Poverty was pervasive here, but less dramatic than in cities. Here, in this country setting, a derelict farmhouse or a crumbling barn in desperate need of a fresh paint job might be considered quaint, conveying an air of rustic charm.

The town of Brown Station rose out of nowhere. There was not a hint along the road that ran into it, ultimately turning into its main street, that it was there. No sign informed the traveler to anticipate it.

Like many other towns in this region, its most distinguished building was the church, white and Methodist. In the blazing heat of midday everything looked closed. What few stores there were, were what you would expect to find in such towns: a grocery, a hardware store, a haberdashery, a barber shop with a decrepit Indian figurine standing outside. The displays in many of the windows appeared not to have been changed for years.

Hollister was looking for the school. He'd been given an address, but wasn't sure what good that would do him since none of the streets he passed seemed to have names.

Some distance into town, he spotted a man wearing a wide-brim black hat; seeing him from the back, with a knotted pigtail hanging halfway down his back, Hollister thought he must be a hippie, an exile indulging in illegal pharmaceuticals under the spell of nature. But upon coming abreast of him Hollister saw that it was not a hippie at all, but an Indian. An Indian advanced in years. Hollister honked at him.

"Excuse me, sir, can you tell me where I might find the school?"

No answer. Not even an acknowledgment that the man understood what he was talking about.

"The school? You know where the school is?" Hollister tried emphasizing each syllable, but that had no impact either.

"Thanks anyway," he said, and drove on, leaving the Indian behind in a cloud of dust stirred up by his car.

At a Getty station he got out of his car and went in search of an attendant. The heat was worse outside than it was in the car; sweat oozed in profusion from his body, and his face couldn't have looked any less burned than it felt.

The attendant was an acne-scarred youth who, while more communicative than the Indian, wasn't a great deal more helpful.

"School's closed for the summer," he said.

That, as Hollister knew, wasn't entirely true, but seeing

no reason to dispute the attendant's statement, he said merely that he was meeting someone in front of it. This made enough sense to the attendant and he proceeded to give, in far more elaborate detail than was necessary, the directions Hollister had requested.

It turned out that he'd passed the school a few blocks back. Like virtually every other structure in Brown Station, it was indifferently constructed, its architecture born of necessity rather than inspiration, with yellow bricks and a shingled roof.

No one was waiting for him outside. He was twenty minutes late and he supposed that Mrs. Grolier, the woman who'd arranged to see him, had retired inside to escape the heat. He couldn't blame her.

Of the many memories Hollister had of school, practically none of them were favorable. Although he was now past fifty years of age, some of the same dread he'd felt entering school, especially on Monday mornings, filled him again. He pressed a black buzzer and waited.

A woman of indeterminate age, maybe forty, maybe sixty, appeared. Her lean, smooth face was framed by neatly coiffed hair that in turning to gray had left several blond strands like a souvenir of her youth. She squinted at him as if her thick lenses, worn on a gold chain over her chest, were insufficient to put him in focus.

"Mrs. Grolier?"

"Yes?" Then recognition dawned on her face. "You must be Mr. Heimeister."

"Hollister," he corrected her.

Motioning him in, she said, "I am so glad you've come. I told Lettie—she's the principal here at Station School—that we could count on you. You can't imagine the trouble we have obtaining the services we require from Albany. The bureaucrats don't care what happens in places like Brown Station, not when all we can muster on Election Day is twenty-two voters."

Nearly all of them Republicans, thought Ned Hollister, a member in good standing of the Democratic machine.

"You said that there was a possible health problem here," said Hollister, fearful that if he didn't immediately get to the business at hand he might be here all day, listening to Mrs. Grolier ramble on.

"Oh yes, that is correct, Mr. Hollister, is it? I have asked Dr. Pike to meet us here." Squinting down at her watch, she added, "He should have been here by now, but of course he has to come all the way from Kingston and sometimes it takes him a while, especially if he has to see an emergency. Now, he believes that it's hysteria."

"Hysteria?" Hollister repeated. Having been unable to ascertain over the phone the exact nature of the health problem—Mrs. Grolier had only stressed that it was "alarming"—he had no idea what she was talking about.

"Yes, that is what he termed it." Here she paused. They were outside a door designated JANITOR. "But between you and me, I think that what these poor children are suffering from is not hysteria at all. And believe me, I have seen enough instances of hysteria to know the difference."

"What precisely is the problem?" he asked, hoping to learn what this was all about before Dr. Pike arrived from Kingston.

"Come this way, Mr. Hollister."

She led him down the corridor to a room with a big black 5 on the door.

He supposed that room 5 looked little different from rooms 1 through 4 except that just about all the windows had been knocked out. The glass had been swept up, but it had not been replaced. In one corner six chairs were stacked. They were chairs that had seen better days; not one of them had all four legs left to it.

"You see, Mr. Hollister, most of the families here in town are too poor to send their children to camp. Oh, there's the YMCA day camp, but that's fifty miles from here as the crow flies and you know that it costs money to hire the bus to take them back and forth."

It takes money to do anything, Hollister thought; it even took money to have him stand here wondering why this particular classroom was in a shambles.

"So, although our resources are very limited, what with such a small tax base, we at Brown Station School try to make up for it. The children meet here every weekday morning and we do our best to keep them occupied. Some of the parents volunteer their services to take the children on field trips." She began to elaborate on these field trips, and for the next ten minutes there was nothing that Hollister could do to get her to change the subject.

At last, though, she seemed to recall why she'd sent for him, and said, "Now, I don't want you thinking that just because many of our youngsters come from poor families, they are anything other than polite and well-behaved."

"That was the furthest thing from my thoughts, Mrs. Grolier."

"Oh, occasionally some of them act up, but that's normal for six- and seven-year-olds."

"That's the age group that meets here?"

"Yes. We have one or two who are eight, but that's our limit."

Taking in again the sight of the windows knocked out of their moorings, Hollister began to wonder how six- and seven-year-old children did all this.

"I wasn't in the classroom at the time," Mrs. Grolier said, "but the reliability of Miss Day—that would be Alicia Day—is unimpeachable."

"Miss Day was the woman taking care of the children?"

"That's right. Unfortunately, she took ill after the incident."

"Ill?" He raised his eyebrows. Precision was not this woman's strong point.

"Well, her nerves were never the best, and you can imagine what a shock it was to have something like this happen to her."

Pressed for details, Mrs. Grolier proceeded to tell him that just three days previously, one of their best-behaved children, "a marvelous little boy" by the name of John Grimes, had suddenly gone berserk. "It was like a fit actually, from what Miss Day told me. He was frothing at the mouth, and he began hurling everything in sight—his lunchbox, his food, his chair."

"Hurling them at anyone in particular?"

No, she said, he was just throwing things, apparently choosing his targets at random. One girl was struck on the head and was later briefly hospitalized with a concussion.

"Did Miss Day try to stop him?"

"Of course," Mrs. Grolier said, sounding a bit indignant that he would have thought otherwise. "But the boy proved too strong."

"How old is Miss Day?" He imagined a woman well along in years, with a frail constitution and a bad heart.

"In her late forties. She is not at all a weak woman, Mr. Hollister. Under ordinary circumstances she would have had no difficulty controlling the boy."

"And what about the other children?"

"Three of them joined in the rampage; the others were content to cheer them on."

"So they broke all these windows?"

"With their fists."

Hollister's astonishment grew. "You mean to tell me that a six-year-old boy smashed all this glass with his fists?"

"Johnny and Barry Simon and Debby Kramer."

"How long did this rampage go on for?"

"Forty minutes. It took five adults, including our janitor, Mr. Tildon, to restrain the children."

"Tell me, Mrs. Grolier, did anything that you know of occur that might have triggered off such a fit?"

Shaking her head vigorously, Mrs. Grolier insisted that there was no reason to suspect that anything was amiss. "It just happened out of the blue."

At that moment the buzzer sounded, alerting them to Dr. Pike's arrival.

Dr. Pike looked to Hollister like one of those doctors from an earlier era who was now reduced to performing tonsillectomies on schoolchildren. He was a gaunt man with skin that was transparent enough to reveal a welter of blue veins on the backs of his hands. He gave off a faint antiseptic smell he'd probably brought with him from his office in Kingston.

As Mrs. Grolier had indicated, Dr. Pike's all-purpose diagnosis was hysteria. One boy went nuts, his friends followed suit.

"What do you think caused the first boy, Johnny Grimes, to go nuts, as you put it, in the first place?"

"These things happen. I am no psychiatrist. All I can tell you is that I examined the three children responsible and found nothing physically the matter with them."

As he spoke, a look of exasperation settled on Mrs. Grolier's face, but the doctor seemed not to notice.

"Where are the children now?" Hollister asked when he was through.

"Why, I sent them home. If their families wish to speak to a child psychiatrist, that is their business. There's nothing more I can do."

"Isn't it true, Mr. Hollister, that sometimes this sort of thing could be caused by a . . . well, a physical contaminant? Asbestos in the insulation or lead in the paint?" Mrs. Grolier asked.

"I don't know whether asbestos or lead could be blamed in this case, but certainly it's a possibility that can't be ruled out. What do you think, Doctor?"

Although Hollister had scant interest in Dr. Pike's opinion, he felt it best to include him out of politeness.

Shrugging, the doctor allowed that although such agents had caused outbreaks of illness in the past, he doubted that this was true here. "It was hysteria," he said again.

Once he'd departed, giving both Hollister and Mrs. Grolier a gruff good-bye, Mrs. Grolier turned to her guest and said, "I knew that you would need to speak to him eventually and I thought: Why not get it over with now?" Screwing her face up, she said, "You don't really believe it was hysteria, do you, Mr. Hollister?"

"Until the children are given thorough examinations I am really in no position to speculate." The whole affair, however, sounded very odd to him. He stepped closer to the windows and gently laid his hand along the jagged ends of glass, as if to confirm the reality of the destruction. *A six-year-old child did this,* he kept thinking.

This was a most unusual case, but he wasn't sure that it constituted a hazard demanding the attention of his office. But Mrs. Grolier seemed to think that other investigators would follow in his wake. Why else would someone as important as he take the time out to stop by the Brown Station Public School unless he was aware of the urgency of the situation?

Hollister refrained from saying that the only reason he'd paid a personal visit was that her story had provoked his curiosity. Now he didn't know whether his curiosity was satisfied or not.

"We'll be in touch, Mrs. Grolier," he said, thinking that this was a nice, neutral remark.

"There is one more thing I didn't tell you before, Mr. Hollister."

Her voice lowered and she assumed a confiding air.

"And what would that be?"

"Those children . . ." Her face had become flushed all of a sudden.

"Yes, what about them?" Hollister was in a hurry to be off and this woman was wearing out his patience.

"Well, they . . . how should I put this?" She seemed to summon up the courage to break through her reserve. Sounding more outraged than shocked, she said, "They began to fondle their genitals quite defiantly after they were finally subdued. The little girl, too, can you imagine? I had no idea that children so small could do such a thing. But Miss Day assured me that it was true."

"They were masturbating? Every one of them?"

"Every one. Just what do you make of it, Mr. Hollister?"

"I'm as mystified as you are," he said, at the same time easing himself out the door.

"Imagine," she said, shaking her head in wonder, "even the little girl."

fifteen

It took longer than Jessie had expected to speak to the detective in charge of the case, and by the time she was through, she discovered that Neville's funeral was already over. Aside from the anger she felt for having missed the funeral, she was also upset because she had so little to show for it.

The detective, a man by the name of McCormick, seemed to her too young, too lacking in experience, to give her confidence that something would be done. The thick mustache he wore made him look like half the grad students on the streets of Boston and Cambridge.

Impatiently, he asked her to repeat what she'd told him over the phone from Atlanta.

"You say he excused himself to go to the door?"

Jessie confirmed that this was true.

"Did you actually hear him talk to anybody?"

"I thought I heard a man's voice."

"You *thought* you heard a man's voice." McCormick might not be a seasoned detective, she thought, but he was not immune to the sarcasm characteristic of his older colleagues.

"I can't be sure, but it seems to me, after what happened to Pat Flanigan—"

"Pat who? Oh yes, that's right, you told me. The lab technician or whatever she was, the one who was killed."

She noted that he was taking none of this down. Either he possessed an infallible memory or, more likely, didn't consider her story crucial enough to record.

"And you think that her killer was Mr. Green's killer?"

"That's basically correct."

He leaned across his desk, clasping his hands together and adopting a concerned expression that he must have learned from one of his partners somewhere along the line. It was the expression you used when you wished someone to think that you cared when, in fact, you didn't give a damn.

"The problem, as I tried to tell you, Dr.—or is it Ms. Palmer?"

"Miss Palmer will do just fine."

"Well, Miss Palmer, the coroner has ruled Mr. Green's death a result of an accidental fall. Knowing him as you say you did, you certainly are aware that he had bad legs and needed a walker to get around."

"I'm fully aware of the problem he had with his legs," Jessie snapped, "but that has nothing to do with it."

McCormick held up his hands in a gesture of mock surrender. "Hey, Miss Palmer, I'm only telling you what the coroner said." He sat back in his chair. "Did I tell you where Mr. Green's body was found?"

She said she assumed it was close to the door.

"No, actually, he was sprawled out in the middle of the living room."

"Surely his killer could have put him anywhere he wanted to."

"According to the coroner's report, he sustained his fatal injury by falling against the corner of a marble tabletop."

"But he could have been pushed."

"That may be, Miss Palmer, but there were no signs of forced entry."

Jessie pointed out that any man who could have penetrated the maximum containment lab at CDC headquarters was certainly capable of murdering an aged man, and a cripple at that, alone in a house in Cambridge.

The detective still wasn't buying it.

"You don't know this man," Jessie protested.

McCormick could barely restrain his amusement. "And you do?"

In a strange way she was beginning to. He was closing in, hovering not so very far away. One day he would make his presence known.

"Listen, Miss Palmer, we've checked for fingerprints and come up with nothing. We've found no signs of a struggle, no signs of breaking and entering, no witnesses who say they saw a stranger—even a strange car—anywhere close to Mr.

Green's residence. The only conclusion we've been able to reach, compatible with the facts as we know them, is that Mr. Green slipped and fell against the edge of a marble tabletop. It is not such an extraordinary occurrence. It happens all the time. You're in the medical business, you know about these things."

In an effort to assuage her he added, "Now, it's possible that he did go to the door and talk to someone. They talk for a minute or two, Mr. Green says good-bye, shuts the door, secures the chain, and is on his way back to the phone to resume your conversation. Maybe he's in a bit of a hurry, anxious not to keep you waiting, especially since you're calling long distance. Say he gets careless, trips and falls. Isn't that a reasonable hypothesis?"

Jessie had to admit that it was; the only problem she had with it was that it was wrong.

In parting, the detective assured her that should any new facts come to light, he would get in touch with her again. "Thank you for your cooperation," he said.

She didn't have it in her to give him the courtesy of a reply, especially not after she saw what time it was getting to be.

Although she was too late for the funeral, Jessie did make the reception held at the house of a professor, retired like Neville, who had taught for nearly twenty years at Harvard Medical School.

The house was like so many Jessie had been to in Cambridge, charming and crammed full of books. Gordon would have loved it. Among the seventy or eighty people who'd gathered to honor and drink to Neville's memory, only a few faces proved familiar. One was a nattering but likable fellow who reminded Jessie that they'd once attended one of Neville's seminars together. He said that his name was Melvin Jacobs. He acknowledged that he was a perpetual grad student, "till eternity" as he put it, since he was convinced that not even death would put an end to his studies. He was thin and tall and pale, with an enlarged Adam's apple that bobbed with every consonant he uttered.

After a time Jessie felt relaxed enough with Melvin to talk about her interview with Detective McCormick. Melvin was astonished at first, then intrigued.

"You really think that somebody murdered Neville?"

Jessie nodded. "I'm positive of it, even if no one else believes me."

"Oh, I believe you."

"You do?"

"Well, yes. You see, I met Neville last Tuesday and he was acting so strangely, so out of character, that I had a feeling something was going to happen to him. In retrospect, I think he might have had a premonition of his death."

"And why do you say that?"

"Well, we met purely by chance. I was on my way to the subway and he was coming in the opposite direction. He invited me to have coffee with him. I was in no hurry and so I said sure, coffee will be just fine. We chatted for a few minutes and then he asked me if I could do him a favor."

"A favor?"

"Yes, he said that for years he'd been collecting scrapbooks and he wanted to know whether I'd be willing to take care of them for a while."

"Did he tell you what was in those scrapbooks?"

"Not really. He said that he'd been collecting bits and pieces of information about medical oddities for years, that was all. I couldn't figure out why he'd chosen me to hold them, but I wasn't about to refuse. You didn't refuse Neville anything."

"He didn't mention why he wanted you to keep them?"

"At first, I thought maybe he's afraid of fire. But that didn't make sense. My apartment's no safer than his house is. Besides, if he was so worried about the safety of his scrapbooks, why didn't he do something sooner? He seemed so anxious to get rid of them that I told him I'd be happy to come by and pick them up. But he didn't want to wait. I had to go with him and get them right away."

"They're at your place now?"

He nodded. "My wife nearly killed me when she saw them. I figured we could easily find space for them. But it was a little more than a few scrapbooks."

"Melvin, where do you live?"

"Just off Kenwood Square."

"Do you mind if I go back there with you and take a look at those scrapbooks?"

Melvin reflected on this idea for a moment before he said, "Well, sure, Jessie, I don't see why not."

Melvin's wife, a woman of indifferent looks who wore her red hair knotted into a ponytail, accepted Jessie's appearance with little enthusiasm. After setting down a cup of cinnamon iced tea—"the only kind we've got, I'm afraid"—in front of Jessie, she quickly retreated to the kitchen, where she remained for the duration of Jessie's visit.

Although Jessie had examined some of Neville's books before, she'd never had the opportunity to see them all gathered in one place. Melvin had not exaggerated the size of the collection. Uniformly bound in black leather, bulging with clippings meticulously pasted on thick cream-colored paper, they formed a small mountain at her feet and another one on the bridge table.

"Too bad he didn't like to use computers," Melvin said. "He could've gotten all of this shit onto a hard disk and still had room left over."

"Well, Neville was a little on the old-fashioned side. I suspect that computers frightened him; that one day, by mistake, he'd press a button and lose everything down an electronic black hole."

Fortunately it wasn't necessary for Jessie to pore over the entire collection; what interested her most would be found in the last volume—if it was to be found at all. Where it could be located in the stacks of books was another question altogether.

There was enough dust from them to set both her and Melvin coughing; the air in the room where they sat was beginning to smell like a desert during a sandstorm.

It would be ironic, and frustrating as hell, if the last volume was not there. And it was nearly half an hour before they did find it.

Flipping through the book, Jessie came on the clippings Neville had previously shown her: BROOKLINE MAN ON WILD SPREE; MOTHER OF THREE HELD ON CHARGES OF ATTACKING 12-YEAR-OLD SON; WOMAN SLAYS TWO IN NIGHTCLUB INCIDENT. There were additional clips from other papers—the Providence *Journal*, the Manchester

Leader, the Woonsocket *Call*—and a scattering of dispatches sent out over the regional and national wires of the AP and the UPI. But there were precious few facts in any of these other articles that she hadn't already known.

While she examined these clips, Melvin continued to peer over her shoulder, his cigarette turning into a stalk of ash without his being aware of it. The intensity of his myopic gaze unnerved Jessie, but since she was here at his pleasure, she decided it was best not to say anything.

Turning the pages, she came on a reference to a book entitled *The Childhood of Man* by L. Frobenius, pages 472 to 477. To this reference was appended the note: "Possible origin of disease?"

Intriguing, but cryptic—at least without the book. "Does this mean anything to you?" she asked.

"Frobenius? L. Frobenius? If he doesn't have anything to do with biochemistry I wouldn't have a clue. You're talking to a cultural cretin. Hell, I haven't so much as looked at a newspaper in weeks!"

The graduate student syndrome, she thought—the world reduced to two or three shelves in the library stacks and that was it.

It was still only early evening. "The bookstores should be open now," Jessie said. "I'll go out and see if I can't dig this one up."

"Tell you what," said Melvin. "Why don't I do that? I'll just scoot over in my car and you can stay here and keep reading."

"You wouldn't mind?"

"Not at all."

He seemed to be telling her the truth; he was delighted to have something to do other than absorb yet more minutiae about the molecular structure of the murine cell, which was what, Jessie gathered, his thesis was about.

While he was gone Jessie came upon a chart of some kind with the names Atwater, Chong, and Leiter, each linked by an arrow to someone named Will Ziegler. She was certain that she'd never encountered this name before. Chong and Leiter were in turn connected by another arrow to the initials B.U. which Jessie presumed referred to Boston

University. "How Atwater fit in exactly?" Neville had written in fine, meticulous script at the very bottom of the page.

Jessie proceeded to copy this information down, duplicating the arrows and the positions of the names.

Several blank pages followed. Jessie went back, but soon satisfied herself that there was nothing more about the three cases that had come to Neville's attention.

Melvin's wife went about busying herself in the kitchen, deliberately ignoring Jessie, which was just fine with her. She didn't think that she would enjoy much success trying to make conversation with the woman.

Presently Melvin returned; his hurried footsteps up the three narrow flights of stairs leading to the apartment Jessie took as a hopeful sign. When he burst through the door the excitement was visible on his face, more flushed from whatever he'd read in the book than from his quick climb.

"I don't know what it all means, but it sure is strange," he said, and placed the book down in front of Jessie, opened to page 472.

Her eyes ran over the text. She took in phrases that were about as unsettling as any she had ever read:

"When I asked my men what part of the human body they liked best, they always struck their thighs. . . . The most delicate morsel of all is the fat about the kidneys. . . ." "A man told me that immediately after beginning to wear a small piece of human fat. . . ." ". . . those who die a natural death . . . the dead are consumed by their own relatives. . . ." "This also seems to harmonize with their fondness for the flesh of the Chinese. . . ."

"Why do you think Neville was so interested in all this gruesome stuff?" Melvin asked. "It makes you want to blow lunch, doesn't it?"

Jessie was trying to answer that question in her own mind. A few odd facts, gleaned from years of omnivorous reading, now began to assume a certain relevance. "Remember I told you that this virus acted on the brain and the central nervous system somewhat the way Alzheimer's or Creutzfeldt-Jakob disease did?"

"Only you said it acted much faster?"

"So it would seem."

"Yes, but what does this have to do with Frobenius? He's an anthropologist, not an expert on disease."

"Well, there may be a relationship. I recall reading about a bizarre disease peculiar to one tribe in New Guinea. It was called kuru."

"You're saying that what happened to these three people was caused by kuru?" Melvin looked incredulous. When Jessie didn't immediately reply, he went on, "I mean, wait a minute, Jessie, this is crazy. If I'm not mistaken, you believe—"

"Not me—Neville."

"All right, Neville. Neville believed that these people were infected by kuru or something like it?"

"That's my reading of it."

"It follows then that the way they got it was through—" He couldn't utter the word.

"Through cannibalism. That seems to be what Neville is driving at."

"Shit." Melvin slumped down in his chair. "Cannibalism? In Boston?"

"Maybe not in Boston."

"Where then?"

Jessie had no answer.

sixteen

As director of the field service, Lou Valdespino was in charge of assigning investigators from the CDC to whatever localities requested their assistance. With his lean face, dark eyes, and carefully maintained goatee, he looked as though he could have posed for a painting by El Greco. A Mediterannean heritage was evident in his features and in the dark complexion of his skin, which in summer grew darker still.

Sitting in his office on the fifth floor of Building 1, on the morning of the fourteenth of July, he received a phone call from Ned Hollister.

Valdespino knew Hollister from the days when the latter was with the Center for Prevention Services. He didn't believe that Hollister deserved the position with the New York State Health Department—with any health department for that matter—that he now enjoyed. In his view, Hollister was lax and indecisive, apt to make snap judgments. Besides, he was something of an alcoholic who spent much of his time contriving pretexts so that he could indulge his habit. Consequently, Valdespino was not especially delighted to be hearing from Hollister first thing in the morning.

"There's something unusual happening up here I thought you should know about," Hollister began.

As Hollister related his story, Valdespino realized that, in this instance, the old fool might not be as off the wall as he usually was. The symptoms manifested by the children of Brown Station, New York, bore a remarkable similarity to cases in Boston and California that had already come to the attention of the CDC.

Valdespino broke in on him at one point to ask whether he'd heard of the break-in and murder that had occurred less than a week before in the hot lab.

"I read something about it in the *Times,*" Hollister said. "There were some specimens destroyed, too, weren't there?"

"The specimens were taken from three individuals in Boston who sound like they might have been afflicted with the same thing that these children of yours might have."

"I didn't realize that there was a connection."

That didn't surprise Valdespino; Hollister was not someone who was very good at making connections.

Valdespino wanted to know how he'd reached the conclusion that the children were physically ill, and not just victims of hysteria, as a local physician had asserted.

"After getting back to my office from Brown Station, I asked one of our physicians to go out there and examine the kids himself. The clown I met—Dr. Hysteria—didn't exactly inspire trust."

"And what did your man find?"

"Among the symptoms he reported were an irregular gait, foam on the mouth, hyperventilation, bed-wetting, and episodes of myoclonic jerks and variable ataxia."

"In all the children?"

"The severity of the symptoms differed from child to child, and in two there was no evidence either of foaming or bed-wetting. What was common in all five—"

"Five? I thought you said there were only three."

"There were three in the original cluster—they were the ones who went berserk at the school, but since my visit to Brown Station last Tuesday two more seem to have come down with this thing. We're still not sure how it's being transmitted."

"And what was the one symptom they had in common?"

"Extensor plantar reflex. Their big toes won't go down. It's the damnedest thing."

"Any of these children hospitalized?"

"One is, in Sullivan County Hospital. The others are still at home, but I expect that they'll have to be hospitalized too before long."

"And what was your man's diagnosis?"

"He said that he'd never seen anything like it, that if he had to make a diagnosis at all it would be 'progressive dementia caused by a possible virus-like infection.' In other words, it wouldn't be anything he'd care to place his bets on."

Hollister, who'd once been a veterinarian employed by thoroughbred stables in Kentucky, had a particular interest in bets and the odds that tended to favor them.

"I've put some of our officers on the investigation, but we're obviously dealing with a complicated situation here and any help you people care to provide would certainly be appreciated."

Although Hollister did not sound alarmed, Valdespino discerned considerable anxiety. Ned Hollister was a man who didn't want to be held responsible for anything. From what Valdespino had heard, he'd become acting health commissioner by default. The commissioner had died quite suddenly of a coronary, and the man next in line for the job had recently resigned to go into private practice. This left a void which Hollister filled in the belief that nothing more catastrophic than an outbreak of rubella or botulism poisoning was likely to happen before the governor appointed a new director. The last thing he wanted, the last thing he was prepared for, was to have to cope with a rare disease that attacked the brains of small children and might conceivably be contagious as well.

Valdespino promised to do what he could, assuring Hollister that he would get back to him before the end of the day. A moment later he buzzed his secretary and said, "Would you ring Gordon Markoff's office, please, and tell him I'd like to meet him this afternoon. Around one if it's convenient."

Gordon turned up at half-past the hour, being delayed at lunch by a garrulous World Health Organization representative from Pakistan. He knew he must look drained and sleepless, and if he didn't look it he certainly felt it.

No longer director of the CDC, Gordon wasn't sure why Valdespino would want to see him. Attached to the International Health Program Office, he seldom had dealings with Valdespino, who was concerned principally with epidemic outbreaks within the borders of the United States.

It didn't take long before Gordon understood the field director's purpose in setting up this meeting.

After briefing him on the situation in Upstate New York,

Valdespino said, "The one person I thought of immediately to send up there was Larry Fallon. It seems to me this is obviously something for Special Pathogens. Besides, he's already encountered a similar case out in California."

Although Gordon knew very well whom he was alluding to, he remained silent and let Valdespino finish.

"When I spoke with Larry he suggested two EIS officers. One I'm not sure you know. His name is Ron Cochi."

No, Gordon said, he hadn't met him.

"He's bright, hardworking, very easy to get along with."

"Who's the other officer?"

Valdespino hesitated for a moment before saying, "Your wife."

Gordon had a feeling that that was coming.

"Larry told me about her involvement with that cluster in Boston and recommended that she be included in this investigation."

Valdespino made no mention of the incident in the maximum containment area; it was assumed that just about everyone connected with the CDC was aware of it.

Raising his eyes toward Gordon, Valdespino seemed to be expecting some reaction. But Gordon maintained his silence, trying to frame his answer in his mind.

"I took a look at Jessie's record and what I saw there was really quite impressive. I concurred with Larry's suggestion. I think she's ready for something like this. But I didn't want to talk to her until I had a chance to tell you. If you have strong objections to her undertaking this, then that'll be the end of it. We have enough talented people in the EIS so that finding someone else shouldn't prove much of a problem."

Gordon was tempted to say that he needed time to think it over, but another day, even another few hours, would change nothing. He knew what he was going to say, he knew as soon as Valdespino had put the choice to him.

"I appreciate you taking me into your confidence like this," he began, "but in spite of what you may think, I don't have any say in the matter. Talk to Jessie herself. Whatever she wants to do is her own business. It sounds like quite an opportunity to me."

Valdespino settled back in his chair. No doubt, he preferred to avoid becoming entangled in sticky domestic situations. Gordon was giving him an out which he seemed to appreciate.

"Terrific. I'll talk to her this afternoon. I expect to have the three of them in New York by this evening."

Fate, Gordon thought, or its first cousin, blind chance, wanted Jessie in on this investigation and he realized that there was really nothing he could do to stop it from happening.

"I have just one favor to ask," he said to Valdespino.

"And what would that be?"

"I'd like you to include me on the investigation."

As he expected, the request surprised Valdespino.

"Could I ask you why?"

He probably felt that Markoff simply wished to keep tabs on his wife, but there was more to it than that.

"I happen to like a challenge," Markoff said. He would have added something about the operation of fate in one's life, but he didn't think that Valdespino would understand.

seventeen

The Sycamore Motor Court, advertising an Olympic swimming pool, color TVs in every room, air conditioning, and beds with mattresses that did interesting things once a special vibrating switch was turned on, was selected as the temporary headquarters of the CDC investigatory team. The motor court was located off a winding road that led up along the Hudson and into the heart of the Catskills. About fifteen miles south was a giant chicken farm, and when the wind's direction altered unfavorably, a noxious odor of the shit from two million chickens came drifting through the motel rooms.

Another eight and a half miles north of the Sycamore Motor Court, in a suitably bucolic setting, was the home of the Dai Batsu Zendo, a Zen monastery. Hare Krishna and the Emissaries of the Divine Light also had established retreats in the area. There was something about the region that religious institutions—including those of a more conventional stripe—found conducive to the worship of God in his various manifestations.

The Sycamore Motor Court had been built in expectation of better times that never arrived. Aside from the famous resorts—the Concord and Grossinger's and Shadow Pines—which managed to prosper through depressions, recessions and inflation, a great many hostelries had either folded or were just barely hanging on.

From what Gordon could see, no one would choose to stop at the Sycamore Motor Court unless he was suffering from exhaustion. So there was no problem at all obtaining accommodations for the epidemiologists. At the same time the management was happy to put at their disposal a reception hall, which became their command post—their war room.

The first thing Gordon did upon inspecting the reception

hall was to put up a large colored map, given to him by Hollister, showing the entire Catskills area in extravagant detail: its mountains, its rivers, its towns and villages and principal highways, but also its dirt roads, its hiking trails, and its railway sidings, long since fallen into disuse.

Into this map Gordon stuck five yellow pins to represent the cases in the cluster that had so far occurred in Brown Station. The isolated case in California and the three cases in Boston, of which there was now no record at all, Gordon was not immediately concerned with. Eventually it might be possible to make the connection, but for now the CDC would concentrate its investigation in the Catskills.

Even if the specimens received from Boston hadn't been destroyed, the CDC could not have gone in without an invitation from Massachusetts. At the moment, if an epidemic situation seemed to threaten anywhere, it was here.

It was past one in the morning by the time the CDC team was settled into the Sycamore Motor Court. Gordon had left Jessie asleep and Fallon and Cochi drinking at the bar. The bar seemed to be the only part of the motel that was alive at all. With closing time at one in the morning, it was a magnet for drunks and insomniacs in need of conversation more intimate than what they could obtain from phoning in to late-night talk shows. Since he suffered with great pain the kind of conversation that tended to prevail in bars, Gordon decided not to join his colleagues. But being too restless to sleep, he thought a drive through the surrounding countryside might be in order.

The car he chose to use for this drive was a Toyota, provided courtesy of the state health office. After spreading out a road map, he began in the direction of the mountain from which the motel derived its name.

With the roads so infrequently illuminated, he was obliged for the most part to rely on his high beams. At one point a creature—a raccoon? a squirrel? a chipmunk?—leaped in front of him, soaring into the air, but not so high that it could escape the impact of the Toyota. There was a thump, followed by a screech that could have been produced by any animal, even a human in agony. An instant later blood splattered the windshield like a sudden squall.

"Goddamnit to hell," Gordon muttered, pulling the car to a stop.

He got out and looked back in the road, thinking to spot the corpse of whatever he'd just hit. With flashlight in hand, he peered underneath the car. Nothing. The narrow one-and-a-half-lane road, paved in whatever parts it wasn't caked mud from a recent storm, revealed the imprint of tires from a four-wheel drive, but no dead creature.

It was possible it had lived, but he couldn't imagine, with so much blood on his windshield, that it would survive long. When he set the wipers going he noticed that bits and pieces of fur had collected on the glass along with the blood.

When his view was reasonably clear he started out again, but with an uneasy feeling in his stomach, as if this roadside mishap, however minor, portended far worse to come.

The road had more twists and hairpin turns than the map had led him to expect. What he found strange was the speed at which he was proceeding. Sixty, then seventy miles an hour. He didn't know why, but it felt right. The road was not made for such speeds, there was no urgency required, but nonetheless the speed felt right. It was as if he needed to get somewhere in a hurry.

Rounding a dramatic bend in the road, he saw Mount Sycamore looming about four miles away. Its summit was molded almost smooth, like the surface of an egg, testifying to all the eons of erosion that had reduced it to its present height.

About halfway below the summit his eye caught a cluster of lights—enough lights to indicate the presence of a medium-sized city. There were lights of various degrees of brilliance and hue, blinking or shining fixedly. In some instances, the lights appeared to be moving, suggesting the passage of traffic along the city's thoroughfares.

Gordon was so astonished by this spectacle that he stopped his car and got out again. According to his map, there shouldn't have been so much as a hamlet situated on the slope of Mount Sycamore, much less a city.

Nothing he could think of could account for such a bizarre sighting. Though he might still be suffering the residual effects of jet lag, he didn't believe that he was quite so tired that he should begin hallucinating, projecting lights onto a landscape where they had no right to be.

To make certain he again consulted the map, but he hadn't made any mistake. Nothing—no city, no town, nothing but pines and balsam firs and an old, abandoned rock quarry—should have been up on that mountain.

"They say that it's caused by swamp gas."

Turning in the direction that the voice had come from, Gordon discerned a figure emerging from the woods on the other side of the road, his features cast into weird relief by the light of the high beams of Gordon's Toyota.

As the man came closer Gordon saw that he was old, his face a road map in itself; to say that it was wrinkled was to do it no justice at all, for it was so indented, so crisscrossed, so intricately lined, that there hardly seemed space available for a square centimeter of skin. A black, wide-brim hat rested atop his head; a shawl of dark purple and yellow was draped over his shoulders. His eyes were as dark and as slanted as an Oriental's, and they bore in on Gordon with disconcerting intimacy. The only thing that Gordon could say for certain was that he was an Indian.

"My name," he said, "is Joe—Joe Hunting Bear."

He carried his body with difficulty, as if it were a burden he could have done without.

Gordon didn't know whether to introduce himself or not. The night had turned so strange, and in such a short space of time, that he wasn't sure what he should do. He had a feeling he was a lot more exhausted than he'd reckoned and that, all things considered, he'd have been better off staying put in the Sycamore Motor Court.

Joe Hunting Bear took his time in getting to Gordon and when he did, he raised his eyes to Mount Sycamore and said, "Those who say that it is swamp gas are wrong."

He spoke with precision, but his voice seemed to have gone over gravel in its passage out of his throat.

"I am ninety-seven years old," he said, "and I have seen what happens on this mountain and I know."

Gordon, searching out his withered, desiccated face, could believe that he was aged, but he did not for one moment believe that Joe Hunting Bear had endured on this earth for almost a century.

"Then what exactly am I seeing?"

In some way Gordon was grateful to receive this unexpected confirmation that he wasn't crazy, but he wasn't sure just how much he could count on this old Indian man's sanity, either.

But Joe Hunting Bear seemed not to have heard his question. "I am the last member of the Shoharie tribe," he said. "Once my people lived on this mountain you see. Once they hunted here, once they fished here. Now they are gone, they are like the air. Except for old Joe Hunting Bear." He said this without a trace of emotion.

"How did they all die out?"

"They died out. It happens. But you ask the wrong question."

"And what is the right question?"

"The right question is how does Joe Hunting Bear live on?" He meant this as a rhetorical question, for he hastened to respond to it. "I ask every day why this happens. The Great Spirit will not answer me. But the Great Spirit will not take me from this earth. I do not know why."

Gazing toward the woods, dark and impenetrable, at least now in the depths of the night, Gordon asked if he lived nearby.

"I live wherever I can," said Joe Hunting Bear. "Here or not here. What is the difference? Do you care?" It was another question whose answer he wasn't interested in.

Gesturing toward the mountain, with its dazzling display of lights, Joe Hunting Bear said, "What you see there is not from swamp gas. What you see there is a city."

"A city?" Gordon was about to point out to him that there was no possible way a city could be up on that slope, but he was cut off by Joe Hunting Bear.

"It was told to me by my father and by his father before him, that the day would come when the dwarf Hadui would drop from the sky. Hadui very bad, very evil. This is his city you see there. It fills up little by little with people he steals away." Joe Hunting Bear's voice sounded tired and very far away. "This city of Hadui's, by morning, will disappear. But when darkness falls, until the new moon, you will come here and see it again. This is the city of the dead."

eighteen

When Sean Laramie awoke it was the middle of the night, and so pitch dark that for a moment he thought he might have gone blind. He held out his hands in front of him, bringing them closer, practically within an inch of his eyes; satisfying himself that he could still see, he tried to remember where he was.

What day was it? That wouldn't come to him either. The pain that had lodged inside his skull was so intense, so relentless, that it demanded all of his attention. How could a man think with such pain?

As his eyes adjusted to the near-total absence of light, he began to discern something of his surroundings. A door, a closet, a window.

Blinds were down in the window. If he could get a look out, maybe that would give him some idea of where he was. But as soon as he tried to lift himself off the bed, he discovered that his body was restrained by two leather straps, one drawn taut over his midsection, the other over his ankles.

Why would anyone want to prevent him from leaving his bed? He couldn't understand it. He supposed that if he could ever recall why he was here—or, for that matter, where here was exactly—he would discover the reason for the restraints. But at the same time he understood that it would hurt more if he tried to remember.

About the only favorable aspect of the situation was that he'd somehow managed to work his right hand out of its restraint. One free hand was all he needed. After struggling for a minute or two, he succeeded in freeing himself entirely.

He was clad in a johnny, tied in back. Off the bed now, he began to search for a light but couldn't find one. Opening the sliding door to the closet, he was disappointed to find no clothes. He walked to the other side of the room and peered through the slats of the blinds. Facing him was an airshaft; there was nothing to see there but a gray brick wall. He had no more idea where he was than when he'd woken.

God, his head hurt. It felt like somebody had set off a stick of dynamite inside his skull. At moments his vision would blur or thousands of flickering spots of light would imprint themselves on his retinas. He wished like hell he knew what was wrong with him.

There was an odd, unpleasant smell in the air which he couldn't identify. Whatever else he did, he needed to breathe in air fresher than this. He put his hand to the doorknob and turned it, first to the right, then to the left, but it wouldn't give. Was this a hospital or a prison of some kind?

He now did the only thing he could think of, which was to hammer on the door with his fists and cry out.

To his amazement the lock snapped back and the door came flying open, but with such suddenness that it nearly hit him in the face.

A uniformed man appeared, a badge glinting on his chest. He stood in the doorway in a way that made it impossible for Sean to squeeze by him.

"Where am I?" Sean asked. His voice was hoarse and his throat was extremely raw.

"How did you get out of the bed?" the man asked.

The question seemed beside the point. By what right did this man dictate to him whether he should be in bed or not?

"Get back in there," the man said, taking a step forward.

Sean didn't move.

"Did you hear what I said?"

Another step forward.

Sean still didn't move. The spots in front of his eyes were worse, blotting out the sight of the man altogether.

When Sean felt the man's hands on him, something like an electrical charge shot through him. Seizing hold of his arms, Sean propelled him back, pushing him into the wall. His head made a loud thunk on impact.

Although the spots didn't vanish completely, Sean was able to see that the man was reaching for the gun lodged in a holster strapped over his shoulder.

Sean wasn't sure what he was doing. He was not in control; his body was acting on its own. The kick that he delivered to the guard's chest surprised him almost as much as it did his victim. He was rewarded with a crackling sound as the ribcage splintered apart. The guard's jaw dropped open and blood gushed out, some of it spattering Sean.

The guard crumpled to the floor. But he was still alive. He was attempting to speak, but his words were unintelligible with all the blood welling up from his punctured lungs.

Sean gripped hold of his neck and, applying all his strength, succeeded in choking the man. The man made a long, rasping noise and thrashed and bucked, but this frenzy was momentary, cut off the very instant that his neck snapped; to Sean, it sounded little different than if it had been a dried stick of kindling he'd broken.

Sean quickly stripped out of his blood-soaked johnny, undressed the guard, and put on his uniform. It fit poorly, being much too tight, and blood was drying on the tunic, but it would have to do.

Stepping out into the corridor, Sean saw that he was all alone. The incandescent light fixtures stung his eyes. He could see doors everywhere, but no windows. A ventilating system hummed loudly; it was the only sound he could hear except for the squeaking of the guard's boots which he'd expropriated. Like the uniform, they were the wrong size, and he didn't know how much longer he could stand them.

The doors on either side of him were designated only by a letter of the alphabet. A smell of antiseptic hung in the air; apparently the ventilating system was doing nothing to dispel it.

As he walked he kept his hand by his hip, close to the pistol. A bank of three elevators revealed itself at the far end of the corridor. Next to it was a fire exit and it was this door he chose, hoping to avoid other security guards.

He found that he had to descend eight floors before he reached the ground level. Here there was no way to escape notice. White-coated physicians and nurses were everywhere. More uniformed guards than he could possibly have expected were situated throughout a lobby that looked more like an exclusive art gallery than an entrance to a hospital.

What an amazing place this lobby was, with framed paintings that Sean was positive he'd seen in art history books, and medieval sculptures: the Virgin and Child reproduced in bronze, terra cotta, and stone.

At any moment he figured someone would stop him, demand to know how the blood got on his uniform. But scarcely anyone glanced at him as he walked by, doing his utmost to remain composed. His eyes were fixed on the revolving door.

Surely, by now, someone would have discovered the body. It would not be long before he'd begin hearing the alarms. Yet he maintained an even pace, not wishing to excite any unwanted interest.

And then he was out. Cautiously he turned around and directed his gaze up at the letters engraved in stone above the revolving door he'd just gone through.

RINEMAN-SACHS CLINIC, they said.

The name meant nothing to him. At this point, though, he knew he'd have to put as much distance as possible between himself and this strange place where he'd just spent no telling how many days or weeks.

The air was warm and sweet, and he was gratified to be back on the streets again, anonymous, unfettered in movement. Keeping his hand close to the pistol on his hip, he set off into the Manhattan night.

nineteen

The house had an air of sadness and neglect about it, so much so that if it had been a human being Jessie would have been inclined to diagnose his condition as critical and recommend that no extreme measures be employed to resuscitate him should his heart cease beating.

The lawn was overgrown and thick with weeds, and what path existed to the door was marked by a succession of footprints whose imprint insured that nothing would grow there in the future.

This was the house of Johnny Grimes, the youngster who, if the credibility of his teacher Alicia Day could be relied upon, was the first one to go berserk in the classroom and start smashing the windows.

Jessie had a two-page questionnaire with her, drawn up for the purpose of pinpointing where the virus may have originated.

She tried the bell but heard nothing. Then she knocked as hard as she could.

Nothing. She knocked again, her resolve strengthened by the faint sound of country and western music coming from within.

At last a woman, whom Jessie estimated to be in her late forties, with her hair gathered up into a bun, and skin that might have been coated with a fine layer of ash, came to answer.

"Mrs. Grimes?"

Suspicion knitted the woman's brow, caused her eyes to narrow. "Yes?"

Jessie gave her name and added that she was with the CDC and was interested in talking to her about her son.

"Which son?"

How many sons did she have who were ill? Jessie wondered. But she said, "Johnny. I understand he's not been feeling well lately."

Going on a rampage and frothing at the mouth would certainly constitute not feeling well, she thought.

Mrs. Grimes seemed to take forever to absorb this information.

"Well," she said, "Johnny's seen Dr. Pike. And there was somebody around here yesterday asking questions."

That would be Bill McKee, one of the physicians working out of Ned Hollister's office in Albany.

"I know that it might be inconvenient, Mrs. Grimes, but if you don't mind, I'd like to ask you some more questions—and speak to Johnny if I may."

"Johnny's asleep."

"I can come back later."

Without another word Mrs. Grimes motioned Jessie into her house; the sigh escaping from her lips Jessie construed as a signal of resignation.

The smell of chicken broiling in the stove reached her as soon as she stepped in. The heat inside was stifling, unrelieved by either air conditioning or a fan. Sweat glistened on Mrs. Grimes's arms and dripped with awful slowness down her face. She directed Jessie to sit down on a seat in front of a nineteen-inch Zenith TV. A game show was on.

It was dark in this room; barely a trickle of light seeped through the part in the curtains. Jessie wondered what it would be like to grow up in a place like this.

She unfolded her questionnaire and began by asking when Mrs. Grimes realized that her son wasn't acting normally.

"Johnny's a good boy, nothing's the matter with my Johnny," said Mrs. Grimes, a hardness settling in her voice.

"If he's sick there's nothing to be ashamed of, Mrs. Grimes."

Jessie had the feeling that this was going to be a long haul.

"Dr. Pike's our doctor. He says that it's all nerves. Johnny's been acting up a lot lately because of what happened."

She stopped there, obliging Jessie to ask her to elaborate.

"His daddy left him." She paused before adding, "His daddy left me. The son of a bitch."

"I see. . . . Well, I'm sorry."

One glance at Mrs. Grimes, and Jessie understood that not for a single second did she believe that she was sorry. How could Jessie possibly have any idea of the tragedy that her life had become?

No matter what question Jessie posed to the woman, she discovered it next to impossible to elicit an answer—at least not the answer she sought. When she asked about Johnny's eating habits, she received a harangue about the soaring prices of food and the woeful inadequacy of government assistance programs. When she asked about Johnny's friends, Mrs. Grimes launched into an interminable tale about how her son had fallen in with "the wrong element."

Jessie began to play along, discarding the questionnaire for the time being, allowing Mrs. Grimes to go her own way in the hope that sooner or later she'd drop enough clues to give Jessie the answers she needed.

"Why do you consider his friends to be the wrong element, Mrs. Grimes?"

"They run wild, they're a bad influence. Most of them are older than Johnny. They're always playing down by the creek."

Jessie sat up. "Which creek?"

"Shoharie Creek—at the end of town, not far from the railroad tracks. Nighttime, the older kids go parking around there, smoke dope. I've heard some stories."

"Did Johnny ever go swimming in this creek?"

"Could have, I don't know. You might want to ask his sister, Molly. Molly's twelve. Her job's watching Johnny when I'm not at home."

"Where is Molly now?"

Without replying directly, Mrs. Grimes hollered into the gloom. A minute later a thin girl with skin as pale as her mother's appeared. She stood anxiously in the doorway, deliberately avoiding Jessie's gaze.

"Molly, you tell this woman here the truth now. She wants to know whether Johnny ever went swimming in Shoharie Creek."

Molly remained silent, biting her lower lip.

"It's important we know, Molly," Jessie said.

"Sometimes I let him."

"What about you, Molly? Did you go swimming in that creek?"

She shook her head vigorously. "It smelled funny. I wasn't going in no water that smelled funny."

"In what way did it smell funny?"

She shrugged. "I don't know, it just did."

"Did Johnny go swimming in there often?"

"He's a good swimmer, Johnny," the mother broke in. "His daddy always said it was important to teach a kid to swim even when he was just a few months old."

Jessie told her that she ought to be proud of her son, then quickly returned her attention to Molly before Mrs. Grimes could get another word in.

Jessie asked Molly if she was acquainted with the four other children afflicted with the suspected virus.

She nodded.

"Did they go swimming in Shoharie Creek?"

"Maybe."

"Did you ever see any of them go swimming?"

"I don't know. Maybe."

She was acting as if she were a prisoner of war, fearful of divulging the slightest shred of information to the enemy.

Presumably, though, interviews with the other children would confirm if they'd been exposed to the waters of the creek, so it wasn't necessary to press Molly any further.

"Thank you, Molly. You've been of tremendous help."

Molly's eyes darted to her mother; it was obvious she was hoping to escape.

"Molly's a straight A student, aren't you, Molly?"

"I got a C in geography," Molly said by way of qualification.

"She's not sure where anything is," Mrs. Grimes said. "That's her problem."

Jessie was relieved to finally free herself from Mrs. Grimes's company. Had she stayed, she would no doubt have had to hear all about the vanished Mr. Grimes. Although the man was surely a heel for leaving his wife and four children without means of support, Jessie couldn't help sympathizing with him. To endure years and years of Annette Grimes's monologues would drive anybody mad.

* * *

Shoharie Creek wasn't really much of anything. Its appeal lay entirely in its isolation. Firs and birch trees kept it shaded from the worst of the sun; large rock formations, worn smooth by water, surrounded it on three sides, providing a favorable resting place when one tired of swimming.

There was nothing especially unpleasant or "funny" about the smell and, to Jessie's eye, the water looked, if not exactly pristine, at least unpolluted. But, of course, without careful testing there was no way of telling for sure. If a virus was present in this water, it still might be impossible to determine; viruses were so small and baffling in their behavior that they were often undetectable.

Still, at this juncture, the creek seemed the most likely source for the spread of the disease, more certainly than by person-to-person contact. Otherwise one would expect that members of the children's families would also have come down with the disease. So far that hadn't happened.

Even if it were found that the creek was in some way contaminated, it would still not explain how Mardi Lloyd or the three victims in Boston had taken ill. Jessie didn't believe that those victims had ever swum in Shoharie Creek nor been in contact with the children who had.

Exploring further, Jessie came upon the railway tracks Mrs. Grimes had mentioned. They were rusted and overgrown. And although she saw no one around, there was abundant evidence of human presence: empty beer cans, empty soda cans, cigarette butts and the empty packs from which they'd originally come. There were empty bottles of wine and booze whose labels testified to either the execrable taste of the purchaser or the depleted conditions of his finances, possibly both. There were discarded condoms which told of the other purpose to which this area was put once darkness fell. A junked car, a 1967 Studebaker that was once all red and was now mostly all rust, sat beside a towering pine tree like some piece of environmental sculpture. A cursory inspection of its interior revealed that its back seat, in spite of the frayed and stained upholstery, was not going unused.

When she returned to the Sycamore Motor Court, Jessie found that Gordon and the other members of the team were still away, presumably conducting interviews of their own.

She went into the war room, where a serviceman from the New York Telephone Company was installing half a dozen lines for the use of the CDC. There she examined the map of the Catskill region in hope of tracing the Shoharie Creek to its source. Perhaps she would find a chemical plant nearby whose discharge into the water might explain the presence of a disease-causing agent. She had no difficulty pinpointing the obsolete railroad that once transported passengers to Albany from parts farther south, but the creek, if the map was any guide, was not there at all. Since she'd seen it with her own eyes, the only conclusion she could draw was that the map was mistaken.

She decided to test one of the phones that the serviceman had just put in and called the mayor's office. The mayor wasn't in, she was told; she was advised to try his hardware store. Obviously his honor's obligations took second place to earning a living.

"Eddie White here," the mayor–hardware store proprietor answered.

Jessie explained who she was, but this was unnecessary. Brown Station was too small a town for someone not to know what went on in it five minutes after it happened.

"I have a question about local geography."

"Shoot."

"Shoharie Creek."

"What about it?"

"Where does it come from?"

"Beats the hell out of me," Eddie White said. "My theory is that it comes up from some underground spring."

"You have no idea where its source might be?"

"Could be anywhere. Far as I know, no one's ever followed it all the way to where it starts. What of it?"

"Just curious." Jessie was not prepared to share her hypothesis with anyone in town, especially its mayor. "Well, then maybe you could tell me why I can't seem to find the creek on the map I have."

"It's a recent map?"

"It was printed in the last year or two."

"That's the reason," said Eddie White.

"What's the reason?"

"It's not recent enough. For the last, I don't know, fifty,

sixty years—at least as far back as I can remember—it was dried up. Then, just this spring, it began filling up again. Maybe it was the heavy rains we had. Poured like a mother April and May. And the creek came back. You look on an old map, one published about the turn of the century, and you'll see that Shoharie Creek's clearly marked. Now that it's back with us again it didn't make any sense going to the trouble of naming it something else."

In spite of the mayor's explanation there was something in what he said that disturbed her. It was only then that Gordon's account of his meeting with the Indian came back to her. Hadn't Gordon said that the Indian had claimed to be Shoharie—the last of the Shoharie.

"Mr. White, do you know of an Indian—?"

Before she could continue he said, "Oh, hell, you mean crazy Joe Hunting Bear. He been bothering you?"

"Not at all. I've never even met the gentleman."

"Well, he's a kook. Goes around saying he belongs to some tribe that's all died off but him."

"I believe that's what he told my husband."

"Don't you or your husband pay him any mind. I bet he also told him he's a thousand years old or something. I figure he must be no older than sixty-five. But you know how these people get; they weren't meant for living too long, they don't age like we do. Old Joe, he's nothing but trouble. We're always having to arrest him for hunting out of season or fishing on private property. Next time he shows up you just ignore him. He'll go away once he realizes you're not about to give him a handout."

Having been adequately apprised of Joe Hunting Bear's standing in the town of Brown Station, Jessie thanked the mayor and hung up.

Rather than take Eddie White's advice and ignore Joe Hunting Bear, she resolved to try and find him. It was just a hunch, but she had a feeling that if anyone knew where that creek began, kook or not, he did.

twenty

According to the 1980 census, Brown Station had a population of four hundred and twenty-six. Since then it was widely agreed it had lost anywhere from fifty to eighty, most in their twenties who went to Albany or Binghamton or drifted downstate, principally to New York City, hoping to find job opportunities unavailable in this part of the Catskills.

So it was little surprise to Larry Fallon to see that the clientele of the town's one tavern, which also doubled as the town's restaurant, was getting on in years, losing hair, losing teeth, losing eyesight, gaining only in the gut. Those who were younger and still stuck in Brown Station would drive to the bar at the Sycamore Motor Court or make a night's outing of it and drive farther on, all the way to Ricci's Pizza joint where there was always a chance of picking up some half-decent girls with not a single thing going on between their ears.

Fallon was interested in taking in some local color, which was why he accepted Bill McKee's invitation to down a couple at Kendrick's Tavern, whose two windows were kept illuminated by a Miller, Bud Lite, and Genesee neon logo and a Coca-Cola clock that didn't work any longer.

A rotund, soft-spoken man, McKee seemed to be one of those rare individuals who want for nothing. From what Fallon knew of him he was happily married, with three teenage children, none with any major problems—delinquency, drug abuse and such. He liked his job and suffered from no ambition to be doing other than what he did.

McKee had grown up not far from Brown Station and as a result he enjoyed a great familiarity with the area and its inhabitants. As the two men sat at a table close to the door, putting away glass after glass of ale, he delighted in pointing out the people he knew, either personally or by reputation.

"Fellow seated over there, name of Jim Dyal," he'd say, calling Fallon's attention to a shrunken man in need of a new set of teeth. "Best damn fisherman around. Woman next to him, everyone says she's his wife. She's not his wife, at least they were never married. Though, I suppose, you spend twenty-eight years together, you're married in the eyes of the law anyhow."

The door swung open. A man sauntered in, intimidatingly tall, with the build of a bear and the look of someone who's just made a killing at the track.

It was his uniform, however, that distinguished him; he was obviously a police officer although his appearance in this saloon seemed to have nothing to do with the enforcement of law and order.

He greeted a couple of men in the corner and went over to join them. His laugh was raucous and carried through the bar.

McKee regarded the man with a skeptical eye, saying, "The cop that just walked in? His name is Tom Emmett. Operates out of Boiceville, but his jurisdiction extends from here to West Hurley." Then he lowered his voice. "It's common knowledge Tom's been on the take for years."

"That so?" Fallon rather enjoyed being filled in on the local gossip even if the people involved meant absolutely nothing to him. "No one's ever done anything about it?"

"Let's just say that he has friends. And a big family. Lots of cousins. And he does perform his job, I've got to say that for him. Aside from the usual vandalism and petty theft we don't see much crime around here." He paused, then added, "Except for one incident."

"What might that be?"

"It's the strangest goddamn thing." McKee settled back in his chair and drained what was left in his glass. "You familiar with Shadow Pines? The resort?"

"Of course."

"Well, the way I heard it, about a week, maybe a week and a half ago, one of the people on their staff went berserk and . . ."

"And what?"

"I know this is going to sound unbelievable, but rumor has

it that this fellow went berserk and killed someone. Not just killed him. Decapitated him."

Fallon let out a whistle. This went way beyond mere gossip; this was of a different order of human phenomenon altogether. "Decapitated him? You say it was rumor? Something like that I'd assume would make the papers. The TV news would eat it up."

"That's what's so odd about it. You ask up at Shadow Pines, they'll tell you it's bullshit. They'll laugh in your face. But the story goes that this fellow—the berserk one, not the one who lost his head—was a coach or an instructor, maybe basketball, maybe swimming, who the hell knows? Nothing about him that you'd think of as psychopathic or anything. Then one day, for no reason at all, he gets into a fight, slices some poor guy's head off."

An idea was beginning to take form in Fallon's mind. Yet he did his best to remain composed, to hear McKee out. "Let me guess. Tom Emmett was called in on the investigation?"

"You got it. Somebody who works for the resort must have known of his reputation. It stands to reason that the publicity you get with something like this is not going to encourage a flood of tourists. Most people don't fancy a great deal of blood and gore on their summer vacation."

"That would take some doing, to fix a murder—a decapitation—like that," Fallon said. "What happened to the body?" He was about to ask what happened to the head, but decided that this might be going a little too far.

"Nobody knows."

"All right, what happened to the beheader?"

"Nobody knows." McKee stared balefully at his empty glass. "I need another drink."

"I should say so." Fallon got up to do the honors. At a place like Kendrick's, table service was an amenity no one expected.

When he returned he said, "Now don't get me wrong, Bill, I'm not suggesting you're making this up, but isn't it a little weird, telling me about a murder where no one knows what the hell happened either to the killer or his victim?"

"Oh, it's a little weird all right. I'll grant you that. More than a little weird." Redirecting his gaze toward Tom Emmett's table he said, "All you've got is one corrupt cop." He looked back toward Fallon; noting his abstracted expression, he asked him if there was anything wrong.

"No, no, I was just thinking of something."

What Fallon was thinking was that McKee's story wasn't as incredible as all that. Mardi Lloyd, too, had gone mad, and in much the same way as the subject of McKee's tale, committing a senseless murder in a fit of inexplicable rage. Inexplicable until a CAT scan revealed that practically half of her brain had rotted away. Both Mardi and McKee's murderer had been at Shadow Pines—a connection that certainly bore further investigating. Especially since Brown Station was not very far away.

It occurred to Fallon that both Mardi and the vanished killer had been infected by the same source that the five children in town were.

"Bill, will you excuse me? I need to talk to your boss."

McKee glanced at his watch and announced that it was nearly midnight. "Ned'll probably be asleep. I hope it's important, because Ned likes his sleep."

"Oh, it's important all right." About the last thing that Fallon cared about was Ned Hollister's sleep.

True to McKee's prediction, Hollister was already in bed and in no mood to talk about the possible link between Brown Station and Shadow Pines. Half the time Fallon was afraid that he'd dozed off, unable to stay awake long enough even to complete his own sentences, let alone listen to someone else's.

When, however, Fallon had made himself understood, Hollister agreed that they could do worse than conduct an investigation on the premises of the resort. "Of course, you have to realize it might not be so easy getting your people on the grounds."

"Why's that? Surely your office has the authority."

"Well, it's complicated," Hollister said, hedging. "Particularly with the Northeast Classic coming up."

"The Northeast what?"

With all the noise in the place Fallon thought that maybe he hadn't heard right.

"It's a golf tournament." Hollister sounded a bit annoyed that Fallon was unaware of it.

"Tennis, baseball, sailing I know, but I'm afraid golf doesn't hold much interest for me. Anyhow, I don't see what a golf tournament has to do with our investigation."

"As I said, it's complicated. It involves a lot of people. People high up."

Unlike Gordon, Larry was not well acquainted with Ned Hollister, having, in fact, met him only once, the day before. But it didn't take long to catch on to his way of doing business: he was a man who subscribed to the don't-rock-the-boat school of life. Larry could hear it in his voice.

"How high up?"

Fallon was thinking that maybe he was alluding to an important state official, the senate majority leader possibly, or even the governor.

"I don't want to get into that."

My God, Fallon thought, the man was becoming infuriatingly tight-lipped. How were they ever going to work with him?

"Ned, you have to appreciate the implications of what I'm saying. It's vital that we have an opportunity to see if the source of the virus is on that property. And we can't rule out the possibility that there are others who are infected—or else are carriers."

He was pointing out things he shouldn't have to, but he didn't know how else to break through to this man.

"All right, listen, I'll see what I can do and get back to you or Gordon tomorrow morning once I talk to Koppleman."

"Who?"

"Koppleman—Stanley Koppleman. He's the attorney Shadow Pines has on retainer. Anything like this, you have to go through him."

"I'm sure if you emphasize the danger inherent in the situation, he'll come around."

Echoing his favorite phrase of the evening, Hollister said, "Well, actually, it's a bit more complicated than that," and hung up.

twenty-one

"You pick the damnedest places to stay in," noted Stanley Koppleman upon entering the East Broadway apartment Hal Jarvis had chosen for his temporary home.

Unlike the apartment in L.A. where Koppleman had met him the last time, these digs were spacious, a whole floor-through to be exact. But it was a shambles. While it was furnished, not a single chair or table or couch looked whole. What the attorney realized was that Jarvis wasn't just hiding out in obscure holes-in-the-wall—he actually liked them. At least he wasn't cooking anything today.

"Be careful," warned Jarvis as Koppleman took a seat by the window. "The back leg tends to fall off."

"I'll watch it."

The summer afternoon had turned grim; sullen clouds were flooding the sky, turgid with rain.

"I think this is what you wanted." Jarvis thrust into his hands a manila folder stained in the lower right-hand corner with his thumbprint.

The attorney pulled out a sheaf of typewritten pages and began reading.

"One page each," he noted.

"Except for Markoff. He rates two."

What Jarvis had found wasn't quite enough for Koppleman, with the exception of Ned Hollister. From the documentation—and hearsay—that Jarvis had collected, Hollister emerged as the only one of the four who could be blackmailed without the need to exercise the imagination.

Otherwise, as far as Larry Fallon, Jessie Palmer, and Gordon Markoff were concerned, their records—at least after a quick perusal—seemed reasonably unblemished.

But this didn't mean that they could not be gotten to. According to the data on Fallon he was in line for a position in the Department of Health and Human Services. Although Jarvis hadn't learned the precise nature of this position, it was evidently one that offered its occupant considerable prestige and access to the inner circles of power in Washington. Larry Fallon was clearly an ambitious man, a rising star—and there was his vulnerability, there was Koppleman's leverage.

Palmer was less important now that the Boston operation was protected and Neville Green was out of the way. But in the event that she proved too troublesome, he was certain that he could deal with her in an effective manner. It had been his experience that women were reached by other means than men; further, it was his conviction that no one could reach them better than he.

There was another member of the CDC investigation named in this documentation—Ron Cochi—about whom Jarvis could discover virtually nothing save that he'd also gone through EIS school in Atlanta. It didn't matter; he was in a subordinate capacity, with so little authority of his own he could hardly be worth bothering with.

No, the only one who gave Koppleman pause was Markoff. As a former CDC director, he carried more weight than would ordinarily have been the case. Worse, he seemed to think that he was on a god-given mission to rid the world of disease. Had he been a Shiite Moslem he probably would have rigged up a couple of thousand pounds of dynamite in his car and driven it—with him in it—into an Israeli military installation. Koppleman decided he must have something of a messianic streak; absolutely incorruptible. Take him into a basement jail cell, torture the hell out of him with electric prods, he still wouldn't talk.

For such as Gordon Markoff the attorney recognized that he would have to employ other, more ingenious tactics. Tactics that meant making a few well-placed phone calls to Washington, D.C. Tactics that meant calling in some long-overdue debts.

Jarvis was standing across from him, slugging down Colt .45 malt liquor from a quart bottle, as expectant as a schoolboy waiting for his teacher to grade his exam.

"You did well, Jarvis."

The compliment might have been appreciated but it was

no substitute for hard cash. Hard cash was what followed immediately.

Jarvis counted it with a practiced hand. Koppleman had the feeling that if Jarvis were blindfolded, he would still be capable of telling a fifty from a ten-dollar bill. It was a magic some people had, a kind of emotional understanding of money.

Jarvis looked up at him quizzically. "I'm an honest guy, Mr. Wilder, and I have to tell you that there's more here than is due me."

"I know." Did Jarvis actually believe that he would be so careless as to overpay him by six thousand dollars?

"You have another job for me, is that it?"

How astute. "That's it all right. The night before last a young man named Sean Laramie escaped from a clinic uptown. He's like the ones in Boston."

"Fucked up?"

"You might put it that way, yes. But unlike the ones in Boston he's still operating on his own power. He killed a security guard and took his uniform." Koppleman now reached into his pocket and plucked out a photograph of Laramie taken when he was accepted as a tennis instructor at Shadow Pines. In addition, he presented Jarvis with an envelope containing Laramie's application form as well as the relevant particulars from his admission form at the Rineman-Sachs Clinic.

"It's very important you find this man." The last thing Koppleman needed was for the police to pick up Laramie on a charge of murder and then connect him with the clinic and, ultimately, the resort. He'd already had enough on his hands convincing Laramie's family that their son was overwrought by problems of a personal nature and that he'd run off one night without leaving behind any clue as to where he was going. "I'm afraid as soon as he stepped off the grounds of the resort he was no longer our responsibility," he'd told them.

Then, too, he'd had to contrive a scenario to explain the security guard's violent end so that it would not be blamed on Laramie. After all, Laramie had been admitted to the clinic under a pseudonym, not an uncommon practice for an institution that routinely treated politicians, ailing movie stars with AIDS, exiled potentates living under the shadow of assassination, and Mafiosi who carried on the kind of lifestyle that made insurance companies very nervous.

Fortuitously, another psychopathic patient, confined by the court to the clinic for an indefinite incarceration given his history of butchering children, was available to take the blame. As a result, no manhunt had been instituted for Laramie. But that situation could not be expected to persist for long; sooner or later Laramie would make his presence known by some particularly vicious act.

"How do I find this guy?" Jarvis asked.

"Read the newspapers," Koppleman said. "They should give you some idea. Otherwise my only advice is to get lucky."

At times, but very dimly, Laramie would remember Mardi Lloyd. Passing by record stores, he'd occasionally see her mother's picture hanging in the window and think of her. But the problem was that he couldn't really fix her face in his mind. It was no better when he tried to recall what it had been like to hold her, to fuck her; it all slipped away like a movie he'd seen in childhood. Even when an image did spring to mind, he couldn't be sure whether it had actually happened or whether he was making it up.

He was certain of one thing, though, and that was that she was sick and that by now she was probably dead. And in those rare moments when lucidity would return to him, and things were more distinct, more coherent than they'd ever been before, he understood that what had gone wrong with her was what had gone wrong with him.

It was the strangest sensation he'd ever felt, what was happening inside his head; it was as if a pair of hands were squeezing his brain, crushing it little by little like putty. The pain was so enormous at times it seemed to burn right through him. Lights would flicker and dance in front of his eyes and then he would black out.

What struck him in particular was how easy it was to mix with people. Here he was, walking around wearing a blood-stained uniform, unshaven, with a mad glint in his eye (he'd looked in enough mirrors to know), a gun on his hip, and hardly anyone so much as glanced at him.

But mostly he stayed indoors. The heat weighed down on him too heavily. And he was never certain when he might lose consciousness and collapse. What had him worried was that the cops might find him lying in a doorstoop and haul him down to a precinct house; they'd want to know who he was and what he was doing in a security guard's uniform.

So he decided to stay close to Grand Central, for there, in the subterranean arteries that ran below the tracks, others eked out a living who had no home to call their own. Scarcely anyone in authority ever hazarded a visit to this underground universe; the homeless, the mentally unbalanced, and the criminals had it to themselves.

Sean was seldom hungry, but his thirst was unrelenting. He suspected that this was as much attributable to his illness as it was to the summer heat. The water fountains in the terminal failed to alleviate his parched throat sufficiently, so he took to stealing bottles of refrigerated soda, juice, and beer from the delis and markets inside and within the immediate vicinity of the terminal. No one ever tried to stop him; he didn't know whether this was because his shoplifting went unnoticed or because the sight of his gun discouraged anyone from calling him to account.

He had lost all notion of time in his depleted state. As far as he could figure, a week or more could have passed since he'd escaped from the clinic. But maybe it was closer to a day.

It was difficult to formulate any plans. Sometimes the thought occurred to him that he shouldn't bother, that he probably wouldn't live long enough to execute even a short-range plan. But maybe it was in the nature of the human being to look toward the future even when no future was possible. Maybe it was only because he was overcome by a need for sex so strong that it, too, like his thirst, might have been another symptom of his illness.

Whatever the case, Sean was determined to find the most desirable woman he could. When he did he would take her, fully, completely, until she would no longer be of use to any other man.

twenty-two

That night Gordon woke to the sound of rain pattering against the window. Way in the distance, thunder rumbled and flashes of lightning turned the room eerily green. In the sudden illumination he could see his wife, her face turned toward him, the sheets bunched about her waist. The storm, on its way through the Catskills, grew loud but failed to awaken her. But it might well have penetrated some part of her mind, for she stirred and turned over and at one point seemed to open her eyes and gaze at Gordon. But when he spoke her name there was no answer, save for an extended sigh. She threw out her hand and lay supine. Again the sky turned a livid green, casting the rolling contours of the mountains into relief; again Gordon could see Jessie, the sweep of her hair on the pillow, the hollow of her neck, the tips of her breasts. Thunder swelled into a great cacophony and Gordon thought of Washington Irving's bowlers. Then the darkness enfolded them, and again Jessie was swallowed up. It was really quite remarkable, how untainted this mountain darkness was.

He might have returned to sleep, but one way or another he lost track of the advancing storm's ebb and flow. At one point, though, roused to alertness by a peal of thunder sounding as if the earth were being split asunder, Gordon looked toward the window and saw something hanging there.

He got out of bed and stepped over to the window. He left the light off for fear of waking up Jessie.

His vision was unfocused from sleep, and the darkness yielded very little even after his eyes accommodated themselves to it. He stood by the window, his hands on the sill. A coating of water lay along it from the rain that had penetrated through the screen. Even this close up he couldn't quite see what the object was.

Then a bolt of lightning raced across the heavens, touching down on the summit of Panther Mountain, creating in the process more than enough light for Gordon to see clearly.

An animal, a beaver, was dangling there, suspended by a rope, presumably nailed to the outside wall. It had been recently gutted, its stomach neatly slit and gaping open; its insides, coiled and sopping wet with blood, dribbled to the ground. The worst part of it was that the angle of the rain had driven the carcass repeatedly against the screen, saturating it with blood. When Gordon brought his hands up to his face, he saw that they, too, had blood on them, that what he'd thought was water on the windowsill was not water alone.

It wasn't fear he felt then, not fear, not panic, but something else: a sense of inevitability. First, the animal he'd run into on the road. Now this. One a matter of chance; the second a warning, a message. But in his mind both incidents were connected. It was as if the vanished creature struck by his car and this savaged beaver were one and the same.

Groping about, he found his sneakers. He kept casting sidelong glances toward the bed, thinking that Jessie would wake and discover what was wrong. It was likely that the warning was intended for both of them.

She remained asleep. He wondered at her obliviousness to danger. For Gordon, who seemed to have developed a sixth sense for it, her blindness, whether willed or not, worried him greatly.

It was quarter of six, and with a more favorable sky, light would already be edging over the horizon. But with the clouds that hung on in the aftermath of the storm, what small light there was, was muted and sickly.

No one was about, though Gordon wasn't surprised; he didn't think that whoever had gutted and then strung up the beaver would have stuck around to see how his little entertainment was received.

In the war room Gordon found a pair of rubber gloves, a plastic trash bag, some paper toweling, and a pail of water. With these, he went back outside to remove the evidence.

The rope holding the beaver was attached to the wall by a nail.

After depositing the remains in the trash bag, Gordon set about washing the screen, outside first, then in. By the time he'd slipped back into bed, less than half an hour had elapsed. To look at the screen now, one would have no idea that some dead and bloody thing had been hanging there just a short while before.

But its odor lingered in the air, in the room, and on Gordon's hands in spite of the assiduous washing he'd given them.

"Gordon, do you smell something funny?" Jessie asked, finally awake, her eyes blinking rapidly as she tried absorbing the eight A.M. light—a violent blazing light since most of the clouds had dissipated.

Gordon said that he did and made a show of walking over to the window and breathing in deeply. Specks of blood he'd neglected to wash away in the darkness seemed to leap out at him. They were so small, that unless one knew to look for them it was doubtful they'd be noticed.

"Yes, I do smell something odd," he said. "It's coming from outside."

"You think there's an abattoir nearby?"

"The damn chicken farm is bad enough," Gordon said.

"You think that's what it is? A lot of butchered chickens?"

"Could be."

It was only after she was on her second cup of coffee that Gordon broached the subject that had been on his mind for the last few hours.

Actually, it was she who initiated the conversation. Three years in his company had taught her to know when he was getting ready to say something to her.

"What is it, Gordon?"

She also knew him well enough to sense when what he was about to say was not going to please her.

"I'd like you to go back to Atlanta."

For an instant she didn't say anything; disbelief caught the words in her throat.

When at last she found her voice she said, "You mean you want me to quit the investigation?"

He wasn't looking at her; his eyes were focused on the

mountains far in the distance; a blue haze had settled over them, blurring their contours.

"That's right. We can work things out with Valdespino, say that there wasn't enough for you to do here, get him to put you on another investigation." Before she could put in a word he went on, "Besides, until we hear from Hollister that we can get on the grounds of Shadow Pines, there really isn't anything more we can do." This wasn't entirely true. The investigation in Brown Station was finished—and Jessie knew it. Having not thought this whole thing through, Gordon was saying more or less what came into his mind. He didn't believe it would be this difficult, not until he'd started.

Jessie's face hardened; her eyes burned with anger. Looking at her, Gordon realized sadly that there was no way he could get her to understand, certainly not without telling her about the beaver in the window. Maybe he should have left it where it was, maybe the sight of it would have put such fear into her that she would've been happy to head home on the next flight out of Sullivan County airport.

But after a moment's reflection he decided that this wasn't likely; after all, if neither the sacking of her office nor the murder of a colleague had discouraged her, how could he think that a small dead animal would do the trick?

"Jess, I don't think you have any conception of just how dangerous this whole thing is. Look what happened to Pat Flanigan. Look what happened to Neville."

"Oh, so now you believe what I said and not the opinion of the Boston police department?"

She had a point; when she'd first told him the news about her former professor he'd been quick to assert that it was probably an accident, a judgment corroborated by the Boston coroner's office. But then, as now, his only concern was with Jessie's well-being.

"All I'm saying is that this involves more than tracing the source of a virus. We seem to have stumbled onto something that should be the concern of the FBI, not the CDC."

"Boston's over with," Jessie said flatly. "The bodies are gone, the specimens are gone." She paused for a second before adding, "Neville's gone. What's happening in Brown Station is another story."

"I'm not so sure."

He could see how much effort she was expending to keep herself in check. It was rare that she displayed her temper; but when she did, the only reasonable course of action he ever considered was to run for cover.

"One way or another, I'm not leaving, Gordon."

What else had he thought she would say?

"Jess, I know how hard it is for you—"

"Hard!" The word was virtually spat out, her voice carrying fire with it. "Hard! How the hell am I supposed to go back to Lou Valdespino and offer some lame excuse why I didn't work out? No matter what I told him you know what he's going to think: Poor, submissive little Jessie probably can't even go to the corner grocery store without her husband's permission. You're not my father, you know. I have one of those already. I don't need another."

Tears were gathering at her eyes, but she quickly wiped them away. Gordon knew how much she hated showing emotion in front of him. He felt badly for her, but he could hardly tell her this without her taking it the wrong way too. What an idiotic situation. Like quicksand: the more he struggled the more he kept sinking in.

"Listen to me, Jess. If you were walking out into the middle of the road and I saw a car bearing down on you, don't you think I'd do everything I could to get you out of its way?"

"This isn't the same thing, Gordon." Her voice was quavering. She took long pauses between words, probably afraid that if she didn't, the words would die in a sob.

"I'm telling you it is. I don't want you to think that if you leave now, anyone's going to think the less of you. For Chrissakes, for all I care, you can tell Lou that you couldn't stand working with me and would prefer to be assigned elsewhere. He'll understand that. Everyone'll commiserate, I'm sure." He laughed, hoping that she would see the humor in the situation. She did not.

"That wouldn't be true. I'm not going to tell Lou or anyone else some stupid lie you made up on the spur of the moment because you were so goddamn afraid I'm going to get into trouble. What happens the next time when Lou wants to send me to some godforsaken place in Africa where there are hundreds of people dying of hemorrhagic fever or something no one knows the first thing about? What do you plan on doing then, Gordon?" Here she began to imitate his manner of speech though without attempting to duplicate the timber of his voice. " 'Now, Jessie, I think you might want to consider this carefully. This could be very risky and because I don't want anything to happen to you, why don't you go and ask Lou to send you to Seattle so you can check on how our measles immunization campaign is coming along?' "

"Jess, you know it's not like that."

"But it is, Gordon, it is exactly like that."

He wasn't sure what he was going to say next, but he knew it would have to be persuasive enough to soften her resistance, if not change her mind. But before he could get another word out, the phone rang.

"Goddamnit," he muttered, picking up the phone so violently he nearly smashed the glass tabletop with it.

He expected it to be Hollister, but it wasn't.

"Is this Gordon Markoff?" a woman asked, and when he acknowledged that it was she continued, "Please hold for Congressman Bradstock."

Trent Bradstock? What the hell did he want? The last time the two had had any communication was three years previously, when Markoff was still the director of the CDC.

When Bradstock came on the line, Jessie stormed out of the room.

"Jess!"

Gordon was tempted to tear after her, but it would not do to hang up on a United States congressman before he'd had a chance to say hello.

"Gordon, how are you?" Bradstock didn't sound as if he were much interested in his answer. "And the family?" he added.

"Fine," Gordon said. What was he going to say?

"I'm afraid I have some rather disturbing news for you."

It wasn't ten o'clock in the morning yet, and this was turning into one hell of a day.

"I'm listening."

"I don't know whether you've been following the hearings our subcommittee is conducting about expenditures for health care."

"I'm aware of them."

"I just received word that you're going to have to testify before the subcommittee in connection with your activities while you were the CDC's director. There's a possibility they may want to question you about some of the things you've been up to since then. Especially about that clinic you operated and authorized funding for in El Salvador."

"El Salvador? What the hell does that have to do with anything?"

"I'm not sure. But it's my impression that there's somebody on the subcommittee who wants to nail your ass to the wall."

"Nail me? For what?"

"I wish I could tell you. All I know is that there are certain people up on the Hill—not just in Congress either—who don't particularly hold the CDC in high regard. Too liberal or something. Too many do-gooders. What did you call them—yellow berets?"

"That was a kind of in-house joke during the Vietnam War."

"You have to realize there's been a change of sentiment here since the Carter administration. Maybe they think you're trying to eliminate disease in the wrong people, what do I know? But I have a feeling they're going to want to take a look at a good deal of documentation, including patients' records, from the years you were in charge of the agency."

"You know I can't do that, Trent. It's unethical."

"I know, I know. I want to help you, Gordon. That's why I called. But I can't do anything unless you get down here."

"I'm working on an investigation now, I can't leave."

"You're going to have to, I'm afraid. The subcommittee's racing to conclude the hearings before the summer recess. You try to put them off, they'll goddamn well subpoena you."

The timing couldn't have been worse.

"What's the latest I can get down there?"

"I'd say that the latest is today; this afternoon if possible.

I'm sorry I couldn't have given you more advance warning, but I didn't hear about this myself until I got into the office this morning."

"When are the hearings scheduled?"

"Tomorrow morning, all the way through to Friday. They're probably going to call you Thursday or Friday."

"That's awfully soon."

"I know. I don't understand it myself. But that's how it is. I'm telling you somebody's trying to nail you on this."

"Do you have any idea who it might be?"

"We can talk about all this when you get here." He proceeded to give Gordon his private office number. "Call from the airport and I'll have somebody come and pick you up."

Gordon was enraged. Everywhere he turned it seemed there was someone out to get him. His disposition didn't improve when he walked into the war room and found only Ron Cochi there. Cochi, a bright but humorless young man too eager to make an impression, would ordinarily not have gotten on Gordon's nerves. But today he did. Today everybody did.

Cochi was sitting by the five phone lines, waiting for one of them to do something.

"I haven't heard from either Sullivan County Hospital or Ned Hollister yet," he said when he saw Gordon. "But there's an article you might be interested in about the cluster group here." He held up that morning's edition of the Sullivan County *Democrat*. "There's an interview with a couple of the kids' mothers."

"I'll take a look at it later. Do you know where Jessie went?"

"I think she and Larry were going down to Shoharie Creek, maybe see if they can figure out where that water's coming from. That fellow from the state health department, McKee, went with them."

"Would you do me a favor? Call around and find out if there are any flights for New York City leaving from Wurtsboro or Sullivan today?"

"You leaving us?" Cochi asked, beginning to leaf through the slender county phone book.

"That's right."

"How long?"

"Not long unless they clap me in jail for refusing to comply with their fucking subpoena."

Having not the slightest idea what he was referring to, Cochi frowned. "Excuse me, I didn't quite catch what you said."

"Nothing. Just make the call, will you, please?"

twenty-three

Riding in Bill McKee's car to Shoharie Creek, Jessie said hardly a word. Her two companions, sensing that there was a great deal of anger brewing in her, refrained from engaging her in conversation.

When they arrived at the creek, parking by the railroad tracks, they discovered that a small crowd had gathered. Evidently word had gotten around that the creek was considered to be contaminated. Even Mayor Eddie White, a gaunt, white-haired figure with a set of glowing crowns in his mouth, was putting in an appearance, pumping hands and greeting his constituents. Having only that morning banned all swimming in the creek, he wanted to make sure he received proper recognition for his act. The truth was that without Larry's urging, he might never have done anything about it at all.

But as soon as the three CDC investigators arrived, the crowd's attention focused on them. The implements they carried excited more interest than anything else: nets, white enamel pans, waterscopes, plant hooks, tubes, bottles and vials of a kind that suggested a very unusual fishing expedition. The wardrobe they sported was odder still: long pants and long sleeves, gloves and face masks.

They were after just about anything that moved in or over Shoharie Creek: flies, worms, mosquitoes, mites, beetles, snakes, and water bugs. They were hoping that one of these creatures might turn out to be the carrier of the disease. If they succeeded in pinpointing a carrier, they would be one step closer to determining how the disease originated.

According to specifications of the CDC's Center for Infectious Diseases, these specimens first had to be collected live, then killed by either freezing or exposure to ether. That done, they would be labeled, packaged, and sent to Atlanta for analysis in CDC laboratories.

The state health department officials also planned to test the water itself in the event that it might be the means by which the disease was transmitted. The investigators couldn't entirely discount the possibility that the microbes were airborne, contained in spores or droplets of water. Like any other form of detection work, epidemiology required considerable patience and a great deal of tedium.

The barrier that had been put up consisted of nothing more than a couple of strands of wire strung out for a distance of about thirty feet to which were attached handpainted signs reading:

WARNING
WATER HAZARDOUS
NO SWIMMING AT YOUR OWN RISK
(By order of Eddie White, Mayor)

The three investigators paused before one of these signs, trying to make out the precise meaning of the final injunction.

"What he means is 'swim at your own risk,' " McKee said, squinting as if by somehow readjusting his focus he might better comprehend the message.

"No, I think he means no swimming whatsoever," said Jessie.

Fallon didn't bother venturing an opinion, but instead slipped under the top wire, holding it up so that the others could follow.

A stony embankment sloped down to the creek. With last night's rain, the creek had become swollen.

Wearing knee-high boots, they waded out into the creek, each investigator finding his own section of it to do his scavenging.

After less than an hour of collecting and etherizing untold numbers of bugs, Jessie was exhausted. The heat, oppressive to begin with, was made worse by the mask and the protective garments they wore. When Jessie began she could only distinguish the sound of the mosquitoes among thousands of insects that called Shoharie Creek their home. But in time, her ears became more sensitized to the multiplicity of signals in the air: buzzing and droning and humming and weird little clicking noises. What an incredible racket!

Big, unidentifiable bugs, with gossamer-like wings and heads shaped like bullets, circled her head with seemingly malign intent. Magnified multifold, they could play a significant role in a drive-in horror movie. The mosquitoes, like a shrill Greek chorus commenting on the action, repeatedly dive-bombed her, and were repeatedly frustrated by the absence of flesh to sink whatever they had in place of teeth into. From time to time a hornet, perhaps disturbed in its lair among the surrounding bushes, would hover above her, evidently conducting a reconnaissance patrol. To her relief it did not make any effort to attack although its presence alone, scarcely six inches above her head, could hardly be considered reassuring.

Jessie kept getting wetter. Wet with creek water and with sweat oozing from every pore, she felt that she would soon shrivel up from dehydration.

The portion of the creek she'd staked out for herself formed something like a triangle drawn by a small child with a wobbly hand.

At its tip the creek appeared to reach a cul-de-sac. A wall of rock rose up from it, preventing further passage. But there was no question that the water was feeding in from somewhere, perhaps underneath the rock or through a fissure in it below the surface of the water. Peering through the waterscope, however, Jessie couldn't see an opening.

She decided to see whether there might be any trace of a stream, even if it lay underground, in the woods bordering this end of the creek. Jessie climbed up to the top of the rock and looked back to see Larry and Bill knee-deep in water, casting nets like maniacs, occasionally shouting imprecations at those insects too quick for them to snare. Both were so preoccupied by their work that they failed to notice her.

Black flies were thicker here than they were closer to the water. In spite of their incursions and the danger that they might be carrying the infection, Jessie pulled down her mask. She realized that she was obtaining temporary comfort at the risk of losing her mind—and her life—sometime in the future. Yet the risk was minimal; if the disease organism was present in an insect population like these black flies, it stood to reason that half the town of Brown Station would be infected, which was—up till now—not the case.

Stripping off her mask, Jessie also found hundreds of spiderwebs hanging from the low-lying branches of the trees in this part of the woods. Stretched so thin as to be nearly invisible, these webs caused her to stop every few feet and tear them apart. They felt like a soft downy fabric against the side of her face, but the sensation was far from pleasant. She kept clawing ahead of her, spitting out strands that had somehow become caught between her lips.

About to turn back, Jessie was arrested by the sound of a report, followed a moment later by a second. Birds Jessie hadn't known were anywhere nearby, fluttered into the air with screeches of protest.

Gunshots.

It wasn't hunting season, Jessie knew. It wasn't even close to the start of hunting season. She didn't make any movement apart from brushing the black flies from her face.

There was a disturbance in the bushes behind her. Wheeling about, she saw leaves and slender branches trembling as they responded to someone's approach. She caught a glimpse of him, in bits and pieces, through the latticework of vegetation. Black wide-brim hat first, then half a face, then the glinting barrel of his rifle resting over his shoulder. Another second, and he emerged entirely from the brush, revealing at the same time a wooden pole from which dangled four small animals: a raccoon, a chipmunk, and two beavers, blood dripping from one or two of them.

Right away, Jessie knew this was the man Gordon had told her about, the Indian.

If he was surprised to see her he failed to show it. His face, in the half-light of the woods, looked more Asiatic than American Indian; Tibetan, say, or Mongolian. His eyes fell on her, taking in her strange outfit drenched in sweat and creek water and spattered with mud. Which one of them presented the stranger sight was a question that Jessie would not have wished to know the answer to.

For several seconds the two of them stood motionless. Four squawking crows careened above them, no doubt still enraged by the sound of the Indian's gun going off.

Then the Indian began to advance toward her. She suppressed the urge to run, reassuring herself that this man meant no harm to her even though there was no disputing the unsettling impression he made with his gun and the dead animals bleeding into the mud.

When he was within half a foot of her he stopped and stared, unblinking. This seemed to be turning into some kind of a test. She stood her ground, returning his steadfast gaze as best she could.

"I am Joe Hunting Bear," he said slowly, as if it were a weighty thing to pronounce his name, and perhaps it was. Trying to introduce herself in turn, Jessie found that she had no voice. She nodded and remained mute.

Joe Hunting Bear put his gnarled hand out and touched her shirt, then lifted his hand to her mask. "Go away from here," he said. "If you stay here this is where you will die."

That said, he continued on past her, receding into the woods in the opposite direction from which he'd come. The last thing she saw was the face of one of the dead beavers, with its cold black eyes staring back at her.

twenty-four

Years ago, Hal Jarvis had worked for a private detective agency. The man who ran the agency was a crook, but this didn't become known until much later. The last Jarvis heard of him he was doing seven-to-ten in Soledad for embezzlement and concealing evidence of criminal activities from the police. At the time Jarvis was employed by this agency he'd been straight. Like a man who's found religion, he occasionally looked back on his honest years with a mixture of amazement and horror; even now he was aghast at the opportunities for illegal profit that he'd let slip by him.

Which was not to say that the time spent at this detective agency was wasted. The techniques he acquired for snooping, for hunting down people who would prefer to remain lost, and for not allowing a trail to become cold proved invaluable in his new line of work.

This was why he approached his latest assignment from the ever mysterious Mr. Wilder without being daunted by its inherent difficulty. New York was a large city, with thousands of nooks and crannies in which to hide, but when the quarry's condition was taken into account, the odds narrowed considerably.

A man in wretched shape, unable to take care of himself, probably still wearing a stolen security guard's uniform, presumably penniless, would have a limited number of options at his disposal. Being on the run from the law would reduce those options further; it made it unlikely that he would seek refuge in a men's shelter for fear that someone might see he was ill and notify the police.

To be sure Laramie hadn't already been picked up by the police, Jarvis paid a call on the station house close to the Rineman-Sachs Clinic. He showed the desk sergeant the photograph, claiming that Sean was a stepbrother with a history of mental disturbance. "He just walks off and forgets where he is," he told the officer, adding, "He has a thing for uniforms."

But no one matching Laramie's description had been seen by the police in the Twenty-Third Precinct or in any of the other station houses he called on.

Turning his attention to the city's three major transportation terminals, all of which tended to attract the homeless and mentally deranged, Jarvis buttonholed shopkeepers, vendors, the women who did the cleaning, security officers, cops, and indigents and bag ladies who slept on benches in the waiting rooms for lack of anywhere else to go. Having eliminated both Penn Station and the Port Authority Bus Terminal, he continued his search in Grand Central. Here his luck changed.

The proprietor of a quick-photo development store was sure he recognized Laramie from the picture Jarvis showed him. "He looked like he was growing a beard so I can't be absolutely certain," the man said, "but I know for a fact he was wearing some kind of uniform. I remember it because it had a bloodstain on it."

That sounded right to Jarvis. He asked the man where he might find Laramie should it turn out he was living in or around the terminal building.

"What you want to do, if you've got the stomach for it, is to go look underground—below the tracks. They've got all those heating pipes down there. I've read that that's how those people who live down there get their water—from leaking pipes. Me, I've never gone down there. Never want to, either."

He did consent to show Jarvis the stairway that, if followed far enough, would lead to the subterranean cavity. Jarvis thanked him for his trouble and gave him some cash to insure his silence.

It was rank and claustrophobic underground; the walls vibrated continuously with the sound of arriving and departing trains. Scalding water dripped from pipes extending along the ceiling. The lighting was lunar: stark and ghostly. At intervals, no lights were functioning at all, and Jarvis kept tripping over huddled figures asleep in the darkness.

After nearly an hour, even with the aid of a flashlight, Jarvis failed to locate anyone who resembled Sean Laramie in the least. He was on his way back up into the terminal, thinking that he would have to put many more hours, perhaps even days, into the search, when he spotted Laramie.

It was the tattered uniform that gave him away. He was walking with a shambling step, barely able to keep himself upright.

Jarvis set out to follow him. At first it appeared as if Laramie had no purpose, that he was on his way toward the Lexington Avenue exit simply because that direction was as good as any other. But then Jarvis noticed that he did have an objective; a redhead, wearing a pair of shorts and a T-shirt with holes for the arms cut so large that they exposed her breasts to anyone who cared to look, even to anyone who didn't care to look. Without seeing her face Jarvis couldn't tell if she was pretty or not, but the manner in which she walked, with bold, determined strides, and a hypnotic sway of her ass, was a compelling enough sight in itself. The rhythm of her step might have been dictated by the music that was coming out of her Walkman.

It was a wonder that Laramie could keep up with her, but somehow, in spite of his uncertain gait, in spite of the tide of commuters surging through the terminal, he never let her get very far ahead of him.

Maybe he's sick, Jarvis thought, *but if he can still muster the energy to pursue a redhead with an ass like that, he can't be that sick.*

Anytime Jarvis wished to, he could have grabbed hold of Laramie, hustled him to his car, and easily dispatched him. Grand Central, nearing rush hour, was perfectly suited for such a maneuver. With so many people, who would be the wiser?

But the truth was that Jarvis was curious to see what would happen when and if Laramie caught up with the girl. As long as he had him in sight he wasn't worried.

The pursuit went on longer than he'd imagined, however. The redhead continued downtown, maintaining the same hellbent pace as earlier. But it was not as if she were trying to run from Laramie; she wasn't even aware that he was following her. Jarvis felt sure that her concentration was devoted entirely to whatever was coming through her Walkman.

Occasionally Laramie stopped to get his breath. Jarvis figured he would collapse, maybe even save him the trouble of killing him. But each time, Laramie managed to recover and, with redoubled energy, continued the pursuit.

At the corner of Twenty-ninth Street and Lex the redhead turned. About halfway down the block, on the south side of the street, she reached her destination: an old brick building with barred windows on the ground floor and a sign on the door saying: NO VACANT APARTMENTS

She took a set of keys from her hip pocket and stepped up to the door. Jarvis was close enough to see that she was singing, snapping her fingers at the same time, truly oblivious to everything but the music.

Laramie was still half a block away and it didn't seem likely that he could catch her before she vanished inside.

He began shouting, but his voice, harsh and raw, couldn't reach the redhead with her headphones on. Laramie realized this, and all at once, he drew to a halt and freed his automatic from the holster.

Jarvis didn't do anything. This was like a movie. He wasn't expecting Laramie to actually fire, but this was exactly what happened.

The bullet struck the door, smashing its glass panel. Jagged fragments showered the girl, who screamed and toppled over; blood covered her. Before she could pick herself off the ground Laramie was on her.

Astonishingly, neither the shot nor the screams of the girl attracted much attention. Jarvis spotted an elderly couple at the Park Avenue end of the street, but as soon as Laramie had fired they quickly doubled back. A few faces appeared in the windows of the surrounding buildings, but no one was venturing out of doors. It was possible that the uniform Laramie was wearing, however frayed and soiled, discouraged people from interfering. One way or another, the crazed look in his eyes convinced Jarvis, standing in the shadow of an ailanthus tree across the street, that he wouldn't hesitate to shoot anyone who attempted to stop him.

The redhead probably had no idea what was happening. All at once she found herself hoisted to her feet. Her terror was so enormous, she fell instantly silent. A sliver of glass was protruding from her right shoulder, but she seemed not to be aware of it. Pressing the gun to her stomach, Laramie began to lead her back the way she'd come. Curiously, the headphones remained in place, but whether there was any music coming through them or not was anyone's guess.

Just before they reached the end of the block Laramie dragged his captive into a narrow alleyway that cut between two ugly tenement buildings. There followed a terrific clamor from trashcans being overturned. Then another scream, one that died abruptly. Jarvis could guess what was happening. Without exhibiting any urgency whatsoever, he proceeded to the head of the alley and stood there quietly so as not to disturb the show.

Laramie was struggling with her clothes, and struggling with his. Her blood was getting all over him; that much Jarvis could see. Otherwise, in the darkness, with the obstruction provided by the overturned ash cans, little else was in view. Jarvis went closer.

Laramie must have sensed his intrusion for all at once he looked behind him, at the same time keeping a restraining hand on the redhead. Jarvis could see now that she was in too much pain to put up any resistance. Her T-shirt had been hiked up to reveal a pair of splendid breasts, but these too had been lacerated by the flying glass.

But in spite of her injuries the girl still appeared in better shape than Laramie. Having not gotten as close to him as this before, Jarvis was appalled to see how ravaged he looked. The skin of his face seemed ready to fall off. He was already a dead man and in the desolation of his eyes Jarvis could tell that he knew it.

At the moment Laramie's eyes met his own, Jarvis blew him away. He pitched back, clutching his chest, released a groan and lay motionless. The redhead raised her eyes toward him, her half-naked body trembling with sobs.

"Thank God," she muttered, perceiving in Jarvis her savior. She plucked a sliver of glass from her stomach.

Kicking the corpse out of the way, Jarvis then set about to finish what Sean Laramie had started.

When Jarvis was satisfied that nothing had been left undone, he placed a call to Mr. Wilder, assuring him that he'd found and disposed of Laramie, depositing the body at the bottom of the East River, a customary graveyard for many who disappear suddenly. (He saw no reason to add that this was not the only body he'd gotten rid of, that being his own personal business.)

Satisfied, Wilder said, "What I'd like you to do now, Hal, is drive up to the Catskills. There's a small town called Brown Station. You can find it on any map."

"And what do I do when I get there?"

"There's a motel just out of town, off Route Seventeen, called the Sycamore Motor Court. Take a room there and wait for my instructions."

twenty-five

Jessie returned to the motel and went to her room. Finding neither Gordon nor a message from him, she proceeded to the war room. No phones were ringing. Ron Cochi sat at a table, listlessly reading a paperback with its front cover stripped off. Nothing for him to do: no war, maybe not even a skirmish.

"Ron?"

Hearing his name, he sprang out of his chair, perhaps thinking he would be reprimanded for indolence regardless of the fact that there was nothing for him to do.

"Haven't heard from the hospital, haven't heard from Hollister, haven't heard from anybody," he said, rattling off these non-events as if to preempt the expected upbraiding.

Jessie wasn't interested in any of this at that moment. "Have you seen Gordon today?"

"Earlier. He said to tell you he had to leave for Washington immediately. He wanted to say good-bye to you, but you were already gone with Larry and Bill McKee and there was only one plane out from Wurtsboro today for New York and he had to be on it. So that was why he didn't come down to Shoharie Creek to see you before he left."

By the time he'd finished he was out of breath.

"Washington? Why was he going to Washington?"

"I don't know, he didn't say. He sounded in a hurry though, so it must have been important."

"I don't understand."

Gordon often left for various corners of the world at a moment's notice, but his departures weren't usually this precipitous.

"He told me to tell you that he'll call you this evening and let you know what's going on."

"I see."

Ron seemed to have taken the coldness in her voice as a

reflection on him personally. "I'm sorry, that's all I can tell you."
"Thank you, Ron."
Jessie went back to her room. It was four in the afternoon and their work was finished for the day. All that remained to be done was to package the hundreds of specimens they'd collected and ship them off to Atlanta.
It seemed to her that a drink was in order. She took a tranquilizer first, however. She didn't often resort to them, but she could think of no more appropriate time than this to indulge herself. Gordon hated tranquilizers. When it came to taking any kind of drug, even aspirin, he held with the notion that since he didn't need it why should anyone else? Only impending surgery—some grave need like that—warranted their use. Fitful nerves, in his view, did not constitute a grave need.
Jessie knew better than to have a drink, too, but she didn't care. The more she thought about what had passed between Gordon and her that morning, the more incensed she became. In one way, she was relieved that he'd left; in another she was furious. He'd gotten away without giving her any opportunity for rebuttal.
The staff of the motel was so happy to have the extra business the CDC was providing that they offered to open up the outdoor lounge. All the Cinzano umbrellas were raised, the garden furniture cleaned and polished. A waiter, with the deferential manner of an old retainer, appeared as soon as Jessie sat down, with a plate of complimentary hors d'oeuvres.
"What have you got that is tall and frozen with a lot of fruit in it?"
"A summer drink, madam?"
"Exactly."
"Our bartender makes a wonderful drink he calls a Sycamore Surprise."
"That sounds just fine."
While waiting to be surprised—pleasantly, she hoped—she decided to go for a swim. It would be a refreshing change to immerse herself in water that wasn't suspected of harboring a lethal organism.
Larry Fallon was sitting at her table sampling her Syca-

more Surprise when she emerged from the pool. He frowned.

"What's wrong, don't you like it?"

"Tastes like a strawberry sundae. What the hell do they put in these things?"

She found it more to her liking. "I have no idea. You can't even taste the alcohol."

"That's a bad sign. You put down a couple of those and then you fall over."

As for him, he was content to drink something as pedestrian as a beer.

"Anybody hear from Hollister yet?" she asked.

Larry said no, not a word had been received from the state health department.

Jessie was acutely conscious of the way he was looking at her, his eyes traveling over her bare legs, still glistening with water. Having never seen her in a bathing suit before, he seemed to be giving her a careful appraisal. Or was it a reappraisal?

He was saying something to her about Ron Cochi, about the specimens they'd gathered that day from the creek, but she was having a hard time paying attention. Whether this was because the drink, together with the Valium, was beginning to take effect or because she was too sensitive to Larry's presence next to her, she couldn't be certain. Whatever the reason, she felt no need to say anything. It was soothing just to sit right where she was, soaking up the last real warmth of the sun, listening to the ebb and flow of words, the resonance of his voice.

Occasionally he would ask her a question and then she would have to shake herself from her reverie. "I'm sorry, what was that you asked me, Larry?"

"I said where did you get that suit? There should be a law against you wearing something like that."

She laughed a little uneasily. It was a one-piece suit, deep red and cut into a deeper V. "I bought it on a shopping trip to New York at Saks. Actually I don't know whether you could call it a shopping *trip*. It was more like a shopping *spree*. I think Gordon was a little scandalized when he saw me in this."

All the time she was saying this to Larry, she directed her

gaze away from him, toward the unoccupied pool. "It's a trick bathing suit—a Norma Kamali."

"A trick bathing suit?"

"See!" She reached for the zipper and slid it all the way down to where it ended at her navel, noting with ill-concealed pleasure the expression of momentary alarm that came over Larry's face.

The suit didn't come flying open, as he probably expected it would, but rather remained in place, held by a series of ties. Which was not to say that the view wasn't made a little more generous.

"That's the trick of it?" he said. "I see."

"I'm not sure I liked the suit, but I liked the trick." She rezippered it.

Something is getting away from me, she thought, but decided that it was all right. For now.

The waiter reappeared. 'Would madam like another?" he inquired.

It astonished her that there was nothing but melting ice and a strawberry left at the bottom of the glass. "Why, yes," she said. "I think I will."

To Larry she said, "I am going to pay for this."

"Put it on the tab." Then he realized what she was referring to. "Oh, I shouldn't worry too much about it."

"I'm not worried." And she wasn't.

What really surprised her about her second Sycamore Surprise was how it went about changing her mood. If the first had caused her to become unusually taciturn, the next one had the opposite effect. It was as though something had come undone in her brain, loosening a sudden barrage of words. Soon she was saying things she had no intention of saying. This wasn't like her at all.

It was the first time that she'd ever discussed Gordon with another man. When she thought about it for a moment, it was the first time that she'd ever discussed him with another person—period. It was not in her nature to talk about her private life. Even her close female friends would complain that she was too secretive. But what they called secretive she called discreet.

Even now she steered clear of anything that Larry, or anyone else for that matter, could regard as too personal to be aired in public. She tried to stick to the subject at hand, which was to say the investigation and her role in it. But as soon as she mentioned how Gordon was opposing her presence in Brown Station, there was no way to separate what was personal from what was not.

"I always think that I can handle it," she found herself saying. "I always think that I'm strong enough. Like what happened today, with that Indian. He tells me I'm going to die and my first reaction is: What is this shit? I'm going to listen to some crazy Indian who's never laid eyes on me in his life? That was how it was when Neville died."

"I can't believe that," Larry said.

"No, really. It wasn't that it didn't affect me. Sure, it affected me horribly. But I was able to keep a distance from it. Can you understand that?"

"Yes, I can."

She looked over at him; he was hanging on her words, she could see that. There was such an expression of intensity on his face that it seemed for a moment that perhaps he could share the pain she was feeling. How strange not to know that it was there all the while, waiting to spring.

"All the time what was on my mind was how to prove that he was killed. I was so preoccupied by that and now by this investigation that I never allowed myself to . . . well, to respond to it in any way." She paused; she didn't like the word *respond*. It wasn't right. "I don't know, maybe I've always blocked my feelings like that. I used to believe that that's what doctors did, that's what epidemiologists did—not let their feelings interfere with carrying out their job."

Again she looked over to Larry, waiting for what he would have to say, sure that he would have to say something. She needed him to say something, but all he did was ask her to go on.

She did.

"Sometimes I think that Gordon's living in another world; it's too rarefied, too something, I don't know, but I don't seem to belong in it."

"I'm certain that Gordon doesn't want you to feel that way."

"Of course he doesn't." Again she paused. "I shouldn't be telling you all this."

"It's all right, I'm not going to say anything, believe me."

She believed him. Suddenly there were tears in her eyes. This was ridiculous. God, she hated herself for acting like this. She turned her face away from him, hoping he hadn't seen the tears. Casually, she tried wiping them away.

"Are you okay?" He was leaning over, his hand extended as if he meant to take hold of hers, but he didn't. The hand hung in the air for a moment and was then withdrawn.

"Fine, really. I just had something in my eye."

She could have done better than that.

With absolutely inopportune time the waiter was back, soliciting them for another round.

"I'm finished, thanks," Jessie said, getting up from her chair.

As she scrawled her room number on the check Larry said, "What do you plan on doing for dinner?"

"I don't think I'm hungry."

"If you insist." The disappointment in his voice was palpable. It reflected itself, too, in his downcast expression. "I tell you what."

"What?"

"Later on, if you feel like getting out, Bill and I are going into town."

"You mean into Brown Station? What in God's name is in Brown Station to do after seven o'clock at night?"

"There's Kendrick's."

"That bar."

"It has its peculiar interest, believe me."

"I think I'll pass if you don't mind."

He wouldn't give up. "Tell you what. We'll be going in around nine. Before we do I'll come by your room. Maybe you'll feel differently then."

As soon as he'd said this it struck her that he wasn't just reacting to her out of sympathy, out of a desire to soothe her rattled nerves until her husband returned. All she had to do was to take one look at his eyes; there was a strange light in them whose meaning was unmistakable.

"Maybe," she said, but in such a soft voice that she wasn't sure he'd heard.

But he heard, he heard just fine.

* * *

Fallon was convinced that Jessie would decline to accompany him to Kendrick's that evening. It seemed to him that, by telling him as much as she had about her life, she'd crossed a previously inviolate border. In his experience, when that happened, one of two things occurred: either the woman kept going, advancing into an emotional terra incognita where all bets were off and everything was up for grabs, or else she realized how far off the beaten path she'd strayed and called retreat. He expected that henceforth, Jessie would prove more reserved with him, more guarded than before.

Yet he was flattered that she'd chosen him to open up to. Maybe it was just a matter of being in the right place at the right time. But he didn't think so. There was something—even in his own mind he was loath to apply the tired cliche *chemistry*—that had drawn them together. It was not uncommon for women to become attracted to Fallon; he'd come to accept it almost as his due, giving it no more thought than a multimillionaire would a profitable coup in a real estate transaction. To those who expressed envy at his knack for gaining the affections of women with such apparent ease he would say, "Yes, you're right, but once I get them I can't seem to keep them." What he didn't add, for it hardly reflected well on him, was that he wasn't sure he wanted to.

Larry tried to think through what he would do if Jessie surprised him and did not call retreat. Suppose she opened up to him further? Suppose another trick?

In some way, he hoped that she did become reserved with him, reverting to their previous relationship, one which was entirely professional in nature. Because if she didn't, if she did not decide to turn back across the border she'd crossed that afternoon, he didn't know what he would do.

When Larry went to call on Jessie a little past nine, he was taken completely by surprise as she opened the door and announced that she'd be ready in a minute.

Jessie had cheered up considerably since the afternoon. The sky-blue blouse she was wearing, knotted at her stomach, and the long yellow, rather filmy dress she had on, came as much of a revelation to him as her ingenious red bathing suit. Previously, all he'd seen her in were practical outfits apparently intended to divert attention from the lushness of her figure. The perfume she'd put on was like an intoxicant; he gathered it into his lungs with pleasure.

He thought to say that it was possible she'd gotten an erroneous impression of what Kendrick's was like. She was dressed to kill, at least to maim, and there was no question in his mind that she would not have looked out of place at "21" or Maxim's; but Kendrick's?

It occurred to him, after a moment's reflection, that she was dressed up because there was a need in her to dress up, to feel like a desirable woman again after trudging about all day long in the muck and suspect waters of Shoharie Creek. It also occurred to him that there was an even more compelling motive: she was dressing up to please him.

Shocked? Well, maybe he wasn't shocked exactly. These things had happened before, albeit not with the wife of a colleague. Worried? That wasn't the right word for it either. But scared? Yes, he thought, he was a little bit of that, although he was reluctant to admit as much even to himself.

Where do we go from here? he wondered. He wasn't just thinking of Kendrick's Tavern.

Bill McKee was there when they arrived; if he didn't look morose he looked the next thing to it. Even the sight of Jessie failed to buoy his spirits.

Because McKee generally conveyed a nonchalant air, his melancholy aspect was that much more noticeable.

He did not hesitate to tell them what was wrong. "I heard this afternoon that we're not going to be let into Shadow Pines," he said.

"Why the hell not?" After stressing the urgency of the situation last night on the phone to Hollister, Larry was sure that there would have been no problem.

"You have to understand. I didn't talk to Ned directly. It was his secretary I spoke to. She thinks Ned's a complete ass, by the way."

"An opinion with which you concur." Fallon didn't mean this as a question.

McKee raised his eyebrows but refused to respond.

"What she told me," he went on, "was that this morning, Ned was prepared to authorize an investigation on the grounds of the resort and by this afternoon he'd changed his mind."

"And she has no idea why?"

"Not exactly, but she says that at two-thirty Ned had an appointment with an attorney representing the resort, fellow by the name of Koppleman. It wasn't on her appointment calender which means that the meeting was set up on the spur of the moment. She says that Ned and this Koppleman character spent an hour together."

"I don't suppose she has a clue about what they said?"

"That would be too much to expect," McKee said.

"But we could draw an inference."

McKee looked from Fallon to Jessie and said, "You can draw any inference you'd like." A remote smile flickered on his lips. "But knowing Ned, I have a feeling that your inference and my own are probably pretty close." Directing his eyes toward the bar, he suddenly changed the subject. "Can I get anybody a beer?"

While Bill went to fetch the drinks Jessie turned to Larry, saying, "When I spoke to Gordon tonight he said something like this was probably going to happen."

"Something like what?"

"Like what Bill said. He's convinced that there's someone trying to sabotage the investigation. I think that Gordon could have come up here, poked around, and if nothing much materialized in a few days, he'd decide to cut out. He's always looking for where the action is. But as soon as he has a feeling that people are deliberately putting obstacles in his path, it pisses him off. Then he turns into a stubborn son of a bitch and stays put. You can pound him over the head with a sledgehammer, he still isn't about to move."

For all her misgivings about her husband, Larry noted, she still admired him. He had the feeling she was more subject to Gordon's influence than she realized. It struck him that he really didn't like Gordon. Until now he'd thought Gordon might have become a friend.

He asked Jessie what had caused Gordon to leave so suddenly for Washington.

"Some hearings he has to testify at—that was all he told me."

"What kind of hearings?"

"It has to do with the CDC's budget. He thinks it's a complete waste of time, but I guess he doesn't have much choice in the matter."

"Did he say when he was coming back?"

"The end of the week—maybe."

Three or four days wasn't a great deal of time, he thought.

Bill returned with three mugs. As soon as he did so he looked to the door. The others followed his gaze.

"My, my, what a surprise," Bill said.

Into the bar stepped Joe Hunting Bear. This time, though, he was carrying neither a gun nor the carcasses of animals he'd shot. Instead, he had a canvas bag, the kind that people use to carry gym shorts and sneakers.

The looks he drew from the other patrons made it clear that he wasn't especially welcome in Kendrick's. The bartender, a stout man with a bullet head and a perpetually splenetic expression, regarded him warily but made no move to run him off.

Though the Indian was doubtlessly aware of the ill-tempered nature of his reception, he showed no sign of it. His features were composed, not peaceful exactly, but untouched by any emotion.

Larry saw Jessie stiffen. Her hand found his under the table and squeezed it hard. The contact was all the more pleasurable for being unexpected.

After a few moments Joe Hunting Bear advanced farther into the bar.

"What do you think he's up to?" Larry asked.

McKee said he had no idea. "But whatever it is, I have a feeling it's going to involve us."

Sure enough, the first table Joe Hunting Bear approached was theirs. Larry observed that Jessie was having immense difficulty restraining herself. That incident at the creek shook her up far more than she let on.

Without saying a word he pulled a chair up to the table and lowered himself delicately into it. Then he unzippered his canvas bag, removing several articles, each of them hidden in pieces of wrapping paper.

There was no hint of recognition in his eyes; he gave Jessie the same indifferent look he did McKee and Fallon.

"For sale," he declared, unveiling the first article.

"We don't want any," Bill said. To Jessie and Fallon he added, "What he can't sell to the locals he's trying to palm off on us."

Although Jessie would certainly have been relieved to be rid of him, Larry was inclined to let the man show them his wares out of curiosity.

Larry leaned forward to better inspect a small figurine made of some sort of clay.

"An original Shoharie, no doubt," McKee said, doing nothing to disguise his skepticism.

It was a curious piece all right, with its heavy-lidded eyes and drooping mammaries and very prominent pubis. "Looks like a goddess, a votary object," he said.

"No Shoharie," asserted Joe Hunting Bear.

"I think he's right," Fallon said. "It doesn't look like anything that would come from around here. For that matter, it doesn't look like anything that you'd dig up on the North American continent."

With the Indian's permission he picked it up, holding it gingerly, afraid it might fall apart given the least bit of pressure.

Already Joe Hunting Bear was in the process of revealing yet another mysterious object, this one a pendant made of slightly tarnished gold and lapis lazuli. A third piece revealed itself as a headless torso, also of clay. Then came half a dozen necklaces, composed of brightly colored stones and small jewels that glimmered in the indifferent light of Kendrick's Tavern. None of these items, at least to Fallon's unschooled eye, looked as if they originated from anywhere nearby.

"Where did you get these things?" he asked.

"In the mountains," Joe Hunting Bear replied cryptically.

By now even Jessie, in spite of her reservations, was showing interest, paying particular attention to the necklaces.

"How much do you think these are worth, Larry?"

He didn't want to get into that question just yet. But he had a sense that they couldn't be worth a great deal. On the other hand, he didn't believe they were junk or imitations, either.

The next article they were offered was a necklace, but

unlike any Fallon had seen before. It was composed of shiny metal pieces cut into irregular shapes; what was most peculiar about it was the dial that hung from the necklace like a pendant. On closer inspection, Larry saw that it wasn't a dial, but a magnetic compass, although it was missing the needle that went with it.

With a stubby finger Joe Hunting Bear pointed to himself. "I make this. You like."

It was not a question. That they should admire his handiwork was something he evidently took for granted.

"And where did you get this?" Larry asked, knowing what the answer would be before he asked.

"In the mountains I find."

Joe Hunting Bear took hold of the necklace and draped it over Jessie's neck. For the first time since his arrival in the bar his cracked lips formed a smile.

Jessie looked bemused. The necklace gleamed silver against the blue of her blouse.

"You're bound to attract attention wearing that," McKee noted.

As Jessie went to take it off Joe Hunting Bear held out his hand. "It is yours," he said. "It is my present to you."

Was this the same person who'd warned her that she was risking death by remaining here? Fallon wondered.

Jessie didn't seem to know what to do. "Really, I can't."

But the smile was gone from the aged man's face and his expression had hardened. It was obvious that he would be insulted should his generosity be rebuffed.

"It is my present to you," he said again.

Jessie left it on.

One additional item was left. A watch. A Patek Phillipe perpetual calender watch to be exact. "Tick-tock," said Joe Hunting Bear.

But one thing that this watch didn't do, not any longer, was tick-tock. Something very vital among its interior workings was no longer functional.

It was one of those watches that told the time in four different zones and gave the date. The time, EDT, that it was frozen at was 11:21 P.M. The date: 5.18.85.

"Not much we can do with this," Fallon said. He was beginning to think that maybe Joe Hunting Bear had stolen this odd collection of loot from a camper. But what would a camper be doing with artifacts from some ancient culture? And how did the Indian acquire the compass that went into the making of his necklace—if indeed it was his to begin with?

"All these things, fifty dollars."

"Sorry," Fallon said, almost instinctively falling into the role of negotiator.

Since Joe Hunting Bear had made a gift of his necklace to Jessie, it seemed only polite to make a purchase, which was probably the Indian's intention from the start.

"How much for all these things?"

Fallon gathered up a couple of the necklaces. "I'll give you twenty," he said, believing that he was being more than fair.

"Thirty-five, all yours." Joe Hunting Bear swept his hands over the table to emphasize that he meant the sale as a package deal.

It was just as easy to settle for thirty-five than to go on haggling far into the night.

"But you can keep the watch, we haven't any use for it," he said when the money had changed hands.

Joe Hunting Bear, however, refused to accept it. "You buy, you keep," he said.

A grimace creased his features when he stood up from the table and he pressed a hand to his back. Muscles stiffening, bones becoming weaker, Fallon guessed.

After he'd departed, the three inspected their purchases in silence. It seemed that no one knew exactly what to say. It was as if the Indian's visit had been endowed with more significance that any of them could account for. The clay figurines, the ancient jewelry, the useless watch, and the necklace with a dial hanging on the end of it were totems of some kind of *memento mori*. Together they might have composed a message, but without the key. Fallon doubted that they would ever succeed in deciphering it.

"What are you going to do with all of this shit?" Bill asked, his irreverence all at once lifting the pall that Joe Hunting Bear's appearance had cast over them.

The question was addressed to Fallon who, after all, had sprung for the lot of it. "I'm giving it to Jessie."

"Well, it looks as if you're being showered with gifts tonight," Bill said.

"I appreciate it, Larry, but what am *I* going to do with it?"

Fallon told her that he was certain she would think of something. "Maybe you can even get somebody to fix the watch for you."

"It's probably one of those imitations," said Bill, taking it in hand to study it more scrupulously. Then he turned it over and noticed an inscription on the other side. "Maybe not. Maybe it is genuine at that," he said, "if somebody went to the trouble to engrave it."

"What does it say?" Larry asked.

Bill slid a pair of glasses from his front jacket pocket, then he read, " 'To my beloved Will. Love always, Ellen Leiter.' "

twenty-six

House of Representatives
Subcommittee on Community Health
Washington, D.C.

The Committee met at 2:15 P.M., in Room 2178, Rayburn House Office Building. Hon. Marshall Falk (co-chairman) presiding.

Chairman Falk: The Committee will come to order.

The Committee is holding its ninth day of hearings on appropriations of the Centers for Disease Control over the last five years with particular focus on appropriations overseas.

We have already heard from representatives of the Carter and Reagan administrations, including two former secretaries of the Department of Health and Human Services. We would now like to hear from representatives of the Centers for Disease Control today as well as a few people expert in the area of international health and epidemiology.

I regret the absence of my co-chairman, Mr. Bradstock, who has to be out of town today.

It was indicated that the Committee may have to consider going into executive session. We will have an open meeting, however, as long as questions do not require classified answers. If they do, we will then go into executive session.

We are pleased to have with us today Gordon Markoff, former director of the CDC and currently the deputy director of the CDC's International Health Program Office.

—Excerpt from Hearings Before
the Subcommittee on Community
Health: House of Representatives:
Ninety-ninth Congress. First
Session: August 11, 1985.

The glare of the lights on him caused Gordon to blink frantically before settling into his seat. Across from him were the subcommittee members, arrayed like inquisitioners, with grim expressions and eyeglasses glinting in the lights' reflection so that it was impossible to see their eyes.

Gordon regretted the absence of the one person he believed could help him. Trent Bradstock's departure for his home state of Utah had come as something of a surprise. Not until the previous evening had Bradstock troubled to mention that he was going to be away.

And so Gordon was on his own, left without any dependable ally.

Chairman Falk, pink-faced, imperious in manner, opened the proceedings.

"Mr. Markoff, would you tell this Committee about the link between the CDC and international health organizations?"

Succinctly as he could, Gordon replied that since bacteria and viruses and parasites showed no respect for frontiers, neither did the CDC. "We are involved pretty much on a day-to-day basis with organizations like WHO."

"That is the World Health Organization," Falk said for the record.

"Correct. There's a constant exchange of data between WHO and the CDC in Atlanta and the National Institutes of Health in Bethesda, Maryland."

"Could you tell this Committee about your own personal involvement in the CDC."

Gordon proceeded to sketch out his career for the benefit of the panel.

"Is it true, Mr. Markoff, that prior to becoming the

director of the CDC you were responsible for establishing a clinic in a town in El Salvador known as El Divisio?"

"That is true, Congressman."

"Thank you, Mr. Markoff." Falk now turned the questioning over to Congressman Gibbs from Pennsylvania.

"Mr. Markoff," Gibbs began, "when you arrived in El Salvador in 1979 what were the conditions there?"

"They were hardly tranquil, Congressman, if that's what you mean."

There was a burst of laughter from the people sitting in the rows behind him.

"But they got worse?" Gibbs went on.

"Yes, they got worse. Much worse."

"What about this town, El Divisio?"

Gordon had a feeling about what he was getting at, but gave no sign of it. "What about it?"

"Was it secure?"

"Secure meaning that it was firmly in government control?"

Gibbs acknowledged that this was what he meant.

"Not always."

"Sometimes it was in the hands of Communist guerrillas?"

Gordon looked straight at the congressman, but Gibbs's eyes were focused on the document he held in his hands, not on Gordon.

"It was in what you might call disputed territory. I'm told that it would fall under the control of the guerrillas, but government forces always succeeded in driving them out—at least until recently. Now I understand that the guerrillas have consolidated their control over the town, but that could change at any moment. The situation is, as they say, fluid. In any case . . ."

"In any case what, Mr. Markoff?"

"In any case, I would not want to characterize them as Communists."

It was remarkable to see the change that came over the faces of the Committee; they surely had no appreciation for his last remark.

"Are you trying to tell this Committee that the guerrillas are not, in fact, Communists?"

"I make no distinction about ideology, Congressman."

Gibbs nodded impatiently, scribbling some notes to himself at the same time. The interrogation was now assumed by Walt Spengler, representative of the state of Delaware.

In spite of Spengler's youthful appearance, Gordon expected that he'd be no friendlier than the previous two questioners. He was right.

"Mr. Markoff, this Committee has learned that, just prior to the fall of El Divisio, you were present at the clinic."

Gordon said that this was the case.

"Why were you in El Divisio earlier this month?"

Gordon explained that, since he'd founded the clinic, he tried to visit as often as he could, at least once a year, to see how it was doing.

"Were you aware that some of the personnel working at your clinic were leftist sympathizers?"

Gordon bristled. His heart pounded fiercely, and he tightened his hands until the knuckles were white. "I'm afraid, Congressman Spengler, I don't know what you are talking about."

Spengler pretended to look perplexed and glanced down at his notes.

"Mr. Markoff, are you acquainted with a man named Roberto Neblino?"

"Yes, he worked for me at the clinic—he was a paramedic. A very good one."

"Were you aware that Mr. Neblino was an active supporter of the guerrillas and a member of an outlawed Marxist party?"

Gordon's first impulse was to deny this allegation categorically, but then he reconsidered. It was possible that Spengler was in possession of information he was ignorant of. After all, what did he know about Roberto's political leanings?

"Congressman Spengler, I have no idea who told you that Mr. Neblino was affiliated with the Marxists. Whether he was or not has nothing to do with how he performed at the clinic. He treated every patient with the same care and so far as I know, he never asked about their loyalties."

Spengler apparently didn't think much of Gordon's answer. "I take it that you have no reason to believe that Mr. Neblino was not a Marxist."

"I have no idea what he was."

Spengler nodded gravely, and Gordon thought for an instant that the grilling might be over. But there was more to come. "Three weeks ago, on the night of July fourth, there was a battle for El Divisio. Are you aware, Mr. Markoff, that your clinic was used to treat guerrillas wounded while the battle raged?"

Gordon recalled furtive movements, strange sounds, all during that night, but if any of the injured were taken to the clinic, he knew nothing about it. What infuriated him, though, was the possibility that Roberto and the others at the clinic had deliberately kept him in the dark as to what was going on. Quite likely, they'd done this for his own good. But now he was paying for it. Either these congressmen believed that he was lying or that he was a complete fool.

Nonetheless, he decided that this time he would deny the accusation.

Spengler did not seem surprised. "Then I don't suppose that you know anything about the activities of Mr. Neblino and his comrades on that night and the nights preceding the fourth."

"What activities are you referring to, sir?"

"The activities I am referring to pertain to the use of the clinic's facilities for the purpose of aiding the guerrillas." Spengler, removing his glasses so that his eyes could fix themselves directly on Gordon, was moving in for the kill. "Your paramedics had a radio transmitter on the premises of the clinic. They were in hourly contact with the guerrillas, monitoring movements of government troops through the town."

Gordon hoped his face didn't reveal the shock—and anger—that he felt.

"I know nothing about any radio transmitter."

"Thank you, Mr. Markoff. Your testimony has been most interesting," Spengler said, restoring his glasses to his eyes.

"There is no question in my mind, Mr. Markoff, that you are a patriotic American," Chairman Falk said, reasserting his control over the questioning. "I am sure that if you had any idea that money appropriated by this Congress for the budget of the CDC was being used to subsidize Communist terrorists, you would have acted to stop it. Is that a fair assumption?"

"I suppose so, Mr. Chairman, but even if what you and other members of your Committee say can be corroborated, I don't think that U.S. taxpayer money was at any time used to subsidize Communist terrorists, as you put it."

"Oh no?" Falk affected to look confused. "The clinic in El Divisio was established with CDC funds?"

"That is true."

"The paramedics who were responsible for administering the clinic were paid out of a special budget for international health care?"

"They were volunteers. They were paid a small stipend for living expenses and given shelter and food."

"But those stipends, the money for food, did come from that fund?"

"To a degree. And there was some money from the government of El Salvador."

"Money which the United States provided as part of an economic assistance program," Falk said. "So in either instance it was money that came from this government."

No sense disputing that. "But may I remind you, Mr. Chairman, that most of that money, if not all of it, was used to treat peasants who, without that clinic, would not have had any medical care whatsoever."

"Including Communist guerrillas injured on the battlefield?"

"Yes, including Communist guerrillas. To the best of my knowledge, they are human beings too."

Falk excused him without further questioning, but he was made to understand that this was only a temporary reprieve. "We would like you to be here tomorrow morning, Mr. Markoff, to respond to some other questions regarding certain appropriations you authorized while serving as director of the CDC."

Markoff said nothing, but quickly escaped from the room, ignoring the glances thrown his way by the spectators sitting in the gallery.

From the Sam Rayburn Building Gordon went directly back to his room at the Mayflower Hotel. More than ever he was convinced that he was the victim of a vendetta. But which member of the subcommittee might be behind this campaign was as much a mystery to him as why the campaign would have been undertaken in the first place.

Nor was Bradstock of much help in this regard. Either he truly didn't have any idea or, for reasons of his own, chose not to voice his opinion to Gordon.

He did, however, provide Gordon with all the available data he had about the five members of the subcommittee and its general counsel. For two days Gordon had been poring over this documentation, the vast bulk of it a matter of public record.

After that morning's questioning the man who most interested Gordon was Walt Spengler. While it could not be said that anyone on the subcommittee—apart from the absent Trent Bradstock—was sympathetic toward him, Spengler had proven himself especially hostile.

Thus it came as something of a shock to discover that, far from being a rabid right-wing fanatic, Walt Spengler was actually a moderate Republican. In spite of the impression he'd given that morning, the picture that emerged from the literature depicted him as anything but a hawk. The most surprising piece of information was that he'd twice voted against military aid to American-backed rebels in Nicaragua while at the same time going on record warning of the danger of sending U.S. forces into El Salvador.

Hours went by as Gordon studied Spengler's speeches, his campaign literature, newspaper clippings, letters to his constituents, a photograph of him and his wife posed in front of their Wilmington home from *Town & Country* magazine. But nothing he found told him what the congressman might have had against him until he came upon a photo that ran in the Wilmington *Times-Journal*.

The photo showed Congressman Spengler on a golf course, about to take a swing in front of a group of spectators. "Fore!" read the caption. "Rep. Walt Spengler about to execute a magnificent thirty-five-foot sand wedge shot into the cup at No. 9 yesterday at the Northeast Classic. The congressman finished at three-over-par 72 in the annual event held at the Shadow Pines resort, New York." The picture had been taken a year ago.

Gordon now had no doubt why he'd been summoned to Washington with such little notice. It was obviously an attempt to thwart the CDC's investigation in the Catskills.

Spengler must be doing a favor for the management of Shadow Pines, either that or paying back a debt. By keeping Gordon pinned down in Washington, he was accomplishing two objectives at once: putting Gordon temporarily out of action and undermining his credibility. Who, after all, could trust a dupe of the Communists?

He wasted no time in getting on the phone to Bradstock. The congressman didn't sound surprised to hear from him; on the other hand, he didn't sound particularly pleased either.

"So you think it's Spengler who's behind this?" he said when Gordon had finished.

"Absolutely. Of all the subcommittee's members, he's the one who makes the most sense."

"Damn, and I always liked Walt," Bradstock said. "Still, I'm not sure how much you've got to go on. A picture taken at some golf game doesn't seem like a great deal of evidence to me."

"Maybe not, but it's enough evidence as far as I'm concerned."

"What do you propose to do now, Gordon?"

"Leave."

There was a rather long silence on the other end. "Leave? You mean leave Washington?"

"That's right."

"Didn't you say they wanted you to come back tomorrow and testify?"

"I won't be there. I'll be goddamned if I'm going to participate in this charade."

"They'll subpoena you. I'll try to stop them, but I doubt that they're going to listen to what I have to say. It won't do you any good to be in contempt, Gordon. Do yourself a favor and be there tomorrow. Then it'll be over with and you can forget that the whole thing ever happened."

"It won't end there. Next they'll demand all sorts of confidential records. When I refuse to hand them over they'll subpoena me anyhow. So what the hell is the difference?"

"Gordon, I have no indication that anything like that will happen."

Gordon didn't know whether to believe him or not. But in any event he'd made up his mind.

"Listen, Gordon, if you're going to take off like this at least let me know where you'll be."

"I'd tell you, Trent, but I don't know myself. But I'll be in touch." With that he hung up, uninterested to see if Bradstock had any further words of advice for him.

When the phone rang an instant later Gordon was tempted not to answer it, certain that it must be Bradstock calling back. But it was not. It was Lou Valdespino phoning from Atlanta.

"We just received a report here about a new cluster of cases of that suspected virus," Valdespino began, skipping over the formalities.

"Where?"

"New York City. But the oddest thing about the report is that it didn't come from a physician. It came from the chief medical examiner's office. Guy named Bob Zaborowski. He sounded very secretive over the phone, said that he'd be in trouble if someone found out he was making the report. I figured you'd be the best person to talk to him." He then supplied Gordon with Zaborowski's phone number.

"He say how many cases were in this cluster?"

"Five. All of them from the same source."

"And what was that?"

"One of those exclusive Manhattan institutions catering to VIPs. Maybe you've heard of it? It's called the Rineman-Sachs Clinic."

Gordon had, vaguely. Upon concluding the conversation, he tried to get in touch with Zaborowski. There was no answer. Gordon decided to take the Eastern shuttle to New York and call him as soon as he got in.

Gordon then phoned Brown Station. Reaching the war room at the Sycamore Motor Court, he got hold of Ron Cochi. He asked to speak to his wife.

"She's not here."

"Is she in her room?"

"No." There was a certain edginess to his voice that Gordon didn't like. "I'll have her give you a ring when she gets back."

"Can you tell me when that might be?"

After a few moments of hesitancy, Cochi admitted that he could not.

"Do you have any idea where she is?"

"No," Cochi said, "I don't. No one tells me anything around here."

twenty-seven

If it weren't for Larry, Jessie would never have gone back to Boston. Certainly she wouldn't have done so without letting Gordon know. But of course, Gordon would be adamantly opposed to the idea, and since it was just for the day there was no reason for him to find out about it.

Yet, were the choice hers alone, she would have stayed in Brown Station, waiting for Ned Hollister to change his mind about allowing the investigators into Shadow Pines.

But when Larry was made aware of the connection between the mysterious Will Ziegler, mentioned in Neville's notes, and Ellen Leiter, he'd insisted on a visit to Boston. He said that he had a friend at Boston University, a professor of genetics, who surely could help in tracking down Ziegler. Neville's notation that Ziegler was in turn linked to B.U. had proved to be right on the mark. He'd been a professor of anthropology there.

It was Larry, too, who suggested that they pay a call on the Leiter family. From all accounts that Jessie had seen in the papers, Ellen Leiter was of middle-class background. How then did it come about that she could afford to make a gift of a Patek Phillipe perpetual calender watch Larry guessed was worth close to eighteen thousand dollars? How, for that matter, did she come to know Will Ziegler so well that she would want to give him anything at all?

And the most puzzling question: How did Ziegler's watch end up in the possession of an aged Indian who made his living poaching in the Catskills?

It was Larry's conviction that if they could learn more about Ziegler, then there was an outside chance that they could determine the source of the disease.

Jessie had a feeling that maybe this was something better left to the Boston police. But Larry pointed out that the only crime they might be currently investigating was the theft of Ellen Leiter's body. "What do they care who Will Ziegler is—or was?"

But it was not because of Will Ziegler or the memory of Neville Green that she'd agreed to go to Boston; it was because of Larry.

She knew she shouldn't be feeling like this. She could not make sense of her emotions; one minute she was composed, the next she was brushing tears from her eyes, surprised, even aghast, that she'd been crying. She hadn't slept much for the last three nights and what sleep she'd managed was insufficient, restless, clouded with agitating dreams. At the same time she was conscious of a heightened sensitivity—that and a state of giddiness that used to overcome her every time her brother persuaded her to go on one of those amusement park rides, a weird mixture of terror and pleasurable anticipation. Up, and down, and over, and through, and hope that eventually your heart stops beating quite so fast and your stomach succeeds in catching up with you.

It wasn't like this with Gordon. *I am in another realm of experience,* she thought. *This should have come sooner, years ago.* Now she had a job to perform, a marriage to maintain with a man she loved even if it was a man she could seldom understand.

Although Larry phoned ahead to set up an appointment with his friend, the genetics professor, it was impossible for him to meet them. But aware of Larry's interest in Will Ziegler, he'd left a message for them that he'd arranged for them to see someone in the anthropology department who might be able to shed some light on the man.

The person they were to meet, Professor James Nieberg, was a bewhiskered man in his fifties whose somewhat disheveled appearance seemed entirely appropriate to the disorganized state of his office. On a warped shelf, above his head, were enough heavy tomes to kill him if they ever came tumbling down.

"Will Ziegler, Will Ziegler," Nieberg muttered. "What a strange bird he was."

The use of the past tense did not escape either of his visitors.

"He was in this department?" Larry asked.

"In a manner of speaking. He never got tenure. Too unorthodox for this university, you see." He paused, then added, "Actually, he was a little too unorthodox for just about any university you can think of."

"Unorthodox how?" asked Jessie.

"Come with me. I'll be more than happy to show you."

Nieberg led them out into a luridly lit corridor. They proceeded to an elevator which they rode up to the fifth floor. The only other people they saw were a few disconsolate students who looked as if they'd rather have been at the beach.

"This is, or should I say used to be, Will's office. Nobody's gotten around to emptying it out yet."

The door was unlocked.

Will Ziegler's office, in contrast to Nieberg's, was meticulously organized even though it was far more crowded with books and objets d'art than the space was intended for.

Nieberg settled into the swivel chair behind the desk as if he, and not the absent Ziegler, belonged there. Masks, gaudily painted and carved into a bewildering variety of expressions, gazed down at them from the walls. A spear that might have been from Africa or the South Seas dangled from a hook in the far corner. A pair of hideous-looking dolls, made of clay and straw, with glinting ruby-colored stones meant to be eyes, decorated the desk. On the blotter rested a small green bottle with some kind of powder inside; a dry black substance served as its cork; from it protruded a chicken feather.

Most of the books were inside a cabinet with glass doors. Books about witchcraft, shamanism, magical hair, animalism, snake cults, and obeah. Some sounded typically anthropological in their obscurity: *Ritual and Symbolism Among the Gahuku-Gama* and *The Nyakyusa Concept of Religion in Its Relation to Social Order.*

Nieberg seemed amused by their reactions. "It looks more like a museum than an untenured professor's office, doesn't it?" He reached forward to take hold of a heavy plastic cube into which photographs had been sealed on four of its faces. "This is him," Nieberg said, handing the cube to Jessie.

Will Ziegler looked like a man absolutely enamored of

himself; he was what a romance writer might have called ruggedly handsome, sandy-haired, with electric-blue eyes, his features set off by a cocoa tan; a wide-brim green desert hat shadowed his brow and in the gray thatch of chest hair, revealed by the open neck of his safari jacket, a small gold amulet of some kind could be seen.

"He looks like somebody's idea of an updated Lawrence of Arabia," Jessie noted.

"You must understand that Will was quite a character. He was always running off somewhere, to one part of the world or the other, and bringing back some of the souvenirs you see here. I was once over to his house on Beacon Hill. You wouldn't believe the kind of artifacts he had there. That really was a museum. I have no idea what happened to the collection but I have a feeling it's gone the way of its owner—vanished into thin air." A melancholy expression came over his face. "Too bad he had to leave the way he did. To tell you the truth, he added a lot of life to this department. We could've done with more of him."

While he spoke Jessie studied the cube, examining the other three photographs. One was of an Oriental woman. Pretty, with exquisite features. This could be Lucy Chong, she thought. A radiantly healthy Lucy Chong, not the deranged, ravaged woman she recalled seeing. There was a second photo that could have been Ellen Leiter although Jessie didn't have the newspaper photo with her to make any comparison. Who the third woman was, the brunette with doe eyes and a weird smile, there was no way for her to know. But Jessie didn't doubt that she'd played a role in Ziegler's life similar to the others.

Catching Jessie's eye, Nieberg said, "Oh yes, he did have a way with the women. He was quite the Casanova."

"Are you familiar with any of the women here?" Jessie lifted up the cube so that he could better inspect it.

"Have no idea. It was a waste of time trying to find out. They changed from month to month anyway. One of the reasons people liked to attend the faculty parties we give periodically was to see which girl he'd show up with. Otherwise they make for rather dreary affairs."

"Did you ever hear of somebody named Perry Atwater?" Jessie asked.

Nieberg frowned. "Perry Atwater . . . that sounds familiar. You know, if I'm not mistaken, he was that sullen lad who used to hang around this department. One of those overage sixties types who burned his mind out long ago. Always looking for a guru, somebody to believe in. Timothy Leary, Baba Ram Dass, Carlos Castaneda . . ."

"Will Ziegler?" Jessie put in.

"Yes, I suspect that he regarded Will as a kind of guru. Will never thought much of him, but he was useful as a gofer. People around here used to call him Ziegler's nigger."

From out of his briefcase Larry pulled the figurines and necklaces they'd purchased the night before from Joe Hunting Bear. "Professor, I was wondering if you could identify these objects for us, give us some idea where they might have come from."

Nieberg studied the goddess with particular interest. "I couldn't say for certain," he said after a minute or so, "because my field is Asian studies, but these appear to be South American. Pre-Inca. Nazca maybe, or Chanapata."

"They're from Peru then?"

"Peru? Or Bolivia or Ecuador, anywhere the Incas extended their rule." He stared at the goddess as if he expected her to disclose her origins. "Where the hell did you get hold of this thing?"

"It's a long story." A story Larry wasn't interested in relating. "Tell me, Professor, did Will ever visit the Catskills?"

"The Catskills?" This must have sounded very funny to Nieberg because he broke into laughter. "I suppose it's possible."

"May I ask what you find so amusing, Professor?"

"Nothing really, I'm sorry. It's just that I'm so accustomed to hearing that Will is off in some remote corner of the globe, Malawi or Lake Baikal or God knows where, that somehow I find the notion of Will in the Catskills just . . . well . . . incongruous. But you're talking to the wrong person. He left here, and for all I know, perhaps Boston, sometime last February. I spotted him walking around Newberry Street once or twice, but then he just dropped out of sight."

"Could you tell us who might have an idea of his whereabouts since this winter?" Jessie asked.

"I don't think so. Maybe Van would know. Van Haddleston, he's the chairman of the department. But he's off on vacation in Greece, so you'd have to wait a bit to talk to him."

Thanking him for his trouble, they rose to leave, but then Nieberg stopped them. "Oh, there is one more thing I should tell you about Will."

"And what's that?" Larry asked.

"He was partial to experimenting with drugs."

"What kind of drugs?" Jessie had the feeling that this might turn out to be a key piece in the puzzle.

"Any kind really. Legal, illegal, and drugs hardly anyone knows about yet so that they haven't been classified one way or the other."

They sat back down.

"That wouldn't have been such a grave offense," Nieberg went on, "if he'd been discreet about it. But he would open his house to students and start serving them drugs too. He soon gathered what you might call a cult following. Needless to say, it didn't take too long before word got around campus as to what he was up to. From that point on his days at the university were numbered."

"You said that some of these drugs he experimented with aren't classified." Larry, Jessie saw, had turned on a miniature cassette recorder cupped in his hand. Nieberg didn't appear to notice.

"I wouldn't know anything about them, but I suspect they were drugs derived from mushrooms and exotic plants and such. I remember Will citing a statistic that the CIA had some twenty-six thousand drugs they hadn't even gotten around to screening. That was back in the early seventies. Whether that remains true to this day I wouldn't have the slightest."

"Professor, do you think it's possible that Will might have been smuggling in drugs, not just for personal use, but for profit?"

This notion seemed to puzzle Nieberg. "I really hadn't thought of that. Will, a drug smuggler? True, he had a pilot's license and owned one of those small planes."

"Cessnas?"

"Yes, I think that was it, a Cessna. And I keep seeing these reports about drug smugglers flying in from God knows where, but I never associated such goings-on with Will Ziegler. I mean Will was crazy, no question about it, but I didn't think that he was *that* crazy."

"Yet you could see him getting involved in something like that, drug running?" Jessie pressed.

Nieberg considered this for a moment, then slowly nodded. "Yes, I could see him getting involved in something like that. But not so much for profit."

"What then?" asked Larry.

"For the hell of it. Just like everything else he did."

A boy, eleven or twelve years old, came to the door when Larry rang. He regarded Larry and Jessie without much interest, maybe because he was accustomed to people he didn't know coming around and pestering him.

They introduced themselves. But Jessie could tell that the CDC meant nothing to him. The FBI maybe, but not the CDC.

"What's your name?" Jessie asked him.

"Paul."

"Is there anyone else home we can speak to?" Larry asked.

The boy shook his head. "My aunt's out running errands and Uncle Sy isn't home from work yet."

"Then could we ask you a few questions?" Jessie said, sensing that if the boy was going to talk to anybody it would be her rather than Larry.

He hesitated, shifted his weight from one foot to the other. "Maybe," he said.

"It won't take long, but it's very important."

He was pale, with big eyes which were fixed on Jessie with unsettling intensity.

"It's about your mother," Jessie said.

Larry's right hand disappeared into the coat pocket where the recorder was lodged.

"Mom's dead," the boy said without a trace of emotion in his voice.

"I know she's dead and I'm very sorry."

"She hit me. Before they sent her to the hospital she hit me."

The flatness in his voice was even more noticeable now. So many people—police, psychiatrists, relatives—had been questioning him that his responses had become automatic, lines from a script; at the same time the pain—visible in his eyes—was forced deep below the surface.

"I know that, Paul." She waited for another moment to see whether he had anything to add, but he didn't. "Did you ever hear of a man named Will Ziegler? He was a professor at Boston University."

Jessie could see immediately that the name was unfamiliar to him.

Larry, too impatient to let Jessie assume all of the questioning, asked Paul if his mother had ever worked at B.U.

Again the answer was no. "My mom worked as an executive secretary at an insurance company in the John Hancock Building. The windows were always falling off."

"The what?" Larry asked. "What about the windows?"

But Jessie knew what he was referring to. "They used to have problems with the building all the time. No matter what the architects and contractors did, the windows on the upper floors came loose every time there were high winds."

Paul seemed to warm to the subject. "Mom got an office so that she wouldn't have to be close to the windows. She hated the sound they made when they broke."

"Paul, did your mother ever go on any long trips? To South America possibly?" Larry asked.

"Mom never left the country except once to Canada. She took me and Annie, my sister, when I was nine. We went to Niagara Falls and Toronto. Jeffrey, my younger brother, wasn't born yet so he didn't go."

At that moment a gangly woman, with a birdlike face and straight hair down to her shoulders, came into view, walking briskly in their direction.

"That's my aunt," said Paul.

Seeing Larry and Jessie, the woman quickened her step even more.

"Who are you?" she demanded. "The boy's gone through enough." To her nephew she said, "Paul, go inside now."

The woman had no interest in learning their identity or

their purpose once she'd discovered they weren't from the police.

"I'd thank you to get off my property," she said.

Larry refused to let himself be cowed. "One question, Mrs.—"

"Strohmeyer, Betty Strohmeyer."

"Did your sister—"

"I told you I have nothing to say to you."

". . . sister, Ellen Leiter, know a man named Will Ziegler?"

His words arrested Betty Strohmeyer in midmotion. Her face darkened, her body tensed. "That son of a bitch," she hissed.

She knew him all right.

twenty-eight

"A goddamned conniving bloodsucking bastard," Mrs. Strohmeyer called him. "If it wasn't for him my sister would still be alive today. May she rest in peace, though the good Lord only knows where she is."

Her cheeks reddened with the fire in her veins. Her voice rose to such a shrill level that Jessie wouldn't have been surprised to see the window behind her shatter and fall to the ground just like the ones in the John Hancock Building.

"If you find that son of a bitch you can tell him that I haven't forgotten him. He'll never know a moment's peace so long as I'm alive. And I'll tell you one thing, I am going to live a good many years yet. My mother, may she rest in peace, lived to be ninety-seven and my father would have lived that long, too, if he hadn't drunk himself to an early grave."

It was all that Larry could do to get a word in now that this woman had gotten started. "How did your sister know Ziegler?" he kept asking until at last he elicited a reply.

"She went to that night school course he gave," said Betty Strohmeyer, almost as if she took it for granted that they should have already known.

"A course in anthropology?" Jessie asked.

"She never finished school, Ellen, never graduated. Always felt like she was missing something. Look what happens! She falls for this Svengali and the next thing you know she's staying out all night, ignoring her children. I could hardly get her to talk to me over the phone."

"Was Ellen taking any drugs that you know of?"

"Taking them!" Her laughter was mirthless. "If that's all it was! She was peddling them for that man." Suddenly her voice fell. "Just before she took ill she was planning to go with him to the Caribbean, some island, and I know for a fact that she had close to one hundred thousand dollars with her. In cash! Lord only knows what became of it. We could do with a bit of that money, do something useful with her ill-gotten gains."

Now Jessie understood how Ellen could afford to buy a Patek Phillipe watch worth a small fortune.

"Do you know what kind of drugs she was using?" Larry asked.

It was possible that the drugs Ziegler had in all likelihood smuggled back to the United States might be a source of the virus. It was not necessarily the case that the drug itself caused the disease, but it might have been contaminated and in that way become a vehicle for transmitting the disease.

But Betty could only conjecture what drugs—or dope—her sister had been indulging in. "Whatever I found in the medicine cabinet I burned," she said. "I don't care whether it said aspirin on the label—there was no telling what might have been inside."

In her messianic zeal to purge out all the evil influence left behind by her sister, she'd probably destroyed the most important evidence they could have laid their hands on.

"Do you happen to know someone named Lucy Chong?" Jessie asked.

"The Chink woman?" Betty was not one to disguise her prejudices. "I met her once with my sister. A tramp!" She nearly spat the word out. "You should have seen the dress she was wearing; it left hardly anything to the imagination. She was one of Ziegler's paramours I'd wager."

"Does the name Perry Atwater sound familiar to you?"

"Never heard of him."

Although Betty Strohmeyer was prepared to rant on, and indeed did for several more minutes, they realized that she'd provided them with about as much information as they could hope for. For someone who'd made it clear at the outset that she had no intention of talking to them, she proved almost impossible to break off.

"You tell that murdering son of a bitch Ziegler that I'm not going to let him forget what he did to my sister!" she screamed after them.

Turning to acknowledge her words, Larry said, "You can be sure we'll let him know, Mrs. Strohmeyer."

On the Eastern shuttle back to New York they entertained themselves with Betty Strohmeyer's recorded voice; even at a low volume it raised the hair on the back of their heads and caused a few astonished looks from the passengers in nearby seats.

But it was not for amusement's sake alone that Larry was playing back the conversation; rather it was for the purpose of seeing whether they might have missed something.

"You know what I think," Larry said. "I think that Betty was jealous of her sister. I wouldn't be surprised, from the way she referred to Ziegler, whether she wasn't smitten with him too."

What Larry said made sense to Jessie. Loveless and embittered, Betty Strohmeyer might well have harbored a resentment toward her sister so deep that not even Ellen's death could do much to diminish it. Only by luring Will Ziegler into her bed would she ever achieve the triumph over Ellen that she'd been seeking all of her life. And Jessie doubted that that would ever be.

It was close to midnight when they returned to the Sycamore Motor Court. The lobby was empty, as was the war room. The Hewlett-Packard computer, which was hooked directly into the central computer back in Atlanta, showed only a dead screen. But hanging out of the Juki printer was a message from Lou Valdespino's office:

Confirmed dead of suspected viral syndrome: six.

Perry Atwater, Boston
Ellen Leiter, Boston
Lucy Chong, Boston
Mardi Lloyd, Los Angeles
Johnny Grimes, Sullivan County, N.Y.
Debby Kramer, Sullivan County, N.Y.

Unconfirmed dead of suspected viral syndrome: five.

Cluster group unidentified, New York City

There was a second part to the message as well:

> Tests prove positive for virus in three specimens from Shoharie Creek. Specimens are pupae of the mosquito A. Aegyptus. These pupae, also known as tumblers, are aquatic, active, and can maneuver by employing leaflike tail appendages. It is possible that the infected specimens were hatched at another site and then moved through the water system to the creek.

The question that could not be answered by any laboratory was where the mosquitoes' progenitors were hiding out. Nor was it certain that the mosquitoes were the source of the virus; they might well be picking it up from an infected animal. But Jessie did note one particular comment that came at the very end of the CDC's communication:

> It is presumed that the infectious mosquitoes are female rather than male. Only females are bloodsuckers and therefore are more likely to be vectors of the disease. Many females must have dinner first before they can lay their eggs.

Jessie wasn't at all sure she appreciated Valdespino's sense of humor. "Dinner first," she scoffed, tearing the transmission from the printer.

She tried calling Gordon and was startled to discover that he was no longer registered at the Mayflower and that he hadn't left any message for her. She phoned the desk, but no one there picked up. It was possible that Gordon had gotten hold of Ron Cochi and let him know where he was, but Ron was asleep and she was not about to disturb him.

"Sometimes I have this feeling that Gordon will just vanish like those people you read about in the papers who go out for a pack of cigarettes and never come back," she told Larry.

"You know what happens to those people?" said Larry. "Ten years later they turn up, married to another woman, with three kids, holding down a job completely different from the one they used to."

All this talk about bigamy was making Jessie a bit uneasy. Come to think of it, almost everything was making her a bit uneasy. Worse, she couldn't put her finger on what was bothering her the most.

Larry's room was located four doors from hers. The silence that fell between them was like a coded message. Jessie had all sorts of notions as to how to go about interpreting it.

"You're welcome to come in for a nightcap if you like," Larry said, but in a casual, offhand tone that suggested he might not be entirely serious.

"You're not tired?"

Stupid question.

"Not really."

"Well then, just for one."

There were small refrigerators in each room. Larry had seen to it that his was fully stocked with a supply of mixers and a bottle of Absolut vodka.

He poured her a dangerous amount. She sat on the bed. His suitcase was open on the only available chair.

They toasted to the success of the investigation. "We're homing in on the source of this," Larry said. "It's got to be in those mountains somewhere." He raised the blinds enough to permit a view of the Catskills.

From his room it was possible to see the southern slope of Mount Sycamore.

"That's funny."

"What is?" Jessie joined him at the window.

"Do you see any lights up there?"

"Lights?" She followed his gaze.

"About halfway up to the top."

Now she saw what he was talking about. "It looks like the lights of a small city."

"It does, doesn't it? Only trouble is, there is no city there."

"You know, I think that's what Gordon was referring to. He was saying something about lights on Mount Sycamore, but at the time I didn't really pay close attention to him."

"It's probably some phenomenon that's produced by atmospheric conditions. Keep staring at those mountains—

and sky—long enough, you're bound to see all sorts of things that aren't there."

"UFOs?"

"I wouldn't be surprised."

She was acutely aware of how close he was to her; while she continued to stare at Mount Sycamore he watched her out of the corner of his eye.

Her drink was gone.

"Another?"

"I don't know," she said, but then sat back down on the bed and allowed him to replenish her glass. "Are you trying to get me drunk?"

It occurred to her that she *was* drunk.

"Yes," he answered.

"At least you're forthright about it."

He sat down next to her. His shirt was rumpled and damp. Cleaners benefited more from airplane rides than anybody else, she thought.

Her clothes were a mess too. She was trying to fill up her head with as many different things as she could—what she would wear the next day, when Gordon would call, whether she would put off taking a shower until the morning—all in an effort, altogether futile, not to have to think about what was happening at that moment.

His touch, the sudden but gentle press of his hand against the back of her neck, was expected, was welcomed, but even so she stiffened in response.

"You're too tense," he said.

He was certainly right about that. Her neck was in knots and an extraordinarily mobile pain radiated through her back.

Closing her eyes, she leaned back, luxuriating in the slow kneading movement of his fingers. His hand moved down. He was claiming more territory for himself. But that was just fine with her.

"Do you think you could crack my back? It helps sometimes if it's cracked."

He said that he'd be willing to try.

She lay down on the floor. Straddling her, he maneuvered his hands underneath her blouse, then planted them firmly, one on each shoulder. Bore down. With the crack came a loosening of muscles, a release of warmth.

"What did you say?"

She hadn't said anything, she'd only murmured in pleasure, that was all. No words.

Lower down he repeated the action. The crack was louder, more decisive this time.

It was strange, how when things began to seem inevitable, they assumed their own logic, their own rules. It was like entering another dimension, and though this was not exactly the way she would've expected to enter this dimension—the result was still the same.

What was worse was that she felt no guilt, no anguish, and if she held anything against herself at this moment it was anger for failing to feel neither guilt nor anguish. There was too much desire for this man to allow for any conflicting emotion—not now.

When his hands traveled far enough, she cried out. Half turning her head, she tried looking into his face, into his eyes, but the angle wasn't quite right and she could barely make out his features. He continued to work her back; a soothing warmth coursed up and down her spine. His hands alit on her buttocks and followed their sloping contours to her legs. Grasping hold of his right hand, she brought it between her legs.

She turned over and raised her hips, making it easy for him to undo the buckle of her belt. Her skirt slid off with practically no effort of her own. It might have been designed for coming off more than being worn.

For a moment he paused, appearing to study what he'd just revealed of her, eyes full of admiration.

She reached up to embrace him, to pull him down. She was greedy for his lips; she wanted to lose herself wholly in sensation.

He was rocking her in a motion that, had she her wish, would have gone on forever. As if from very far away the sound of the air-conditioning unit, its unceasing thrum, reached her. But the sound of her own body giving way was louder. *I am gone,* she thought, *gone far away.*

* * *

The scene formed gradually; his eyes had to sort out the tangle of limbs, the blur of flesh, accustom themselves to the way the crosshatched pattern on the screen distorted what he was seeing. At any moment he was ready for one of them to look up and catch sight of his face. But they were getting so lost that Hal Jarvis was running little danger of that happening.

They moved to the bed; what clothes they had on were sloughed off quickly. The woman had fine breasts. Her head was thrown back, her eyes were open.

Jarvis watched her eyes as he lifted the Canon automatic camera and shot his first picture.

twenty-nine

"You know what's been happening at the medical examiner's office," Bob Zaborowski was saying. His manner was that of someone who, were it not for the influence of gravity, would fly apart at any moment. He was smoking with fiendish enthusiasm. Pared down to maybe a hundred and twenty pounds, he looked like he was starving himself to death. All he needed was a good cause to sacrifice himself for.

"I have an idea," Markoff said.

"Once that *Times* piece came out, the only question was how deep's the shit?"

"The *Times* piece?"

"You remember the one? How Haverkos was fudging records, turning death by strangulation into death by coronary occlusion. That was because it was the cops who did the strangling."

"Now I remember." Haverkos, the chief medical examiner, had denied all the allegations. "But what does this have to do with the cluster group you called Atlanta about?"

"I'm getting to that," said Zaborowski.

The way he was glancing about the bar—a dark, downtown joint not far from where he lived called Formerly Joe's—you might have thought of one of Haverkos's spies was sitting nearby, recording their conversation.

"Sorry, I didn't mean to rush you." Markoff was being polite. After forty minutes in Bob Zaborowski's company he was in a hurry to be off.

"Listen, what I'm trying to tell you is that right now, given the *Times* article and shit, we have what you might call a very confused situation in the medical examiner's office."

"Confused?"

"That's right. It was only by chance that I discovered that

five stiffs had come in with the same pathology. I was assigned to assist Haverkos with an autopsy on a twenty-one-year-old-male. Wasted away. Real bad shape. But it wasn't until we got to the brain that it became clear why he'd gone out. Damn if nearly half of his brain wasn't already rotted away. Haverkos said something under his breath like 'another one,' and I asked him what he meant by that, and he said nothing."

"What did he put down in the autopsy report?"

"He put down AIDS."

AIDS, in addition to causing cancer and a variety of bizarre infections, also destroyed brain tissue.

"But you're saying it wasn't AIDS?"

"The pathology didn't match up. I wanted to get a look at the stiff's record. Haverkos said it wasn't available. But I made some inquiries on my own. That's how I found out there were four others who'd all come into our office with their brains rotted out. More or less like the stiff I'd seen. All within the last couple of weeks, and all from the same place."

"The Rineman-Sachs Clinic?"

"That's right. I heard that's where the Shah stayed when he was here in the States. Even Castro was in there for a problem he had with his eyes during the opening of the General Assembly one year. People, rich fuckers, say they have a mental breakdown, or say one of their kids is hooked on smack, that's where they send them."

"And all their deaths were ascribed to AIDS?"

"No, that's the funny thing. One was supposed to be meningo-encephalitis due to naeglaria."

Naeglaria was a parasite found in certain bodies of water in the United States—mostly in the South—that could invade the brain, infiltrating through the nostrils, ultimately causing death.

"How old was the victim?"

"Twenty-four. Another male—a black. It makes no sense. The vast majority of naeglaria victims are young, preadolescents. But still it's possible. But then we received two victims with tick-borne rickettsioses. Both victims apparently did exhibit the signs of rickets—the rashes, the hemorrhaging, the petechiae. But I'm told when their brains were examined a substantial portion of them was rotted away. And that isn't something rickets will do."

"Were either of these cases ever reported to the CDC?"

"Not so far as I know, but it's possible."

"What about the fifth case?"

"I wasn't able to find out much about it. But again the victim was missing part of his brain. When I say this, I mean that the brains weren't exactly shot through with holes, but they'd turned to mush, full of lesions."

"I understand. Bob, why did you conclude that these five cases might be related to the cases in Brown Station?"

"Well, it seemed to me that the stiff I'd looked at bore all the signs of the viral syndrome you'd described about the kids who lived up there."

Doubtless, Zaborowski had read about the ailing children in the Morbidity and Mortality Weekly Report—the MMWR, as it was more familiarly known—published each Monday by the CDC. The news bulletin charted epidemics and mortality statistics, broken down by region and state. In addition, it carried articles about events of interest to the medical community, and often the public at large, calling attention to environmental health hazards, outbreaks of hitherto unknown illnesses, and running updates or afflictions of particularly topical interest like AIDS and toxic shock syndrome.

To corroborate his story Zaborowski produced, in a manila envelope, a copy of the official autopsy report together with his original notes. "You can see how Haverkos altered the facts," he said.

After Gordon had perused the two documents he asked Zaborowski if he could get hold of the autopsy reports and notes pertaining to the other four.

"I wouldn't even try," Zaborowski said. "It would be my ass. I'm taking enough of a risk as it is."

"But you say that all the cadavers came from the same place?"

"That's right. All from the Rineman-Sachs Clinic."

"What was the disposition of the bodies once they were released from the medical examiner's office?"

"I wouldn't know that." He implied that he had no intention of trying to find out, either.

"Have you any idea where they came from before they were taken to the clinic?"

"None whatsoever."

Zaborowski was becoming more agitated. Too distracted to meet Gordon's eyes, he concentrated his gaze on the door, stiffening whenever someone new walked in and looking quickly away.

"Listen, I've told you all I know. I should get going."

"Bob, I'd like to get into the clinic."

Zaborowski was dubious. "They've got pretty top-notch security there."

"Is there a way in?"

"You mean if you're not rich and famous?" He considered the problem. "Maybe."

Maybe, Gordon figured, meant yes.

"Do you think you could help me?"

Stubbing out his eighth Vantage filter of the evening, he said, "It depends."

"On what?"

He turned to face Gordon. "It seems that I got a problem. Now I know what's going to happen to Haverkos, you can't kid me. They'll nail his ass to the wall. Then you know what's going to happen?"

"Then they're going to come looking for the people under him?"

"You're not as out of it as I thought. When they take a look at this shit"—he gestured to the falsified autopsy report in Gordon's lap—"they'll want to know who was in on it with Haverkos. And you watch! That fucker will get a slap on the wrist and in three, four years maybe, he'll wind up as medical examiner of Tulsa, someplace like that. Me, I'm small-fry. You know what they do to small-fry? Ten years in the slammer with time off for good behavior."

"You want me to testify on your behalf if it comes to that?"

Zaborowski nodded, taking a long drag on his latest cigarette.

"Maybe that won't be necessary. Maybe only an affidavit, I don't know. But your word would count for something, I know that, a former head of the CDC."

Gordon had no reason to tell him that in spite of his

previous status he might not make the best character witness in the world, not while he was under the cloud of a congressional subpoena himself.

When he didn't immediately answer, Zaborowski frowned. "Is that a problem? If that's a problem tell me now."

"It's no problem. I'll be happy to put in a word on your behalf. If you want, I'll put it in writing."

"That sounds like a good deal. Don't elaborate any, just say that you're satisfied that I'm on the up and up, that if there was any malfeasance committed as far as you know I had nothing to do with it, I was just an unwitting victim of circumstances."

An unwitting victim of circumstances, Gordon thought; *so are we all.*

When Gordon had written out his statement attesting to Bob Zaborowski's good character, the pathologist asked him if he had a car.

"No, I was planning on taking a cab."

"Then we'll go in mine," Zaborowski said.

At a quarter to eleven they were parked four blocks away from the Rineman-Sachs Clinic. This was not because Zaborowski could not find a closer parking spot; he didn't even search for one closer. Gordon reasoned that his paranoia had something to do with his choice.

It was another one of those sweltering Manhattan summer nights when every step seemed to require more of an expenditure of energy than it could possibly be worth.

The clinic was located on a block that was quiet in the way only very wealthy neighborhoods can be quiet. There was hardly any sound aside from the chorus of air conditioners up and down the street.

An imposing edifice of six floors, with its gray cement and steel cylindrical walls and wraparound windows, the clinic looked less like a medical facility than the headquarters of some obscure but extraordinarily well-endowed philanthropic foundation. A foundation that went in big for horticulture by the evidence of the towering palms, hibiscus, jasmine, and bougainvillea visible through the window that began on the ground floor and rose three stories. Although it was impossible, from where they were standing, to identify the paintings hanging on the walls of the lobby, Gordon didn't doubt for an instant that they would do a museum proud.

As Gordon started toward the canopied entrance Zaborowski grabbed hold of his arm.

"No, not that way," he said. "We go around."

"Around?"

"In back. It'll be easier for us to get in that way."

"How do you know about the clinic?" asked Gordon as they started to walk back the way they'd come.

"I've been here with Haverkos a few times. And I have a friend who did some work in the pathology department. He used to tell me these stories about the place like you wouldn't believe."

Zaborowski was walking quickly now, stabbing at the air with his cigarette as he explained how the clinic worked. "It may look like something from the front, but it's all for show. No one—no one of importance anyway—enters that way. Most of the patients they treat aren't exactly angling for publicity. The last thing they want is some paparazzo leaping out of the bushes, snapping their picture for the tabloids."

They turned the corner as Zaborowski continued, "The real entrance is around here. Also the real exit. The living and the dead both want their departure to be as discreet as their arrival."

The Seventy-sixth Street side was even quieter than the Seventy-fifth, which the clinic fronted. Halfway down the block a gray limousine was idling with its lights killed.

As they continued walking, a driveway, half-hidden by high, carefully trimmed bushes and a gnarled old oak tree, came into view. The driveway followed a sharp gradient into what appeared to be a garage. There was a sign posted at the entrance to the driveway reading: NO PARKING/NO STANDING ANYTIME. VIOLATORS WILL BE TOWED.

Zaborowski directed Gordon's attention to a narrow windowless door to the right of the garage entrance. A moment later he produced his identification showing that he worked for the medical examiner's office.

"I shouldn't be doing this," he said. "They'll probably have my ass if they ever find out what I've done."

"I'll never tell."

"Oh, I know you won't, but they have other ways."

"You mean Haverkos?"

"I mean Haverkos and friends. Follow me. And if anybody asks, just say that you're with the medical examiner's office."

As they stepped to within half a dozen feet of the door, it slid open. A security guard, who bore a remarkable resemblance to a popular black movie actor whose name slipped Gordon's mind, greeted Zaborowski.

"Hey, my man, how are you doin'?"

Zaborowski said that he was doing okay. He called the guard Leo. It seemed as if they were old friends.

"Man, you sure are one busy mother. Seems like every time I look around there you are."

Gordon noted that there was no one else around. He suspected that Leo wouldn't have been conversing so familiarly with his visitor had he had any company.

"What's the matter with your friend?" Leo asked, fixing his eyes now on Gordon.

"He's new, just started working for us. His name's Gordon."

"Say, Gord, my man, aren't you a little old to be starting work like this?"

"He came from the medical examiner's office in Detroit."

Leo let out a burst of laughter. "Lot of bodies in Detroit, they tell me." Then his expression changed, becoming darker. All business now, he asked why they were coming at this late night hour. "I haven't heard that anyone went out tonight."

"We got a call down at the office, saying that another kid from unit five struck out."

"If that happened, I'm sure I would've heard about it. But I just got on duty so maybe somebody just forgot to tell me."

As he was about to pick up the house phone, Zaborowski asked if he minded whether they just went up to unit five and checked for themselves.

Leo went ahead and dialed anyway, ignoring the request.

"Yeah," he said when he'd established contact, "this is Leo down at the gate. We have a couple of people from the medical examiner's office here. They say that they got a call from you about a death tonight on your unit."

A frown formed on his lips as he listened to the reply. Zaborowski avoided acknowledging the glance that Gordon threw at him.

When Leo replaced the receiver he said, "Nobody seems to know a thing about it, Bob."

"The call came in less than an hour ago. Maybe whoever you talked to isn't aware of it."

For someone as nervous and distracted as Zaborowski, he wasn't doing a half-bad job at this. Gordon thought he sounded rather convincing.

"I don't know," Leo said.

"Look, I only have so much time, Leo. You know what's going to happen. I'll get home, sit down to dinner, and then they'll call me again, telling me to get my ass on back here. All I want to do is run up to unit five, take a look around, and make sure no one struck out. It'll take ten minutes, no more."

Leo silently deliberated for a few moments before relenting. "Well, I don't suppose it could hurt to check it out. Make sure you sign in though."

Gordon used a false last name which Leo saw no reason to corroborate. He was then handed a visitor's pass with an adhesive backing and instructed to wear it at all times while he was in the building.

Once inside, they proceeded along a subterranean corridor that took them past three supply rooms and a pharmacy closed down for the night. Close-circuit video cameras followed their progress until they reached a bank of elevators.

Here Zaborowski said in a low voice, "This is as far as I go."

"You're not coming with me?"

"Not on your life. I'm splitting. I figure I've put my ass on the line as much as I care to for one night."

"And what do I do?"

"You take the elevator to the third floor. When you get off, what you don't want to do is follow the signs to unit five. You want to go in the opposite direction. There's a small holding room—you can't miss it. That's where they store any stiffs they've got waiting until we arrive to take them away. Go straight through the holding room to the exit. That exit will lead you into unit five itself. From then on you're on your own."

In spite of the prominent NO SMOKING sign on the wall just behind him, Zaborowski was lighting up another Vantage. His hands were trembling.

"I'll tell Leo that I had to run and that you can handle the situation yourself. When you come down just sign out and say good night. I know him, he won't ask any questions."

They shook hands. Zaborowski's hand was like syrup floating through Gordon's grip. Then he was gone, walking briskly back the way they'd come.

The elevator was slow to arrive. When it did, it proved to be the size of a large bathroom and opened on both sides.

The visitor's pass affixed to his chest was all that he needed, he found, for no one gave him the slightest notice as he stepped off the elevator.

Just as Zaborowski had said, the holding room was unguarded. Empty beds were deployed on either side. There was a smell that reminded Gordon of either incense or a tolerable woman's perfume. He guessed that it was what they used here to purge the lingering odor of the deceased. He continued on.

A spectral light, like a desert haze, was visible through the small oval window of the door ahead of him.

He opened the door and saw, way at the end of another corridor, a nurses' station. The brunette nurse sitting there did not immediately notice him, although he had to assume that, somewhere, his course was being monitored by close-circuit TV.

Off both sides of the corridor were rooms, each shielded by an opaque plastic curtain.

He drew open the curtain of the first room he came to and stepped in.

A woman, bone-thin, with eyes set deep in the hollowed-out skull that her face had become, sat upright, blinking furiously. She could have been no more than twenty years old Gordon judged, but her deterioration was such that she resembled a frail woman decades older. A saline solution seeped through a tube into her arm; another tube was inserted into her right nostril and held there with a small bandage.

She said something that Gordon couldn't hear. He approached the bed.

"I've already had my shot," he heard now.

She was freezing, holding herself, rocking back and forth as if in hope that this motion might warm her. Yet it was not cold.

Gordon looked for the chart that was usually located at the end of the bed, but it wasn't there or anywhere else that he could see.

Closer to the woman he began to notice rashes on the underside of her face.

"What's your name?" he asked.

"Elsie Simmons."

He told her that his name was Gordon, nothing more. It seemed to make no difference to her.

"Do I know you?"

No, he said, she didn't know him. So many doctors had probably come by to examine her since her confinement that she could no longer distinguish between one and the other.

He took hold of her hands, turning them over so that he could inspect her palms. Just as he suspected, they were covered with rashes. When he looked at the soles of her feet, he saw that the rash had spread to them as well. Something else struck him. Her big left toe was turned upward—extensor plantar reflex. The same symptom that characterized the children stricken in Brown Station. But none of them had rashes like this woman's.

"How long have you had these?" It was difficult for him to stare into her wasted eyes. There was a great deal in them that he did not wish to see.

She stared at him so blankly that for a moment he thought she hadn't heard him. But then she said, "The rashes you mean? I got them after I came here. Whatever they give me, that's what causes them. They all say no, they say what they give me is to help me, but I know different."

He asked her if she was sure of this.

She repeated her words.

"Elsie, why were you sent here?"

"I don't know." Her lips pursed, she lowered herself farther under the covers.

"You don't know? Come on, Elsie, you must have some idea."

"I'm cold," she said. "I'm freezing."

His eyes scanned the room for another blanket, but there was none that he could see.

He decided to take another tack. "Elsie, did you work at a resort called Shadow Pines?"

Nothing.

"Elsie!"

Footsteps sounded down the corridor, coming closer.

"It wasn't so bad for a while," she said.

"What wasn't?"

"Until I got sick."

"Shadow Pines, you mean?"

"Their pay was shit. Oooh, God, I'm so cold." Her head wobbled, her jaw fell; spittle was thick on her lower lip.

The footsteps grew louder. The curtain was swept open. The brunette nurse, her face contorted first in irritation, then in bewilderment when her eyes fell on Gordon. "What—?" was about all that she managed to get out.

"Sorry for the intrusion," said Gordon, stepping around her.

The apology, as he'd anticipated, failed to mollify her. But it was the security people that concerned him, not her. Returning his attention to Elsie, he said good-bye, knowing that this good-bye would be a permanent one.

But the girl was no longer interested. Her body was shaking, not just from the coldness but from spasms that carried the force of electricity. It was as though she was being hit from one side, then from the other, her whole body out of control.

"Wait just a minute," the nurse was calling after him, but he wasn't waiting, he was too occupied in trying to make a hasty exit.

No question, she would alert security. Back in the holding room he quickened his pace.

He decided on the stairway.

Racing down several sets of stairs, conscious of the rasp

of his breath, thinking that he ought to get more exercise if he was to continue doing things like this, he finally reached the door on the lowest level, but when he opened it he discovered that he was not in the underground corridor he'd entered. He was in the principal lobby area—the museum.

Although there were five security men circulating through the lobby area, not one of them appeared to take any interest in him. Maintaining a studied pace toward the revolving door, he began to think that he would not be stopped.

But then he was arrested by the sound of his name being called. He turned in the direction of the voice, and saw, approaching him, a man in a burgundy-colored three-piece suit that looked as if it had been pressed directly on his body: not a wrinkle anywhere. His expression suggested that they were well-acquainted although Gordon had not the slightest recollection of him.

"Mr. Markoff, I don't believe I've had the pleasure," the man said, belying the familiarity of his manner. He held out his hand for Gordon to accept. "Let me introduce myself. My name is Stanley Koppleman."

thirty

On summer nights in Brown Station there was nothing to do, no way to blow off steam. Most of the people in town stayed put, contenting themselves with sedate supper parties and barbecues supplemented by watermelon, gossip, and corn on the cob, or they played card games on the porch under mosquito-repellent lights.

For three teenagers like Hugh Craven, Scott Trowbridge, and Gary Kramer, life in Brown Station was sheer torture, an ordeal of waiting until they could get it together to find a job in Albany or Rochester, even New York—somewhere, anyhow, where there was a little action. They were too young to drink at Kendrick's, so when they needed beer or cheap wine or half-decent gin they'd drive out in Scott's Rabbit to Mike's, a package store where they could buy whatever poison they wanted.

Mostly, the three youths amused themselves by repairing to the woods of Mount Sycamore where they would proceed to get loaded. Someone always had some weed, and if the occasional Quaalude or gram of cocaine found its way into their possession, well, so much the better.

From time to time they would steal down to Shoharie Creek and spy on the lovers who came from neighboring towns to fumble and screw and make a mess of the upholstery in their fathers' cars.

On this particular night, decorated by a lemon sliver of a moon, the three decided to do something different to pass the time.

"Know what I heard?" Gary said. "I heard that old Jim Dyal keeps a shitload of cash in his house; never trusted those fucking banks."

Gary was a strapping kid, with two front teeth missing, both lost in a bitterly contested fight some time back. He was always aggressive, but more so lately, a change everyone in town attributed to the death of his younger sister. Gary never talked about it, though, and even his best friends were wise enough not to say anything that touched on the subject.

"So he's got a shitload of cash, so what?" Scott said.

Scott was a dark-complected kid, five-five, and embarrassed about his height. He wasn't sure he'd be accepted by the others if it weren't for the fact that he was the only one who owned a car.

"So maybe we could go pay old Jim a visit," Gary said. "What does fucking Jim Dyal need with all that money? He's got, I bet, ten, twelve thousand stashed away. We split it even, we still got enough to go to New York, set ourselves up so no one will find us."

Taking another swig of the Colt .45 he held in his hand, Scott shook his head, saying, "Yeah, so what are we going to do, walk in and go, 'Hey, Mr. Dyal, you don't mind, we'd like to have a look at your stash, maybe help ourselves to a few bills'? Come off it, you guys."

"Shit, man, I got a plan," Gary said, standing up so that he was now silhouetted against the darkness of sky and pinewood. "You think I'm that dumb? Look what I got here!"

He reached into his jacket pocket and produced a gun—a .22 automatic, nothing fancy, certainly nothing that was going to stop a man at fifty feet.

"Aw shit," Scott muttered, "where the fuck did you get hold of that?"

"It was my father's."

"Is it loaded?" Hugh wanted to know.

In answer Gary cocked the weapon and fired it into the air. The report sounded like a mortar shell going off in the silence of the woods.

"Jesus Christ! Would you put that thing away!" Scott reached out as if to grab it, then stopped himself.

A broad grin formed on Gary's lips. This was the kind of power that he enjoyed. "We just threaten the old man, we don't hurt him."

At first it was only a game they were playing, figuring out how they would go about relieving Jim Dyal of his fortune, but then as the night wore on, and the level of their intoxication grew, the three began to take the notion more seriously—even Scott. Scott, however, remained skeptical that they could pull it off.

"Oh, fuck it, man, you don't want to come, you don't have to," Hugh said. "That'll mean we just have to split the cash two ways instead of three."

Scott seemed not to have thought of this. "Suppose I drive you by his house and wait outside in the car?"

"The getaway car?" Gary laughed. "You've seen too many fucking movies." But you could tell the idea appealed to him.

It was nearly midnight by the time they headed off the mountain, nearly one o'clock by the time they were sitting in the Rabbit in front of Jim Dyal's two-story house, one of the more imposing in all of Brown Station.

"Are we going to actually fucking do this, man?" Scott asked.

"What's your beef?" Gary demanded to know. "All you've got to do is sit here in this junkheap of yours until we come out."

Scott nodded dubiously.

Gary showed no hesitation in getting out and marching straight up the stairs to the front porch. Hugh was a little slow to follow.

"He knows me, don't worry, man, we've gone fishing together a thousand times," Gary said by way of assurance.

Five minutes had to elapse, during which Gary could have raised the dead with all the racket he was making pounding on the door and ringing the bell, before Jim Dyal came to answer.

He appeared in the doorway in a ridiculous silk robe, a diminutive, stooped figure with a crinkled face. Groggily he peered out through the screen door, relying on the porch light he'd just switched on to see who his late-night callers were.

"What can I do for you boys?" Jim Dyal asked. "Something the matter with your car?"

Waiting for a reply, he studied their faces. And because his gaze was so fixed he failed to notice the .22 that Gary held in his hand.

"You got some bread for us?" Gary said, advancing a couple of paces forward. His motion frightened Dyal, who stepped back even though the screen door still formed a barrier between them.

"What are you talking about?"

"Money, man, you have money for us." There was in Gary's eyes a menacing gleam, a radiance of pure insanity. Even Hugh, standing next to him, was becoming scared.

"Money? Money?" Dyal had yet to remark upon the gun. Or else, because of the shadows, he hadn't realized what it was.

The screen door wasn't latched. Gary opened it and walked in. Hugh was right in back of him.

"Hugh? Is that you, Hugh?" Dyal asked, as if he were appealing for an explanation from him.

"It's me, Jim," Hugh answered as deferentially as he would had they met by chance on the street.

Dyal's eyes registered the gun. "What the hell is this, boys? Just what do you think you're up to here?" He kept his eyes on Hugh. "What would your dad think of this if he knew what you were doing?"

Hugh said nothing, averting his gaze.

"Fuck you, old man," Gary said. "Give us your money."

At that instant, Jim's common-law wife Mary came to the head of the stairs and called out to Dyal, "Honey, what's going on?"

The sound of her high-pitched voice set something off in Gary. He leaped back as if he'd been hit, raising his eyes to identify the source of the voice.

"Goddamn bitch!" he yelled, training the .22 on her. He fired twice.

The old woman released a howl like the sound of a cat in heat, and tumbled down the stairs to the landing, thrashing there in pain.

Jim Dyal's momentary paralysis gave way to a frantic need to take action. With his arthritic hands he tried to wrest the gun from Gary's grip.

"What are you doing?" Hugh shouted uselessly.

Easily breaking free of the old man's hold, Gary brought the butt of the .22 down on his head. His shiny bald scalp turned immediately red with blood. But he refused to fall down. Instead he staggered away, into an adjoining room. A barely audible groan escaped from his caked lips.

"What the fuck are you doing, man, hurting an old guy like that?" demanded Hugh, attempting to restrain Gary.

Gary brushed him aside. "You get in my way, man, I'll waste you like that bitch."

The bitch he was referring to, Mary Lawe, was not yet wasted; the two bullets in her chest were not fatal.

A moment later Jim Dyal returned, his face soaked with perspiration, a trail of blood running through his hair and into his right eye. He was brandishing a kitchen knife in his hand.

The sight of it caused Gary to laugh. When he fired this time it was at such close range that the bullet hardly had any distance to travel at all. A part of Jim Dyal's face fell away. Blood bubbled from the wound in his temple.

With dreadful slowness he collapsed, sinking first to his knees, then allowing his head to tilt toward the floor until his brow was just touching it. He was still alive. The knife slipped from his grasp.

"What's he going to do, take all fucking night to die?"

Hugh wasn't talking. His mouth was open as if he intended to say something, but he simply could not get a sound out.

Gary looked at him with obvious irritation. "Asshole, why don't you see if you can find the goddamn money instead of standing here with your tongue hanging out?"

Hugh seemed as incapable of movement as he was of speech.

"Hey, what's the matter with you? Go look in the bedroom upstairs."

To get to the bedroom meant that he would have to step around Mary Lawe, who hadn't moved from the landing since she'd been shot.

As Hugh tried to vault over her, she reached out and took hold of his pants leg. "Please, please," was all she said.

At which point Hugh drove his foot down on her face, then into it. It yielded as easily as plaster. Then he gazed down at her with an expression of great perplexity as if he couldn't quite understand what he'd just done.

"Come on, asshole, you want to see if you can find that money?"

Gary's words put Hugh in motion again, but when he got to the head of the stairs he couldn't help looking back down at the body of Mary Lawe; he seemed to be expecting her to show some sign of life, but this was patently not going to happen.

Jim Dyal, meanwhile, was still in the process of dying. But he didn't appear to know how to go about it. His breathing was labored; he sounded like a marathon runner who knew he had no chance of making the finish. His prayerful posture remained fixed. The blood flowing out of him was dripping all over the pinewood floor, seeping into the cracks.

Gary was mesmerized by the sight of him in his death throes, curious to see how long it would take him to die. But he was running out of patience.

"You old fuckers think that everybody's got all the time in the world," he muttered.

Picking up the kitchen knife, he wondered what it would be like to feel the blade slide into flesh, into muscle, what it would be like to feel it becoming stuck in bone.

The first thrust threw Jim Dyal into a paroxysm. "Still life in you yet," Gary said, not without a certain awe.

Another five thrusts, each one deeper than the last, brought Jim Dyal's life to an end. But Gary was incapable of stopping. He didn't stop even when he heard Hugh call down to him, exultantly crying out that he'd found the money—more money than they could ever have imagined. Fifty-dollar bills, hundreds too, floated from his hands.

At last Gary grew weary when he saw that there was little left to carve up. Moreover, he was covered with blood, head to toe. Hugh was aghast at the spectacle but said nothing, fearful that he too might incur Gary's astonishing wrath.

In silence, the two gathered up the money from its hiding place in the upstairs bedroom, cramming it into plastic bags that Mary Lawe must have saved from her shopping trips into town.

Stepping onto the porch, they looked for the car, but it was gone.

"The fucker!" Gary said, but with little anger in his voice.

Most of his anger had been expended, and besides, Scott's

flight in the Rabbit might have been something he was expecting.

"What do we do now?" Hugh asked, his voice quavering.

"What do we do now? We walk, that's what we do. Unless you want to stay here all night."

"But—"

"But what, asshole?"

"Look at you, you're covered with blood."

Gary shrugged, indifferent to the grotesque appearance he presented. Hugh was trying to keep a certain distance from him, not just because his friend was acting so unpredictably, but because of the smell he gave off. The smell of dead Jim Dyal.

They began walking. Church Street, which ran past Jim Dyal's place, continued on into the center of town. A couple of blocks from there, down Pine, and they would be home.

It was as dark as it ever got in Brown Station. Gary stayed on Church, walking down the middle of the street, which was hardly a problem considering how little traffic there was. Hugh would have proceeded through the woods if it were up to him, but he was afraid to be on his own. It was as though he believed Gary would protect him, that as long as he was in Gary's presence nothing too terrible would happen.

But it did.

A pair of headlight beams struck them, casting them into relief like an accusation, revealing two local boys to the driver of the approaching car, one of them awash with blood.

The car veered to avoid them, then pulled to a stop about twenty feet from where they were.

"Let's get the fuck out of here," urged Hugh, already breaking into a run.

His words seemed to have no impact on Gary who, with a dangerous calm, set down the plastic bag bulging with looted cash and drew the .22 from his belt.

"You're crazy, man, you're fucking nuts!"

The car door opened and the driver emerged. "You boys all right?" they heard.

"Oh shit! You know who it is?" Hugh said, tugging at his friend in hope that he'd come to his senses.

If Gary did know, it didn't make any difference to him.

His first shot was wildly askew, striking not the advancing driver, but the back fender of his Oldsmobile.

The man let out a curse, dropped to the ground, and brought out a gun of his own—a .44, one much more powerful than the weapon Gary held.

Hugh didn't wait; he dived to the ground, hoping that God and the darkness would conceal him from view.

The man fired three rounds before Gary could fire a second time. He was thrown back by the first, then, succeeding in restoring himself to his feet, was knocked on his backside again. With miraculous obstinacy he tried once more. The explosion of the third bullet in his heart insured that he would not be getting up again.

Hugh waited a moment, and then satisfied the shooting had come to an end, drew himself up, raising his hands in trembling anticipation.

The badge on Tom Emmett's chest glimmered as he came closer. He looked puzzled as he glanced down at Gary Kramer. Several crumpled fifties had fallen out of the bag and these caught the police officer's eye as well. When he stepped up to Hugh, Hugh could smell the Genesee ale on his breath. There was no question in his mind that he was on his way home from Kendrick's Tavern after a long night of boozing.

"Well, boy," said Tom Emmett, "I guess you know you're under arrest."

Hugh said yes, he expected that.

thirty-one

The ringing phone wasn't what caused Larry Fallon to awaken. He'd been dreaming, and the dream had somehow turned sour and it was the need to escape it that had drawn him back to consciousness. With the phone coming alive, though, the dream was lost, vanished completely.

"Fallon here."

Next to him, Jessie was stirring. He was so disoriented that for an instant he hadn't remembered she was there. For that matter, he was having to struggle to recall where he was. It came back to him when he looked out the window to see Mount Sycamore.

"Larry, this is Bill McKee." His voice conveyed urgency, but no more so than the hour, which by the readout of the bedside clock was 2:14 A.M.

"What is it, Bill?"

"Two local kids just robbed and killed Jim Dyal and his wife. Our sheriff, Tom Emmett, killed one of the kids and took the other into custody."

"You think it might be the virus?"

"From what I hear, they were both stoned, loaded to the gills, but I'd say that it's worth checking out. You don't want to wait on this, either. If Emmett did participate in a cover-up at Shadow Pines, there's no telling what he'll do in this case."

McKee went on to say that the body of Gary Kramer had been sent to Sullivan County Hospital where an autopsy—routine in such cases—would be performed. The surviving youth, Hugh Craven, was locked up in a holding cell in the Boiceville courthouse.

After he'd hung up, Jessie turned to him, fully awake now, propping herself up on her elbow. "What was that about?" she said, thinking it was Gordon on the phone.

When he told her it was McKee, she looked relieved.

"The courthouse is closest," she said. "We can start there and go to the hospital."

At the risk of disappointing her, he said that it would be better if they separated. "I'll deal with Emmett," he said, "and you can observe the postmortem. I don't think we have the time to do both things together."

"It might take hours for them to get around to the autopsy," Jessie said. "I'll just be waiting around there."

"But we don't know that. Something like this, they might get right on it."

There was really no argument. Whatever else had passed between them, the fact was that Fallon was still the senior member of the investigation.

Even though they were going in different directions Fallon waited for her by the motel office. As he waited, a spanking new Chevy pulled up. Its motor was left idling while a man on the passenger side got out.

He was wearing a jacket and tie despite the warmth of the night. There was the unmistakable air of authority about him. He barely glanced at Fallon on his way into the office. No one was there.

"You looking for a room?" Fallon asked. "I think the manager's asleep. He isn't used to getting guests this late."

The man shook his head. "I don't want a room. I'm looking for a man."

When Fallon said nothing he continued, "You staying here?"

"That's right."

"Then maybe you know him. He's with the Centers for Disease Control. His name's Gordon Markoff."

Rather than responding directly, Fallon, doing his best to maintain his composure, asked what interest this man had in Markoff.

A wallet unfolded in the palm of the man's hand, revealing his photograph and identification. The words *Federal Bureau of Investigation* clearly registered.

"There's a subpoena out on him," the agent added.

"Well, I'm sorry, I don't have any idea who he is."

The man regarded him skeptically, but that might have been the way he looked at people as a matter of course. "Have a nice evening," the agent said as he started back toward his car. The words probably came so naturally to his tongue that it made no difference to him that evening was long gone.

At that instant Jessie appeared. The agent took no note of her.

"I saw you talking to that man. What did he want?"

"Oh, nothing. Just directions how to get on the road to Albany."

Except for the light on in a ground floor window, the courthouse appeared shut down for the night now coming to an end.

Two county patrol cars were parked outside. Another car Fallon recognized as belonging to Mayor Eddie White was parked across the street—illegally.

A brass knocker on the door was the only means to demand attention from within.

A barrel-chested police officer soon appeared. Fallon showed him his credentials.

"Centers for Disease Control?" the officer said. "I can't see where this is any business of yours."

"One of the participants in the killing was a brother of a victim of a lethal virus. We want to find out if the boy you're holding here is also infected."

Everyone in the area had naturally heard of the affliction that had stricken five of the town's children; most of the residents were personally acquainted with one or more victims of the disease. So Fallon's words had their intended effect.

"Let me talk to the chief." The officer was no doubt referring to Tom Emmett. This was not someone Fallon was especially looking forward to meeting. Not after what he'd heard about him.

Surprisingly, though, Emmett proved to be rather amenable to his visit. "I don't think this has anything to do with that damn disease," he told Fallon. "These kids have always been trouble. Especially that Kramer."

"But not trouble like this?"

"There's always a first time. In my line of work you see everything."

"Yes, I imagine you do," Fallon said, having no wish to

offend him. He just wished that Emmett would not feel compelled to wear his shades inside the courthouse. He was a formidable enough presence without them.

"I didn't want to shoot the poor bastard," Emmett said. "I've known him since he was yea high. Hell, I thought he was injured, all that blood on him. How was I to know he'd butchered Jim Dyal? And then he had to go and shoot at me."

"Why didn't he run?"

"Maybe he'd seen too many westerns, beats the shit out of me. Some people, they get off on the idea of a shootout at the O.K. Corral. They're not all there." He tapped his temple with his finger to underscore his assertion. "Besides, he was wired, fucked-up on drugs."

The more he talked the more Fallon believed that the dead Gary Kramer was a victim of the virus, his brain deteriorated to such an extent that he'd turned permanently psychotic. The drugs he'd consumed would only have accelerated the process.

"What about the Craven kid?"

"No mind of his own. Ever since I can remember he was following Gary's lead. Peer pressure is what did it—that and the dope he was smoking or shooting up on or whatever they do to get it in their bodies."

"I'd like to see him, ask him some questions."

Emmett posed no objection, but advised him that Craven had been with a lawyer. "Damn fool told him not to say nothing to nobody."

There were two holding cells in the basement of the courthouse; about half an inch of water covered much of the floor, which Emmett attributed to a leak in one of the overhead pipes.

Hugh Craven was rocking back and forth on a cot, obviously chilled. He was clad only in a pair of jockey shorts; the tattered blanket he'd been given wasn't nearly enough cover to warm him.

"Clothes were all bloody," Emmett said, explaining why Craven had been left like this.

The lawyer was nowhere in sight, but his influence made itself felt from the first moment that Fallon entered Hugh's cell.

Rather than trying to draw Hugh out about the crime, Fallon chose a different approach. "Would you mind if I take a look at your toes?"

The question took the youth by such surprise that for several seconds he didn't know what to say. Undoubtedly, he believed this was some kind of trick on Fallon's part.

"Something wrong with you, man? You one of those . . . ?"

He couldn't think of the word. Fallon supplied it for him. "One of those perverts?"

Hugh nodded.

Fallon told him that he was a doctor, which wasn't *exactly* the truth; but he had a feeling that communication would be more easily established if the boy believed it was true.

Without waiting, Fallon drew the blanket away from his feet. There was nothing unusual about his right foot, but one toe was raised on the left. "Can you lower that toe?" he asked.

It seemed that this was the first time that Hugh had given any attention to the way his toe had arched up. "No, I guess not. Is that supposed to mean anything?"

Yes, Fallon thought, *it means that you're sick and are going to die*. But all he said was, "Probably not."

Fallon now had to determine where the boy might have picked up the virus. Although he could not completely rule out human contact, there was no evidence, at least until now, that the contagion had been transmitted this way.

"Has anyone in your family been ill lately? With anything? Even a common cold?"

The nature of his questioning appeared to confuse Hugh. Expecting to be asked about what had transpired in Jim Dyal's house, he was instead being called on to remember whether anyone close to him had recently had the sniffles.

"I don't think so. Why?"

Fallon proceeded to the next question, ignoring his. "Did you or any of your friends ever go swimming in Shoharie Creek?"

"No, there's a much better lake south of Brown Station we go to. But somehow we never got around to doing much swimming this summer. Most of the time we hung out on Mount Sycamore."

Now, Fallon thought, *we might be getting someplace.* "Anyplace in particular on the mountain?"

"Yeah, it's about halfway up the slope. It was a place Gary found. You can see just about all the valley from there. Weird place, man."

"Oh, and why's that?"

"That crazy Indian . . ."

"Joe Hunting Bear?"

"Yeah, Joe the fucking Hunting Bear. He lives in the woods up around there, always shooting chipmunks and deer. We hear him sometimes, but we never see him, which is just fine with us."

"That's what makes it weird?"

"Not really. See, there's part of a plane wreck up there—what's left of the fuselage and a part of the cockpit."

Fallon immediately thought of the improbable necklace Joe Hunting Bear had constructed from a nonfunctioning compass and scraps of metal.

"How long has that wreck been there?"

"Oh, since spring. Late May, I think. One night in a storm one of those prop planes crashed into the mountain. Nobody knows whether the guy piloting it lost control or ran out of fuel or what happened."

"Will Ziegler," Fallon said to himself.

Hugh didn't seem to hear him. "These small planes, you know? The pilots don't bother filing flight plans half the time."

"What you're saying is that no one's determined the identity of the pilot."

"You got that right." Hugh was obviously happier to be discussing a plane crash of three months ago rather than squirming through another interrogation. "They searched that place for days, but they could never find a body. They figure whoever it was must have gotten blown to bits when the plane went down."

Fallon held out a notebook and opened it to a blank page. He asked Hugh if he could draw a map for him indicating the location of the wreckage.

Hugh took the notebook and, with Fallon's felt-tip pen, proceeded to draw a fairly good representation of the mountain and its surroundings, with special emphasis on the trail leading to the site. "You can't miss it if you follow the trail high enough. It's just that hardly anybody ever goes high enough."

Before Fallon could leave the courthouse, Emmett's deputy informed him that he had a call. It was from Jessie.

"They still haven't gotten around to the autopsy of the Kramer boy," she said, "but I did have a chance to look at the body."

"Don't tell me. You found the extensor plantar reflex."

"How did you guess?"

"Why don't you meet me back at the motel. We can get the results of the autopsy later on. For now, I think we've found out what we wanted to know."

When Fallon returned to the Sycamore Motor Court, he found that Jessie still wasn't back. He went into the war room to study the survey map of the Catskills.

From the point that Hugh Craven had marked about halfway up the southern slope of Mount Sycamore, he drew a line down to Shoharie Creek. He was certain that the water containing the infected mosquito larvae must be flowing down underground from somewhere on that mountain. He remarked with interest the way the boundary lines were drawn; while the southern slope was state property, the northern belonged to the Shadow Pines resort.

Somewhere, he believed, very close to the remains of Will Ziegler's prop plane, was the ultimate source of the virus. Tomorrow he and Jessie, and perhaps Ron Cochi, would head up the mountain and see if they could find it.

thirty-two

"I don't see where there's anything to be gained by beating around the bush," Koppleman said, his tone so casual that he might have been engaging Gordon in cocktail conversation.

Over Koppleman's right shoulder a trapezoidally shaped window was crowded with the lights of midtown skyscrapers, a view available only from the penthouse floor of the Rineman-Sachs Clinic.

"I've always appreciated candor," Gordon said in reply. "It's such a remarkably rare thing to find these days."

Even if the circumstances of their meeting had been more propitious, Gordon doubted that he would have liked this man—or even found it in himself to tolerate him. Stanley Koppleman wore his corruption openly, without the slightest embarrassment. He reminded Gordon of some of the more venal politicians he'd encountered in his travels to the Third World, unbound by restraints, either constitutional or moral. For such people, ridding disease from their country mattered only insofar as they could derive some profit from it.

Koppleman, who'd been standing up until this point, dropped down into his chair with a sigh, folding his hands, and gazed at his involuntary guest with a strangely sympathetic expression.

"You have a penchant for controversy, Mr. Markoff. Even your colleagues at the CDC would admit to that." He waited for Markoff to respond. When this didn't happen he went on. "I'm told that you have made representations to the New York State Health Department to investigate certan property belonging to the Shadow Pines resort." His statement, couched as it was in lawyerly language, contained traps that Gordon only hoped he would see before falling into them.

"We have reason to believe that a health hazard exists on the property and may, in fact, be originating on the property of the resort."

"And you think that you have discovered evidence at this clinic that would bear out your theory?" The way in which he pronounced this last word underscored his skepticism.

"I believe so, yes."

"Do you seriously think that you could prove, before a court of law, that your theory was correct?"

"As a lawyer you naturally think in those terms, Mr. Koppleman, but we don't operate that way. If there are reasonable grounds for suspecting that a health hazard presents an immediate danger to the community, then we act. I don't think the victims of this virus give a damn as to what a judge or jury might think about the evidence."

"I see your point, but frankly it doesn't interest me. At this juncture, you have nothing to implicate the resort in the spread of this disease. Whoever your sources are, I seriously question their motives. There are certain individuals who like to make trouble. I'm sure you know the type." Warming to his subject, Koppleman leaned forward, causing the chair to groan. "For instance, word has reached me that there's a pathologist working out of the chief medical examiner's office who insists that certain cadavers recently autopsied have shown signs of this virus of yours." Koppleman reached over to the desk and took hold of the MMWR of the previous week which had carried a report about the affliction.

Continuing, he said, "Now I happen to know, on good authority, that this individual has been engaged in an ongoing feud with his superior, Dr. Haverkos. I am no expert in public health, Mr. Markoff, but it seems to me that you'd be sadly mistaken if you relied on a man like this for your information. Any more than it would be if you accepted the word of some poor half-demented girl who's so sedated she can barely recognize her own name."

It astonished Gordon, and dismayed him utterly, how much the attorney knew. One step ahead of him in every way. But if he was filled with fear it was less for himself than for Zaborowski.

Koppleman, tired of sitting, stood up again. He went to

the window and gazed out. Gordon wondered whether this was his office or one temporarily on loan to him.

"As a lawyer I am necessarily a compromiser, a bargainer," Koppleman was saying, his eyes fixed on the dazzling lights of Manhattan. "Rather than expend so much energy and time on this thing, why don't we agree to a date when your people can go into Shadow Pines?" Turning to Gordon, he said, "I had in mind the eighth of September."

That was two and a half weeks away. Not only was it after Labor Day, when a large percentage of the vacationers would be leaving the resort, but it was also well after the closing of the Northeast Classic.

"In two and a half weeks a lot of people can die and a lot more can get sick."

"Then let's say, just after Labor Day."

Gordon wondered whether this man actually believed he could settle this the way he would a plea-bargaining session.

"If I could get in there tomorrow, I would," Gordon said.

"Did you know that the FBI is interested in your whereabouts?"

Koppleman dropped this with the same offhandedness that had characterized everything he'd said to Gordon.

Somehow Gordon hadn't considered the repercussions of running out on the subcommittee hearings. He'd assumed Bradstock would have figured out some way to quash the subpoena.

"Now, I am aware that you are highly regarded by many people in the field of public health. They seem to think of you as a kind of latter-day saint, tireless in your devotion to putting an end to suffering and disease. Don't think that I don't find such a quality admirable."

He's leading up to something, Gordon thought.

"It would grieve me to see such a reputation ruined." Koppleman's expression altered; the coarseness in his face, the hardness in it, emerged fully. His eyes narrowed and his nostrils flared.

"But you know," he said, putting his face not more than twelve inches from Gordon's, "I could do it! Why do you think you were called before that subcommittee in the first place?"

"Spengler's in your pocket."

"Spengler?" Koppleman laughed. "No, I'm afraid not. Spengler is too inconsequential to bother buying. He'd cost more than he'd be worth." He allowed Gordon several moments to venture a second guess, but Gordon did not. "No, it was Bradstock."

Gordon only now began to understand the enormity of this man's power; it was the power of genius gone astray.

"Naturally, I can put an end to this little problem," Koppleman said, his eyes resting now on the telephone and on the Rolodex beside it.

"I imagine you could."

"On the other hand, if you persist in your demand to go into Shadow Pines before Labor Day, I would have to take measures. You can be certain that this matter of a subpoena would be the least of your troubles."

All at once it came to Gordon what had happened to the patient he'd seen in unit five. She was likely suffering from spotted fever; the rashes spread widely over her body testified to that. But she'd not been brought into the clinic with spotted fever; it had been given to her while she was here, intended to camouflage the existence of the virus which was responsible for her consignment to this institution in the first place. And when she died—and it was all but certain that she would—it would be easy enough for a pathologist to determine that spotted fever was responsible for her demise. Such duplicity would probably buy Koppleman the time he needed. What Gordon couldn't figure out was why the Northeast Classic meant so much to him.

It gave Gordon pause. Any man who could condone—even perpetrate—the deliberate inoculation of microbes into a human being was capable of delivering on his threats.

"I am quite serious," Koppleman said as if he were able to read Gordon's thoughts. "I can make life more unbearable for you than you could ever imagine."

Gordon stood up. "Am I free to go?"

Nodding, Koppleman said, "And when can I expect your answer?"

"You can have it now."

"Well . . . ?"

"The moment we get permission from the state to go into Shadow Pines we are going in. That is *my* last word."

Koppleman appeared to accept this declaration with equanimity. As an astute judge of character, he should not have been surprised by Gordon's reply. "I'd give the matter some thought if I were you. In fact, if I were you I would wait until tomorrow before making my final decision. I could tell you now exactly what I'm planning to do should you persist in your unreasonable attitude, but frankly, I'd rather have it come as a surprise."

thirty-three

Not halfway up a mountain in the middle of the Catskills the air was so humid they could have been in monsoon country. Clouds floated across the sky, breaking suddenly to let in bursts of sunlight and glimpses of blue.

In its zigzagging course the path up the slope passed an empty bluestone quarry that was scarcely visible with so much overgrowth smothering it. White birch trees, some denuded by lightning or charred by forest fire, were conspicuous among the pine and butternut trees. From time to time the landscape would change abruptly, yielding to bedrock sparse of vegetation.

But the bedrock was simply traversed; it was the oxalis montana ferns and dwarf cornel that made the going difficult. The decaying organic matter provided a surface so spongy that it sucked them down into it. It was moist and muddy like walking through wet tissue paper.

The earth smelled of rotting leaves, rotting pinecones, rotting everything—that and moisture. It was a dank but not altogether displeasing odor.

Jessie supposed she was expecting something dramatic: half a fuselage, all of a tail, a cockpit sufficiently intact so that it would be possible to sit in the pilot's seat and play with the useless controls. But when they finally came upon the wreckage at the point where Hugh Craven had indicated, they found only a mangled hulk of metal, blackened by fire, rusted where it wasn't blackened. A part of the controls was visible; insects, not all of them readily identifiable, were swarming everywhere, laying eggs in the holes where the gauges used to be and deploying themselves along the razor-sharp edges of glass which were all that was left of the windshield.

Of the pilot, Will Ziegler, there was nothing to be seen. Jessie assumed that anything of interest that could be salvaged from this wreck had been taken either by Joe Hunting Bear or by Hugh and his friends.

Certainly the youths hadn't taken pains to conceal evidence of their presence here. Quart bottles of Bud and cans of Colt .45 were strewn about. Cigarette butts and what looked like dead joints had been discarded in such plentiful supply that it was a wonder they hadn't set the woods on fire.

The three epidemiologists were beat. It had taken them five hours to reach the site. Jessie felt less like flesh than like sweat, her whole body consistency turned to water. But this was not so bad; the effort of getting here, risking a permanent crook in the back from the weight of the pack she'd carried, served to take her mind off Larry and Gordon. Against such diabolical humidity and such exhaustion, neither passion nor guilt stood much of a chance.

Late in the afternoon they began collecting specimens, taking their initial sampling from a circumscribed area close to the wreckage. The task was, if anything, more grueling than it had been two days previously at Shoharie Creek. The black flies continued to harass them until they vanished all at once just before sundown.

The air grew heavier and more oppressive; the turgid gray clouds covering the sky hastened the approach of darkness. There was a feel of rain and the smell of it too.

Work suspended for the day, they returned to the campsite for drinks. Larry had thought to bring along a bottle of martini mix, together with the gin and vermouth and, of course, the olives.

Looking at him as dispassionately as she could, Jessie decided that Larry really should have been a nineteenth-century explorer who reveled in the adventure of an imperial expedition into whatever hearts of darkness happened to be available at the time. She had the feeling that he might even envy Will Ziegler and the life he led, at least until the moment his Cessna slammed into the mountainside.

After a time Larry proposed a walk. Ron understood that the invitation was addressed to Jessie, not to him, and said he would stay behind. Jessie wondered what was going on in his mind, but didn't think that either she or Larry had given him any grounds for suspicion.

For a while Larry and Jessie walked without saying a word. What Jessie had in mind to say she couldn't. Was it possible that in affairs of the heart everyone was reduced to being a sophomore in high school all over again? That there was never a time in your life when you could act like an adult in such matters?

Certainly she did not feel like a married woman, she did not feel like she was thirty; no, what she felt like was sixteen—insecure, jittery, filled with longing that had no real target but just wanted to pounce on anything in sight.

"Are you sorry it happened?"

The words were Larry's, but on hearing them Jessie thought for an instant that they'd come out of her mouth.

"No," she said, maybe too quickly, "no, I'm not sorry. I'm . . ."

"You're what?"

"I'm confused." That seemed like the most sensible, surely the most accurate, appraisal of her condition.

"So am I."

She looked at him in surprise, astonished that he'd said such a thing, for really she could never believe that Larry Fallon—any of the Larry Fallons of the world—could feel confused. She didn't think he could be anything other than self-assured, intent on getting what he wanted.

He stopped and gripped her shoulders, succeeding in arresting her motion as well. "I'm confused only because I don't want to do anything to hurt you."

"Yes," she said. It wasn't that she meant to agree with him; she was only acknowledging what he had to say, that was all.

"I like Gordon, I have a great deal of respect for him."

Of course, she thought, *everyone has respect for Gordon. Not love, not friendship maybe, but respect.*

"But I am in love with you."

"Don't say that."

"And why not?"

"You don't know me. How can you be in love with me?"

This was a rational argument, of course, and in situations such as this, rational arguments had practically no relevance at all.

"What would you suggest, that I spend the next few

months—the next few years maybe—trying to get to know you and then tell you I love you?"

"Then maybe you won't."

"I want you. Is that better?" His eyes locked on hers and would not let go.

Love? It was possible. Passion? Of that there was no question.

Larry took hold of her, hurrying his hands under her shirt, anxious for the feel of her bare skin. Their kiss had something desperate about it. It took them both some time before they realized that they were getting wet from the rain beginning to come down.

"Maybe we should go back," Larry said.

In silence they began retracing their steps. Then, through a cluster of yellow birch and pine trees, Jessie noticed what appeared to be a lake—or maybe not.

"What is that?"

Larry looked to where she was pointing. Then he started toward it. As they got closer they saw that it was in fact a lake, but a lake very different from any that either of them had ever seen. It was very black, and even with rain spattering it, its surface remained calm and motionless. The odor was of things gone dead many months before.

Not far away was a heap of downed branches fortified by twigs, pinecones, and brush that had been used to dam the lake. Not a single beaver responsible for this bulwark was in sight.

"This is it," Larry said.

From the expression on his face he could have been admiring a landscape by Monet, not a dammed-up lake blacker than night.

"This is what?"

"This is the source of the virus. I'm sure of it." His voice rose in excitement. "I'll lay odds that this is where the underground river's coming from. The larvae are hatched here. Some of them are carried down the slope into Shoharie, some of them, when they turn into adults, eventually find their way to the other side of the mountain."

"To Shadow Pines."

"That's right."

"But how can you be sure?"

"It's a hunch. But we've got to come back here tomorrow and take as many specimens as we can. This is the place, mark my words."

His enthusiasm didn't allow for doubt; even Jessie, who had other things on her mind besides mosquito larvae, was caught up by it.

When they returned to their camp they found Ron preparing to leave. Gesturing to the sky which, with the rain, had turned more sullen than before, he said, "Way over to the north, beyond Panther Mountain, a big storm's brewing. I think I want to get down from this mountain before it hits."

His eyes came to rest on the tent. With the fitful wind that had begun to blow, it was flapping loudly, suddenly seeming very frail.

"We're staying on. There's a lake about a quarter of a mile from here that we want to investigate in the morning," Larry said.

Jessie felt that he had no right to speak for her; he could at least have solicited her opinion, found out whether she wished to remain or leave. But the truth was that she had no wish to go back down with Ron. It would be better to ride out a thunderstorm than face Gordon.

Ron looked at them both as if they'd taken leave of their senses, but all he did was to shrug and gather up the day's specimens and cram them into his backpack. "I'll see you when you get back," he said. "Do you have any messages you want me to pass along?"

He seemed only mildly surprised when he learned that no one did.

Once darkness fell, the rain came with more punishing force, sounding like machine-gun fire against the roof of their tent. Jessie began having second thoughts about the wisdom of their choice. The wind roared and snapped off branches and sent them flying. The lightning was bright enough to penetrate through the canvas, and thunder followed so quickly on its heels that barely a second passed between one and the other.

Not that she was necessarily unhappy. The storm stilled—at least temporarily—the debate going on in her mind. In Larry's arms, pressed against him, her legs between his, she felt at peace. The driving rain, the drama of thunder and lightning, the attacking wind, only fueled her desire for this man.

It was like this in the beginning of history, she thought, making love in unreliable shelters while the storm raged without, all heat, all passion, fearful that the sun will never reappear, dimly conscious of death lurking not far away. It was terrifying and exhilarating.

It was like this in the beginning of history and it will be like this at its end. She arched herself up and watched Larry's head dip between her legs.

thirty-four

It wasn't until ten in the morning that Gordon arrived back at the Sycamore Motor Court. He couldn't quite get used to the fact that he was a fugitive; it wasn't like him to hide and bother to cover his tracks. Yet he realized that he would have to take some precautions if he didn't want to be hauled off to prison on a contempt charge. He felt as if he was trapped in a bad dream and that he should be able to shake himself awake to escape it.

But perhaps, he reasoned, *there remains latent in all of us the survivor's instinct.* It seemed to come almost natural to him to stay out of sight as much as possible, slipping past the motel office, heading to the room where he hoped to find Jessie and the others.

The door was locked. He had the key and opened it. No one was there. He phoned his room. No answer. His eyes fell on a note that had been left for him by his wife. "We are collecting specimens on Mount Sycamore and will be back tomorrow. Love, J."

He was disappointed; he was desperate to talk to her, to relate to her all that had occurred since he'd left for Washington. They'd spoken only once over the phone since then and it was such a brief, inconclusive conversation that there was no way for him to tell whether her anger toward him had abated. While he still believed it was risky for her to continue with the investigation, he had come around to accepting it.

What he most feared was that her resentment would linger, that she would add fuel to their dispute when he was ready to put an end to it.

There was a message from CDC headquarters in Atlanta that must have come in over the modem since Jessie and Larry and Ron had left for Mount Sycamore; no printout had yet been made from it. The message was from Lou Valdespino at the field office:

> Confirmed dead from Catskill virus: 14.
> Unconfirmed dead: 11.
>
> Confirmed cases of infection (current): 9.
> Unconfirmed cases of infection (current): 8.

The eight unconfirmed in the last category included the female patient Gordon had seen in unit five of the Rineman-Sachs Clinic. It was he who'd come up with the figure, basing his guess on the number of rooms in the unit, but he was aware that his approximation could be wildly off base.

He read on:

> In all confirmed instances where an autopsy has been performed the same phenomenon recurs: a proliferation of astrocytes: gaping white vacuoles where nerve cells should have been found, and a multiplicity of plaques. Preliminary laboratory tests conducted here and at the National Institutes of Health in Bethesda indicate that this virus resembles a family of slow-moving viruses, both infectious and genetic in nature. These include Alzheimer's disease, Creutzfeldt-Jakob and Gerstmann-Straussler syndromes in humans and scrapie in sheep.

This coincided with the information the CDC investigatory team had already gathered. The more significant findings came next:

> The Catskill virus, like those slow-moving viruses, also is able to withstand high temperatures (up to forty-five minutes in boiling water) and immersion in formaldehyde that ordinarily inactivate viral organisms. But in two significant respects this virus differs from the others.
>
> First is the rapidity with which it acts on the brain; it apparently does not require a long incubation period that is characteristic of kuru or JCS. Second, it impairs

both the central nervous system like kuru and the intellect like GSS.

The conclusion of the message pertained to a report by one of the Bethesda neuropathologists who'd examined various specimens of brains removed from the dead victims.

> The virus seems to target the limbic system of the brain in addition to the central nervous system. Both the hippocampus and the amygdala have been found to have a high density of plaques and elongated fibriles. It is known that the rabies virus also attacks the hippocampus, triggering off outbursts of rage and frenzy. Disturbance of the amygdala is associated with compulsive sexual behavior.

Compulsive sexual behavior. What a tantalizing note to close on, Gordon thought.

After printing out the message, he went back to his room. Except for Jessie's bag hanging in the closet and the toilet articles she'd left behind in the bathroom, there was nothing to hint at her presence. The maid had restored the room to its normal anonymous state. There were still traces of beaver blood on the window screen, though; the room wasn't entirely anonymous.

Gordon was too exhausted to sleep and there was, besides, too much on his mind. At four thirty in the afternoon he gave up the struggle and got dressed.

He drove his rented car into town, deciding that he would have a bite to eat at Kendrick's.

While he sat there waiting for his chili, rain began to fall. Soon the window ran so thick with water oozing down that everything in view on Church Street was either blurred or distorted.

"Big storm's coming," the man serving him the chili said. "Already knocked out the power lines in Boiceville and West Hurley."

Gordon thought of Jessie hunting for specimens on the mountain. He couldn't imagine that if the storm grew too bad she and Larry wouldn't decide to come down. He couldn't envision Jessie confronting a late-summer storm.

A scattering of people who didn't look like they belonged in a place like Kendrick's started to appear, refugees from the rain. A few had been caught unprepared and they stood in one place, their clothes soaked and transparent, waiting to dry out before they gave thought to what to do next.

About the time that Gordon finished his chili, a man who was bundled up in rain gear came in. He snapped shut his umbrella, then pulled down the hood of his slicker, revealing an unusual head of hair; parted straight down the middle, it was white on one side and straw-blond on the other.

He glanced around, seemingly in search of someone; then his gaze rested on Gordon.

"You're Markoff, aren't you?" he said, stepping closer to Gordon's table.

An FBI agent? Somehow he didn't look the type. Gordon saw no point in lying.

"And what would your name be?"

The question seemed momentarily to stump the man. "You can call me Hal if you need to call me anything at all." Without being invited, he took the chair opposite Gordon's.

Having met a great many people in his time, several of whom he'd long forgotten, Gordon tried to think if he knew Hal. He concluded that he did not.

"I have something that might be of interest to you," Hal said.

"I doubt it."

Unfazed by this response, Hal went on, "No kidding. This will really interest you." He began to reach under his slicker for something.

Gordon had no patience for this. He stood up from the table and drew some bills out of his wallet to pay.

"You don't want to go just yet, not before you take a look at this."

He found what he was groping in his pockets for and threw it on the table. It landed beside the empty stein face down. A photograph.

Gordon's curiosity was piqued, but he resisted the impulse to turn the photo over. Something was working on his nerves and he didn't appreciate what was happening in the pit of his stomach.

"It's yours to keep. There's more where it came from."

Gordon was sure that this was one of Koppleman's emissaries, but when he mentioned the attorney's name Hal shook his head and, smiling without warmth, said, "I haven't any idea what you're talking about."

Then, adjusting his hood back in place, he turned and walked out the door.

No one else in the bar appeared to have observed this exchange. Gordon grasped hold of the photograph and, still without glancing at it, slid it into his front pocket.

After leaving the bar he ran to his car, parked half a block away. The rain was worse, hammering on the roof and hood, making a considerable racket. Church Street was completely deserted.

Twenty minutes went by as Gordon deliberated about what he should do. He removed the photo from his pocket and ripped it in half, then in quarters, keeping his eyes rigidly glued to the windshield.

Then he stopped. His whole life had been devoted to acquiring the truth. Only by knowing exactly what a virus or a bacterium or a parasite did, only by knowing exactly how it was formed, could there be any hope of defeating it.

He laid out the four parts of the photo on the dashboard, still keeping them face down.

One by one he turned them over.

It wasn't a very good photograph; it was too dark for one thing, and not quite in focus. But there was no questioning what it showed; that was clear enough. The two bodies, the faces: there was no mistaking them.

thirty-five

Ron Cochi was sopping wet. He was up to his ankles in water. His coat, described on the label as waterproof, had long since become so saturated that it felt as if it weighed more than the backpack whose straps were eating into his shoulders. He knew he should have had a haircut before he'd left Atlanta, because he couldn't keep his hair out of his eyes or from slapping the side of his face every time there was a fresh onslaught of wind.

Either one of two things had happened: the car they'd come in had been towed away by the highway patrol, or he'd gotten confused in his descent off Mount Sycamore and come out at the wrong spot, perhaps miles from where they'd parked. It was impossible to tell where he was in relation to the mountain or the road, and it would have been impossible even if he was familiar with the area; the torrential rain was obliterating every distinguishing feature of the landscape.

He did manage to find a sign to Oneonta, but that didn't prove of much help since he couldn't recall whether he wanted to head toward Oneonta or away from it. After an hour of wandering back and forth in the darkness, he gave up his search for the car and decided to hitchhike.

Unhappily, there were few vehicles passing by, either heading toward Oneonta or away from it. Those that did, didn't stop for him.

After a while, no cars, not even four-wheel drives which were better suited to such conditions, came by. He didn't realize why until he came upon a towering pine that had come crashing down into the middle of the highway, blocking traffic in both directions. Ron doubted that this was an isolated instance. Other trees would have been felled by the storm and were undoubtedly contributing to the blockade.

Not until the storm had subsided and road crews set to work would there be any hope of restoring service.

He clambered over the downed pine, ripping his trousers on a particularly sharp branch, and continued on. Every now and again, he considered taking refuge under one of the more sheltering trees still standing, but the frequency of the lightning deterred him.

He had a flashlight with him, but he was sparing about its use, fearing that the batteries would die and he'd be left without any way to see at all.

But now, maybe a dozen yards ahead of him he was positive he saw a figure. A man like him sloshing around in the water.

He turned on his flashlight, and its beam caught Gordon Markoff.

Ron, gathering his matted hair out of his eyes, looked again, thinking that his perception might be failing him in spite of the flashlight. But no, it was Gordon all right, determinedly marching through everything the storm had put in his path.

"Gordon!" he shouted, trying to make himself heard over the din of thunder and groaning pinewood. "It's me, Ron Cochi!"

While the circumstances did not allow for a protracted exchange of formalities, Ron at least expected a greeting more polite than a demand to know what had become of Larry and Jessie.

"They're still up there," Ron said, pointing to the mountain behind him, which was now scarcely visible in all the rain and gloom.

Gordon looked toward the mountain with incredulity. "How could they still be up there?"

"They've set up a tent. I guess they hope to ride out the storm."

"Where exactly?"

"You aren't planning on going up there, too, are you?"

Gordon repeated his question with more insistence. So Ron attempted to give him directions.

Gordon handed him the keys to his car. "I had to leave it off the road back about half a mile," he said. "You shouldn't have any problem finding it."

If Gordon was insane enough to climb Mount Sycamore tonight, Ron thought, then let him. As long as he now enjoyed the prospect of a roof over his head he was happy. But the conviction was growing in him that he was working with lunatics.

At one point, about a quarter of the way up the trail, Gordon paused and raised his eyes, hoping that the distance he'd yet to traverse wasn't quite as much as he suspected it probably was. It was then he spied the lights that he'd seen several nights before. They glimmered in the rain, ghostly and beautiful; they seemed to hover in the air, blinking and flashing for several moments at a time, then becoming still.

This uncanny phenomenon remained in sight for another twenty minutes, but no matter how high he climbed, the lights seemed to get no closer.

When the trail turned and entered a particularly dense part of the woods, Gordon was no longer able to see them. Out of curiosity, he doubled back to a point where he'd held them in view. But they were no longer there. The city of the dead, Joe Hunting Bear had said it was. A strange destination indeed.

The lights would have disturbed him far more on another night. The rain and wind would have long since shaken his resolve on another night. But it was anger and pain that carried him tonight. It was possible that he would have welcomed a bolt of lightning, for he could not imagine that the shock it could produce in him, no matter how lethal, could compare with the shock he'd already received. Something in him was already dead.

He hardly noticed the mud thickening in whorls about his feet, or the temporary spells of blindness that the drenching rain was responsible for. His wife's name reverberated in his mind. Jessie, Jessie, Jessie, Jessie. What was once an incantation, even a prayer for him, was now a curse.

He did not know what he would say to her when he found her. For that matter, he had no idea what he would say to Fallon—or do to him. This situation was so new, so perplexing, that all he could bring to mind were scenes from old movies and novels he'd read years ago. There was always the cuckolded husband bursting in through the bedroom door, there was always the naked couple taken by surprise in bed. And what came afterward? Stupid words, garbled, too easily drowned out by shouted threats. Outrage. Numbness. Burning hatred.

Without Jessie, he wasn't convinced he could go on. At the same time he knew he would. Life would just get much lonelier.

And he climbed. He began to rely on the recurrent flashes of lightning that cast the landscape into sudden relief, making it nearly as bright as midday.

When he was close to where he believed the campsite to be, he heard something odd, like a rumbling freight train higher up on the slope, but it was not thunder.

No, what he was hearing was the sound of the mountain itself coming apart.

The sound woke Jessie. For a moment she was completely disoriented and had no idea where she was. *Completely disoriented.* The darkness was strange and penetrating, carrying the smell of newly fallen rain. Beside her Larry slept on.

The sound repeated itself, louder this time. She had the urge to rouse Larry and ask him if he could figure out what it was when a roar filled her ears; it might have been a powerful bomb going off. She undid the flaps of the tent and looked out. A black tide of mud and sodden earth, bearing with it pine and birch and alpine plants, was rolling down the slope in their direction.

For several seconds Jessie could do nothing but stare at the avalanche, numbed with fear. There was no chance to get out of its path; it was approaching them with incredible speed, accelerating as the gradient of the slope became more pronounced.

"Larry!" she shouted.

The last thing she heard before the black tide engulfed her was her own name being called, but what confused her was that the voice wasn't Larry's. It was Gordon's.

The first thing that Gordon could think of was to grab hold of a butternut tree. Although he could see the tent, he was powerless to bridge the fifty or so yards that lay between him and it. For a few seconds he had Jessie in view; then she was gone, submerged, like the tent, in the flow of mud and water that was now coming toward him.

He scraped and clawed, clambering higher up the tree. The crest of mud swelled, uprooting trees that looked at least as big as the one he held on to desperately, giving him no confidence whatever that this butternut would survive.

He saw the shredded tent pass by, swaths of olive green canvas that were soon sucked into the caldron of mud and mangled vegetation. But no sign of Jessie or Larry.

Then the avalanche reached him. He felt an enormous slap in the chest. His face took a massive pummeling as well. The force of these blows was nearly enough to dislodge him from his precarious position. The tree itself swung back until it was practically doubled over, its top branches brushing the ground, but it did not break. By some miracle the trunk was sufficiently resilient not to give completely.

Gordon lost all track of time; gradually he became aware that the tide of mud had passed and he was still alive. A considerable residue of mud had been left behind, however, and he was buried up to his shoulders in the stuff. More mud covered his face and burned into his eyes. When he tried to move, everything seemed to hurt. Besides, there was so much muck in his way that it was all he could do to put one foot in front of the other.

He kept calling out to Jessie, but heard only the echo of his own voice in response. He realized the storm was dying, the rain reduced to a chilly drizzle. The winds, too, had subsided. And toward the east a ribbon of gray light on the horizon signaled not just the approach of a new day, but a renewal of clear skies.

Little by little he groped forward. The landscape seemed so changed now, so deformed and chaotic that directions like up and down no longer served much of a purpose. What was once slope now had the look of mud-strewn plateau, pockmarked by craters overflowing with brackish water.

After nearly an hour he succeeded in reaching higher ground where the mud was not nearly so thick and tenacious. He discovered that he was bleeding, but with so much mud plastering him, he couldn't determine where the blood was coming from. He also had a feeling that one or two ribs must be broken; it was especially painful to breathe vigorously.

Now, as if from far, far away he began to hear a voice. Someone was crying for help. His heart lifted. He thought it might be Jessie, but then he realized that it was a man's voice—Larry's.

He stopped. It would have been just as easy to go on. That the notion of doing this even entered his mind shamed him. But he couldn't entirely dismiss the pull of the temptation. Probably not more than half an hour before his arrival, Larry had been screwing his wife. Even in the face of this catastrophe Gordon's rage had not lessened. And why should it? A revolt of nature did not make an act of betrayal any more palatable.

It would be a bitter irony if he rescued Larry, only to discover that Jessie had been killed. But it seemed to be his fate, to be trying forever to save people—even from themselves. With a curse intended for whatever god would cause mountains to collapse and human hearts to change so suddenly, he headed in the direction the voice was coming from.

When Jessie managed to hold on to consciousness long enough to realize what had happened, she saw that she'd been flung up on a bed of mud. She couldn't move, but she didn't know whether this was because she was badly injured or because she was trapped in the mud. When she lifted her head, hoping to see where she was on the mountain the only thing in view was a stretch of terrain that looked like it belonged on another planet: denuded and blackened, with only a few trees scattered here and there to indicate where any woods had been.

There was nothing left of the beaver lake. Along with everything else, it had washed down the side of the mountain. From over the crest of the mountain she heard the sound of a chopper.

In the newly risen sun it shined as bright as a jewel. Jessie tried to prop herself up with her arms, hoping that the pilot would spot her. She even thought to shout, but realized that there was no way she could make herself heard at such a distance, certainly not above the noise of the rotors.

She saw something out of the corner of her eye that she

hadn't noticed before. Twisting her neck to obtain a better view of it, she saw that she was staring into a face. For all the decomposing and rotting it had suffered, there was enough skin left on it to give her a good idea of who it was—or had been. This was the face—the severed head—of Will Ziegler.

thirty-six

Too many flowers, Jessie thought. Chrysanthemums, roses, anemones, peonies: she liked flowers but not in such profusion that they obscured her view. Hospitals were bad enough without having to endure a room with no view.

Three days, seventy-two hours more, and she could go home, but she wasn't sure exactly where home was. It was a problem she'd never quite had before.

Friends and colleagues came and went during visiting hours. Her mother, having flown up from Florida, was a constant, and not entirely welcome, presence. She kept asking about Gordon, questions that under ordinary circumstances could easily have been answered, but were now fraught with emotion. Her mother, for the last eight and a half years a widow, was only now beginning to voice all the resentment she'd held for her late husband, and she had always been suspicious of Gordon. "If Gordon hadn't gotten you involved in this business you wouldn't have gotten hurt," she said.

When the phone would ring, Jessie was sure it would have to be either Gordon or Larry, but she didn't know which one she was afraid of hearing from more. At least she was alone, separated from them both. While doctors had approved her transfer to Emory, so that she could be closer to home, Larry's injuries were regarded as graver; from what she understood, he was still at Sullivan County Hospital in New York. And there was no telling where Gordon was. So far, neither of them had called. *They're both cowards,* she thought, then reminded herself that she, too, was a coward in her own way.

Something had changed in her since that night on the mountain, but she couldn't pin it down precisely. What she realized, though, was that she needed time on her own, that she wasn't going to rush into the arms of any man.

On the third morning following her arrival in Atlanta the door to her room opened and Gordon walked in.

He took a deep breath as if testing the air for its sweetness. She thought it interesting, and rather unsettling, that he looked first toward the patient who shared the semi-private room, a retired schoolteacher recovering from surgery to restore circulation to her legs, before his eyes lit on her.

He appeared older, tired and somehow depleted. Something had gone out of him and she had an idea what it was.

"How are you feeling?"

"I'm all right. They say they'll let me out of here in a few days."

She wanted to know what had happened to him in the days since the storm. He told her that he'd had to clear up a few things in New York. She knew better than to try to coax more of an explanation out of him.

"I have to leave Atlanta for a while," he said then.

The news upset her. It was one thing for them to separate, another for him to leave. She realized it was probably selfish of her, but she didn't want Gordon to be too far away.

"Where are you going?"

"I can't say for now. But I'll let you know."

He wasn't looking at her. *He knows,* she thought with despair, *he knows.*

At that moment the door opened again and her mother walked in. Seeing Gordon she said, "Oh, I'm sorry, I didn't know you were here. How are you, Gordon?"

"Getting along, Mrs. Palmer."

Studying his face, Mrs. Palmer frowned, obviously convinced that he was doing anything but getting along. "That's good to hear," she said. "Well, I'll leave the two of you alone and come back later."

"There's no need," Gordon said. "I was just leaving."

After he'd gone the older woman turned to Jessie and said, "Why, he's certainly acting strangely, isn't he?" When she didn't receive an answer, she returned her gaze to her daughter. Noticing the tears in her eyes, Mrs. Palmer said, not without a certain satisfaction in her voice, "It's over, isn't it? It's finished with."

thirty-seven

Larry Fallon spent his days testing his memory. Lying in bed in a private room at Sullivan County Hospital, he had a great deal of time in which to do this. Neither the books given him to read nor the television proved distracting enough.

What he remembered from the night of the storm was like a dream, clouded with images that seemed to lack chronological order or coherence. One moment he was lying next to Jessie, the next he was being buried in mud. After that he had no idea.

He wasn't in such bad shape but he looked like hell. Black eyes and discolored skin, abraded in his tumble down the mountain, discouraged appraisal in the mirror. Strips of tape wound about his chest, intended to accelerate the mending of his bruised and broken ribs, made him feel as if he'd been fitted into a suffocating corset. Walking was possible, but since his left ankle was so swollen from a sprain, it was also painful.

But he would certainly recover from these indignities. It could have been worse. His night on Mount Sycamore might have been his last.

And it would have been if not for Gordon's timely appearance. When he tried to force from his memory any recollection of this rescue, he came up blank. A black hole. He'd found out about it only because Lou Valdespino, phoning him from Atlanta, had told him.

Guilt was a stranger to Larry. He liked the idea of being rescued, but he didn't like the idea that it was Gordon who'd been responsible. Had Gordon any notion of what had gone on between him and his wife, no doubt Larry would have been left where he was, at the mercy of the elements.

Valdespino had also informed him that Jessie was in

Atlanta, recovering there. He did not so much as hint that Larry had been wrong to camp out on the mountain even knowing a storm was on its way. And what difference would it make? There must have been worse, with heavier rains and higher winds, that had come through the region in the last several years. But none of those had caused half a mountain slope to come sliding down.

A nurse left him a copy of the Albany *Union-News*. It carried a story about the impact the storm had had on Mount Sycamore and offered a commentary by a geologist named V. X. Philips.

Mr. Philips wrote: "We've learned subsequent to the storm that a lake, perhaps an acre and a half in size, was situated about a third of the way down from the summit of the mountain. This lake was formed by beaver dams that effectively impeded drainage. Over time a considerable amount of earth was displaced by the water in this lake, seriously eroding the structural base of the slope. When the storm swept into the area it dumped so much rain into the lake that there was no more room to accommodate it. It overflowed and, as it did so, brought down a substantial chunk of the mountain with it."

How was Larry to know this would happen? Of course, there was no way he could have. He had enough guilt; if he began to blame himself for putting Jessie's life in jeopardy—having already put her marriage in jeopardy—he would end by driving himself crazy.

Nonetheless, he remained in a deep funk. His ex-wife, Cynthia, called, but she was not one to give him the lift he needed. His children sent him letters, saying they hoped he would get well soon; their messages were rendered in Crayola crayons. This helped, but not enough.

I should call Jessie at Emory Hospital, he thought. *I have to talk to her.* And say what? He didn't know. He couldn't quite organize his thoughts, not with his memory of their night together so uncertain.

Larry might have become completely despondent had it not been for the unexpected appearance of a man who announced himself as Dr. Surwawady. He was an Indian, formerly of Bombay, he said, now a resident pathologist at Sullivan County. He spoke with a clipped British accent and seemed oddly enthusiastic for a man whose job it was to study disease and trauma in the dead.

Surwawady was surprised that Larry had not been told that a body had been discovered on Mount Sycamore in the aftermath of the storm. "Not a whole body, but bits and pieces of a body. And it seems as if the head and these pieces were thrown up from a lake."

"The beaver lake?"

"Yes, this is the lake I am referring to. It is thought that these are the remains of the pilot of a small plane that crashed into the mountain last May. You know about this crash?"

Larry said that he did. *Will Ziegler,* he thought. *We found Will Ziegler.*

"Did you conduct an examination on these remains?"

"Yes, of course," Dr. Surwawady replied. "There is little question this man was killed by trauma resulting from the crash. There was evidence of severe burns on one side of the skull compatible with a diagnosis of trauma."

But this wasn't the most important thing the pathologist had to tell him. "I was on the telephone to your Mr. Valdespino," he said, "and he told me to let you know the results of the examination we carried out on the brain."

"What did you find?"

"Oh, it was in wretched condition, Mr. Fallon. I have never before seen anything like it. So many holes."

"Astrocytes?"

"Very many astrocytes."

"Plaques?"

"Oh yes, many plaques."

It sounded like Will Ziegler's brain was riddled with the virus. It might have accounted for why he crashed. Yet what excited Larry was the possibility that Will Ziegler was the source of the virus.

The pathologist confirmed what Larry already assumed: uncounted numbers of insects with an affinity for water had eaten away at the infected flesh and very likely had transmitted the virus to animals and ultimately to humans. And there was no way of knowing how many other bits and pieces of the late Will Ziegler had been scattered over the southern slope of Mount Sycamore, providing further sources for the spread of the disease.

After Surwawady left, Larry got on the phone to Valdespino. The two men agreed that they'd probably hit upon the source of the virus; and that the virus was probably being harbored in Shadow Pines.

"Unfortunately," Valdespino said, "Hollister still won't permit us onto the resort."

"What the hell could possibly be his excuse?"

"Insufficient grounds, paperwork to be done, you name it. Mostly, he's never in his office when I call. Or he's there and won't take the call. A more likely possibility."

"Now what happens?"

"We try to get evidence so overwhelming Hollister can't refuse. If he does, I'll have to go over his head."

"You don't think the evidence is overwhelming now?"

"It's at the highly circumstantial phase."

"And?" Larry knew there was more.

"And the state still has jurisdiction in this matter. At this particular point, Hollister represents the state. We can't come in without an invitation."

"Have you been able to reach Gordon since I spoke to you last?"

That had been two days before.

"Not a word."

"What about Jessie?"

"She's coming along fine. You should give her a call."

"She say anything about Gordon?"

"Not to me she hasn't. In the meantime, I keep getting calls from this guy named Garrison, says he's with the FBI. He seems to want to know what happened to Gordon too."

"It's that subpoena."

"I suppose that must be it." Valdespino's voice betrayed a certain weariness. "Well, I'm not about to give them any information." He paused, adding, "Not that I have any. But if he ever gets in touch with you, Larry, tell him I need to speak to him."

"I'm sure he'll surface sooner or later," Larry said.

"Yes, but the question is where. And what trouble is he going to get us all into when he does?"

thirty-eight

WELCOME TO SHADOW PINES: A Resort for All Your Vacation Needs!

Shadow Pines is fifty-two rustic buildings featuring a huge, lavishly furnished central lodge, twenty guest cottages, three restaurants, five bars and a discotheque, convention facilities, stables, sixteen tennis courts, three Olympic-size swimming pools, movie theater, saunas, Jacuzzis, gymnasium with the latest Nautilus equipment, located in the heart of the Catskills.

You can mix, mingle, jingle a glass or rock to music in our famous Saturn Disco, or relax in the quiet setting of the Hunter's Lodge or any of our other fine bars.

Each room offers the ultimate in contemporary luxuries. . . . No detail has been overlooked in an effort to put you at ease.

One would have to be awfully starved for reading material, Gordon thought, to bother with nonsense like this brochure. As it happened, he was now occupying one of the rooms offering the ultimate in contemporary luxuries, and although it wasn't exactly the elegant environment that the brochure described, he had to admit that it wasn't bad. The kingsize bed almost demanded to be shared with someone else. But Gordon was alone.

So far as anyone knew, Gordon had left New York. And the last he'd heard, the investigation was now under the nominal direction of Ron Cochi, pending either Gordon's or Fallon's return. Gordon imagined that Cochi was scared out of his wits to have to hold down a position of such responsibility. But practically speaking, he was responsible for nothing more than monitoring the screen of the Hewlett-Packard computer for whatever new information might be forthcoming from Atlanta. Without permission to take the investigation into Shadow Pines, there was really nothing the CDC could do.

It was the absence of any movement that prompted Gordon to come to the resort himself. He was acting without authorization. Also, he was employing an alias, having no wish to alert Koppleman to his presence here.

He'd had no problem in renting a room like any other vacationer to Shadow Pines. But he was disappointed to learn that he could stay for only three days; afterward everything was booked because of the upcoming Northeast Classic.

Somewhere on the grounds he believed he would find the evidence Valdespino required to circumvent Ned Hollister and appeal directly to the governor. Unfortunately, three days was not a lot of time.

Gordon was in no position to start asking questions of the people he met. Any suspicious behavior on his part would speedily come to the attention of the management—and inevitably Stanley Koppleman himself. With preparations for the golf tournament getting underway, security was more ubiquitous than ever. A small army of private bodyguards and at least a dozen secret service men with dead-serious looks on their faces and transmitters in their ears had been added to the regular security staff.

But Gordon didn't believe that the reinforced security made for an insurmountable problem. The real danger that threatened him was inside himself and had only grown worse since his visit to Jessie's room the previous morning. He'd come hoping for some sign from her that there still remained something between them. But he'd gone away convinced that any attempt he made toward reconciliation would be useless.

It was better he put her out of his mind, out of his life; otherwise she would distract him from his true purpose. The bitterness would eventually poison him if he let it.

In his more generous moments he would think that maybe, after all, she was better off with someone like Larry Fallon, a man who was younger and exceedingly ambitious, who would in advancing his career eventually pull down a salary much larger than Gordon could ever hope to.

So he resolved to concentrate on just one thing: to conclusively prove that the virus had been here and might be here still.

As he circulated through the resort, he found that there was nothing abnormal or the least bit out of place. He observed no one with twitching limbs, incapable of standing; he noticed no one behaving oddly or with unexpected violence. To his practiced eye nothing in the vicinity of the kitchens or the public gathering places seemed to hint at unsanitary conditions. Nor did he discover an environment that pests, either insects or rodents, would find inviting. He did see a couple of men in white outfits lugging around exterminating equipment, but he didn't think that this meant anything unusual; their visits were probably routine.

After two days of hunting and poking around he'd come up with nothing. The only part of the resort that he hadn't taken a look at was the section reserved for the VIPs. But he shortly learned that there was a way in—a legitimate way—if he was prepared to fork over a tidy sum of cash to do it.

There were two golf courses on the grounds of the resort; the larger one was located on the other side of the artificial lake. Designed by a protégé of Donald Ross's who created the famous Oakland Hills course in Michigan, this eighteen-hole course was one of the main attractions of Shadow Pines. As such, it was open to any guest. The only difference was that the VIPs could use it free while the less celebrated and well-heeled had to pay. With no other opportunities available, Gordon signed up for three the next afternoon, the only time that was still not taken.

The following afternoon, when the sun was at its most scorching, Gordon found himself with his rented clubs standing twenty-five yards from the third hole. From the literature he'd been given, this hole was heavily lipped with rough grass and filled with fine light-brown sand. He had no idea what to make of this information. His problem was that he was a bad golfer, an abysmal golfer. He couldn't stand the game.

The fairway extended several thousand feet, bordered on one side by a woods planted with a variety of trees—red maples, crimson king maples, Norway maples, walnuts, pines, green ash, and blue spruce. Except for one other golfer, receding from view in his electrified blue golf cart, Gordon was alone.

Beyond the woods were twenty guest cottages. Although he was certain he wouldn't be allowed to get too close to them, he still thought it worth a try. Whipping his three-iron, he attempted to put the ball somewhere among the trees. It didn't work. He selected a number four iron, driving the ball far enough to lose sight of it among the pines and green ash. Then he pretended to go off in search of it. Although he could see no one anywhere around him, that did not necessarily mean he wasn't being watched.

The woods didn't go on very far before culminating in a row of six-foot-high hedges, absurdly fashioned by the resort's gardeners into a bewildering variety of shapes, with particular emphasis on spheres and ovoids. Beyond the perimeter they defined, stretched a lush green lawn, cut so evenly that it was conceivable that it had been done by some poor slob down on his hands and knees with a scissors. Four guesthouses, each of two floors, of oak and blocks of finely chiseled stone, came into view. Gordon couldn't see anyone at first, but he could hear voices through the screens. Human voices or radio voices.

After perhaps ten minutes had passed a man emerged from the rear door of the house nearest him. He had a slightly furtive air and he hurried down the steps leading from the sundeck and was soon gone from sight. But the quick glimpse of him that Gordon had was enough; it was Representative Trent Bradstock.

Well, he thought, this little adventure of his might not draw him any closer to tracking down the virus, but it was not without its interest.

Ten minutes later another visitor showed up at the guesthouse: Stanley Koppleman. Gordon wondered who the occupant was who was proving so popular this afternoon.

He had his answer in a moment. A woman, spectacularly proportioned, with magnificent red hair the color of fire, appeared at the screen door. Her skin glistened with water; a towel was wrapped around her midsection. A post-Bradstock shower, thought Gordon.

She and Koppleman exchanged a few words before the woman allowed him to enter.

After that nothing happened. Gordon waited as long as he felt there was no danger in doing so. But he realized that someone would eventually come looking for him and, reluctantly, put an end to his vigil.

By the time he returned to his room it was nearly five o'clock. This was his last evening, and for all his trouble he'd come up with nothing except that Trent Bradstock consorted with prostitutes—for that was what he believed the redhead to be.

Rather than stay in his room as he'd done the last two nights, he decided to explore the bars and restaurants. Perhaps he would find something that had so far eluded him.

He saved the Saturn Discotheque until last. The decibel level was painful; the dazzling frenzy of lights that kept shooting through the room began to make him dizzy.

The dancers were young and fresh and tan and seemed to have come from another world. He smelled their perfume and their sweat.

In the corner farthest from him, repeatedly brought into the light by the strobe, Gordon spied the woman he'd seen earlier that afternoon. She was in a China blue dress, slit way up to her thigh, with a neckline that dropped nearly to her navel. Her dancing was hypnotic, her legs moving with such speed as to defy the eye to follow them. Her face had a glazed, inward look as though she were lost in a world of her own; no communication of any kind seemed to be going on with her partner.

Gordon decided to wait; eventually, when she sat down, he would try to talk to her. Surely, any friend of Trent Bradstock and Stanley Koppleman must have a few interesting stories to tell.

thirty-nine

Her name was Morgan Lee. It was also Noelle Lee. It was also Penny Hunter, Michelle Drummond, Tracy Fairchild, and Kim Sazarak. She was a redhead, a honey blonde, auburn-haired, and brunette. She was an actress, a hairstylist, a fashion designer, a buyer for a department store, a model, a dancer, and a graphics artist. She was twenty-five years old and what she was most afraid of was growing old in a hurry. What she was doing was growing old in a hurry.

Before Stanley Koppleman had discovered her, she'd been an exotic dancer. She liked to think of herself as an exotic dancer anyhow but, when translated, all *exotic dancer* worked out to be was a topless-bottomless dancer at a New York club that no longer existed. It was a club downtown on the East Side; the men who came there, who were usually not as sleazy as she would have suspected, would give her money, sometimes generous amounts of it, to reward her for her efforts. She didn't like to disappoint them as some of the other girls did, going through the motions. She believed that her tips would work out better if she put some energy into what she was doing. And it helped. The tips *were* better. By the end of each set she would find up to a hundred dollars thrown her way or slipped into her crack. No question, enthusiasm paid off.

But the money she'd received then was nothing like what she was making now. Wherever she went she traveled first class; and if the men she fucked were as twisted in their tastes as the ones she took upstairs for twenty bucks between sets, they were much happier to part with their cash.

Koppleman was her protector; he was also her pimp. They had never fucked. Koppleman had a wife to whom he was faithful, but Morgan didn't think that this was because of any bizarre notion of fidelity on his part; more likely, he wasn't interested in other women. Or any woman at all. Power was his trip; Morgan recognized that from her first meeting. She knew enough about power to understand when a man was infected by it, when there was nothing else in the whole world that meant as much.

Koppleman sent her all over. Sometimes he would instruct her to pick up certain men and tell them stories about herself. Sometimes he would tell her to try to obtain specific information. Other times it didn't seem to matter to him what she did, whom she laid or gave a hundred-dollar blowjob to.

Well, it was all right with her. Sooner or later she would put enough together so that she could buy a house in the country somewhere and settle down. She had an idea that she would find a man who had nothing twisted or crazed about him, who would buy one of her stories, think of her as a model or an actress, or anything that wasn't a call girl, and marry her.

She'd been married once. She'd met him while working in Boston at the Ritz Carlton—another one of Koppleman's contracts. He told her he was an explorer. She didn't believe him. She didn't think that there was such a thing anymore. She told him that the world had already been explored enough and that maybe he ought to think of getting into another line of work. He'd liked that, he found her highly amusing. His name was Will Ziegler and it turned out that he really was an explorer.

Given how much they were both on the road, they didn't get to see a great deal of each other. But they kept in touch. Or rather she kept in touch, for it was seldom that Will wrote or called. But then one day, without warning, he'd turn up, bringing her souvenirs from someplace she'd never heard of, regaling her with stories that coming from anyone else she wouldn't have believed for two seconds. But with Will she believed; she bought his stories hook, line, and sinker.

It wasn't just souvenirs and stories he brought her. Now and then he would make a gift of some strange drug he'd picked up on his travels, assuring her that she never experienced anything like it before. He'd be right. These drugs would make her hallucinate like crazy. One time he told her that he had something special, but that the only way to take it was by drinking piss.

Now, Morgan had done many kinky things in her life—it went with the territory—but there were some things that she refused to do, and one of them was drink piss.

Meantime Koppleman was taking an ever greater interest in Will Ziegler. When he learned that Will was on his way to Peru and Bolivia, he proposed that they might work out an "arrangement." Will agreed, claiming that he could bring back several hundred thousand dollars' worth of the purest cocaine Koppleman had ever tasted. Koppleman said that he wasn't interested in it for himself, but that he needed it for his clients.

"Your clients are probably used to shit," Morgan remembered Will saying. "They won't know what to do when this stuff hits them."

To which Koppleman had replied, "We'll see how long it takes for them to get used to it."

Everything had gone splendidly until the night of May eighteenth. That was the night Will flew in from Boston in his Cessna to deliver the half million worth of toot. He was planning to land at a small airstrip adjacent to the resort.

She had not been at Shadow Pines that night. But Koppleman described it to her: first, the sound of the plane slamming into the mountain, causing all the windows of the lodge to rattle; then, the bright orange glow above the ridge of the mountain—"just like Halloween," he said.

Koppleman never told anyone that he knew who the pilot was. He only talked to her about the incident. "I thought that the bastard knew how to fly," he would say.

It was as if he believed that Will had crashed just to spite him. "A complete write-off," he concluded, referring not to Will, who was as expendable as anyone else, but to the half million he'd already shelled out for the toot that he would now never get his hands on.

Even though three months had passed since Will went down, Morgan still hadn't recovered from the shock of his death. She'd built him up so much in her mind that it was still hard for her to believe that he could be so easily destroyed. She no longer derived any pleasure at all when she came up here to work the Northeast Classic. It was just a job. All she could ever think about when she looked toward that mountain was the glow from Will's burning plane. In some way, she realized, she kept having the feeling that he wasn't actually dead, that one day she would hear the drone of his Cessna and raise her eyes to the sky and see it pass over the peak of Mount Sycamore.

Tonight was one of the last she would spend by herself until the tournament ended. Three other girls were working with her, but they were new recruits of Koppleman's and she wasn't looking for any more friends. God knows, she had enough friends. So she'd come out dancing on her own; it was one of the few ways she knew of to lose herself. Work up a good sweat in the motion and the music, what else mattered?

When her legs began to buckle and give way and her throat was aching for a drink, she left the dance floor and fought her way through to the bar. The man standing next to her was studying her.

"What are you staring at?"

"You're a friend of Stanley Koppleman, aren't you?" he said.

He was tall, she noticed, and not bad-looking, but his eyes held such intensity that they made her uncomfortable.

"That's a strange line to use for a come-on." She ordered a Seabreeze and slipped away from the bar. The man followed.

"I'd like to introduce myself."

She was off-duty tonight; she saw no reason to be particularly polite. "Most men would."

"My name is Gordon Markoff. I'm with the Centers for Disease Control."

This gave her pause. Then she said, "Well, I suppose everybody's got to make a living."

"I'd like to ask you a few questions—in confidence."

"What is this, some kind of survey like that guy Gallup does?"

"If you care to think of it that way, yes."

"What do I get out of it?"

"Maybe your life."

She didn't like the way this conversation was developing at all. "Sorry, but I've had a long day. I think I'm going to bed now."

"There is a very insidious and lethal virus present on the

grounds of this resort. It is being spread by mosquitoes," Markoff explained.

A whacko, Morgan thought, a complete lunatic. "I told you I have to go."

Markoff proved a persistent son of a bitch. As she walked out of the disco he kept abreast of her. "What this disease does is attack the mind; it rots it out in a few weeks and causes people to act violently before they collapse and die."

She began to quicken her pace, thinking that whoever this guy was, he must get his jollies from terrifying single women. But she decided that she had nothing to worry about. The grounds were well-lit and as soon as she came to the bridge that led to the restricted part of the compound the security guards there would detain him.

"Listen," he said, his voice growing more demanding, "your friend Koppleman is trying to conceal evidence of this virus. But already there have been at least a dozen people from here who've come down with it. There'll be more unless we shut the place down."

Morgan recalled seeing a young woman—a housemaid—a couple of days ago who could hardly stand. She was outside one of the guest cottages, her whole body shaking convulsively. She also recalled overhearing Koppleman discuss a decapitation, something to do with one of the cooks. At the time she'd assumed that he was talking about a scene from a movie or a TV show he'd seen. Supposing, though, it had actually happened? It was possible she'd be able to come up with all sorts of stories of interest to this man. Maybe he was for real.

But then she thought: *Why should I help him?* All she would be doing was putting herself at risk if Koppleman found out she'd said anything.

"Sorry, Mr. Markoff, I wish you a lot of luck, but there's nothing I can tell you."

They were approaching the restricted section of the resort. She spotted two figures in the darkness—security men.

"You don't believe me, do you?" he said.

"It's not that I don't believe you. But I really can't help you, it's as simple as that."

"Look, just last week we located the source of this virus. It was submerged in a lake around the other side of that mountain." He pointed to Mount Sycamore which stood silhouetted against a sky full of whatever constellations came out in late August. Somebody had told her once what they were, but she had forgotten.

"What was it? The source I mean."

"The body of a pilot who crashed a few months ago."

"Will," she said.

"What did you say?"

"Nothing. Listen, really, I have to go."

She was about to break into a run when he grasped her wrist. "If something—anything—should come to mind call me at home or this number. It's a service. I'll call you back within twenty minutes, guaranteed."

A card was pressed into her palm. "All right . . . well, thanks."

Then she was gone, back over the bridge into the restricted area where the Kopplemans of the world ruled and where the Markoffs of the world could not enter.

She couldn't sleep. As much as she tried to remember what Will looked like, the only image that came to mind was a maggot-infested body floating on the surface of a mountain lake, mosquitoes gathering up a virus from his putrescent flesh. She felt contaminated, leprous. Bad enough that she'd had to worry about the clap and herpes and AIDS.

She reached for the phone and dialed the number Markoff had given her. *He wants a story,* she thought, *he's going to get one.*

forty

There was no question in Ned Hollister's mind why Stanley Koppleman was so insistent about seeing him. He felt an obligation and had made room for him on his appointment calender. He was praying that Koppleman decided at the last minute to cancel. The closer the hour of his appointment approached, the more jittery he became.

"No phone calls," he instructed his secretary over the intercom.

At three forty he began pacing, unable to concentrate on any work. Four o'clock was when Koppleman would appear, and Koppleman was always infuriatingly punctual.

There was no indication either in his expression or in his manner that the attorney was the least bit put out. But then he was never one to betray his emotions.

It was the next to last day in August, chilly and gray. If Hollister was looking for a favorable portent, it was not to be found in the meteorological conditions.

Koppleman took a seat. He lit a cigarette with a gold Dunhill lighter and said something to the effect that his doctor had told him he would be better advised not to smoke them. Hollister had the feeling that he meant this remark as a kind of joke, something to break the ice.

"So I gather from what you told me over the phone that you plan to let the CDC investigators into Shadow Pines." Nothing in Koppleman's voice hinted at any displeasure, but Hollister knew it was there.

"I'm afraid there's nothing I can do to stop them. The man who's heading up the investigation in Atlanta received the go-ahead from the governor. Apparently, he's gotten hold of some very persuasive information."

"Any idea what that information might be?"

"I wish I could tell you."

"I assume you don't know what the source of this information was either."

"I told you, it's all gone beyond me at this point. I'm out of it. I'm sure I'm going to be called on the carpet for what I've done for you already." He hoped that he might somehow enlist Koppleman's sympathy, make him understand how far he'd extended himself.

Koppleman waited for a few moments, appearing to consider his answer. Then he said, "Well, I find this most regrettable."

"Mr. Koppleman, you must understand that there was nothing I could do."

He could hear the strain in his voice, how close he was to losing control, and knew that Koppleman could detect it too.

"I understand."

For an instant Hollister thought that this was his way of saying that he was off the hook, but then he realized this wasn't the case at all.

"You know, I told you what I would do if you failed to keep the CDC's investigators off the grounds of Shadow Pines."

"Now, wait just a minute—"

Koppleman refused to allow him to finish. "In my business, when an arrangement is reached, that's it. I don't expect anyone to abrogate terms that have been mutually agreed upon."

Fighting to keep the panic out of his voice, Hollister reminded him that he could guarantee just so much. "Don't you remember what I said at that first meeting?"

"I remember. And I remember telling you what would happen if those investigators disrupted the start of the Northeast Classic. Since it appears that they will do just that, I am afraid I have no alternative but to do what I said I would." He paused, then added, "I expect you'll be interested to see what the New York *Post* says about you tomorrow."

Hollister slumped down in his chair, thinking it extraordinary that the day he'd long dreaded had finally come. "There's no way that the story can be stopped?"

"Not unless the CDC investigation is stopped."

As this was something that Hollister could no longer exert

any control over, the question was moot. "Well then," he said resignedly, "I don't suppose there is anything else to discuss."

Koppleman agreed. "Remember, Dr. Hollister, I am a man of my word."

"I'll bear that in mind, but I rather doubt that we'll be doing any further business together."

Koppleman turned back at the door and said, "Think of it this way—we've both lost."

The following morning, August 31, Hollister did what no one expected him to do and showed up for work. It was not so much an act of courage as one of defiance. He did not, however, buy his morning paper as he regularly did, certain that by now the *Post* story would have been picked up by papers all over the state and very possibly by the wire services.

He still held out hope that, for some reason, the story hadn't run, but that hope was dashed by his first caller of the morning, a man he hadn't heard from for quite some time named Sal West who used to work for the Thoroughbred Racing Association. "They've got it all down, Ned," he began. "You're fucked and so are a few of your friends. It's one thing if you want to fuck yourself over. We have no problem with that. But you fuck your friends, hey, that's a different matter."

The threat was unmistakable. Hollister hung up on him and gathered enough courage to look at the morning's papers left on his desk. He saw that he had made not only the *Post*, but the *Times* and the *News* as well as the Albany *Union-News*. Not all of the facts were right, but it scarcely mattered. The thrust of each story was largely the same: how the acting head of the state health department had assisted "criminal elements," as they were termed, in fixing races at the Monmouth Handicap, the Jockey Club Gold Cup, the Pennsylvania Derby, and the Travers. It also detailed how he'd used furosemide, a diuretic that can control hemorrhaging but can also improve a horse's performance, as well as painkillers like phenylbutazone to keep horses going long after they should have been retired—and this was only the beginning. The allegations grew more serious as he read on. Not all of them could be proved, but the conclusion was inescapable: he was finished.

Even so, he might have managed to escape with a year or two in a minimum-security prison like Danberry. But the problem was that others were implicated along with him, people like Sal West who would not forget or allow him to slip gracefully into obscurity.

He stepped over to the door and secured the lock. Then he went to the windows and drew the blinds. Unlocking his top desk drawer he extracted a .32 automatic that he'd been licensed to carry.

He raised the gun to his head and cocked it. Just before pulling the trigger, he realized that this might be the first time in his entire life that he had not waffled or shown any sign of hesitation.

forty-one

On the same day that Ned Hollister took his life, Stanley Koppleman flew to Atlanta. It was five o'clock when he arrived, giving him only an hour and a half before the six thirty sitting at Nikolai's Roof. For others a month or more might be necessary in order to reserve a table at Nikolai's, but a few hours' notice was all that Koppleman required. It always helped to have connections wherever you went. He trusted that his dinner guest would be suitably impressed.

In spite of the rush-hour traffic that clogged the roads from the airport into the city, he had no trouble getting to the restaurant in time to spare himself a reproving glance from the maitre d'. His guest showed up a few minutes later.

"It's a pleasure to meet you, Dr. Fallon," Koppleman said.

Fallon, his face still bruised, using a cane to help him walk, apologized for his condition. "I assure you that I've looked better than this."

"I heard about what happened during that storm. You were fortunate to escape with your life from what I understand."

After they'd taken their seats Fallon said he'd heard quite a lot about the attorney.

This did not come as any surprise. "I presume Mr. Markoff briefed you about our meeting in New York."

"Actually, I wasn't even aware the two of you had met. Gordon and I haven't been in touch for a while."

Perhaps because of Mrs. Markoff, thought Koppleman.

"So where have you derived your information about me?"

"From the papers. There was that piece in the Washington *Post*."

"Oh yes, that one. It made me out to be quite a brigand, didn't it? Unscrupulous and corrupt. I took them to court."

"What was the resolution?"

"It's still being litigated. These things have a way of going on forever."

Koppleman was in no hurry to get down to business. Having lured Fallon here with a vague intimation that his client was willing to cooperate with the CDC's investigation, he saw no need to immediately satisfy his curiosity. "I recommend you try either the faisant à la Normandie or the tournedos Esterhazz. Neither will disappoint you."

Fallon thanked him for his advice, but went ahead and ordered the canard au muscadet.

Evidently Fallon, too, subscribed to the belief that nothing truly serious could be discussed before coffee.

It was Fallon who first broached the subject. "You said over the phone that Shadow Pines might open its facilities to our investigators."

"If you recall, I said that my client—that is, the parent company, Wisdom-Templar—might consider the idea and that I would have to check and see. Well, I have checked and unfortunately, my client's position has not changed."

Fallon didn't appear to be disconcerted. "At this point, Mr. Koppleman, I don't think it really matters. The governor has indicated that he is prepared to intervene on behalf of the CDC. I don't know whether you've seen the papers today—"

"You mean about poor Dr. Hollister. A terrible shame."

"I suspect that whoever the governor appoints to replace him will also go along with us."

"That is entirely possible."

"I'm not sure I understand why you wanted to see me if you have nothing new to offer." There was a trace of irritation in Fallon's voice; perhaps he thought he was wasting time.

Ignoring his remark Koppleman said, "I'm informed that sometime this weekend you and Mr. Markoff and other colleagues of yours will decide whether to run a story about my client in the Morbidity and Mortality Weekly Report."

Fallon confirmed that the subject would be discussed at a meeting set for tomorrow morning—Saturday. At that time a decision would be made whether to publish a story linking the resort with the spread of the virus. If the decision was positive then it would appear the following Monday.

Koppleman was uncomfortably aware of the publicity that such news items in the MMWR could generate. Every Monday representatives of the media would gather at the CDC headquarters on Clifton Road in anticipation of an important story like this. Should Shadow Pines be implicated by the CDC on Monday, the rest of the country would know about it on Tuesday. In many ways this would be far more damaging than having half a dozen epidemiologists on the grounds of the resort.

"I realize it might be a violation of confidentiality for you to reveal how you intend to vote," Koppleman said.

"Not at all, Mr. Koppleman. I see no reason why I can't tell you. The preponderance of the evidence we've collected so far leads me to think that Shadow Pines may constitute a public safety hazard. More to the point, I believe that several of its employees may have been stricken with the virus—cases which should have been reported to the CDC and, unaccountably, were not."

Nothing Fallon said made an impression on Koppleman. It was, more or less, what he'd expected to hear. "As long as we're being honest, have you come up with any smoking gun? Something that would prove, beyond any doubt, that the virus might have spread to the resort?"

"We have a great deal of circumstantial evidence that would lead us to believe that it is. Had your client been more cooperative in the first place, we wouldn't have to be going through all this. If, as you say, the resort doesn't present a hazard we could have inspected it and that would have been the end of it. Your client's behavior has been rather suspect. Even you will have to admit that much."

Koppleman liked what he was hearing. "You are obfuscating, Dr. Fallon. You won't answer my question."

"All right, we don't have any smoking gun, as you put it."

"I won't burden you with statistics, but our resort employs hundreds of workers, providing a much-needed infusion of capital into an area of New York State that could certainly use it. Not to mention the millions of dollars that our guests pour into the local economy. If you publish this highly speculative story you will be hurting far more people than you perhaps realize."

"We don't take something like this lightly, I assure you, Mr. Koppleman."

"One of those people you might be hurting, by the way, is yourself."

"Would you mind repeating that?"

Koppleman began to elaborate. "I am told that you are under consideration for an important position in the Health and Human Services Department. I am told that it has come down to a choice between you and one other person."

"I'll take your word for it."

Koppleman could tell that his dinner guest was trying not to reveal his astonishment. "I would be delighted to see you get the job. I can also guarantee that it will be yours should you reconsider your vote tomorrow."

Fallon bristled. He looked ready to storm out of the restaurant.

"Before you say anything, Dr. Fallon, let me also remind you that I can make sure that you do not get the appointment. Moreover, I can see to it that your position at the CDC is made untenable. No, don't leave—not before you understand exactly what is at stake. Before doing anything rash, take a look at this." Koppleman took out a photograph, the same snapshot that Markoff had been presented with. "This is only one in a series, by the way. I apologize for the quality of the print, but it was a little underexposed, I'm afraid."

Fallon wasn't listening. The blood drained from his face and his hands were shaking so much it was a wonder he could hold on to the photograph.

"And I needn't tell you what this could do to Mrs. Markoff's career—and reputation at the CDC," Koppleman went on.

"You bastard, you fucking bastard," was about all that Fallon could get out before he tore the picture in half and rushed from the restaurant.

Satisfied that he'd gotten his money's worth, Koppleman presented his gold card to the waiter. "The service was excellent," he said, leaving a generous tip.

forty-two

When the phone rang Jessie was just getting ready for bed. It was only nine o'clock in the evening, but this was her first day back home and she found she was tiring easily.

It was Gordon.

She was so surprised to hear from him that the first thing that came into her mind was to ask where he was. Wrong question.

"I can't tell you that over the phone."

With all that had happened to her in the last week, she'd forgotten about the subpoena and the FBI. Still, it shocked her to think that there might be a tap on their phone. She wondered whether the strange clicks she'd heard when she'd made some calls earlier in the day had signaled the presence of a tap.

There was a small silence during which it seemed that both of them were waiting for the other to say something.

"It's good to hear from you, Gordon."

And it truly was; she didn't like the idea that there was no communication between them. That didn't mean, however, that she still didn't feel awkward and nervous. Very nervous.

"I think we should talk."

About what? About getting back together? About a trial separation? About a divorce? She didn't have the heart to ask.

"All right. When?"

She wasn't certain how to go about making arrangements with him, not with the FBI listening in.

"Tomorrow. Do you remember where we used to meet when we were dating?"

She remembered; it hadn't been that long ago. It was always the lobby of the Hyatt, by the fountain.

"What time?"

"Same time as always."

She assumed that must mean five o'clock. He would invariably be late and she used to sit for an hour, occupying herself with a book, growing furious with him while at the same time doing her best to understand that his life was one of constant interruption and emergency meetings, and that if she wanted promptness she would just have to find someone else to go out with.

Almost as an afterthought he asked her whether she felt well enough to travel.

"That won't be a problem," she said, although she suspected that, in fact, she wasn't quite up to driving into town. But it was important enough, so she figured she could make it.

"I have to go now, Jessie. Take care."

"I will. Good night, Gordon."

She'd wished him good night because it seemed better, and much less final, than saying good -bye.

As she suspected, she couldn't sleep. She lay in bed and stared up at the ceiling, noticing even in the dimness a welter of cracks in it that had escaped her attention before. She got up and padded barefoot into the bathroom, deliberating as to whether to take a Valium, having forty minutes before taken a prescription drug to knock out the pain. She didn't know about the drug; it alleviated some of the pain, most notably in her hip, but did nothing to temper the ache in her arms or the soreness in her right collarbone.

She took the Valium anyway, but she had the sense that it would be quite some while before calm descended on her. Thinking that soaking in the tub might make her more sleepy, she began running the water.

Over the sound of the water she thought she heard something, a small disturbance. She turned off the taps and listened with heightened awareness. She could hear nothing, not even the crickets, whose interminable chorus drifted into the bedroom every night in this season. Drawing the bathroom door ajar, she still could hear nothing.

I'm too spooked, she thought, *hearing things that aren't there*.

She went ahead and took her bath, then put on a filmy gown Gordon had once bought for her and daubed herself with some toilet water if for no other reason than she had an idea it might change her mood.

As soon as she stepped out of the bathroom, though, she knew something was wrong. She went back into the bedroom, shutting the door behind her.

He's back. The same man who'd broken into the house before and vandalized her office. She didn't know how she knew this, but she knew. Something in the room had changed; she was not alone. She noticed the bit of mud on the floor; tracked in by the intruder.

She scarcely had the time to make this observation when she was seized from behind. One hand cupped her breast through the gown, the other pressed in against her stomach. She screamed and the hand moved from her breast to her mouth. She bit into it as hard as she could, registering with some satisfaction a cry of pain from her antagonist. At the same time she used her right elbow to jab him in the chest. Although she failed to do him any harm, she succeeded in freeing herself of his hold.

Turning, she caught sight of his face, but it wasn't his face that distinguished him so much as it was his hair, blond on one side and white on the other, parted straight down the middle.

As he advanced toward her she had a glimpse of something glinting in his hand—a hypodermic needle. Desperately she grabbed the first solid object she could lay her hands on, hoping to stun him with it long enough to give her time to flee.

From the top of her dresser, she took the ancient statue Larry had bought for her from Joe Hunting Bear—the earth goddess—and swung it at the man, catching him on the side of his shoulder. The force of her motion caused it to fly from her hands and crash to the floor.

As it shattered, a cloud of white powder rose into the air. The sight was so astonishing that even the man paused for an instant to stare at it. But so had she. And in those few seconds she was distracted, the man regained his hold over her, simultaneously plunging the hypodermic into her arm.

Just before she blacked out she realized that the white substance stuffed inside the statue was cocaine. A fortune in cocaine.

forty-three

Early Saturday morning Gordon slipped, unnoticed, into the CDC compound on Clifton Road. He took the long way around to get to the office of Max Beaumont, the long-time editor of the Morbidity and Mortality Weekly Report, using one of the buildings adjoining Building 1 to get there. He chose his route so that it would lead him into areas where a computerized access card was required to enter. Gordon reasoned that if he were being followed by federal agents or one of Koppleman's people, they would be effectively blocked off, and in that way would lose track of him.

Joining Beaumont this morning to discuss the subject of the virus was the deputy director of the CDC, Albert Thacker, and Lou Valdespino and Larry Fallon. And, of course, Gordon himself.

As far as Gordon could see, the decision to publish was a foregone conclusion. The stories he'd heard from Morgan Lee had been sufficiently credible to convince even Valdespino. Her account, coupled with the other evidence the investigating team had collected, was enough, he believed, to sway both Thacker and Beaumont in the event that either was wavering.

For nearly a decade Max had edited the MMWR. Prior to that, he'd worked out of the Division of Surveillance and Epidemiologic Studies, a division entrusted with the task of gathering statistics which would eventually be used in the MMWR. Well past seventy now, Max had the crusty, slightly dour air of a Shakespearean actor, someone suitable for the role of Lear. Thacker, by contrast, had the thoughtful, reserved aspect of a high school physics teacher whose classes everyone hoped to get out of.

All the others were there when Gordon arrived. He gave a curt nod and took a seat as far from Larry Fallon as he could. It was an effort not to look at him, but he managed.

He was acutely aware of the curiosity he'd aroused, but he didn't allow it to disturb him. God knows, people had expressed curiosity about him many times before. Still, he couldn't escape the feeling that some kind of stigma had attached itself to him, a very real physical mark branded upon his flesh, which everyone else could see and he couldn't.

Yet no mention was made of the subcommittee hearings or the subpoena that hung over his head. Each man seemed to go out of his way to act normally; the only hint that something might be amiss came from Fallon, who sat stiffly in his chair, his whole posture unnaturally rigid.

Valdespino moderated the proceedings, beginning with a summation of the virus's history. "At this point we have forty-one confirmed cases and at least a dozen unconfirmed. Of the forty-one, twenty-eight have died. So far, all efforts to cure or arrest the virus have failed to show any positive results. The course of the disease appears to be inexorable."

He went on to say that certain experimental drugs, some of them exotic and available only through the auspices of the CDC, were being tried on victims of the virus, including HLA-23, which was being used with sufferers from Creutzfeldt-Jakob syndrome. "But it is too premature to say whether these drugs will be any more effective than those that have already been employed and found wanting."

At this point Valdespino touched on the locations of the outbreaks, where there were clusters of victims and not just an isolated case or two. "Up until now there have been two confirmed sites of the viral spread. One is in the Catskills, in the vicinity of Brown Station; the other, in the Boston area."

"We have some news about Boston, don't we?" interjected Thacker.

"I was just getting to that," the field director said. "For several weeks following the initial cluster of cases—Atwater, Leiter and Chong—we received no reports of any further occurrence of the virus."

It struck Gordon as curious that Valdespino neglected to mention the destruction of the specimens from those cases, although he supposed that the incident was too fresh in everyone's minds to bear repeating.

"However, five new cases have been documented in the

past several days in the Boston area. Specifically from a lower-class neighborhood just south of the town of Milton. So far we haven't succeeded in tracing the source of the infection, but the Boston health department is looking into it and I would expect that some of our own investigators will be asked to assist their efforts within the week."

This disclosure came as a surprise to Gordon. Having absented himself from the CDC for so many days, he'd been unaware of any new outbreak. But his intuition told him that there had to be some connection between the Milton cases and the original three.

It was at this point that Valdespino turned his attention to the business at hand, saying, "In addition to the two sites I've already mentioned, there is good reason to believe that a third site of the outbreak exists as well. As you are all aware, this site is the Catskills resort of Shadow Pines. My office has been assured by the governor of New York that surveillance can begin at the resort early next week to see whether or not it constitutes a public health hazard.

"However, evidence already gathered by our investigators in and around the resort indicates that a hazard is in fact present, that several individuals, particularly among members of the staff employed by the resort, have been stricken with the virus. The possibility of a cover-up in this matter, by Shadow Pines and its parent company, Wisdom-Templar, cannot be ruled out, either. What we must decide here today, gentlemen, is whether we wait for the relevant studies in the field to be completed or whether we immediately go ahead with a story in the MMWR linking the resort to the virus."

No sooner had he opened up the question for discussion than the phone on Max Beaumont's desk began to ring. Strange timing, Gordon thought.

Beaumont answered, then looked across the room at Gordon. "It's for you," he said. "You can take it in there," indicating an adjoining office.

Since Gordon had told no one that he'd be present at this meeting, he suspected that whoever was calling was no one he cared to hear from.

He didn't recognize the voice on the other end; it was a man who sounded as far away as the moon.

"I have your wife," he said simply. Before Gordon could

respond, the man put Jessie on. She called his name and tried to say something more, but she was abruptly cut off. The man said, "I suggest that if you don't wish to see her harmed you vote against publication. We'll know what you do."

Then he broke off. Immediately Gordon called home. Busy. He dialed the operator and was informed that there was trouble on the line.

He thought to phone the police, then decided that would only place Jessie in more danger than she was already. He called New York information and obtained the number of Koppleman's firm. According to his secretary, he was out of town.

Although Gordon wanted to leave the meeting, he knew that that wouldn't do much good either. And by not voting, he might also be putting Jessie at risk. He went back into the other office.

"Is anything wrong?" Valdespino asked.

"Nothing," Gordon mumbled, taking his seat.

For the next several minutes not a word that was spoken registered on his consciousness. Asked to comment, he deferred to Fallon, adding that everything he had to contribute was already contained in documentation submitted earlier to Valdespino.

The surprise generated by his refusal was inevitable, but there was nothing to be done about it. Gordon had lost his heart for the whole affair.

Fallon himself had little to offer, confining himself to a brief recitation of the facts, declining to voice his own opinion as to their meaning.

Thacker and Beaumont were becoming increasingly mystified by the responses of the two men most responsible for presenting the case against Shadow Pines in the first place.

"Neither of you sounds too positive about this," noted Thacker.

"I think that the facts speak for themselves," Fallon said.

"What was that?" Beaumont asked, leaning toward him. "I'm afraid I didn't quite catch what you said."

And no wonder; Fallon's voice was so soft. It occurred to Gordon that Koppleman had gotten to him, too; how else to explain his uneasiness? At the same time the kidnapper's last words came back to him: "We'll know what you do."

Although it might have been an empty threat, it was equally possible that the room was bugged. Yet, no matter how he tried to resolve the matter in his own mind, he was so shaken, so crazed with fear for Jessie, that he couldn't see his way clear to know what he should do—or which way to vote.

"If no one has anything more to add," Valdespino said, "I think we should get to the vote."

He began with Fallon. Fallon said he just wanted another minute to look at Gordon's report which he was holding in his hand.

There was no question: Koppleman had gotten to him.

Valdespino was going around the room in order. Puzzled by Fallon's equivocal response, he addressed Thacker.

"The evidence seems persuasive enough," Thacker said. "I vote we go with the story."

"Max?"

"I'm afraid I have to disagree. We have two men here who have been out in the field and from what I've heard today neither seems very convinced. I wouldn't like to take the responsibility of closing down this resort without substantiation from our investigators. Let's wait and see what their findings are. That's only a week away."

By which time the Northeast Classic will have been played and Koppleman will have won, reflected Gordon.

"So that's a no?"

"That's a no," Beaumont said.

"What about you, Gordon?"

After a moment's hesitation Gordon told him that he needed a couple more minutes. For the first time Fallon looked directly at him. A certain understanding passed between the two men.

"Is there something wrong, Gordon?"

"I just would like a minute or so more, that's all."

"Well," he said, directing his eyes first at Fallon and then back at Gordon, "if it will make things easier for you two gentlemen, I will vote yes."

At that moment, almost as if that was all the encouragement he needed, Fallon said, "I realize that I have previously favored running this story Monday, but after reviewing this material, I question whether this woman, Sheila L., is really a credible witness."

The woman he was alluding to was Morgan Lee. Gordon had used an alias to protect her privacy and possibly her life.

Baffled and annoyed, Valdespino asked Fallon if this meant he was casting a negative vote.

"I just think it's better we hold off. Let's give it a week until we see what our EIS people come up with after their surveillance of the resort."

The bastard, Gordon thought. It was one thing to succumb to whatever pressure Koppleman had applied to him—and he assumed it had something to do with the compromising photos—but it was quite another to use Gordon's report as a pretext for doing so.

"The vote stands at two yeas and two nays. Gordon, have you had enough time to consider?"

Gordon's eyes clouded; the faces of the four men looking at him blurred. He thought he was going to be sick.

"Gordon, are you feeling all right?"

Valdespino's voice reverberated inside his skull. He didn't think that he had ever been called upon to make a choice this difficult in his life. If only Beaumont had voted yes, he could have complied with the demand of his wife's kidnapper and voted against publication, knowing that the story would run in any case.

Gordon blinked back his tears and struggled to find his voice.

"I didn't hear you," Valdespino said.

Gordon repeated himself. "I'm voting yes. Yes, we go with the story."

forty-four

When Larry Fallon called the Markoff home, it was with the expectation that Jessie would answer. He hoped to be able to see her; it was better, he thought, to explain why he'd voted as he had in person. He wanted her to know what the consequences would have been had he supported publication of the story. What he couldn't be sure of was whether his decision had been prompted more out of concern for her reputation and career, or for his. Maybe the two motives were inseparable.

But it was Gordon who answered the phone. For several moments Larry was struck dumb. Supposing that he'd acted in the best interests of everyone concerned, he still felt like a heel. He'd betrayed Gordon twice over. It was all he could do to identify himself.

"I don't want to talk to you," Gordon said, and hung up.

An understandable reaction, Larry thought. Nonetheless, he couldn't let it go at that. He and Gordon needed to talk.

It was only while he was on his way to see Gordon that he thought to ask himself what Gordon was doing at home. Wasn't that about the worst place to take refuge when you wanted to avoid detection?

But since Gordon's behavior was often inscrutable, he didn't see that there was much to be gained by dwelling on the question. He presumed he'd find out sooner or later.

Larry wasn't sure what to expect when he stepped up to the door at 54 Corcoran Road. Gordon might not even trouble to answer when he saw who it was.

But he did come to the door. Not that he looked very pleased.

"I thought I told you I didn't want to talk to you."

"Gordon, I think we have to talk." As he was saying this his eyes were searching for some sign of Jessie.

Gordon caught on to what he was doing. "It's Jessie you want to talk to, not me. It doesn't matter. They've taken her."

"They what?" At first he didn't understand.

"Koppleman or one of his goons. She might be dead for all I know."

Larry was so stunned he couldn't think of what to say. "When did this happen?" was the best he could do.

"Friday night, Saturday morning. Before the meeting at any rate."

Now he understood. "That was what that telephone call was about?"

Gordon nodded.

"Yet you voted in favor of the story?" The implications of Gordon's decision were just beginning to dawn on him. "You might have killed her, Gordon!" he blurted out.

Had he given it a moment's reflection he wouldn't have used quite those words. But all Gordon did was say wearily, "Yes, I might have done that, I might have killed her. Hers wasn't the only life at stake." His voice was dry and flat, without inflection.

You self-righteous bastard, Larry thought. *Other lives at stake?* Larry didn't feel so much at fault anymore; what were his betrayals when weighed against what Gordon had done?

"Larry, you have never had any idea what I'm about and I don't expect you ever will. Now if you'll excuse me—"

Before he could say another word the phone rang. Immediately Gordon ran toward the kitchen to answer it.

He's hoping that it will be Jessie, Larry thought. *That's why he came home: to wait for word from her.*

Larry slipped into the house. Having been in it a few times before on social occasions, he was familiar enough with its layout to know where another phone could be found.

Quietly he picked up and heard a woman on the other end, but it wasn't Jessie.

"Yes, I'm sure," she was saying. "I saw Stanley go in with her myself. I wouldn't have known it was your wife if he hadn't told me later."

"Is she all right?"

"I honestly couldn't tell you. I haven't seen her since yesterday morning."

"Guest cottage five you said?"

"Yes, but you'll never get in there on your own. There are too many guys walking around here packing heat. I might be able to help you. When do you think you could get up here?"

"What time is it now? Two twenty. I could be there by ten, eleven at the latest if nothing holds me up."

"All right. Then why don't you meet me at the disco where we met last time, say at around midnight?"

"I'd rather not meet you at Shadow Pines. Do you think you could get a ride into Brown Station?"

"Brown Station? What's a Brown Station?"

"Small town, around the other side of Mount Sycamore. There's a place called Kendrick's there, only bar in town. I'll meet you there at midnight."

"Well, if that's what you want. But don't bring along any cops. I have a thing about cops."

Gordon promised he wouldn't. "I want you to know how much I appreciate what you're doing, Morgan."

"Yeah, all right, sure," she said, and hung up.

Larry replaced the receiver and quickly stepped back into the hallway where he pretended to be waiting. When Gordon returned he gave Larry a puzzled look as if he couldn't quite remember what Larry was doing there. "I might have found her," he muttered. "I've got to go now."

He threw on his jacket and motioned Larry ahead of him out the door.

"Call me as soon as you learn anything," Larry said.

Gordon didn't bother to give him the courtesy of a reply.

As Gordon began to unlock the door to his car, a gray Chevy roared down the street, coming to a stop directly in front of his house. Larry remembered the Chevy and he remembered who the men were who rode in it.

The man Larry had spoken to at the Sycamore Motor Court several nights before emerged, running, from the Chevy. His badge, displayed in his open wallet, glinted in the afternoon sun. "Mr. Markoff," he said, continuing to approach.

Before Gordon could say anything the agent identified himself.

Gordon had the door to his car partway open, considering his chances of escaping. But the FBI agent anticipated that he might try to get away and moved to block him. Then, in a motion too quick for Larry to catch, the agent clapped him in handcuffs.

As Larry began toward them, uncertain as to what he would do, the second agent got out of the car. "Don't interfere in this," he warned.

Even in handcuffs Gordon struggled, but against the combined strength of the two agents there was nothing he could do. "My wife has been kidnapped, you sonsabitches!" he was shouting. "What the hell are you doing?"

The look Gordon threw Larry was full of anger. It was as if he judged Larry partly to blame for his predicament. The agents hustled Gordon into the back seat and then got back into their car. A few moments later the Chevy disappeared in the direction of Briarcliff Road.

Larry knew now what he had to do; he would return to New York and find Jessie himself. It would be fitting if he were the one, not Gordon, who got her back.

forty-five

It was happening again—the lights in front of his eyes, the sensation that he was floating. But that was only the start of it; there were the terrible smells, the tingling of the skin, the uncontrollable trembling, and the twitching of the limbs that at times became so bad that he could barely stand.

He couldn't be sick. Everything was going so well for him. A dude in Queens had agreed to front the coke for him and had shelled out eighty thousand—in cash—with more to come. With all that he expected he could make from the deal, Jarvis could buy freedom for himself.

Now that he could actually see his way clear, he was sick as a dog, and nothing he took for it, including a shitload of the coke he'd skimmed off the top for himself, was helping him.

He'd seen what had happened to the others. Once it started, it didn't take long. And he had a good idea as to how he'd become infected too—from the corpse he'd buried in that junkyard south of Milton.

He was convinced that his employer, Mr. Wilder, understood the risk he was taking, probably wanting him dead: pay him off and send him on his way and hope he croaks.

But Jarvis wasn't the fool Wilder thought him to be. After delivering the bitch he'd snatched in Atlanta, he decided to stick around, do some digging. It didn't take him long to discover that Mr. Wilder was named Stanley Koppleman.

The time was coming, and it would have to be soon, when he'd turn the tables on Koppleman. Not only him. He had the vial he'd taken from the hot lab which was full of concentrated infection. The way he figured it was this: if he was going to go, he was going to take a lot of folks with him.

When Larry Fallon walked into Kendrick's, the first person he noticed was Tom Emmett sitting with his friends at a table toward the rear. If Emmett noticed him, he gave no sign of it.

It was past midnight and the bar was packed.

Having no idea what Morgan looked like, Larry sought out any woman sitting alone. Women who were waiting for a man, Larry found, behaved in a certain way, used their eyes in a certain way that was immediately identifiable.

Of all the women in the place, none was a more likely candidate than the redhead seated at the bar. She seemed indifferent, even oblivious, to the man sitting beside her, who was doing his best to draw her into conversation. The redhead was far more attractive than a crowd like Kendrick's was accustomed to. Moreover, she was dressed in a manner that distinguished her from the others: her blue silk shirt hanging loose over her breasts and her white slacks spoke of conspicuous consumption; even the sumptuousness of her body seemed beyond the capacity of the women of Brown Station to equal.

He went over to her. "Morgan?" he said.

Puzzlement showed in her face. "Yes?"

The man on the stool next to hers looked at Larry and wasn't at all happy about what he observed.

"My name is Larry Fallon. I'm a friend of Gordon's."

This only confused her.

"I'm afraid that Gordon was detained. I don't know when he'll be able to get here, but it might not be for quite some time."

"But what could be more important than what happens to his wife?"

What indeed? Larry thought. "Don't get me wrong. He wanted to come, but, well, there were certain circumstances beyond his control."

"Oh." Morgan didn't seem to know what to say next. Excusing herself to the man by her side, she abandoned her seat. "Are you with the Centers of whatever it is too?"

"For Disease Control, and yes, I'm with them."

This was something that she could identify with. "All right then, let's go."

She led him out of the bar. "That red Porsche?" She was pointing to the car parked directly across the street.

"That's yours?"

"Uh-huh, it was a gift from a friend."

A very special friend, Larry thought. His own car, rented from Avis, was parked half a block away. He told her he would follow.

Before they separated he asked whether Morgan had learned anything new about Jessie. "Well," she answered, "like I told Mr. Markoff, I only got a look at her just once and that was yesterday and so I can't tell you any more than that."

For some reason Larry didn't quite believe her, but that may have been his own paranoia at work, nothing more.

For miles they were the only two cars on the road, her Porsche, his rented Cutlass. After twenty minutes they reached the main parking lot of Shadow Pines.

"Stick with me," Morgan told him, "and don't get lost. Otherwise you won't be able to get into the restricted area."

As they walked through the resort grounds Morgan began to tell him about how many dignitaries had been arriving in the last few days, many of them coming by chopper, the rest by limos, most of them accompanied by bodyguards, some bearing Uzis, the rest looking like they were, in her words, "packing heat." "All you have to do is see how their jackets bulge," she said. With some awe she added, "The President's coming tomorrow."

"You mean the ex-President?"

"What's the difference? They all golf, don't they?"

Tomorrow was Monday, Larry thought. Tomorrow the MMWR would issue its report linking Shadow Pines to the virus. Once the news media got hold of the story, it wouldn't take very long before the ex-President—and others much less celebrated than he—hightailed it for safer precincts.

It seemed to Larry that Morgan was in another world, that what happened to Jessie was of little consequence compared to this invasion of celebrities. She went on about them at such length that finally he broke in to ask, "Why are you doing this, Morgan? Why are you helping us out like this? It seems to me you're risking a great deal."

She shrugged, momentarily at a loss for an answer. Then she said, "Well, I kind of liked your friend, Mr. Markoff. I hate to see bad things happen to nice people like that. Besides, I have a beef with Stanley over what happened to a good friend of mine. What happened didn't have to happen if it wasn't for Stanley. You know Stanley? Koppleman? The lawyer?"

"I know him all right."

They were crossing a Japanese-style bridge that spanned an artificial lake. Koi could be seen in the water below, flashes of gold in the black.

"Is Jessie still being held in cottage five?"

"What? Oh right, that's what I told Mr. Markoff over the phone. Cottage five, right."

"Won't there be someone watching her?"

Larry was prepared to march in and rescue her. Now that he was actually this close, he wasn't sure what he was going to do.

"Oh?" Morgan seemed confused. "Well, don't worry, I'll get you in okay. They trust me."

"What about Koppleman?"

"Stanley? He's not around, forget about him." She began to laugh as if the lawyer were a punchline to some private joke of hers.

A lamp was burning above the porch of guesthouse five. Morgan preceded Larry up the stairs. She rapped on the door.

A man answered. "Jessie in here?" Morgan asked.

The man nodded and indicated that the two should enter. Beckoning Larry to follow, Morgan did just that.

Larry hesitated for an instant, then went ahead. As he stepped in he saw Jessie, pale and frightened, seated in a wicker chair on the other side of the room. She had her mouth open as if to say something.

The sound of footsteps behind him caused him to turn his head. A man with hair swept down either side of his scalp, blond on one side, white on the other, was standing there.

"What—?" Larry started to say when he noticed the gun in the man's hand.

He had no opportunity to say anything more before the man shot him through the head.

forty-six

Early on Saturday evening, just as Betty Strohmeyer and her husband, Sy, were sitting down to watch the local news, the telephone rang. With a look of annoyance Betty took the call, fully expecting that it would be for one of the children. But it was not; it was the police.

"We've found your sister's body, Mrs. Strohmeyer," he announced.

She wondered what the correct response to this should be. It was astonishing; she was as shocked as she'd been the day when Ellen's body had mysteriously vanished.

"We located it in a lot not far from Milton," the officer went on.

"Yes," she said distantly. Sy was looking at her strangely, silently questioning her as to whom she was talking to. She ignored him.

"We wanted you to know before you heard it on the news."

The news? She hadn't thought of the discovery of her sister's body as news particularly. "Yes," she said again. "Thank you."

"I regret to say that the health authorities will not allow the body to be buried again. An autopsy was conducted."

"Another autopsy? There was one done right after she died."

It seemed to her like such a needless indignity.

"We are aware of that, Mrs. Strohmeyer. However, it was necessary to test for the presence of the virus." He paused.

"And you found it."

"Yes, we did." He seemed to be choosing his words carefully. "According to the health authorities, it appears that her body was the source of the infection in the immediate area."

"I see." Just like Will Ziegler, whom she read about in the

papers, Ellen was causing as much trouble now that she was dead as she had when she was alive—maybe more.

"So I'm afraid to tell you that it was necessary—as a precaution—to cremate the body once the autopsy was completed."

"I understand."

"However, the ashes have been preserved and I have been assured that they are perfectly safe. There is absolutely no danger of contamination." He told her where to go to pick them up and again apologized for having brought her such unhappy news.

She returned to the couch. "They found Ellen," she told Sy. But she was saved the trouble of saying more because at that moment there appeared on the TV screen a shot of the junkyard where Ellen Leiter had been disinterred.

The pretty, bespectacled woman who was at the scene for Channel 6 news noted that the police still had no idea how the body had found its way to this derelict site. "But a spokesman for the Boston Health Department did say tonight that the body is definitely the source of the virus that has stricken eight people in the Milton area." She added that it was expected that, with the removal of the body, there should be no further incidences of the disease.

Back in the Channel 6 newsroom the anchorman said that the news of this discovery had caused "widespread relief." This was because it might mean the end of an insidious and bizarre affliction "to which no cure has been found." He cited a spokesman of the CDC in Atlanta who said that, outside of the Boston area, there had been no new outbreaks in the past week.

Sy was anxious to talk about Ellen; there was the problem of how to break the news to the kids. But Betty wasn't interested in voicing her views, not now. Claiming a headache, she went to the bedroom and lay down.

She had a feeling she knew how Ellen had taken ill. It must have been that night she came home, very late, after one of Will's parties. She couldn't go to sleep, she said, which was why she'd called Betty, waking her up to tell her what an extraordinary experience she'd just had. Obviously, she was on some kind of drug; Betty was discerning enough to recognize the signs: the breathlessness in her voice, the hurried cadence, the sense that at any moment something was going to break inside.

"I felt like I was floating, I saw such things, you can't imagine," she'd said. "I've taken acid, but it was never anything like this. For the first time in my life, Betty, I felt whole."

She'd rambled on, speaking of visions, hinting at stirrings of sexual desire unlike any she'd ever had before, causing orgiastic images to percolate into Betty's mind.

But none of this appalled her as much as what she said about the drug Will had given her, and God knows who else, to take. "It came from a shaman—you know, a healer? a Sharanahua Indian healer Will met in the Peruvian jungles," she told Betty, hastening to add, "When I say that it came from a healer I mean that literally, Betty. The drug was in his urine."

"The drug was what? You mean to say you drank it?"

"Will did. My friend Lucy did. Why shouldn't I? You have to try new experiences in life, don't you think? Maybe that's your problem, Betty. You've stopped having new experiences."

It was then that Betty had hung up on her.

It was in that urine, Betty was sure. More than some hallucinatory drug there was disease in that Indian's urine.

After an hour Betty came out of the bedroom and said that she wanted Sy to drive her to the police station. "We have to go and get Ellen's ashes. It wouldn't be right to leave them just sitting there on some officer's desk, would it?"

Late that night, long after Sy was asleep, Betty got up from bed and went into the living room where she'd left the urn. She didn't hesitate for an instant; she'd given considerable thought about what she was going to do.

She proceeded into the bathroom and, knowing how soundly Sy slept, did not bother to lock the door. Using a kitchen knife, she pried open the lid to the urn and poured its entire contents down the toilet. It was the best way she could think of to finally say good-bye to her sister.

forty-seven

Nearly six hours had elapsed since the two agents had brought Gordon to the room he was now sitting in, part of an office the FBI made use of close to Peachtree Plaza. Apart from the unpleasantness that had occurred when they'd picked him up, the two, whose names were Garrison and Wilson, had proved surprisingly deferential, almost embarrassed, as if they had much better things to do with their time than to detain him.

They asked him a few perfunctory questions, confirmed that he had indeed run out on a congressional subcommittee, and then seemed to lose interest. They went out to get him coffee and ham sandwiches from a deli across the street. They told him, almost apologetically, that they hadn't wanted to keep him so long, but that they were "waiting for instructions."

At another time Gordon might have endured the ordeal with better humor, but now he was seething with frustration. He needed to get to his wife; nothing else mattered. He told himself that she was still alive, that Koppleman's threat had been a bluff. At the same time he was aware of how vindictive the man could become; there was no way that he could reassure himself completely.

Garrison told him he could make one phone call, presuming that he would wish to confer with his lawyer. But a lawyer wasn't going to extricate him from this situation.

Instead he put a call into Congressman Trent Bradstock's office. It being midday on a weekend, he certainly didn't expect the congressman to be there. But he assumed that whoever picked up had a way of reaching him if the message was urgent.

This turned out to be the case. The secretary who answered explained that Trent was away until Monday.

"Do you think you could get a message to him today?"

"It's possible."

"Tell the congressman that this is Gordon Markoff calling. Tell him that I happen to be in the custody of the FBI's Atlanta bureau."

"Yes, sir. Anything else?"

"There is one thing more. Could you tell him that I saw him come out of guesthouse eighteen the other day and that I later spoke to Morgan Lee."

"Guesthouse eighteen?"

"That's correct."

"All right, I have the message," she said. "Thank you for calling."

"You're entirely welcome."

Gordon hoped that this message would have its desired effect. That so many hours had passed since he'd left it, however, had him alarmed. Was it possible that Bradstock was in so deep with Koppleman that he would risk his political career for him? Once Gordon leaked word that Bradstock repaired to Shadow Pines not only to improve his golf game but also to have it off with delectable-looking call girls, his constituents might not be so quick to reelect him in November.

At quarter past eight Garrison walked into the office where Gordon had been sequestered to tell him that he was free to go.

"You've received your instructions then?"

"That's right. As I understand it, there are no longer any charges pending against you."

Gordon decided that Bradstock had indeed gotten the message and had no difficulty appreciating its importance.

He asked Garrison if he might make another phone call. Garrison told him that he was sorry, but free or not, only one call was permitted. "There's a pay phone you can use in the lobby."

After phoning the major airlines that operated out of Hartsfield International Airport, he discovered that he was too late to make any of the New York–bound flights. So he decided to try the charter companies.

He called three of them before he found someone named

Len Berry who declared that he would be happy to fly Gordon up to the Catskills that night as long as the price was right.

Berry operated a small fleet of Cessna Skyhawks, each capable of transporting three passengers, out of Brown Airport, a small field about seven miles west of the city. He told Gordon that he'd be waiting for him in the terminal building, at his company's counter.

Next, Gordon attempted to reach Morgan to see if she'd learned anything new regarding Jessie since they'd talked that afternoon, and also to let her know that he was on his way. There was no answer at her cottage. Was that a good sign or a bad one? He had no way of judging but he wasn't going to delay until he knew something concrete.

Len Berry was a solidly-built man with the look of an adventurer, someone you could imagine having worked as a roustabout on an oil rig or a builder of water tunnels. His face was scarred and not very pretty to look at.

Gordon asked him whether other pilots flew his planes for him, because at least on this particular night he seemed to be all there was of Berry International Charter Airlines.

"Sometimes," Berry said.

Gordon was given the choice of sitting up in the cockpit, in what would have been the co-pilot's seat, or sitting in back. "Some people, they don't like sitting up in front. Makes them nervous," said Berry.

Being a well-seasoned traveler who'd taken more than his share of flights in small planes, Gordon was agreeable to sharing the cockpit with him. He'd be no more nervous there than sitting in the rear.

On their way to the Sullivan County airport they had to pass over Mount Sycamore. The mountain, from ten thousand feet up, would have been indistinguishable from all the others around it save for the mysterious lights which glimmered off the eastern slope.

"You see those?" Gordon asked Berry.

The pilot observed them all right, but he had no explanation to offer. "I don't usually get up around these parts. You'd think it was a city, wouldn't you?"

"Way over to the right, what do you see?"

"I'll be damned," Berry said, taking the Skyhawk lower in order to inspect the phenomenon better. "It looks like a small airstrip."

It was then that Gordon remembered Will Ziegler's final flight. Supposing in the midst of a viral delirium he'd mistaken this mirage for an actual landing field? Or perhaps his vision was unimpaired by the disease he harbored in his body; perhaps rain and low-lying clouds had accounted for his fatal error. There was a third possibility which entered Gordon's mind.

Maybe the lights had mesmerized him and drawn him down to his death, exerting the same pull that caused moths to gravitate to flame. Gordon felt in some strange way that he understood Will Ziegler; it wouldn't have surprised him to learn that Ziegler had slammed into the side of Mount Sycamore not because of a hallucination or an accident, but because he wanted to be close to the lights, he wanted to enter the city of the dead.

Sullivan County International Airport was used mostly by light private craft. Built at a cost of six million dollars, it was intended to service the resort casinos that state officials anticipated becoming legal in the 1970s. This never happened, however, and now, particularly this late in the night, it had the look of a Hollywood set that the crew hadn't gotten around to striking yet.

Immediately after refueling Berry took off, leaving Gordon to fend for himself. He tried phoning Morgan again. This time she was in.

"I didn't think you were coming," she said.

"Have you heard anything about Jessie?"

"Not a word. I don't know whether she's still in the guesthouse or whether they've moved her or what. But I think I can find out for you."

"But she's still alive? No one's done anything to harm her?"

There was a long pause. "I wish I could tell you, but honestly, I don't have the foggiest. Listen, I have someone with me right now. Do you think you could meet me later? I can't leave the resort. But you'll be safe in the disco. Stanley would never be caught dead in there, believe me. How about in an hour?"

Gordon said that he would have to live with it.

"Oh, it's not so bad," she said. "Maybe we could even do a little dancing."

If Morgan was joking, he decided, there was certainly a big difference between his sense of humor and her own.

He left the terminal building, which at this hour was practically deserted, and went to find a taxi, an enterprise which wasn't so easily accomplished when there were so few prospects for fares.

Morgan called Koppleman as soon as she had finished talking to Markoff. "I told him I would meet him in an hour," she said once she'd apprised the attorney of his arrival.

"You've redeemed yourself, Morgan." It still amazed him that she would have deceived him.

"What should I do?"

"Take him to his wife. I'll handle everything from there. By the way, you haven't seen Jarvis anywhere?"

"There's no sign of him, but I sure hope you find him soon. I don't like the idea of him wandering around here. He's like the others, he'll waste anybody."

This was probably true. The moment Jarvis appeared at Shadow Pines with Jessie, Koppleman had recognized the symptoms. Paying him off with a sum far in excess of what they'd agreed upon, he'd assumed that that would be the end of it. But Jarvis, for some reason, had chosen to remain behind, very likely hiding out in the woods. Why he'd shot Larry Fallon was beyond him. It wasn't supposed to happen. Koppleman had nothing against the man. After all, Fallon had kept his side of their agreement, and Koppleman believed that an agreement should always be honored.

He attempted to reassure Morgan, reminding her that he'd put two guards on her cottage. "And we've got people everywhere in the compound on the alert for him. There's no need for you to be concerned."

Of course there was. Ordinary individuals, pacific by nature, turned psychopathic and dangerously violent when stricken with the virus. But when it hit someone like Hal

Jarvis, who was psychopathic to begin with, there was no telling what was going to happen. Koppleman only hoped that Jarvis would be picked up by security before he committed any further acts of mayhem.

The next call the attorney took came only a few minutes later. It was from Jeremiah Mack at Wisdom-Templar.

"Mr. Koppleman," he began in a way that left no doubt as to what an unhappy state he was in, "we have a problem."

"I would expect so."

"I understand that the CDC is preparing to implicate us Monday in their morbidity journal."

"The Morbidity and Mortality Weekly Report it's called."

"You were supposed to make sure that this didn't happen."

"I assure you I did all that was humanly possible."

Mack continued, "We also understand that you have committed certain illegal practices—practices that would, if they came to light, reflect very poorly on our company."

"I don't think you have to worry about that happening, sir."

"Oh, but we do. A fellow by the name of Bob Zaborowski was called before the grand jury two days ago. I'm told that he held nothing back."

Koppleman cursed himself; he should have dealt with Zaborowski when he'd had the opportunity. Somehow, though, he hadn't believed the man had the courage.

"Believe me, Mr. Mack, I have no intention of violating any confidence—"

Mack wasn't interested.

"You realize that from this moment on you no longer represent Wisdom-Templar or Shadow Pines."

"My fee will be paid for services rendered?"

"Naturally," said Jeremiah Mack before hanging up.

Koppleman called his wife.

"I'd like you to make the reservations," he said.

She knew what he was referring to. They'd discussed what would happen in an emergency like this many times before.

"For tomorrow?"

"Yes, tomorrow."

"I didn't think it would be so soon," she said.

"There's nothing I can do about it."

After several seconds she said, "I'll do what you ask, but please, Stanley, take care of yourself."

"Don't worry, I'll be home by morning."

Right now, though, morning seemed like a very long time away.

When the tranquilizer's effects wore off, Jessie saw that she was in a large room painted a tranquil shade of green, with shelves full of unopened lotions, beauty creams, skin softeners, moisturizers, and the like. The table she'd been stretched out on was one especially designed for massages. What a strange place to find oneself, she thought.

It was only then that the memory of Larry's shooting returned to her. All she could really remember was the way he'd looked at her a moment before it happened. Had there been so much blood spattered on the wall behind him or was that something she'd imagined? It wouldn't do to think about it. The horror of the incident hadn't quite reached her, which was all to the good. Best to remain numb; it was the only way she was going to survive.

She began to explore her improbable prison. There were doors on either end of the room. One refused to budge but the other opened without any problem. This wasn't an exit, as she'd hoped, but an entrance to yet another room. This, too, was painted a calming pastel shade and had the further amenity of classical music being piped into it. It sounded like a piano concerto, maybe Brahms. Here she found four tables, like the one she'd been on; three of them were occupied. There were two women and one man, all lying supine, all covered from head to foot in mud.

Stepping up to the table closest to her, she looked down. Now she saw that there was no life to any of the three. Their nostrils were packed thick with mud; so were their mouths. Only their eyes, open and glazed, showed through the covering.

She was so shaken at first that it was several minutes before she gave any thought as to what these bodies were doing here.

In the end she could only come to one conclusion: these three were victims of the virus, left here in this apparently unused spa until someone figured out how to dispose of them.

Spooked, she headed back to the isolation of the adjoining room where she'd woken. But when she tried the door she found that it couldn't be opened from this side; she was locked in until somebody came for her. Jessie didn't know what she dreaded more: the waiting or what would happen when the waiting came to an end.

Walking out of the discotheque, Morgan said to Gordon, "You know, I'm sure that your friend was up here. He said he was coming on your behalf, but I didn't believe him."

"Friend? What friend?"

"You mean you didn't know?" She frowned, putting a well-manicured fingernail to her lips. "Oh, I thought you knew. He said his name was Larry something or other."

"Fallon? Larry Fallon?"

She brightened. "That's the one."

How could Fallon have known that Jessie was here? Thinking back to their encounter at his house, he realized that the son of a bitch had probably listened in to his conversation on the extension. "What did you say to him, Morgan?"

"I told him I didn't know shit and sent him away."

That's a good girl, he thought. "You did right."

Just before they came to the Japanese bridge, Gordon asked Morgan if she was sure she knew where Jessie was.

"I told you, they've moved her to the spa," she shot back.

Although she'd proven a credible witness the last time he'd spoken with her, he was no longer certain that he could trust her. She was acting too distracted and edgy in the way people get when they'd rather be anywhere but where they happen to be.

She held up her pass—a computerized card that also opened the door to her cottage—for the security man on duty. Evidently he was accustomed to seeing her with strange men, since he barely glanced at Gordon.

The spa was located in a corner of its own; a pink-and-white stucco building with a glass-enclosed pool occupying the entirety of its roof, it was reached by a winding gravel path. Scaffolding draped one wing of the structure that was still awaiting completion. "They're planning on opening it this coming spring," said Morgan. "They've installed a couple of saunas, whirlpool baths, a gym with Nautilus equipment. They say it cost a million and a half to build."

This was a woman who one day was probably counting out pennies and the next was calculating the interest on a money market account in six figures.

Although a few lights were on, visible through the windows, Gordon could see no sign of any activity within—or without for that matter.

"You're sure there's no one with her?"

Morgan nodded. "Stanley had some people lock her in there. No way she can get out. But this card works." She displayed the same card she'd shown the security man at the bridge. "Any card would. The spa's meant for the use of all the guests staying at the resort."

"This part of the resort, you mean?"

"I never think much about what happens on the other side."

"Let me get this straight. We just walk in and get her out?"

It sounded too easy, but Morgan insisted that there really shouldn't be any problem.

But when they were only a few steps away from the door, she stopped abruptly.

"What's the matter?"

"There's something I have to tell you." She was looking away from him: a bad sign.

"What is it?" He was afraid she was going to confess that something had happened to Jessie or that she wasn't here after all.

But what she had to say had nothing to do with his wife. "Your friend?"

"Larry? What about him?"

"He was shot."

"What are you talking about?"

"This crazy bastard who works for Koppleman shot him in the head. Stanley says it wasn't supposed to happen. But it happened. He's a real psycho, and I think he has that disease. You could see it in his eyes and he was twitching all over."

As much as he loathed the man, Gordon didn't wish something like this on him. "What happened to Larry?"

"I don't know. They took him away. He wasn't dead when they came and got him. They put him on a helicopter, but I couldn't get Stanley to tell me what happened to him after that."

"Jesus."

Morgan approached the door, which was all of bright new stainless steel, and inserted her card in a slot at its side. The door slid soundlessly open.

Proceeding through a gymnasium filled with an interesting variety of contraptions for building muscles, they came at length into a lounge area. The couches and cushioned chairs looked as if they'd never been sat in.

It only now occurred to Gordon to ask Morgan how she knew where in this complex Jessie was being confined.

Instead of answering him, Morgan pressed a button on the wall, causing another door to slide open, revealing a glass panel through which one could see into the sauna room.

A moment later Gordon saw Stanley Koppleman. Looking back at Morgan, he now understood that this was what she'd been expecting to happen.

Gordon silently cursed himself for having been lured here so easily. He had a notion that Jessie might not be anywhere nearby at all, but then when he shifted his glance he caught sight of her—part of her anyhow, half of her face, her bare shoulders—emerging from the whorls of steam.

Koppleman looked spent. He displayed none of his customary cockiness, no spirit or enthusiasm. His shoulders sagged, his face was ashen, and his eyes, sunk into hollows, were red from lack of sleep.

What Gordon couldn't figure out was what was going on here. Why was Jessie in the sauna?

Before he could say anything Koppleman directed him over to what looked like a fusebox at the right of the glass panel. He opened it.

What was inside were not fuses, but gauges that monitored the flow of heat and air into the sauna room and a thermostat to regulate the temperature. The thermostat was set at 120 degrees Fahrenheit.

Koppleman now adjusted it upward, to 145 degrees.

When Gordon noticed the Beretta Koppleman was holding in his hand, he was no longer in any doubt as to why he'd been brought here: he was going to watch his wife be burned to death.

forty-eight

"I tried to tell you, Mr. Markoff, that I'm a man who keeps his word," Koppleman said. "I wanted you to understand that."

Gordon was desperate. "What do you want me to do for you to stop it?" he cried out.

"There isn't anything you can do. The damage has been done. You had your chance and you blew it."

Gordon's eyes searched out Morgan's. But all he received in return was a blank stare. He was seeing her true face now; it was a mask giving away nothing.

"My God, you can't do this!"

But he could, and was.

When Gordon peered inside now, he could see nothing but steam rising from vents in the floor, a thick creamy mist. But after several seconds he caught sight of Jessie, her torso reddening as the heat intensified. He began shouting, tapping on the glass, ignoring Koppleman who said, "It's soundproof, she can't hear you."

But he could hear her—not her voice, but the repeated sound of her fists hammering futilely against the glass.

Then he saw her face: the contorted expression, the pain registering in her eyes, her skin an ugly, blazing red, her hair in disarray, matted to her neck and shoulders by the gathering moisture.

Then he lost sight of her as the steam submerged her once more. He had no way of knowing whether she had seen him too.

He couldn't stand it. Her pain was becoming his own. He dared not look at the thermostat to see what Koppleman had put it up to now.

When he noticed Koppleman turn away to address Morgan, he thought he had his chance. But as soon as he reached for the thermostat he felt a terrific blow on his arm. Koppleman held the butt-end of the gun in the air, ready to strike him again if he risisted.

The pain shot into his shoulder. "You planning on killing me, too?"

"No. As a matter of fact, I have no interest in doing that. Don't think that you'll have any luck going to the police. By the time you leave here I'll be far away."

Koppleman again adjusted the thermostat. "It is astonishing how high it can go," he noted when he saw that Gordon was deliberately averting his eyes from the sight of it.

Just then Morgan said, "What was that?"

Koppleman, frowning with puzzlement, cocked his head to one side and said, "I didn't hear anything."

But a moment later there was a shriek of glass coming apart, followed immediately by a great clamor as an alarm was triggered off.

"What the hell is happening?" Koppleman looked in the direction the sound had come from. Morgan turned at the same time.

"Wait, I see him," she said, pointing toward the far end of the corridor.

No sooner had these words emerged from her mouth than she let out a sigh. As blood began to soak through her blouse, making for a dramatic contrast with the blue silk backdrop of the fabric, she crumpled to the floor.

Gordon saw approaching them the man he'd first seen in Kendrick's, the man who called himself Hal. This must have been the one who'd shot Larry. He was using a silencer, which was why none of them had realized that Morgan had been shot at first.

Koppleman fired back, but the gunman's pace didn't falter. He kept lurching forward, his legs working in spasms, his head bobbing back and forth, his lips twisted, all symptoms of the virus in its final stages.

Gordon reacted now, leaping on top of the attorney while his back was to him, unbalancing him enough so that when he tried to fire again his shot went wide of the mark. At the same time Hal continued to shoot his own weapon, but with his arm shaking so badly the bullets began to strike the glass, shattering parts of it and releasing jets of scalding steam into the room.

Gordon could hear Jessie's screams, but he couldn't get free to reach the thermostat.

As Koppleman struggled with Gordon, attempting to push him aside so he could concentrate on his other antagonist, Hal had come close enough so that he could press his weapon to the attorney's head.

Gordon registered the sound of the *ppphhhhtt* in his ears, the silencer only partially muting the gun's discharge at this range.

His eyes bulging in response, Koppleman fell into Gordon's arms, like a lover embracing him. A speck of blood formed on his lips. When his face fell into Gordon's shoulder, the blood smudged on his cheek.

Gordon heard him say something in a whisper, the voice of a lover too. It was only after he fell to the ground that he realized that his last words had been "You shit."

In the short time it had taken for Koppleman to do his dying, more steam had penetrated into the room, thickening around Gordon, obscuring his view.

The crazed man before him, with his two-toned hair and his twitching eyes, was staring at him. It seemed that he was trying to account for Gordon's presence. The look in those eyes was the same as Gordon had seen in rabid dogs. There was no hint of reason there, nothing but rage and an impossible will to survive.

To hope for mercy from this man was out of the question. The clamor the alarm was making didn't even seem to have any impact on him.

At that moment Gordon saw Jessie trying to squeeze her head through one of the larger holes in the panel, risking cutting her neck on the sharp edges of broken glass.

Hal trained his gun on her. Gordon lunged at him, but too late—the gun went off.

forty-nine

Then the madman was gone, vanishing in the steam. Gordon looked back to where he'd seen Jessie, but she wasn't there any longer.

He pushed the thermostat down as far as it would go, then began to search for the door to the sauna.

He heard footsteps and voices, signaling the arrival of the security personnel. They should have come sooner, he thought.

On the other side of the sauna he located the door. He stepped inside and was all but enveloped by the searing heat. It was much worse than he'd anticipated, but he plunged in, scarcely able to see anything more than he had from the outside.

Then he spotted her, crumpled on the floor, naked, her face covered with blood.

Without pausing to inspect her wounds or see whether she was even alive, he scooped her up in his arms. The heat from her abused skin transmitted to his. How light she was, he thought.

Don't be dead, don't be dead, he kept saying to himself. *Goddamn you, don't be dead.*

As soon as he'd gotten her out he lay her gently on the floor. He saw that her breasts were rising and falling in a feeble rhythm.

She was alive. He began to inspect her injuries, using his shirt to sponge away the blood on her face. People were collecting around him, shouting, asking him questions that he failed to comprehend. All he would say to them was, "Get help, find a doctor, would you?"

Someone said that a doctor was on his way.

To Gordon's relief he saw that the blood was from lacerations she'd sustained from splinters of glass. He couldn't find any bullet wound.

A man handed him a towel which he used to cover her. It might have been the touch of the rough fabric against her skin that caused her to suddenly cry out.

Her eyes flickered opened and she stared at Gordon, taking him in.

"I'm here," he said over and over again. "I'm here and I love you."

She moved her lips, apparently in response. She couldn't make herself heard, but Gordon had no trouble deciphering what she was trying to say: "I love you too."

But she wanted him to understand that there was more. She found her voice although it was barely audible. "Larry . . . shot Larry . . ."

"I know, sweetheart, I know."

"Don't leave me, please."

"I'm not going anywhere," he assured her. And perhaps for the first time in a long while he meant it.

Hal Jarvis fought his way through the brush, scratched by nettles, with a gash in his thigh that continued to ooze blood and cuts and scratches that he couldn't account for. Nothing mattered. He was dying and nothing mattered.

The loss of motor control was so pronounced now that he could scarcely stay upright, and for long stretches of time he was obliged to maneuver on all fours. His mouth tasted of dead leaves and grass.

He had only the vaguest notion as to where he was, but he did have a destination in mind, a place to arrive at before the end.

At last, through a parting in the woods, he held it in view: the water, the pure blue water of the Ashokan reservoir. This was part of an entire system of reservoirs that delivered well over one billion gallons of water to New York City every day.

He scrabbled down a small incline and reached the water's edge. There was a sign posted not far away warning against swimming, boating, and fishing.

His throat was parched, his vision blurring; the tremors in

his limbs were growing worse. And there was a terrific pounding in his head. He knew that it wouldn't be too long before the life simply ran out of him. It was only sheer willpower that had gotten him to this point.

Squatting, he dug out of his pocket the vial he'd been carrying with him ever since he'd been in Atlanta, the concentrate of infectious solution.

Why shouldn't he take as many people as possible with him when he went? Once he emptied the contents into the reservoir he would jump in himself. He'd always viewed his body as a weapon, but he couldn't have imagined that it would remain one after his death, spreading to others the disease that had reduced him to this miserable state.

Lacking practically all coordination, he had a great deal of trouble unscrewing the top of the container. Eventually, though, he succeeded in loosening it.

As he picked himself up with a groan, meaning to pour the concentrate into the reservoir, he heard a noise behind him.

His vision was so bad that he couldn't focus adequately enough to see what had caused the noise.

Then, in the grim gray light of the vanishing night, he saw, emerging from the underbrush, a man with a wide-brim black hat and a shotgun.

"You, stop!" he heard.

Jarvis ignored the command and, stepping to the edge of the water, placed his fingers on the lid of the vial, ready to give it the one last turn it needed before he got it off.

It was then that Joe Hunting Bear lifted his shotgun to his shoulder and fired.

The blast caught Jarvis in the small of the back and pitched him to the ground.

While it was still dark, Joe Hunting Bear burned the body, knowing that it was impure and should not be permitted to lie in the earth. But he did not destroy the vial, although he understood that it was full of evil medicine, Hadui's medicine, that could cause great harm among men. It would make them sick and mad as the one he had just put to death.

But he believed that it was not his responsibility to decide what to do with it. It was the responsibility of Hadui, the dwarf god, who would appear in advance of the other gods—

the gods of the Shoharie, of whom he was the sole remnant. Soon they would fully reveal themselves. Even now, he knew they had begun to do so, bringing down mountains and setting loose on the land this great sickness.

In anticipation of this day, Joe Hunting Bear carefully buried the vial, marking the site with a slab of rock—bluestone—that had come from the abandoned quarry. From now on, this would be a sacred place.

When he'd completed this task, he lifted his eyes toward the slope of Mount Sycamore. He saw to his satisfaction that the lights were still visible, a faint glimmer through the mist. Soon, he knew, there would be many more people to join those who were already there, to inhabit the only city of any importance in this land, the city of the dead.

GOLF TOURNAMENT CANCELED AMID VIRUS SCARE

HUNDREDS LEAVE CATSKILLS RESORT IN PANIC

(Special to the N.Y. Times)

Sullivan County, Sept. 3—The annual Northeast Classic, scheduled to begin today at the Shadow Pines resort, was canceled abruptly on account of a risk to the players and audience from an apparently incurable virus. A report in the Morbidity and Mortality Weekly Report, issued Monday by the Atlanta-based Centers for Disease Control, disclosed that several victims of the virus, known to cause extensive brain damage and death, were staying at the resort when they became ill. Within hours of the release of this report, cancellations began to pour into the booking offices of the resort. An assertion by a resort spokesman that "the CDC report is baseless" failed to stop the tide.

As news of the health hazard became known, hundreds of guests made preparations to cut short their vacations and leave. Sullivan County medical facilities reported a surge of panic-stricken people seeking assurance that they had not been infected during their stay at the resort. Several guests announced their intention to bring suit against the parent company, the Wisdom-Templar Corporation, for knowingly exposing them to the disease. A company spokesman declined to comment on the charges.

The Northeast Classic, which was scheduled for broadcast by ABC Sports, was to have been attended by several high-ranking officials and dignitaries from the federal and state governments. But now a cloud hangs over not only the future of the tournament but the future of the Shadow Pines resort as well.

fifty

It was hard to know what the doctors meant when they talked about "progress." There was, barring a miracle—which no one expected—no progress to be made. The brain was irreparably damaged.

But there was some indication that the patient, Larry Fallon, could understand what was spoken to him—at least on occasion—even if he could respond only with a nod or a smile or what seemed to be a tortuous attempt to articulate a word.

He liked being brought out to the front lawn of the hospital to enjoy the day whenever it was warm and sunny enough. He would sit in his wheelchair with his face raised to the sun, a smile fixed on his lips.

Occasionally he would have visitors, members of his family, friends, former associates from the CDC. They would sit and talk with him for a while, pretending to be engaged in a normal conversation, and then they would go on their way. Some of these visitors would swear that he understood everything they said, and others were convinced that not a word they'd spoken had gotten through.

About twice, maybe three times a year, a radiant young woman would come and visit. She would wear a necklace from which a magnetic compass hung. A magnetic compass without a needle. Her name was Jessie Palmer and, with her, the nurses noted, he would pay special attention, sitting up in his wheelchair, from time to time leaning forward as if he was anxious to catch every word she uttered.

Afterward, when the nurses would return him to his room, speaking to him as if he were a very backward child—for that was how they tended to regard him—they'd ask him if he didn't think his visitor was a very pretty girl and a very nice one as well.

"Jessie, Jessie," he'd reply, repeating her name in a low, incantatory voice. "Jessie, Jessie, Jessie."

It was strange though, the nurses said, how after each one of her visits there would be tears in his eyes. If they were to be believed, it never happened at any other time.